ASCENDANCE OF A BOOKWORM
I'll do anything to become a librarian!

Part 3 Adopted Daughter of an Archduke Vol. 5

Author: **Miya Kazuki**
Illustrator: **You Shiina**

Karstedt
The commander of Ehrenfest's knights. Rozemyne's noble father.

Elvira
Karstedt's first wife. Rozemyne's noble mother.

The Knight Commander's Family

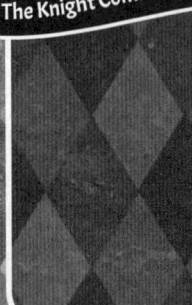

Eckhart
Karstedt's oldest son. Serves as Ferdinand's guard knight.

Lamprecht
Karstedt's second son. A knight who serves as Wilfried's guard.

Cornelius
Karstedt's third son. An apprentice knight who serves as Rozemyne's guard.

Ottilie
An attendant and an archnoble. Elvira's friend.

Rozemyne's Retainers

Angelica
Apprentice guard knight. A mednoble in the middle of growing her manablade.

Rihyarda
Rozemyne's head attendant in the castle. An archnoble who took care of Ferdinand, Sylvester, and Karstedt when they were kids.

Brigitte
A knight and a mednoble. Giebe Illgner's younger sister.

Damuel
A knight and a laynoble who continues to guard Rozemyne.

Cast of Characters

The Archduke's Family

Rozemyne
The protagonist. She went from the daughter of a soldier to the adopted daughter of the archduke, changing her name in the process. But her personality hasn't changed at all — she'll do whatever it takes to read books.

Ferdinand
Sylvester's brother from another mother. He is Rozemyne's guardian in the temple.

Sylvester
The archduke of Ehrenfest. He adopted Rozemyne, making him her adoptive father.

Florencia
Sylvester's wife and the mother of his three children. Rozemyne's adoptive mother.

Wilfried
Sylvester's oldest son, and now Rozemyne's older brother.

Bonifatius
Sylvester's uncle, Karstedt's father, and Rozemyne's grandfather.

Charlotte
Sylvester's oldest daughter, and now Rozemyne's little sister.

Summary of Part Two:

After becoming an apprentice blue shrine maiden, Myne built a workshop in the temple, giving food and work to the starving orphans while busily spending her days developing printing through trial and error with her Gutenbergs. However, she was suddenly attacked by a foreign noble brought in by the High Bishop. In order to gain enough status to protect her family and attendants, Myne resolved to become the archnoble Rozemyne, soon to be adopted by the archduke.

Lower City Family

 **Gunther** — Myne's father.
 **Effa** — Myne's mother.
 **Tuuli** — Myne's older sister.
 **Kamil** — Myne's little brother.

Lower City Merchants

- **Benno** — Head of the Plantin Company.
- **Mark** — Benno's right-hand man.
- **Lutz** — A leherl apprentice.
- **Otto** — Head of the Gilberta Company.
- **Corinna** — A seamstress for the Gilberta Company.
- **Damian** — Grandson of Gustav, the guildmaster.

Temple Attendants

- **Fran** — In charge of the High Bishop's chambers.
- **Zahm** — In charge of the High Bishop's chambers.
- **Gil** — In charge of the workshop.
- **Fritz** — In charge of the workshop.
- **Wilma** — In charge of the orphanage.
- **Monika** — A cook who also helps in the High Bishop's chambers.
- **Nicola** — A cook who also helps in the High Bishop's chambers.

Rozemyne's Personnel

- **Ella** — Rozemyne's personal chef.
- **Hugo** — Rozemyne's personal chef.
- **Rosina** — Rozemyne's personal musician.

Gutenbergs

- **Ingo** — Foreman of a carpentry workshop.
- **Zack** — A smith. Comes up with ideas.
- **Johann** — A smith. Turns ideas into reality.
- **Heidi** — Ink craftswoman. Josef's wife.
- **Josef** — Ink craftsman. Heidi's husband.

Other Nobles

- **Oswald** — Wilfried's head attendant.
- **Justus** — Rihyarda's son and Ferdinand's retainer.
- **Giebe Illgner** — Brigitte's older brother.
- **Georgine** — Sylvester's older sister and the first wife of Ahrensbach.
- **Veronica** — Sylvester's mother. Currently detained.
- **Viscount Joisontak** — A member of Rozemary's family.
- **Viscount Gerlach** — A noble loyal to Georgine.

Other

- **Kampfer** — A blue priest being trained by Ferdinand.
- **Frietack** — A blue priest being trained by Ferdinand.
- **Richt** — Hasse's new mayor.
- **Achim** — A gray priest sent to Hasse.
- **Egon** — A gray priest sent to Hasse.
- **Volk** — A gray priest who wishes to live in Illgner.
- **Carya** — A woman from Illgner who wishes to marry Volk.
- **Dirk** — An orphan forced to sign a submission contract with Count Bindewald.
- **Delia** — Rozemyne's former attendant from when she was a shrine maiden.
- **Lily** — A gray shrine maiden returned to the orphanage after getting pregnant.

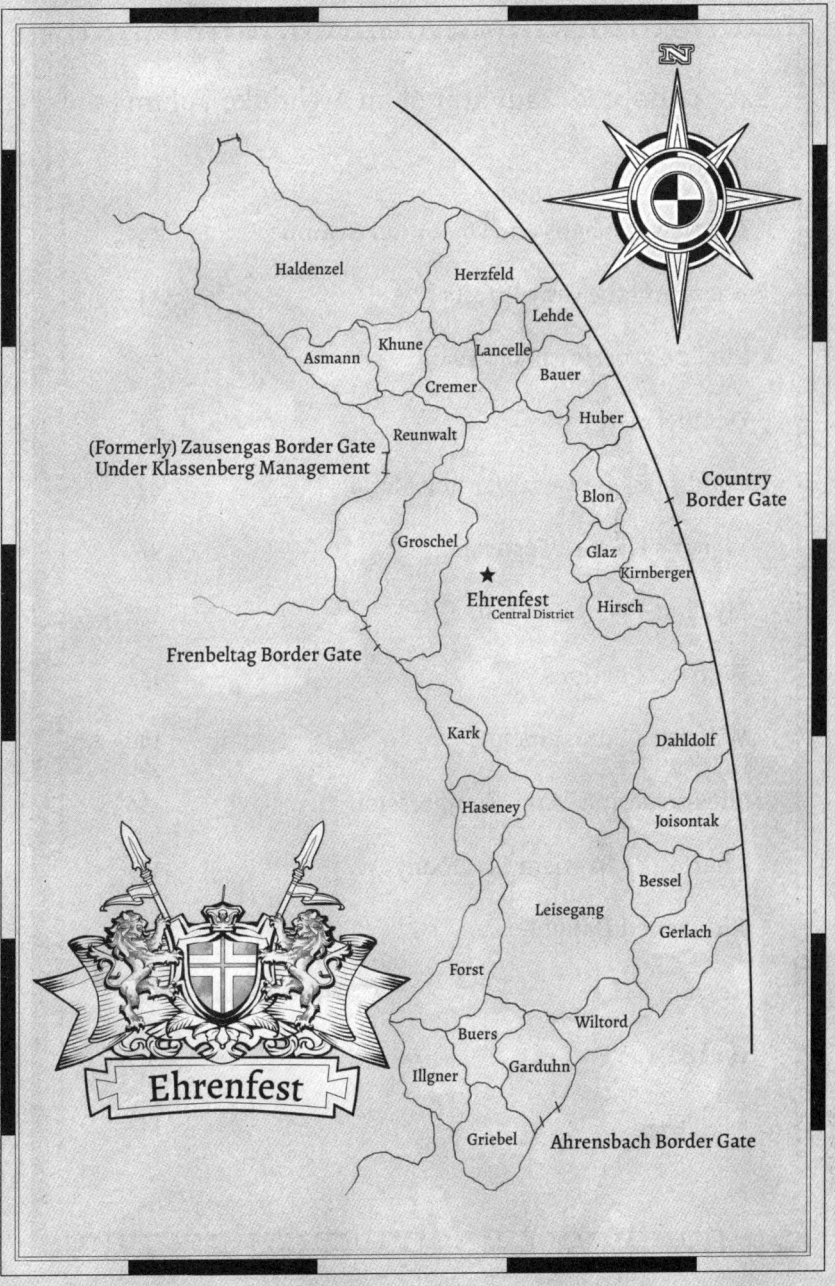

Part 3 Adopted Daughter of an Archduke Volume 5

Prologue	11
The New Orphans and Operation Grimm	26
Hasse and the Gray Priests	44
Ruelle Gathering (Take Two)	59
Damuel's Growth	73
Conditions for Compressing Mana	88
Illgner's Harvest Festival	96
My First-Ever Little Sister	117
Wilfried's Actions	132
Wilfried's Punishment	146
The Jureve and Mana Compression	156
Charlotte's Baptism Ceremony	173
Kidnapped Daughter	188
Rescue	197
And So, the Future	211
Epilogue	217

Extra Story:
Grandfather on the Day of the Baptism					222

Extra Story:
In Place of My Older Sister					254

Extra Story:
Two Marriages					275

Extra Story:
No Rest for Us					293

Extra Story:
Meanwhile at the Temple					316

Extra Story:
The Laynoble Guard Knight					357

Extra Story:
One Handful of a Chef					370

Afterword					380

Bonus Manga					382

Ascendance of a Bookworm: Part 3 Adopted Daughter of an Archduke Volume 5
by Miya Kazuki

Translated by quof
Edited by Kieran Redgewell
English Cover & Lettering by Meiru
Layout by Jennifer Elgabrowny

This book is a work of fiction. Names, characters, places, and incidents are the product of the author's imagination or are used fictitiously. Any resemblance to actual events, locales, or persons, living or dead, is coincidental.

Copyright © 2017 Miya Kazuki
Illustrations by You Shiina

First published in Japan in 2017
Publication rights for this English edition arranged through TO Books, Japan.
English translation © 2021 J-Novel Club LLC

All rights reserved. In accordance with the U.S. Copyright Act of 1976, the scanning, uploading, and electronic sharing of any part of this book without the permission of the publisher is unlawful piracy and theft of the author's intellectual property.

Find more books like this one at www.j-novel.club!

Managing Director: Samuel Pinansky
Light Novel Line Manager: Chi Tran
Managing Editor: Jan Mitsuko Cash
Managing Translator: Kristi Fernandez
QA Manager: Hannah N. Carter
Marketing Manager: Stephanie Hii
Project Manager: Nikki Lapshinoff

ISBN: 978-1-7183-5611-5
Printed in Korea
First Printing: May 2022
10 9 8 7 6 5 4 3 2

Part 3 Adopted Daughter of an Archduke Volume 5

Prologue

"Now then, shall we discuss this elsewhere?" Rozemyne suggested, glancing toward the door to her hidden room in the orphanage director's chambers. That was her signal for this formal discussion to turn casual, and so Fran guided Benno and Mark inside.

In this room, she could speak as Myne rather than Rozemyne, the archduke's adopted daughter, and the retainers allowed to follow her inside were all those who knew her from her commoner days. For that reason, Benno generally only ever brought Mark and Lutz to the temple. Damian technically knew her from when she was a commoner as well, but it seemed that she didn't exactly like him very much, so Benno avoided bringing him when he could.

The lehanges sent from other stores weren't particularly happy about not being brought to the temple to observe the negotiations, but Benno was holding them at bay for now by reminding them how lucky they'd already been to sell goods in the castle.

The lehanges'll stop complaining when we start doing even more business there. It's just that, in these kinda discussions, people being too subtle and overly flattering always gives Rozemyne the wrong idea.

On the inside, she was a commoner raised in poverty, which meant she didn't quite have the level of common sense one would expect from a blue shrine maiden turned archduke's adopted daughter. Even Benno had no way of knowing what might set her off on her next rampage, which is why he had to discuss things with her in frank, clear language. And worst of all, now that she was the archduke's adopted daughter, every word she spoke carried an immense amount of political influence.

"Here is your seat, Master Benno."

Benno sat in the chair that Fran offered him, with Mark standing behind him. Only once Benno had sipped the tea that was served to him did the discussion begin, and he made doubly sure to hold the cup with noble etiquette. Ever since Gil went to Illgner, Fran had started entering the hidden room in his place, meaning noble customs had started to take root even in here.

A sudden fear struck Benno. *If we see even more changes like this, how long is the hidden room even gonna function as a spot for real-deal business discussions? Rozemyne needs to learn to understand noble euphemisms, and fast. Things could get real bad otherwise.*

"So, what's our business this time? I heard you finished some new kind of paper," Benno said, breaking the ice as he set down his cup.

Fran began lining up some gleaming silky paper on the table, placing a letter beside it. Rozemyne's regal expression crumbled in an instant, her golden eyes twinkling as she regarded Benno with a proud grin.

"Benno, this is the paper I just received from Illgner. Could you give it to Heidi at the ink workshop so she can run some experiments? It has a silky smooth surface, so I want her to see if colored ink will stick to it."

"Alright."

Despite having sent Lutz and everyone to Illgner, Benno had largely assumed they would teach the locals how to make paper and nothing more. Never did he expect they would finish making an entirely new kind of paper this fast. He picked up a sheet,

Prologue

feeling his lips curve into a grin as he rubbed its surface with his finger; assuming the ink did indeed stick to it, he could only imagine how many new products they could make.

"I wish I could do some research myself..." Rozemyne muttered.

"Hey, we've all got our roles here. Researching ink isn't a job for the archduke's adopted daughter. You just need to continue building up influence in noble society, all while staying healthy enough to not collapse. Can't let some noble scuffles bring the printing industry to its knees before it even takes off, y'know?"

Rozemyne would spontaneously overstep her boundaries without considering the consequences, so Benno reminded her to stick to her role and not butt into anyone else's work. That wouldn't actually stop her if push came to shove, but he could at least say he tried.

"Making paper is a lot more fun than dealing with nobles, but I understand it's my duty to protect the printing industry now that I've started it. I'm doing my best here," Rozemyne said, puffing out her cheeks in a way that wasn't cute in the slightest.

Truth be told, Benno knew that she was working extremely hard to survive in her position. Even merchants struggled to speak and act properly when visiting the castle, and yet here she was, a commoner girl stuck living as the archduke's adopted daughter, forever surrounded by noble attendants. It took more than a little hard work to survive in that kind of situation.

"Yep, you better protect it. But anyway... This new paper is pretty firm, huh? What's it gonna be used for?" Benno asked, whipping one sheet around a little, holding it up to the light to peer through, then rolling it up.

"Playing cards to start with. They'll be much easier to use that way," Rozemyne explained. Small wooden boards were currently used for the playing cards, but it seemed she wanted to start using this paper instead.

Doesn't look like she's even considered that this'll take valuable work away from the Ingo Workshop, who make those boards every year.

Benno was conflicted. Should he point that out for Ingo's sake, or just let Rozemyne's creative spirit run free, knowing that real-world consequences would only stifle her ideas?

"Ferdinand seemed to like the harisen a lot, but I don't really want him beating my head with it all the time. Oh, Benno, you'll never believe this—Ferdinand was *so* mean to me," Rozemyne began, launching into a fervent speech about just how cruel the High Priest had been when the paper arrived from Illgner.

This is just so... so petty!

Benno slumped in his chair, almost losing the will to live. He just knew that Mark was smiling behind him, and in all honesty, he felt stupid for ever taking this seriously.

Bleh. I guess no matter what happens, Rozemyne's gonna keep inventing more weird junk that she wants for whatever reason. Losing a single job won't put Ingo in too bad of a spot.

Concluding that he would simply let this matter rest until the day potentially came when Ingo was desperate for more work, Benno cut Rozemyne's rant short by asking what price she intended to sell the paper for. She fell into thought, not seeming at all bothered about the topic being so abruptly changed.

"I think we should wait for Heidi to do her research before we consider the price. It really is going to depend on whether or not the ink sticks."

"Yeah, I guess the research should come first," Benno replied, handing both the new paper and the letter from Lutz over to Mark. As he did so, Rozemyne took out her diptych and looked it over, nodding to herself a few times. It seemed she had written down everything they needed to talk about.

Prologue

"What's the status of the pump for Hasse?"

"They're moving the prototype they were planning to put by Johann's workshop over to Hasse's monastery. Johann got all weepy about having to wait for a new one. Can't say I'm surprised, though—their first pump was given to the temple, then he had to make one for the castle, and now this. He was pretty depressed."

"I guess Johann really needs to train someone else to make that part, hm?" Rozemyne said with a contemplative hand on her cheek. While the schematics for the pump were readily available, no other craftsmen had managed to produce one themselves; one part in particular was so precise that Johann was currently the only person able to make it.

"It won't take long for someone to figure it out. Now that everyone knows you're showing favor to fresh talent like Johann and Zack, all the young men have been busting their butts to hone their skills."

"Oh, really?"

"Yep. Head of the Smithing Guild told me all about it. Zack spilled the beans about you wanting to give him and Johann their own workshop, so loads of people are doing their best to improve in hopes of getting one as well."

Now that the pump schematics were public and the archduke's adopted daughter was placing a ton of orders, the smiths of the lower city were all working harder than ever. Rozemyne's golden eyes sparkled upon hearing that, and she broke into a happy smile.

"I will welcome any number of people as Gutenbergs, so long as they have skills as honed as Johann's or creativity as impressive as Zack's. Please, introduce them all to me."

Benno's cheek twitched. He could already picture it—Ehrenfest's upcoming talents having their common sense torn to shreds one after another as Rozemyne turned them all into Gutenbergs.

He needed to maintain the current status quo for as long as possible to keep the peace in the lower city. But even with that in mind, he didn't turn Rozemyne down.

"...Alright. I'll pass that along to the head of the Smithing Guild."

The reason? He knew that as the paper-making and printing industries grew, the load placed on Rozemyne's Gutenbergs would continue increasing to an overwhelming degree. Having more Gutenbergs would at least lessen that burden. Plus, Rozemyne's ideas were profitable; if young craftsmen *wanted* to be knocked all over the place with unreasonable expectations, then that was all the more beneficial for him.

No reason for us to deal with all this alone. The more the merrier.

"Oh, right. Mind if we check out the workshop before leaving?" Benno asked. "We're still getting regular reports, but without Lutz and Gil there, we're not quite as in the know."

Since the two boys' departure, Benno hadn't received any messages detailing the gray priests' thoughts—whether that be what they wanted improved in the workshop, or ideas for new products that sometimes ended up pretty valuable. He wanted to see how things had changed now that their best workers had gone to Illgner, and whether they were at all unsatisfied with the Gutenbergs working elsewhere.

"I don't think the gray priests will say very much to you, Benno, but I don't mind you checking up on the workshop. Fran, please send word to Fritz."

"As you wish."

With that, Fran exited the hidden room. Silence fell almost immediately, perhaps due to their discussion having run dry, and Rozemyne's eyes wavered slightly as she searched for something to say. Soon enough, she clapped her hands together in realization.

Prologue

"Speaking of which, Benno—how's Tuuli doing? Is her work going okay? She's been going there every day now that she's ten, right? She never has a chance to come to the orphanage now..." she said, slumping her shoulders sadly. Lutz being in Illgner meant he couldn't pass letters to her lower city family nor tell her stories about them, so it was easy to guess she was feeling especially lonely. "I have so many letters sitting around that I've written but can't send. Could you not give them to Tuuli for me?"

"Well, the Plantin Company's separate from the Gilberta Company now, so..."

With the Plantin Company currently in the process of moving, Benno was actively trying to avoid going to the Gilberta Company in front of the lehanges from other stores, thinking it best to minimize contact until the transition was completely finished. It would stick out way too much for him or Mark to start giving Tuuli letters.

"I could give them to Corinna, but we really don't want this to go public," Benno continued. There was no problem with Lutz taking the letters from the hidden room and delivering them straight to Rozemyne's family in the lower city, but having Benno give them to Corinna, then Corinna pass them on to Tuuli created too many opportunities for other people to see what was going on. "Having her give the letters to Tuuli would be way too conspicuous, since everyone's gonna want to know what she's telling the new leherl who came from a poor home. We'd be drawing a lot of attention to ourselves, and we don't want that."

"...You're right," Rozemyne said with a sigh, bottling up her loneliness once again. "I suppose I'll make do until the Harvest Festival. It sucks, though."

Benno knew how much Rozemyne cared for her family, so the mature way she was controlling her feelings actually made him feel a little bad. He scratched his head, trying to think of something he could say about them.

"Actually... Hey, how's the Harvest Festival looking this year? Are you going to be moving the priests about again? I can get carriages for you if you need them."

"I am, yes. Please do get carriages. We'll be moving some from Ehrenfest to Hasse, and vice versa."

Benno glanced behind him to see that Mark was already writing it down on his diptych. The two exchanged a meaningful glance; then Mark turned his eyes to Rozemyne.

"Lady Rozemyne, we shall organize the carriages and prepare food. Would you kindly write a letter to the gate requesting some guards?"

"Absolutely! I'll get started as soon as I can," she replied, enthusiasm returning to her voice. She must have remembered that this was a rare opportunity for her to see Gunther.

"Also, I'd recommend doing the orphanage's winter prep with the Gilberta Company again this year," Benno added. "We want to keep it as connected to the Rozemyne Workshop as we can."

"Right. Oh, if you want to strengthen that connection, maybe I could ask Tuuli to take the gray priests shopping for used clothing? Tell her that I'll pay for whatever clothes she needs in return. She'd end up wearing the same ones otherwise, even if they started getting tight on her, right? I wouldn't want her sticking out in Corinna's workshop."

Rozemyne's expectations were correct. Most of the seamstresses working in Corinna's workshop were from wealthy families; she only employed workers with connections to the Gilberta Company, and since her store was such a large one, that meant hiring those

Prologue

from the wealthy side of society. Tuuli was the one exception—the single poor person in the workshop, hired to make hair sticks for the archduke's adopted daughter. Corinna had warned Benno that she would initially struggle to adapt to the culture there, just as Lutz had.

"But Tuuli has Lutz there to help her, she knows how to clean herself with homemade rinsham, she's cute, she has an honest personality, and she's earning the store money with her hair sticks," Rozemyne continued. "As long as she has good clothes to wear, I don't think she'll have any problem fitting in. Just ask Corinna and Otto to keep an eye on her for me."

It was because of Rozemyne's influence that Lutz was given time to adjust to the Gilberta Company and ultimately became a leherl in the Plantin Company, so hearing her say she would stay connected with the Gilberta Company for Tuuli made Benno glad for a variety of reasons.

"Alright. You sure love Tuuli, huh?"

"Of course. She's my angel," Rozemyne said proudly, puffing out her chest. It was then that Fran returned from the workshop with Fritz, everything having been prepared for Benno's visit.

Upon entering the workshop at Fritz's guidance, Benno and Mark looked around. At a glance, the working gray priests all seemed to be doing fine.

"Master Benno, may I ask what brings you here so suddenly?" Fritz asked.

"I just wanted to check up on the workshop. Sales this summer were real high, and we can expect a lot more books to sell at the end of winter this year. Lutz and the others have gone to Illgner, so I wanted to make sure there weren't any problems."

"It is all as my reports said—no major problems have occurred in the workshop."

Noticing Fritz's stiff demeanor, Mark gave a peaceful smile and nodded in agreement. "We certainly believed that things were running smoothly."

Benno followed up with a merchant's smile himself, trying to disarm Fritz. "Lutz always passed on minor issues and such that he heard about while working. We haven't received news of any since he departed, so we were a little curious. Got anything like that for us? It doesn't have to be anything major—just things you might want to be improved now that your best men are gone."

Mark and Benno's explanation made Fritz widen his brown eyes a little. "We improved the workshop many times at Lutz's suggestion, but we never knew he was discussing those matters with you, Master Benno. There were many minor problems when Gil and the others first left, but we have since made various small adjustments and grown accustomed to the situation. In the future, we shall report any improvements we wish to make."

According to Lutz's reports, Fritz was the solid foundation that kept the workshop running smoothly, and he would mediate whenever Lutz and Gil got into a debate. The fact that he guessed Benno's intentions and agreed to them after such a short exchange was very impressive to say the least; had he not been one of Rozemyne's attendants, Benno would have tried to take him into his own store.

"If this long-term trip to Illgner works out, printing and papermaking will start spreading all across Ehrenfest," Benno explained. "I'm guessing Lutz and Gil will be going to one city after another, which means this situation might just be your new standard. That's why it's in everyone's best interests for you to tell us right away if there are any problems."

Prologue

Fritz thought for a moment, then smiled. "As long as Lady Rozemyne remains the High Bishop and orphanage director, everything should be fine. She readily accommodates our every need."

Now it was Benno's turn to be shocked by a realization. What the Plantin Company needed to worry about wasn't how the gray priests were faring while Lutz and Gil were in Illgner, but what they'd do if Rozemyne stopped being the High Bishop and they lost the ability to communicate in her hidden room.

"Fritz, I'm going to be blunt—are there any rumors about Lady Rozemyne stepping down from her position as High Bishop?"

A stir immediately ran through the workshop. All eyes fell on Fritz, who shot Benno a resentful glare.

"No, but she will retire from the position when she comes of age and marries as the archduke's adopted daughter. Everyone in the temple knows this. She cannot get married while serving here."

Benno gulped at the presence of such a clear deadline, but the gray priests simply nodded in support of Fritz's words and returned to their work. And with the workshop checkup complete, Fritz gestured toward the door, signaling that it was time to leave. Benno and Mark promptly obliged, with Benno speaking words of encouragement to a nearby apprentice gray priest on his way out.

"Fritz, are you sure Lady Rozemyne's going to stay here until she comes of age?"

"I heard from Fran that she intends to remain High Bishop until then. However, this does not mean you will always be able to discuss matters with her as you have been. You will surely be forbidden from entering her hidden room long before then, as it is frowned upon to allow those of the opposite gender inside. Hidden rooms are very private, personal places for nobles."

Benno was able to discern from this information that, under normal circumstances, entry would only be permitted to someone like a future spouse. If that was basic knowledge to nobles, then gray priests and a commoner merchant certainly wouldn't be allowed inside forever. Rozemyne's guardian, the High Priest, was only permitting it for the time being because she currently lacked the common sense of a noble, needed connections to her commoner life to remain emotionally stable, and still looked absurdly young on the outside. It wouldn't be strange for their access to be revoked at any moment.

"...How long do you expect we've got before that happens?"

"I can provide no definite answer, but I would guess quite soon after she turns ten and starts attending the Royal Academy. At the absolute longest, you might retain access until her fiancé is chosen."

There were only two years until Rozemyne turned ten. Benno had always known that the hidden room wouldn't be an option for them forever, but that was an even shorter time frame than he expected.

Fritz gave a sympathetic smile, sensing Benno's slight panic. "I am somewhat anxious about this as well. As her attendants, Gil and I have been instructed to continue operating the workshop even after she leaves the temple so that the orphans can continue to sustain themselves using their own money. But Gil still struggles to comprehend that Lady Rozemyne will one day leave the temple. It is therefore my duty as one who has experienced such loss before to prepare for the day that will inevitably come, and to that end, I intend to keep in close contact with the Plantin Company, regardless of Gil's presence or Lady Rozemyne's protection."

Fritz's voice conveyed none of the anxiousness that he claimed to feel, his peaceful smile exuding such strength that Benno couldn't help but blink in surprise. He had worked with Fritz before and received many reports from him, but it felt like this was the first time he was actually having a real conversation with him.

"I intend to increase the frequency with which I visit the Plantin Company. Master Benno, I look forward to working together with you."

"Same to you, Fritz."

If Gil and Lutz being away on long-term business trips was going to become standard practice, Benno needed to strengthen his relationship with Fritz. The two men exchanged a glance, then firmly shook hands.

Upon leaving the temple, Benno and Mark got back into their carriage. It was annoying that they needed to use one when visiting the temple, but they were the High Bishop's favored merchants—there was no getting around it. The doors closed, and only once the carriage was rattling down the road did Benno let out a heavy sigh.

"Mark, we've got two years. We're gonna need to prepare for when we can't discuss things in the hidden room anymore. Do you think we'll make it? Gotta admit, I'm worried about Rozemyne here."

Benno picked up Lutz's letter. His absence alone made it hard to get messages to Rozemyne's lower city family, and Benno was quickly reminded of just how sad she had looked. When access to the hidden room was inevitably restricted, she would get even fewer opportunities to properly speak with Lutz and Tuuli. That would probably place a heavy burden on her heart.

"There is nothing we can do about that ourselves, Master Benno. The most we can do for Lady Rozemyne is train Tuuli to be a personal craftswoman for the nobility, ensure Lutz is capable enough to visit the castle, and entrust Gunther with continuing to guard the priests on their way to Hasse. We have received powerful advice from Fritz—advice we must use as best we can. This is hardly different from our usual situation," Mark concluded with a laugh. He was right.

Prologue

Benno started to relax slightly. "You've got a point—dwelling on this won't change the outcome. Besides, no matter how much we prepare, she always goes way beyond our expectations like it's nothing at all," he said, starting to cackle himself.

Soon enough, the carriage arrived at the Plantin Company, and the driver opened the door for them. When Benno and Mark stepped out, the cool air signaling the approach of autumn brushed over them.

The New Orphans and Operation Grimm

I had a meeting scheduled for this afternoon with Richt—Hasse's mayor—so we were leaving the temple after lunch. Accompanying me were Fran, Monika, my two guard knights, and Ferdinand, who was himself accompanied by his guard knight Eckhart and the scholar Justus.

"I have very much been looking forward to riding in your highbeast, milady."

"Unfortunately, Justus, you will not be riding with me today."

"Guh?! Why not?!"

Justus must not have expected me to turn him down; his head spun in my direction, an absolutely flabbergasted expression on his face. But I hadn't forgotten how annoying it had been the last time he rode with me.

"You talk nonstop, which makes it very hard to focus."

"Milady, please excuse my impertinence, but your language is a little harsh…"

"I think it necessary, otherwise you would attempt to wriggle your way into getting what you desire, would you not? I have learned how to deal with you."

He looked hurt by my remark, but it was his own fault for refusing to listen unless you were harsh with him.

It was at this point that Ferdinand stepped in. "She has turned you down, Justus. Give up and ride on your own highbeast."

"Aah, but my hopes and dreams..." Justus groaned, looking wistfully at my Pandabus.

Ferdinand shook his head, muttering something about Justus being foolish before taking out his own highbeast. "Justus, you can either take out your highbeast or return to the Noble's Quarter. Choose. In the meantime, Rozemyne, we may leave as soon as you are ready."

The journey to Hasse was fairly short by highbeast. When we arrived, we found Richt and the chiefs of the neighboring towns kneeling by the front door. That much deserved some respect, considering they were all busy with the upcoming autumn harvest.

After exchanging our lengthy greetings, we stepped inside. Waiting for us in the parlor were incense, flowers, and freshly squeezed juice, which Fran tested for poison. I then exchanged a glance with Ferdinand, who was holding a glass himself.

Well, looks like they didn't at all understand what that "We shall prepare offerings of sweet fruits and beautiful flowers to you" *line actually means...*

"Richt, how is this year's harvest looking? Has missing Spring Prayer had a noticeable impact?"

"It has. Things will certainly be very difficult for us, as expected. I only hope we can have a proper Spring Prayer next year," Richt said, hanging his head sadly with the town chiefs. No matter how carefully one tended to their fields, the land simply wouldn't produce a considerable enough yield without being blessed. They could hardly expect a good harvest without the help of Spring Prayer.

"I have come to deliver news of a temple decree," I announced. "We shall be sending two gray priests to stay in Hasse this winter, to ensure there are no lingering embers of rebellion."

Richt's head shot up as though he had been struck by lightning, his expression making it more than clear that he was stunned we still didn't trust him. I could empathize with how he felt, since he and the entire city were working together now, but it wasn't appropriate for him to show his emotions so openly when speaking to nobles.

"That insurance is of course important," I continued, "but my true objective lies elsewhere."

"Your true objective?" Richt asked, blinking in confusion.

I nodded as gravely as I could. "Yes. The gray priests will use this winter to teach the people of Hasse how to properly interact with and write to nobles. It seems the long reign of the previous High Bishop has resulted in you developing some quite abnormal practices."

"Truly? What sort of practices, exactly?" he asked, visibly disturbed. It was more than apparent that he didn't realize how odd their behavior had been. He might have remembered how the previous mayor had failed to understand the phrase "climbed the towering staircase," subsequently digging his own grave by continuing to act all haughty.

"You do not understand the meaning behind the phrases you use to end the letters you always send me, do you?"

"The meaning...?" Richt glanced between us nervously.

Ferdinand deliberately shifted his gaze, directing Richt to the flowers in the room. "The phrasing that you used is understood by nobles to mean you will prepare wine, women, and money in return for us granting you favors," he explained.

"What?! W-We had absolutely no idea!" Richt exclaimed, the blood immediately draining from his face. I could understand his reaction; anyone would be shocked to learn that the phrasing they had been using all this time actually meant something very crude.

Meanwhile, the town chiefs widened their eyes in shock, unable to believe that another of Hasse's mayors had managed to disrespect the nobility. They trembled in fear of what new punishment now awaited them, fresh off the heels of their last one.

Seeing all this, Ferdinand waved a wary hand. "It is not uncommon for words to lose their meaning as those in power are replaced, and the lack of wine and women makes it clear that you did not understand what you had written. For this reason, we have no intention of punishing you. But can you imagine how a noble would react if such a letter were their first communication with you?"

"I can. You have my sincerest apologies," Richt said, kneeling and hanging his head low. The town chiefs quickly followed suit.

"We are hoping that you can learn from the gray priests we send to Hasse," I said. "If you do not understand noble euphemisms, problems of this nature will only continue to occur. And I would not like for Hasse to suffer more than it already has."

"We are deeply honored by your concern, High Bishop, and will graciously accept the teachings of your gray priests."

Both Richt and the town chiefs were looking at me with moved eyes: they seemed to be viewing me as a deeply compassionate saint. I really wasn't one, but I thought I would at least use this brief opportunity to make them promise to treat the gray priests well.

"The gray priests sent to Hasse shall serve as my representatives. Should you mock them as orphans or look down on them in any way, I will have them promptly return to the monastery," I asserted, hoping that my threat would prevent any harassment. "I ask that you ensure all of your citizens know that the gray priests are there to confirm your loyalty and teach you to speak to nobles. If no problems occur over the winter, I believe we should be able to hold Spring Prayer for you without any issue. All you must do is continue working hard for a little longer."

"We thank you," Richt replied. The tension drained from his shoulders, and the town chiefs who were gathered also looked a little relieved.

"Now then—what business did you all have with us, Richt?"

"As requested in our letter, we would appreciate it if you could purchase several orphans from us. To speak honestly, we will already struggle to overcome the winter, and nobody else is willing to buy them while the archduke is punishing us."

With people avoiding Hasse for the duration of its punishment, I could easily imagine them being shot down everywhere they went. I of course felt bad for the orphans being sold, but I didn't mind purchasing them myself to help out with a problem I'd caused in the first place.

"I do not mind buying the orphans. But once they enter the temple's orphanage, they will henceforth be treated as priests and shrine maidens. They will never return to Hasse as citizens, and so the younger they are, the better."

After joining the temple, it wasn't easy to leave. The main consideration here was that the children of Hasse who stayed in the city's orphanage were given plots of land when they grew up, but that would no longer be the case for those who joined the temple; they would become gray priests and shrine maidens for life, living the remainder of their days according to the whims of nobles.

"You would not mind purchasing the younger children?" Richt asked, his eyes wide with surprise. Younger orphans were rarely picked, since they couldn't be used for labor until they had grown big and strong enough. They just weren't worth the money.

"I would rather not snatch away the futures of those on the verge of coming of age and receiving their own land. Younger children also adapt to new customs faster, so they will have an easier time adjusting to the monastery. I am told that Nora, one of the orphans we bought last year, is greatly struggling to adapt to temple life due to having been so close to coming of age."

"I see…"

They brought the orphans younger than ten over to us. They were all pretty much in rags, but unlike last time, they weren't covered in bruises. None appeared to be hurt, and they were all being kept clean. I let out a small sigh, relieved that they weren't being abused, then looked at Richt.

"How many do you need us to buy?"

"May I ask that you purchase at least four?"

I agreed to buying four of the pre-baptism orphans. Justus the scholar wrote up the documents for us, then Ferdinand signed them as my guardian, since I was still underage. As this was being done, I smiled at the orphans, who all seemed nervous about moving to the monastery.

"Fear not. You won't be alone in the monastery: Nora and the others are going to be there."

And so, I took the new orphans to the monastery in Lessy. Nora and the others greeted us there, welcoming the fresh faces. We had contacted them ahead of time, so beds, clothes, and the like were all already prepared. It was a huge relief to see the children relax a little upon seeing people they recognized.

"Everyone, these children shall be joining you in the monastery. I hope you will help accustom them to temple life by the Harvest Festival. You are going to be spending the winter here, but they are young enough that we shall be moving them to Ehrenfest following the festival. Please remember your struggles when you first arrived here and assist them in growing as you have."

"As you wish."

And with that, Hasse's monastery received more orphans.

Once the summer coming-of-age ceremony and autumn baptism ceremony were complete, things would get busy with everyone preparing for the Harvest Festival and subsequent winter.

In the midst of all this, I had to select which gray priests would be going to Hasse. I needed two of them to teach Richt and the others noble manners, and four to exchange places with those in the monastery for winter. But it wasn't as though I knew every gray priest in the orphanage, their personalities and abilities included, so I decided to leave the decision to those who were more informed—Fritz, who ran the workshop, and Wilma, who ran the orphanage.

"Monika, send word. I shall go to both the workshop and orphanage after lunch."

"As you wish."

After seeing Monika briskly walk off, clearly excited to see Wilma, I turned to look at Brigitte. This seemed as good an opportunity as any.

"Brigitte, would you mind guarding me on these visits this afternoon?"

Up until now, I had only ever brought Damuel with me to the workshop, so as to avoid leaking any unnecessary information about our profits and such to other nobles. Now that we were establishing a paper-making workshop in Illgner and involving them in the printing industry, however, there was no need to hide anything from Brigitte.

"Now that Illgner has its own workshop, there is nothing in our workshop that I need to hide from you," I continued. "I think it would be best for the sister of Giebe Illgner to see these things personally."

Brigitte widened her eyes, then broke into a smile and knelt before me. "I am honored, Lady Rozemyne. I would like nothing more than to accompany you."

And so, following lunch, Brigitte and I went to the workshop. Most nobles would hate traveling to the basement where commoners worked, but judging by how life was in Illgner, I doubted she would mind.

"Thank you for coming, Lady Rozemyne."

I entered the workshop to find everybody kneeling in wait, and my attendant Fritz gave the customary greeting as their representative. It was one for nobles, which I accepted with a nod.

"Fritz, please have everyone resume their work. I would like Brigitte to see what we do here. Do you recall that Illgner is the province Gil and Lutz are currently visiting? Brigitte is family to Giebe Illgner."

"Understood. Everyone, continue your work."

As ordered, the workers all got back to what they had previously been doing. Some were swishing pulp in suketas, while others worked the printing press, which made loud smacking sounds interrupted only by the pleasant clinking of metal letter types being swapped around.

"Fritz, would you come with me to the orphanage when you have a moment?"

"I am free for as long as you are here, Lady Rozemyne. We can leave as soon as Lady Brigitte has finished looking around," he replied, wearing a peaceful smile as he spoke. As expected, my attendants were the shining image of competence; he asked one of the younger children in the workshop to go and inform Wilma of our upcoming visit, then gave instructions to some other gray priests.

"Brigitte, this is where the paper is made. Over there is the printing press," I explained. "It seems they have already invented a new kind of paper in Illgner, so we should soon begin printing there as well."

As she listened, Brigitte watched the suketas being swished about with great interest. "They've made a new type of paper in Illgner?" she asked with a smile.

We stayed and watched the workshop operate for a short while, but I thought it best that we leave relatively soon so as to avoid interfering with the workers. "Shall we go to the orphanage, Brigitte?" I called out.

She regretfully looked around one last time as everyone paused what they were doing to kneel. I circled the workshop floor to speak to them all.

"I am glad to have had the opportunity to see you work today. Please continue your efforts."

Fritz guided us through the girls' building's basement, where the apprentice gray shrine maidens stopped making soup to sidle against the walls and kneel. They didn't look surprised to see us because of the child who had been sent ahead earlier to inform them.

"It is thanks to your efforts that everyone in the orphanage gets to eat warm soup. I imagine it is tough to make food for so many people, but please continue to do your best," I said, offering them words of encouragement. I made sure to move on reasonably quickly, since keeping the shrine maidens from their duties for too long might cause the soup to burn.

We climbed up the stairs and entered the dining hall, where we found Wilma kneeling in wait. "Monika told me you have something to discuss," she said.

I sat in the chair offered to me, looking up at both Fritz and Wilma. "Please select two gray priests to be sent to Hasse's winter mansion, and four to switch places with those in the monastery. The two sent to the winter mansion will be teaching noble euphemisms and the like to those who write letters and documents, so they will ideally be experienced attendants, skilled at teaching others, and friendly enough with one another to work together well."

Whoever they chose would be stuck in an unfamiliar place with an unfamiliar culture for the entirety of winter. That was a challenge in itself, and things would only be more arduous if the two selected didn't even get along together.

"Please pick two men and two women for the monastery. That can include apprentices. I would appreciate them already being on good terms with Nora and the others as well."

"As you wish."

With my business there done, I returned to my High Bishop's chambers, sipping the tea that had been poured for me by Nicola as I spoke to Brigitte. "So, what did you think about the workshop?"

"I had no idea one could make paper like that. It was quite the surprise."

"Is that all…? Do you not have any thoughts on the gray priests there?"

Brigitte placed a contemplative hand on her cheek, her expression thoughtful. "I did think they were surprisingly hard workers; I don't recall seeing anyone engaged in any idle chatter."

"That's true. They're all very dedicated. But that's not all I wanted you to see," I said, giving her a more serious look. "You know that I will be visiting Illgner during the Harvest Festival to retrieve the members of the Plantin Company, yes? Well, Ferdinand will also be accompanying me. He is my guardian, and he wishes to see the status and results of the first printing workshop built in a noble's province."

"That will be quite the honor," Brigitte said with a smile.

As the archduke's adopted daughter, I would be providing my support to Illgner, establishing the paper-making industry there before doing so in any other province. On top of that, the archduke's half-brother Ferdinand would be visiting as well. Any noble would consider that an honor.

"With that in mind, you will need to instruct Giebe Illgner to educate his people in preparation for our visit."

"Educate his people, you say...?" Brigitte asked in confusion.

"Yes. The people of Illgner are quite close to the giebe and his family, are they not? While I personally like their free-spiritedness, I can't imagine Ferdinand will share my view."

"Illgner truly is a country province, one rarely visited by other nobles. They may act a little overly familiar with the nobility, but they mean no ill."

"But do you not agree that their intention is irrelevant? Entire cities can be destroyed simply for not knowing how to behave around nobles. Surely you have not forgotten the situation with Hasse."

Brigitte paled in an instant, having seen the entire Hasse incident from start to finish as my guard knight. Up until now, I could assume she had only sympathized with the commoners who lived close to the Noble's Quarter, but Illgner would end up in the same situation if nobles started to visit. Ignorance would not be a strong enough excuse for them.

"Illgner has done well up to this point due to the lack of visiting nobles, but that will soon change. I imagine many other giebes will develop an interest in your province once it becomes known that you are making paper sooner than anywhere else. I can predict them wanting to see how the workshops function, how much profit they earn, and so on. What will happen if commoners approach them and act without the proper respect?"

"But educating them all…? Is that truly reasonable?"

Changing one's behavior so suddenly was not an easy thing to do, and it would certainly be hard to educate so many commoners before the Harvest Festival. But Brigitte had no other option if she wanted to keep them safe.

"Illgner embraced the printing industry to earn my protection; there is no backing out now. Its people must learn to act in a way that will not earn the wrath of visiting nobles. There is no other way to protect them."

Brigitte stood up, the blood having completely drained from her face. I gently took her hand in mine.

"As you saw, those in my workshop know how to behave around nobles. I simply ask that you tell the giebe what happened in Hasse, and at the very least have those working in his estate and the workshop learn proper manners. I don't want to see a repeat of what Hasse went through," I said, thinking back on how peaceful of a province Illgner was.

Brigitte nodded, tears welling up in her eyes. "I thank you ever so much for your valuable advice, Lady Rozemyne. I will discuss this matter with my brother at once," she said, her serious work expression morphing to one of grave desperation.

The gray priests to be moved to Hasse were chosen, and I sent word to the Plantin Company asking them to handle various preparations. The days sped past at an alarming speed, with discussions of the upcoming Harvest Festival and ruelle gathering coming up again and again.

Soon enough, it was almost time for the Harvest Festival. Fritz informed me that the selected gray priests were preparing to leave, and so I went to the orphanage to give them words of encouragement. Fran and Zahm were carrying large boxes, while Monika held one that wasn't quite so sizable.

The gray priests leaving for Hasse were all assembled in the orphanage's dining hall. Wilma introduced them one at a time, then concluded the noble greetings.

I first spoke with the two priests and two apprentice shrine maidens leaving for Hasse's monastery. "I have received word from Ingo that the monastery now has a printing press of its own. There are presently few residents there, and none of them know how to print. I am looking forward to your efforts this winter."

We needed more people in Hasse to get involved in the printing industry, and I was genuinely eager for them to do their best there.

"Understood," came their crisp replies.

I nodded at them and then looked to Fran, who opened the box he was holding and distributed its contents to the four. Just like last time, they each received a diptych as a gift.

"This is my gift to all of you who shall be working hard in Hasse. I imagine you all know from my attendants how to use them. Each diptych belongs to you individually and is not something you need to share with others. Take care not to forget to write your names on them."

"We are honored," they all replied. The gray priests spoke with gentle smiles, while the apprentice shrine maidens broke into broad grins.

With that done, I turned to the two gray priests leaving for Hasse's winter mansion. "Achim, Egon—I entrust you both with diptychs as well. I imagine the two of you will struggle more than anyone, having to spend the winter in an entirely different world than the one you are used to, but I trust you to both succeed."

"Lady Rozemyne…"

"You have two jobs, the first of which is to teach all this to the mayor and his associates," I said, gesturing toward the box Zahm had brought. Inside were stacks of boards detailing everything I wanted Hasse to learn about, including euphemisms and letter formats that any noble would know as a matter of course.

Incidentally, these were the very same boards that Fran had so kindly prepared for me when I was a commoner. I planned to organize the lessons and put together an educational textbook once book prices were low enough for commoners to buy them.

"I am certain no problems will arise in the winter mansion, but they may look down on you as orphans. Even with all your compassion, if at any point you find their treatment of you unbearable, leave for the monastery at once. I will not begrudge you, and Hasse's mayor has already been informed."

I then looked toward Monika. Inside her box were playing cards, karuta, and picture books for entertainment.

"It is my understanding that there is little to do for fun in winter mansions, but I hope you can form bridges by reading these picture books to children, playing cards with the adults, and so on," I continued. "I must emphasize that the books are very expensive, however, so let no one else handle them. Should anything happen to them, Hasse will need to cover the costs."

"Understood."

Those raised in the orphanage had been thoroughly trained to handle things with care, so none of them had ever broken anything thus far. But whether this would also be the case in Hasse, I couldn't say. These books were expensive enough that even some nobles hesitated to buy them, and I didn't want them treated roughly. The karuta and playing cards would be fine, since they were made of wood, but the books could end up getting ripped to shreds in no time, which would easily make me madder than the former mayor's rudeness had. There was no doubt about that.

I next signaled for Monika to take out the ink and notepads from her box, the latter of which were made from dud paper. She handed both to Achim and Egon.

"And now for your second job," I continued. "You are to gather and write down stories from the people of Hasse."

"Stories?"

"Yes. Just as nobles have tales about knights and the temple has stories of the gods, commoners have tales that only they know. Hasse might have ones from traveling merchants, or local stories that have circulated through farming towns for generations. They will all one day become material for my books, so I ask you to use this opportunity to write them down. In truth, this job is more important than anything else."

This was my true objective, one I revealed to neither Ferdinand nor the townsfolk who worshiped me as a deeply compassionate saint. What I truly wanted from this was a collection of stories known only to commoners. And the name of my plan? Operation Grimm. I would collect stories from all over the country—tales that had been passed down through oral tradition.

Hasse was only the beginning. Assuming things worked out there, I would send gray priests to winter mansions all over, under the guise of teaching commoners how to properly speak to nobles. I would then gather stories from the noble-ruled provinces while spreading printing workshops. The workers would no doubt jump to collect them for me if a set sum was offered for each one. Then, once Ehrenfest was conquered, I would move on to collecting stories from other duchies as well. My ambitions were endless.

I hope it goes well. Operation Grimm... Eheheh.

My plan was to raise the literacy rate among commoners in the meantime, but books being too expensive for them to buy had really thrown a wrench in the works. There was also the likelihood that more than a few people would discover the joy of reading, only to go insane from not having access to any new books. That was a feeling I knew all too well—one that was much too sad to put others through. From the bottom of my heart, I hoped to make them available enough that even commoners could soon fund book rooms for their winter mansions.

The day came for the Plantin Company's carriage to leave for Hasse ahead of the Harvest Festival. Those heading to the monastery were loading luggage into the carriages, with other members of the orphanage helping them. Meanwhile, those going to the winter mansion were getting ready to travel separately with me, since I was leaving for the festival itself.

"The carriage will have the same number of people on the return trip. But do take care—the orphans in Hasse include pre-baptism children."

"Understood. Ah... It seems the soldiers have arrived."

While the gray priests were loading the Plantin Company's carriages, the soldiers who would be guarding them arrived. Dad was marching enthusiastically at the front. I hadn't seen him in such a long time. I gave him a smile, and upon meeting my gaze, he returned a grin and knelt in front of me.

"Thank you for coming, Gunther. We are enlisting your aid once again."

"Honorable High Bishop, you can always count on us to help when you are in need," Dad said in a polite tone. The other soldiers promptly followed up with lively responses of their own.

"I'll rush over here way faster than, er... I shall arrive swifter than the commander himself."

"I will too. Just say the word."

"Shut it, you two. You're being disrespectful," Dad said, silencing them with a glare.

"I see you are once again accompanied by a hearty group of soldiers," I said with a giggle. "It is thanks to all of you that I can rest easy, knowing my gray priests will remain safe outside the city walls."

"They will indeed. I await the chance to see you again at the monastery."

And so, after the briefest of exchanges, I sent the carriages off to Hasse. With the Plantin Company gone, it was time for me to prepare for my own departure. I planned to bring several books with me to the Harvest Festival this year; I wouldn't be able to survive the heated fervor for long without some good stories to relax with.

"Milady, it is a pleasure to work with you again this year."

"Oh, the pleasure is all mine, Justus."

Justus was coming along as a tax official, while Eckhart and Brigitte were serving as my guard knights. Ferdinand had instructed that Eckhart and Damuel swap places for this mission, since Damuel and Brigitte alone wouldn't have been able to stop Justus's rampages.

"Eckhart, I entrust them all to you. May we meet again in Dorvan," Ferdinand said.

"Yes, sir!" Eckhart replied, then turning to look at Damuel. "Until then, I trust you to guard Lord Ferdinand in my stead."

"Understood."

After enduring an endless list of warnings from Ferdinand for what felt like an eternity, I climbed into my already-prepared Pandabus. Achim and Egon were inside, as well as Fran, Monika, Nicola, Hugo, and Rosina—the latter two coming with me as my personal chef and musician, respectively.

Ella was staying home for this one—our journey was set to be a long one, and Hugo simply had more stamina. Instead, she would be making food for the orphans and my other attendants while I was gone. Fritz and Zahm were staying behind as well, the latter of whom was being entrusted with running the entire temple while Ferdinand was gone.

Who had it harder between us? It was impossible to say.

"Well, Ferdinand, I'm off. May we meet again in Dorvan."

"Do try not to cause any problems."

"We'll see."

"That is not an answer," he sighed, rubbing his temples. But I simply avoided making eye contact and gripped Lessy's steering wheel. I poured mana into him, stepped on the gas pedal, and up into the air we went.

So began my long journey for the Harvest Festival.

Hasse and the Gray Priests

"Now then," I began, "please do ensure that the rooms and food are prepared."

Since we were traveling by air, our journey to Hasse had been a short one. I landed my highbeast by the monastery, at which point all of my attendants and personnel alighted except Fran. When their luggage had been taken out and moved into the monastery, I departed for the winter mansion.

When we were high in the sky above the mansion, I furrowed my brow.

What…? There's nobody there. Did I get the date wrong or something?

The year before, while the people were waiting for us to arrive, a bustling crowd was preparing the large, field-like plaza for the festival. But this year, there were no signs of any people nor any preparations being made. I had sent a letter ahead of time outlining the date of my visit, but perhaps I had written it down incorrectly, or simply just misread something.

Brigitte, who was flying ahead of me on her highbeast, pointed down toward the ground and began to descend. I could see several people kneeling by the front door of the winter mansion, and when I strained my eyes, I recognized them as Richt and the town chiefs.

"High Bishop," Richt said, "thank you for coming."

Hasse and the Gray Priests

While I received my greetings, Fran, Achim, and Egon began taking more luggage-filled boxes out of my Pandabus. When you combined their living necessities, learning materials, and recreational items, there was a surprising amount to unload. Once they were done, I put away my highbeast.

"Richt, why aren't you preparing for the Harvest Festival?"

"...We are naturally refraining from holding such large-scale festivities while out of the archduke's favor. This year, we hope to perform only the ritual and pay our taxes."

Richt went on to explain that it was difficult for them to hold the festival as they usually would with the eyes of their neighbors and traveling merchants on them. But they still needed to hold the baptism, coming-of-age, and wedding ceremonies, which they hoped to do quietly in the gathering hall of the winter mansion.

"I see..." I said, feeling a little nervous. The people here had endured a harsh year without a blessing, they were unable to hold the once-a-year celebration that everyone loved, and now here I was sending two gray priests to keep an eye on them. Would Achim and Egon really be safe here with everyone so unhappy?

I glanced over at the two gray priests, at which point Fran stepped forward to introduce them. "These are the gray priests who shall be staying here and representing the High Bishop this winter. Their names are Achim and Egon."

With that, Achim and Egon crossed their arms in front of their chests and crouched a little. Richt and the others tensed up at the sight: these men may have been gray priests, but they were my representatives and soon to be their teachers. Hasse's very future was resting in their hands, so I could imagine that Richt was nervous to see what they were like as people.

"Richt, please guide us to their room. As you can see, they have much luggage with them, and I would like to see the conditions in which they will be staying."

"As you wish. Please follow me."

One of the town chiefs hurried off on Richt's instruction to send word of our arrival. Richt then led us into the mansion, heading toward the room where Achim and Egon would be staying. Fran and the two priests were carrying boxes behind me, followed closely by Justus and my guard knights. The furor of playing children could be heard at first, but this quickly quieted down as we walked.

It's quiet now, but I can feel eyes all over me...

We climbed a creaky staircase to the living area. Several curious children poked their heads out from around corners or behind cracked-open doors, and while I smiled whenever I made eye contact with one, they always gasped or ran away to hide. It seemed that they considered me quite scary.

It's good to think of nobles as scary—I mean, they're not wrong there. But it kind of seems like the boys are trying to show how brave they are by sneaking glances at me. That's a bit worrying...

Some doors were open wide enough for me to see inside the rooms beyond them. They were of various different sizes, with each one housing an entire family. Some were classroom-sized with a dozen people sleeping on straw mattresses strewn about the floor, while others were small with an actual bed inside. They largely resembled my lower city home—that is, before I started cleaning it from top to bottom.

"This is where they will be staying. It is the closest room to my office. Here, they will be able to minimize contact with the others, if they so wish."

Richt had stopped in front of a two-person room. Considering it had two separate beds, I could guess that he had reserved an especially high-quality room for them.

Fran, Achim, and Egon set their boxes down, then collectively grimaced as they examined the interior.

"My apologies, but could you tell us where the well and cleaning utensils are, so that we might clean the room?" Fran asked. It was probably unbearably filthy for those raised in the always-immaculate temple and orphanage. I could definitely sympathize with them—after all, back in the lower city, the first thing I had done when I got to my feet was clean.

One of the town chiefs blinked in surprise, then hurried off to ask a woman where the cleaning utensils were. I let out a quiet sigh. "Achim, Egon—if you wish to clean this room to make it as comfortable as possible for the both of you, that is perfectly fine. But please take care not to force the temple's lifestyle on everyone else. This is not the temple."

"Understood."

Achim, Egon, and Fran all opened their mouths as if about to protest, but promptly conceded after seeing the cleaning utensils the town chief returned with. Perhaps it would be best to give them some support here.

"Achim, Egon—might I suggest taking a set of cleaning utensils from the monastery tomorrow? If there is anything else you need, you may ask Fran."

"Your concern honors us, Lady Rozemyne."

They both resolved to endure the room as it was for the night, then give it a thorough clean in the morning the next day. It was pretty funny seeing them seriously discuss whether or not they would also need a washtub for cleaning themselves, considering this place probably didn't even have tools for cleaning clothes.

"Richt, is everything ready for the ceremony?"

"Yes, Lady Rozemyne. Please follow us to the dining hall."

The winter mansion's dining hall had a much lower ceiling than the castle's grand hall, and the floor was covered in stains and oily substances, likely due to feasts having been held there. A strange smell wafted through the air as well.

That said, no matter how bad this is, they probably made a real attempt to clean it as much as they could.

The festival was always held outside, so they almost certainly hadn't expected priests and tax officials to be entering the winter mansion itself. I could bear it, but Eckhart had a very stern look on his face.

There was a stage prepared in the hall, and just like last year, I stood at the altar with Justus, Fran, and my two guard knights. Aside from us being inside, nothing seemed to have really changed; I summoned the children who were to be baptized onto the stage, blessing them after reading aloud the picture books about the gods. The coming-of-age and wedding ceremonies were also pretty similar to the year prior, but everyone looked sick rather than celebratory, and there was a heavy air of sorrow weighing down the whole room.

Once the ceremonies were over, I called Achim and Egon up onto the stage to introduce them.

"People of Hasse—despite the difficulties you have endured this year, having had to farm without a blessing, you have worked well. The archduke has instructed that two gray priests be sent to your winter mansion to ensure that no embers of rebellion still linger. Their names are Achim and Egon. They are here to watch over you, but also to teach you."

A stir ran through the crowd at the word *"teach."*

"Recent letters from Hasse were found to contain language that is highly disrespectful. Were another noble to receive such letters, their anger would be palpable. Such a mistake was born simply due to the failures of your previous mayor and your inexperience with nobles, but once again, Hasse was on the verge of making a grave mistake."

Some people were shocked to hear that they were angering nobles once again. Others let out angry cries about the mayor failing to do his job right. I held up a hand to silence them.

"You will not be punished for these affronts. Instead, I have instructed these two gray priests—both highly familiar with how to communicate with nobles—to use this opportunity to teach your mayor and his workers the proper language to use when communicating with nobles. If they study well and remember these lessons, I am sure there will be no more incidents such as this."

The people's anger faded once they understood that not only were they not going to be punished, but they were being offered an opportunity to learn from their mistakes. It was important to use this moment of relief to put my foot down.

"The gray priests are orphans, but understand that they are directly representing me, the High Bishop. If they are at any point treated poorly, they will move to the monastery. I trust that you would not be so foolish as to abuse them right as your punishment is coming to an end, but regardless, take care to be respectful when speaking to them."

At this remark, the people gathered in the hall all wore dark expressions, visible even from up on stage. It was obvious that they expected their punishment to never end.

Well, they did work hard for an entire year without a blessing. I think they deserve at least a little relief.

I pursed my lips in thought, then walked from the center of the stage to the edge, where Eckhart and the others were standing in wait.

"Eckhart, Justus."

"Yes, Lady Rozemyne?"

"Might we permit them to play a little warf? I believe too much restraint is bad for the heart."

Eckhart grimaced at my suggestion, clearly thinking about how furious Ferdinand would get if we deviated from the plan, but Justus actually smiled in amusement. "It is important to take breathers, milady, and the people will surely be moved if they are told you permitted it yourself," he said. "I personally consider it a fine idea, though normal nobles would never take into account the feelings of mere commoners."

With Justus in my corner, I took Achim and Egon over to where Richt was. "Richt, I appreciate your rationale for not holding the festival, but would tensions not explode during the winter if the people don't relieve any of their stresses?" I asked quietly.

His eyes wavered for a moment, then he gave a nod. "You may be right."

"You and I shall speak in the meeting room, and should something take place outside while we are in there, I am certain that I will not notice it. No matter how loud the people might get. There is surely nothing wrong with doing something that goes unnoticed, don't you agree?"

Richt didn't seem to grasp my implication.

I looked toward Achim. "It seems it is already time for you to work. Would you mind explaining to Richt what I mean?"

Achim blinked in surprise, muttering "Did he truly not understand that?" quietly under his breath. Egon appeared to be just as surprised—his eyes were open wide with disbelief.

"I imagine he did understand in some regard, but the people of Hasse have suffered so much as a result of misunderstandings that they have most likely lost all confidence in their ability to interpret things."

"I see. Mayor Richt, Lady Rozemyne is saying that she will turn a blind eye to any festivities that might take place outside while you and she are discussing matters in the meeting room," Achim explained.

"You may interpret that as her giving you permission to play warf," Egon added.

With that, Richt broke into a smile. "Understood. We have many hot-blooded youths in Hasse, and I am sure they will be overjoyed to hear this."

Richt left setting up the warf tournament to one of the town chiefs and exited the dining hall, guiding me and the others to the meeting room. We heard shouts ring out not long after we were gone.

"The High Bishop gave us her approval! Let's go play some warf!"

"YEAAAH! WOOHOO!"

The townsfolk let out loud, fervent cries, as though all the frustration that had been building up inside them over the year was unleashing all at once.

Achim and Egon flinched and turned around, fearfully looking at the doors to the hall. They must have been genuinely frightened, given that they had never heard people roar so loudly that the vibrations could quite literally be felt through the floor. I could only hope that my gesture of goodwill would help make their time here as peaceful as possible.

In the meeting room, we discussed this year's harvest, taxes, and the tithe that would be paid to me. Hasse's lack of a blessing meant that its harvest was smaller than those of the neighboring cities, but its yield was large enough to prove that the townsfolk really had poured their all into their work.

Just like last year, Justus would be sending the taxes to the castle the next morning, with a portion of my tithe being used to pay for Achim and Egon's winter preparations. The rest would be brought to the monastery rather than the castle to help fund its winter preparations.

As our meeting continued, the warf tournament outside concluded. Energetic voices conveyed a lively atmosphere as they all came back into the hall, their bright tones radiating the fun they had just had, which confirmed to me that permitting the tournament to happen had been the right move.

After the meeting was dinner in the dining hall. I already knew from my time in Illgner that the gray priests would be stunned into silence by how commoners ate, so I instructed Achim and Egon to eat with me so that I could instruct them on what to do.

The commoners lined up the food atop low tables that were nothing more than long boards placed over two large boxes, then sat down on straw and started eating whatever they wanted to. Aside from the knives placed by the meat so that people could help themselves, wooden spoons were the only cutlery available; everyone ate with their hands when they weren't having soup-like foods.

As expected, the whole experience was so unfamiliar to Achim and Egon that they froze in place out of shock. They were supposed to be serving Eckhart and Justus, but instead, they were just standing stock-still, their mouths agape.

Eckhart wasn't scolding them because he too was taken aback by the scene. He had apparently never seen commoners eat up close, as he was always on the stage far away from the plaza, and food was only served when the sun started to set. His stern expression reminded me of when Ferdinand had first watched Hasse's orphans eat.

"If their behavior displeases you, I would recommend looking away," I commented. "This is normal to them."

"They may be able to look away, but they cannot block out the noises," Fran replied, regretfully shaking his head as he served my food. He was largely unfazed, since he had seen this often enough with Nora's group and when accompanying me to Illgner.

"Erm, Lady Rozemyne... where will we be eating?" Achim and Egon asked together, both looking nervous. Tables and chairs had been provided for the nobles in our group, but it must have been assumed that the gray priests wouldn't mind eating with the commoners.

"You may eat with us here for today. I imagine it will take some time for you to adjust to the customs here, so I will ask Richt to prepare a table and chairs in your room so that you may have your food there instead. That should allow you to eat in peace."

"We thank you, Lady Rozemyne," Achim and Egon replied, patting their chests with relieved sighs.

My efforts were of course all for the sake of Operation Grimm, but it seemed that sending gray priests to winter mansions all over was going to be harder than I expected. Having them adjust to the lifestyles of commoners after spending their entire lives in the temple was not looking to be a smooth process at all.

I finished my notably modest meal, having not touched most of the food so that Achim and Egon would have enough to eat. By that time, the beer had already started giving the townsfolk rather loose tongues: they started to grumble and complain about things, either because they were emboldened by the alcohol or because they had forgotten I was up here on stage.

"Y'know, I saw them orphans that got sold to the monastery th'other day. Sure looks like they're eatin' a lot better than us o'er there," one man said. "They're lookin' real good, not to mention all weighty now. Where'd those scrawny sacks a' bone go?"

"Haah... I'm so jealous," a woman chimed in with a wistful sigh. "If someone'd told me they have that much food in the orphanage, I would've wanted to go there myself."

Fran gave a frustrated frown upon hearing all that, but I excitedly clasped my hands together in front of my chest, my eyes shining with excitement. We had sent four people to Hasse, but we still needed a lot more manpower for our printing endeavors. And thankfully, our wallets were overflowing due to how well the books for nobles had sold. I didn't want to force anyone to work in the orphanage due to the discrimination they would face, but if they actively wanted to live there themselves, then by all means...

I called out from the stage in hopes of recruiting at least a few people. "If you wish to come to the orphanage, please do. We at the monastery would welcome you. The truth is, we have more printing presses now and are in need of extra assistance."

Everyone chatting at the nearby table let out goofy-sounding noises in shock; nobody had expected a response from the High Bishop herself. The drunkenness was wiped from their faces in an instant, and although they were starting to look increasingly sick, I continued doing everything I could to shill the virtues of the orphanage.

"Those in the orphanage are given three meals a day, as well as beds, clothes, and the like. They are also educated quite thoroughly, so you will learn to speak properly and act with grace. Young children will go on to serve nobles only a few years after being baptized, and believe it or not, the literacy rate of children raised in the orphanage is one hundred percent. They can all write and do simple math, plus we have picture books, karuta, and playing cards all prepared as educational materials to help speed up the learning process."

My description so far made the orphanage come across as a bona fide paradise, but there was no denying that there were also some drawbacks, and I wasn't about to hide them. I wanted people to join fully aware of all the pros and cons.

"There are, of course, some negatives as well. Once you join the orphanage, the world will scorn you as an orphan forevermore. Priests and shrine maidens must also live at the behest of nobles, paying heed to their every word and deed. It is an entirely different environment from a farming town, and the orphans from Hasse who joined previously are still struggling to adapt to its culture."

"Er, uh... H-High Bishop...?"

The townsfolk were looking conflicted; there must have been something that I'd forgotten to mention.

"Let's see... Oh, yes—those raised in the temple orphanage are given no land upon coming of age, are not permitted to marry, and do not receive a break on Earthday, since they must live every day for the sake of the nobility. It is not uncommon to be abruptly sold to a noble you have never met before either, and the orphans themselves have no say in those matters."

The more I spoke, the more their expressions turned fearful.

"I currently serve as the orphanage director and ensure that everyone receives enough food to have their fill, but living conditions were quite abhorrent before I took up the position, and there is no guarantee that they will not revert back to being abhorrent under my successor. Almost nobody wishes to join the orphanage due to its nightmarish reputation and the future being so uncertain, but if anybody wishes to join us there, I welcome you from the bottom of my heart!"

I excitedly spread out my arms, waiting for people to step forward. And yet, despite how honorably transparent I had been with my explanation, enthusiasm to join was quite frankly nonexistent.

"E-Er, well... I've already got land in Hasse, so... Y'know?" one man mumbled.

"Yeah... I'm gonna get married next year, so I can't just go an' break her heart like that," added another.

"R-Right. When everything's said 'n done, what's most important is livin' on the land you know."

I could understand them not wanting to leave Hasse after having lived there their entire lives—I myself had never intended to leave the lower city. There were some things you just didn't want to give up, no matter how poor or hungry you were.

"I can fully understand not wanting to leave your hometown. It is unfortunate that you will not be joining the orphanage, but I can see your reasoning."

As I sat back down in disappointment, everyone else exchanged blatantly relieved glances, picked their mugs back up, and returned to their food. The sight of commoners eating made the nobles with us grimace, but to me, it was a reminder of how my life used to be in the lower city.

You know, I really want to see Dad right now...

I gripped my sleeves tightly. I only needed to go to the monastery to see him, so when the meal was over, I went over to Richt to announce my departure.

"Richt, I shall be leaving for the monastery soon."

"Thank you for visiting today. Everyone had a wonderful time because of you permitting the warf tournament," he said. There was a relieved smile on his face, which was understandable, since it was his job to keep the winter mansion in check.

"I was also glad to see everybody's mood brighten. Oh, incidentally—Achim and Egon will need a table and some chairs in their room so that they can do written work. Please make arrangements for that."

"Understood."

"Also, much like how the people of Hasse do not know the ways of nobles, the gray priests have lived their lives in the temple and do not understand the ways of the outside world. They eat, clean, and live entirely differently from how you do. Please be considerate of that fact."

With my departure announced, Eckhart knelt in front of me as though I were his mistress. "I will be trusting Brigitte to guard you, Lady Rozemyne. Justus and I will remain here, as is customary, so please return tomorrow morning for the tithe."

And so, I left Eckhart and Justus in the winter mansion, returning to the monastery with Fran and Brigitte. Even there, people were having a loud and hearty meal. I headed to my room, listening to the joyous clamor in the dining hall, while Fran went to eat, entrusting Monika and Nicola to serve me while he was away. It seemed that he had gone without food at the winter mansion so that he could have dinner here instead.

I grabbed a notepad made with white paper and a pen from my room, then went to the dining hall myself, having Monika pull a chair up to the table where the soldiers were enjoying their food.

"Gunther, I am currently collecting stories to make into books. Might I ask what stories you have heard in the lower city?"

Mom had told me a lot of stories, but Dad hadn't really told me many at all.

"Stories, hm? My mother did tell me a few when I was young..." Dad said. He fell into thought for a short while before eventually raising his head. "There once was a family, the siblings of which were closer than you would ever believe. Their names were Tuuli, Myne, and Kamil..."

Thus began a story wherein Kamil and Tuuli raced into a forest to save their beloved sister Myne, who had been kidnapped by feybeasts.

"...And so, Myne was safely returned to her family, and she lived happily ever after with her siblings."

"What a wonderful story..." I said, so moved that my nose was dripping and my eyes brimming with tears. I wrote it all down, and immediately the other soldiers began fighting to tell me the stories they knew. They were all completely new to me and very easy to understand, given that they weren't filled with euphemisms like noble stories were. I could visualize everything instantly.

By the time I had written down three stories in total, seventh bell started to ring. I stood up, overcome with a deep sense of satisfaction.

"Sleep well, everyone."

"Sleep well, High Bishop. May you be blessed with good dreams..."

That night, I did have a dream. It was a very happy one, in which I returned to my lower city home as Myne, and spent the day laughing with my family...

Ruelle Gathering (Take Two)

As pleasant as the dream was, I felt an indescribable loneliness upon waking up.

After eating breakfast, I left cleaning the monastery to Hasse's apprentices and the shrine maidens while having Fran and the adult priests stock Lessy with the cleaning utensils, tubs, soap, and such that Achim and Egon needed. At the same time, my other attendants and personnel loaded their things into carriages, which we then sent on their way. Just like last year, they would be meeting up with the carriages containing Eckhart's and Justus's attendants at Hasse's winter mansion before we headed to the next one.

The Plantin Company carriages held the young orphans being moved from Hasse to the temple. I saw off the guards after giving them their little bonuses, and with that, the brief amount of time I could spend with Dad came to a close.

Once they were gone, we departed for the winter mansion in my Pandabus.

"Achim, Egon, will this be enough, I wonder? Please do visit the monastery if you need anything else."

"Thank you, Lady Rozemyne. Now we should be able to clean exceedingly well." The two gray priests rejoiced, giving big appreciative nods as they accepted the supplies from us. It seemed they were going to pour their hearts into cleaning their room, and that was fine by me. In all honesty, it would have been nice if the people of Hasse saw their work and put a little more effort into cleaning themselves.

"Richt, as discussed yesterday, here is food for the both of them. Please consider it part of their winter preparations."

"Understood."

I gave a portion of the tithe to Richt for Achim and Egon, then had the rest piled into Lessy. This would be used for the monastery's winter preparations.

"Now then, I will see you both when you arrive at the monastery," I said to Eckhart and Justus, the former carefully observing as the latter teleported the collected taxes to the castle. And with that, I promptly brought all the luggage to Hasse's monastery.

Whew. This is a lot of work to be doing first thing in the morning...

All I needed to do now was drive Lessy, but that was tiring enough in itself. I decided to sit in my room in the monastery for the time being and sip tea with Brigitte, taking a much-needed rest.

"I was a bit worried about Hasse's winter preparations, but Nora and the others know what needs to be done, and since this is going to be the third time those from the temple are doing winter preparations, they have grown used to it as well. Things are proceeding smoothly," Fran reported.

I gave a nod in response. The gray priests in the monastery were running around busily, carrying the tithe to the food storage area and hurriedly preserving the perishables. They wouldn't be able to work freely with me about, so it was best for me to stay in my room.

"So, Fran, may I read a book while we wait for Justus and my brother to arrive?"

"...My apologies. The books you prepared are in one of the carriages that has already left."

"No way!"

Ruelle Gathering (Take Two)

The copies from the castle's book room and the knight stories I intended to put into my next book had already departed. Who could have ever seen this coming?

As I wailed, Fran held out a picture book bible. "The books you prepared for leisure reading were too bulky to be held during an entire ceremony," he said with a serious expression. "If you are fine with the picture books read to the children during their baptism ceremony, then... here you are."

"Yay! Thank you ever so much, Fran."

I eagerly flipped through the pages, my eyes racing over the letters. That alone was enough to bring much peace to my heart. Just sitting down with a book helped to steady my breath, and a warm feeling washed over me like I was finally alive again. I honestly wanted the whole world to understand what an essential part of life reading was.

Eckhart and Justus arrived at the monastery while I was blissfully spending my time reading books.

"What in the world inspired you to make these books, milady?" Justus asked, peering over my shoulder at the picture bible. I understood his words, but not the meaning behind them.

"I make books to read books. What other reason could I possibly have?"

"Er, rather, why picture bibles in particular?" he asked. But I couldn't exactly tell him it was because all the stories I knew—both from my Urano days and the ones Mom had told me as a commoner—didn't match the aesthetic sense of my target demographic.

"Because I had never read anything but the bible. I feel that one must read new books to make new books, so if you ever intend to gift me any, I would gladly accept them all."

Justus, being Rihyarda's son, was an archnoble, and there was no doubt in my mind that an information-loving man such as him had a huge collection of interesting books. But when I looked up at him with hope-filled eyes, he returned a stern expression much like one his mother would give.

"Milady, you should never say something like that in public. You will only draw ambitious nobles to you."

I would happily accept bribes from anyone if doing so meant getting more books, but I guess Ferdinand would get mad at me for that... I can already imagine him smacking me on the head with that harisen the moment I leapt onto my pile of illicitly gained reading material.

After finishing a lunch consisting of soup made by the gray shrine maidens and bread baked by Hugo, we set out by highbeast toward the next winter mansion.

Unlike Hasse, the other cities in the Central District had reaped bountiful harvests thanks to having received my blessing, so all the people welcomed us with such fanatical enthusiasm that it actually threw me off. The mayors and town chiefs clasped their hands together and all but begged me to bless their land again next year, and it was all I could do to put on a polite smile and say that I would continue to perform Spring Prayer while serving as the High Bishop.

This experience looped over and over again, the energy of the festivals overwhelming me to the point that I collapsed. I forced myself up again by drinking potions, but this happened several more times over the course of our journey.

In the end, we arrived at Dorvan's winter mansion—where we would be meeting up with Ferdinand—the day before the Night of Schutzaria. Given that we were initially scheduled to arrive with plenty of time to spare, it was safe to say that we had just barely made it.

Ruelle Gathering (Take Two)

Eckhart had apparently sent an ordonnanz to Ferdinand informing him of our situation, and since Ferdinand arrived at Dorvan before us, he performed the Harvest Festival in my stead. The buzz from the celebrations had already died down, and it seemed my peaceful days had returned.

"You are late, Rozemyne. I was getting exceedingly worried that you were not going to make it at all."

"My apologies for worrying you, Ferdinand. And thank you ever so much for performing the Harvest Festival here ahead of time. I am truly, truly grateful that it is over..."

We had also started to fear that we wouldn't make it to Dorvan in time for the Night of Schutzaria. I sighed in relief that those worries had gone unfounded, only for Ferdinand to peer down at me with a frown, touching my cheeks and neck with his hands.

"So cold!"

"No, your body temperature is much too high. Your pulse is abnormally rapid too. Fran, do you have enough potions?"

"We have used about half of what we had prepared before our initial departure," he responded instantly.

Ferdinand glanced over at a box in the middle of the room. "I am storing extra potions in there. Take what you need for the rest of the trip. Rozemyne, drink one and then rest for the remainder of tonight. Your gathering will take place tomorrow."

While Ferdinand ordered me to leave, Fran began stocking up on potions with visible relief. I trudged over to the room that had been prepared for me, had Monika and Nicola change my clothes, then drank the potion that Fran had given me and went to sleep. I couldn't be responsible for this year's gathering being canceled when Karstedt was coming all the way from Ehrenfest just to help out.

I promised Lutz that I'd make it this year too. I need to succeed, no matter what.

I woke up the next morning feeling much better. Eckhart had reunited with Ferdinand, which meant Damuel was serving me again. He seemed a lot more dead-eyed and all-around exhausted since the last time we were together, but his face lit up with relief when he saw me. I smiled and finished breakfast, all the while imagining what insane workload Ferdinand must have dumped on him.

"Rozemyne, you are going to be napping this evening, and I imagine you will sleep better if you use your head in the morning," Ferdinand said. "Come to my room. You can write reports for the Harvest Festival."

I had thought I might be able to use my poor health as an excuse to spend all day lounging around in bed with a book, but Ferdinand wanted me to do paperwork with him almost immediately after waking up. How was that any different from a normal day in the temple?

"I see that grimace on your face, but this is for your own sake," he continued. "The sooner these reports are finished, the sooner we can start making your jureve. We cannot simply begin the moment we have all the ingredients—we must first report the results of the Harvest Festival to the archduke."

Ferdinand was assigned as my doctor and apothecary, so with him pushing me like this, there wasn't much I could do. I simply had to give in and work hard for the sake of my health.

I'm going to power through and finish this jureve so that I can finally be healthy, then I'll read books until I collapse from exhaustion! Just you wait!

Ruelle Gathering (Take Two)

I reluctantly made my way to Ferdinand's room, almost having to fight against the alluring pull of the box with books in it. When we arrived, I found that all the attendants he had brought with him for the Harvest Festival were doing work as well, Eckhart included. Both Ferdinand's tax official and Justus were also busy, writing up reports in their respective rooms.

That was Ferdinand for you, the man who lived to work and let no time go to waste. And once again, he was wrapping everyone around him into his obsession.

I spent some time silently scratching out documents, when an ordonnanz suddenly flew in, its ivory wings flapping majestically. It circled around the room once before landing on Ferdinand's desk and delivering a message in Karstedt's voice.

"I'm almost there. Have lunch ready."

"Understood," Ferdinand replied, and once the ordonnanz had flown away, he looked out the window and sighed.

I followed his gaze to see what he was looking at. It was far away enough that it was little more than a speck, but I could make out the griffon representing the knight commander flying this way. To say Karstedt was almost here was a bit of an understatement.

"That is enough work for today. Clean up and prepare to welcome him," Ferdinand said.

Everyone put away their work at once. Ferdinand's attendants then headed to the front entrance to welcome Karstedt, while my attendants started preparing tea and sweets. They were hurrying about without a shred of dignity or grace to their movements, but their organization nonetheless showed just how skilled they were. By the time Karstedt was brought inside, all the preparations were complete.

"You appear to be doing well, Rozemyne," Karstedt greeted me.

"It's all thanks to Ferdinand's potions," I replied, and it seemed my message was conveyed without me having to spell out that I had been a total mess the day before.

Karstedt's eyes wavered as he searched for the right words. "I'm just glad you have recovered enough for your gathering," he eventually managed to force out.

"How are matters at the castle?" Ferdinand asked casually, taking a seat. Karstedt would ordinarily reply that everything was normal and peaceful, but this time he paused to think. Then, he carefully scanned the room.

"There's something I was told to tell you both. Rozemyne, you stay seated there. Clear the room of everyone but the guard knights."

Once all the attendants were out of the room, Karstedt took out the kind of sound-blocking magic tool that affected an entire area, then activated it. Ferdinand took a deep breath before exhaling.

"Karstedt. What in the world has happened?"

"Nothing as of yet, but there are some dangerous signs popping up."

Everyone tensed up a little. Even if nothing had happened yet, the fact that there was danger would put anyone on guard.

Karstedt looked us over, then continued. "I heard this from Elvira, but... Ferdinand, as I've already mentioned to you, the former Veronica faction has shown signs of reviving as the Georgine faction ever since her visit."

"Yes, I remember you mentioning that. But she is the first wife of Ahrensbach; she doesn't have the ability to lead a faction in Ehrenfest."

Veronica's faction had long been the largest faction due to her having served as the first wife of Ehrenfest during the previous archduke's reign, then having raised the future archduke ever since Florencia was wed into the duchy. It retained this prominence even when Sylvester becoming the archduke caused Florencia and Elvira's faction to steadily grow in both size and power.

Ruelle Gathering (Take Two)

That all changed, however, when Veronica was arrested for abusing her position as the archduke's mother to commit crimes: the more neutral members within her faction instantly switched to Florencia's.

"And that is precisely why the former Veronica faction is attempting to reconvene beneath Lord Wilfried."

"Wilfried...? What does he have to do with a women's faction?"

"The point is not for him to be invited to tea parties or anything like that. I imagine they just need a name to unite themselves under. Lord Wilfried was raised by Lady Veronica, and he opposed the archduke's will by inviting Georgine to return to Ehrenfest," Karstedt explained, reminding me of when we had said our farewells. "He's the perfect figurehead to unify both the former Veronica faction and the new Georgine faction."

"But Wilfried didn't intentionally disobey Sylvester, did he?" I asked. "He just wasn't paying enough attention to what was going on."

Karstedt nodded. "Right. I doubt he was thinking about anything at all. But what matters is how the situation looks to the public."

Ferdinand began tapping a finger against his temple. "This is going to be a pain," he muttered, his eyes narrowing as he fell deep into thought. I hadn't the faintest idea what might have been running through his head.

Karstedt continued speaking in the meantime, providing Ferdinand with more intel. "It seems people are saying that, with Lord Wilfried close to Lady Georgine and very likely to become the next archduke, there's no better leader for them."

This information had come up in conversation during all manner of tea parties due to laynoble connections. Most neutrals were laynobles, since they needed to stick to the dominant faction just to survive, and thanks to that, information flowed freer through them than it did anywhere else.

"So despite all we have done to both unite the factions around Lady Florencia and Rozemyne, and restore Lady Florencia's right to rear Wilfried as his mother, the war between factions is only getting worse?" Ferdinand muttered, tightly knitting his brow.

It seemed that all the hard work Elvira had been doing behind the scenes to form a large faction around the current first wife had now been washed away entirely. This was news to me, but she apparently hadn't just been using the tea parties to gather information about Ferdinand and fangirl over him.

"They have made no open moves yet, at most having spread rumors and some information during the hunting tournament. They can't do much more when Lady Georgine is out of the duchy and Lord Wilfried is under the supervision of his retainers. Normally, this whole mess would just fade away over time. But since Lady Georgine is coming back next summer, it's impossible to squash it completely. We should stay on guard in case they become more active."

"Okay, Father—I have a question!" I exclaimed, launching a hand into the air. "What exactly does staying on guard entail?"

Karstedt, Ferdinand, Eckhart, and Justus all replied in turn.

"Speak to Ferdinand before doing *anything*."

"Just... please think before you act."

"Do not speak to or meet with strangers."

"Don't accept bribes, even if they're books."

The flurry of warnings hit me with such force that the most I could muster in response was a weak, "Okay..."

They really don't trust me at all, do they...?

With lunch over, we started a meeting to ensure that everything was in place for the ruelle gathering to proceed smoothly. We knew what to do this time, since we had already experienced

Ruelle Gathering (Take Two)

the Night of Schutzaria last year, and with the knight commander Karstedt, Ferdinand, and Eckhart all working together in an invincible team, it supposedly wouldn't be difficult at all.

"The feybeasts are going to be gathered in a horde, but they're all weak," Karstedt began. "We should use weapons that can kill swathes of them at once."

"During our previous attempt, they didn't appear until the ruelle petals started to fall, so it should be okay for us to delay our departure," Eckhart suggested.

"I agree," Justus chimed in. "And with that in mind, we should let Lady Rozemyne nap for longer than she did last year. She was so sleepy last year that she needed to be kept awake during the battle."

"Wait just a second, Justus! That only happened because I had to contain the goltze for ages!" I protested. "As long as I only need to do the gathering part, I won't need any more sleep than last time."

We all shared our opinions and narrowed down what role each of us was going to play. It was decided that the knights would position themselves in a circle around the ruelle tree, with Justus riding his highbeast and slaying any feybeasts that tried climbing on the branches, just like last year.

"You can fight even though you're a scholar, Justus?"

"I know a bit about combat, since there's no avoiding it while gathering. At the very least, I'm skilled enough to protect myself."

"Considering that he gathered ruelles last year, it is perfectly safe to count on him in battle," Ferdinand said. It seemed that Justus was completely unreliable when put in front of materials that he hadn't gathered before, but when it came to things he already had and thus didn't care so much about, he'd join the fight without issue.

By the time we had settled on when we would depart, discussed the types of feybeasts we could expect to encounter, and established where we would each be positioned, it was already evening and time for me to nap. It seemed that Ferdinand had indeed worked me so hard in the morning that I could fall asleep with ease, but did that mean I was happy about it?

Absolutely not. Curse him.

Beneath the gleaming purple moon that marked the Night of Schutzaria, we converged at the discussed time and flew to the same ruelle tree as the year prior. When we arrived, the moon was almost directly above us in the sky, and the ruelles were already swelling in size. The flowers bloomed as slender, metallic-looking tree branches wrapped around them, filling the air with a thick, flowery smell.

"The petals will soon begin to fall. Let us use this opportunity to slice away any obstacles," Ferdinand said. He whipped out his schtappe and muttered *"riesesichel,"* transforming it into a large, shining scythe that made him look entirely like the Grim Reaper. The aesthetic honestly suited him pretty well, though I would never say that to him; even if a similar concept did somehow exist in their culture, he would just end up getting mad at me.

"Hyah!"

Ferdinand lifted the scythe high into the air, then began slashing away the branches of the trees surrounding the ruelle tree.

"I see. Cutting the branches will decrease the number of feybeasts that can jump this high..." Karstedt muttered, transforming his own schtappe into a giant scythe and promptly hacking away at them as well. Upon hearing his words, I was struck with an intense urge to apologize to Ferdinand.

Ruelle Gathering (Take Two)

I'm sorry for thinking that you looked like the Grim Reaper, Ferdinand. You're the best. My hero.

"Incidentally, what did you use the ruelle flowers you gathered last year for, Justus?" I asked.

"My hobby is gathering materials, not using them, so you will need to ask Lord Ferdinand about that," he replied. It seemed that he only needed a single ingredient for his collection, and once he had that, he gave the rest to Ferdinand. He considered it both an apology for all the problems he had caused in the past, and an advance payment for the future problems he was no doubt going to cause later.

I couldn't help but wonder just how many issues Justus had been responsible for, but then it suddenly hit me—

W-Wait a minute... Am I going to need to pay Ferdinand an apology fee too? But I can't think of anything he would want. Should I just pay with my mana?

Soon enough, the ruelle petals began to scatter. Just like last year, they peeled off one by one, dancing in the wind as they fell. They were large in size—a lot more similar to magnolias than cherry blossoms—and elegantly fluttered down like the white feathers of a bird, spinning and drifting along on the night breeze. The way they fused with the ground the instant they touched it made them all the more extraordinary and ephemeral.

"Rozemyne, perform the blessing now before they arrive," Ferdinand called.

I prayed to Angriff the God of War and blessed everybody, as instructed, then flew up right next to a ruelle, waiting for it to ripen so that I could gather it as soon as possible. From my elevated position, I curiously watched everyone below.

"Here they come."

The five knights readied their weapons, now circling the ruelle tree. It was interesting to see how they all used different weapons: Eckhart wielded a spear, Brigitte the same halberd as last year, Damuel his familiar sword, and Karstedt the scythe he had been using to cut away the branches. Sadly, I couldn't see what Ferdinand was holding from where I was, but I could at least make out that it didn't seem to be a scythe.

I wonder what it is...

My pondering was soon interrupted by the rustling of grass and branches coming from far away. There weren't just one or two feybeasts approaching—there were dozens and dozens of them. And I knew from experience that countless more would soon follow, drawn in by the flowers' smell.

Cat-like zantzes and squirrel-like eifintes, none tall enough to even reach Damuel's knees, leapt out of the bushes and raced toward us, their eyes gleaming an intimidating red.

"Individually, they are weak. Take care to kill rather than wound them," Ferdinand ordered.

"This is going to be a long fight," Karstedt added. "Watch your mana usage, Damuel."

"Yes, sir!"

Damuel, standing between Karstedt and Ferdinand, tightened his grip on his sword.

Damuel's Growth

As I waited in my highbeast for the ruelle to finish growing, I watched everyone fighting below. The knights were stationed around the ruelle tree in a circle, with Damuel positioned between Ferdinand and Karstedt so that they could follow up on any feybeasts that slipped past him. He had the smallest area to protect out of anyone, but that much made sense—it was too risky to give him more than he could handle.

Tiny feybeasts rushed forward from all directions.

After having traveled all over the duchy and having fought all sorts of feybeasts while gathering my seasonal ingredients, I was better able to judge their relative strengths. With this knowledge, I could confidently say that the zantzes, fetzes (which were slightly larger than zantzes), and eifintes racing toward us weren't much of a threat at all. Their strength came only from their numbers, and while this had proven dangerous last year when we had only a few knights, we now had the mana-rich Ferdinand and Karstedt on our side. It seemed like this would be a piece of cake.

"Here I go!"

The first to strike was Eckhart. He rushed a few steps forward, lowering his hips a little before thrusting his spear out with tremendous force. A sharp whistling noise tore through the air, the weapon's tip gleaming beneath the purple moon. His blow had pierced the feystones of several feybeasts, all of which melted away into nothingness.

A single strike—that was all it took for him to kill multiple feybeasts.

"Haah!"

Eckhart pivoted, turning his thrust into a wide swing that swept down all the feybeasts nearby. Some were knocked to the ground by the blunt force of the shaft, while others weakly collapsed after the spear tip sliced through them. Nearby feybeasts moved to attack not Eckhart, but those weakened feybeasts, promptly devouring them. They were trying to eat the feystones to gain even a little bit of strength.

His blue eyes fiercely fixed on the horde, Eckhart next adjusted his grip on his spear, stabbing into the group over and over again. The rapid thrusts sliced through the air, killing feybeast after feybeast.

Wowee... Eckhart sure is cool. He's, like, half as cool as Dad is. Well, maybe more like a quarter as cool. Or an eighth.

As I continued to watch Eckhart fight, I let out a whistle of admiration. I had mostly just seen him helping Ferdinand with paperwork, but when he fought like a knight, he was honestly a sight to behold.

While I was internally praising Eckhart's heroic visage, I heard Brigitte let out a ferocious battle cry. I adjusted the position of my highbeast slightly to look at her.

"Graaah!"

She roared again, stamping one foot down before swinging her halberd in a wide arc. It audibly cut through the air, then through the surrounding feybeasts, all of which immediately began to melt.

"Next!"

Damuel's Growth

Brigitte's amethyst eyes locked onto her next targets without even pausing to watch the already slain feybeasts fully disappear. She lowered her hips into a battle stance, then spun and twisted to swing her halberd from side to side, her skirt flapping about as she moved.

Her weapon followed her movements exactly, never lagging behind no matter how much she twisted her hips. And each time it flashed, its long, slightly curved blade swept through and tore apart several of the feybeasts rushing this way. Brigitte looked so alive as she ceaselessly swung her weapon, exuding beauty and heroic grace in equal parts.

Aaah... So wonderful. I wanna be strong like that too one day...

While I knew that I wouldn't ever be exactly like Brigitte, I wanted to be all cool and knightly too. My dream was to be a wonderful older sister who everybody could count on.

Incidentally... I wonder how Father fights?

I had technically been there to see Karstedt fight during both the Spring Prayer raid and the schnesturm hunt, but he had always been too far away. The former event had also ended after a single major attack, while there were so many knights present for the latter that I couldn't get much of a grasp on his particular fighting style.

And so, I scanned the area for where he was positioned, feeling a small wave of excitement wash over me.

Soon enough, I spotted him. In my eyes, it looked like he was just lazily swinging around a scythe larger than his own body. It didn't even seem like he was putting that much strength behind his attacks; he was cutting down the horde of oncoming feybeasts with casual swipes, much like one would leisurely cut grass.

Aaah! Father! You're so strong! That's the knight commander for you!

Even with how nonchalant he seemed, each swing of the massive scythe resulted in a powerful slashing sound, loud enough that I could hear it clearly from all the way up by the ruelle. It was like the very air was being torn apart, and the number of feybeasts reduced to mist with each attack was simply incomparable to Eckhart's and Brigitte's efforts: at least a dozen were killed with each swipe, if not more. It certainly wasn't my imagination that, despite Karstedt having been given such a large area to protect, he had far fewer feybeasts around him than the others.

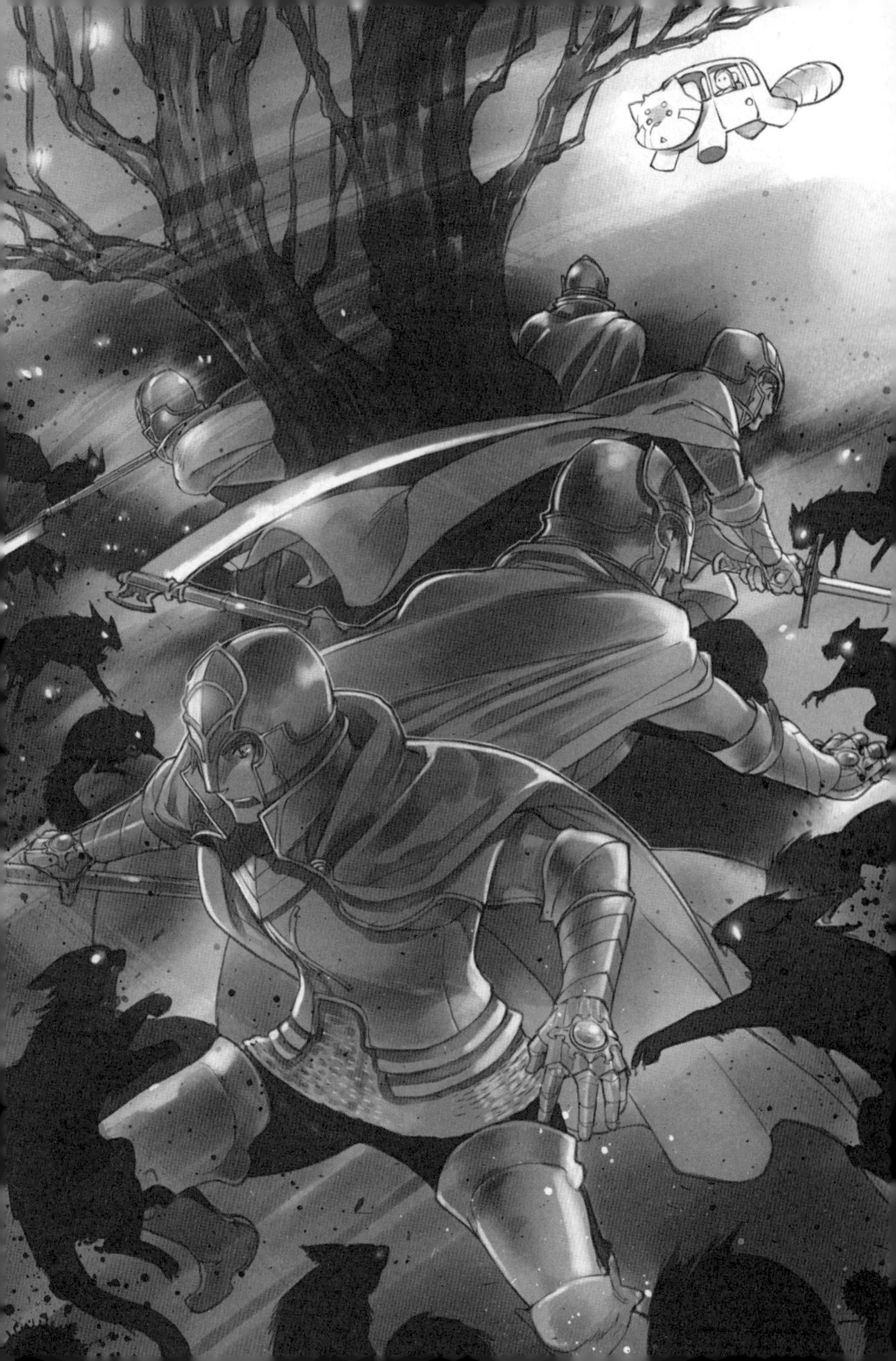

He did come all the way from Ehrenfest just to help me with my gathering... Okay! Dad is still the coolest, but Father gets to be second coolest!

I slapped my knees in excitement while praising Karstedt, when the thunder of a loud explosion suddenly tore through the air.

"Eep?!"

It admittedly wasn't *that* loud, but it came so out of nowhere that I couldn't help but flinch and reflexively cover my ears. I swung my head around wildly, trying to find out what had happened.

Then I saw Ferdinand.

The designated area for him to guard had a gaping circle in the middle completely clear of feybeasts. There was no mistaking it—he was the one behind the explosion. But what could he have done to completely wipe clear his surroundings? It was so unsettling that I couldn't take my eyes away from him, curiously watching to see what would happen next.

Ferdinand simply stood there, watching casually as more feybeasts scurried forward to fill the empty space. I couldn't help but wonder whether I was the only one who got the sudden urge to yell, *"Run! Turn around and run if you want to live!"* at them.

Soon enough, Ferdinand tossed something at the approaching feybeasts. It shone brightly in the air for a moment, then rapidly began to spread out. A second later, it seemed to have vanished completely. I couldn't see it anymore, at least.

Was that... a net?

As it turned out, it hadn't actually vanished after all—it had simply landed on all the feybeasts. As they started to struggle and flail about in a desperate attempt to escape, Ferdinand bent down and pressed a palm against the ground, carefully eyeing the trapped creatures.

"Disappear," he said quietly.

Damuel's Growth

I could see him pouring mana into the net. Its strands shone with the light of mana, and an instant later, I heard the same explosive boom as before. All the feybeasts within the net disappeared, just as Ferdinand commanded.

That's terrifying... That's so, so terrifying.

I could guess that only someone with an overwhelming mana capacity like Ferdinand could manage an attack like that; pouring mana into a net that wide would require both a ton of mana and great skill in manipulating it.

Ferdinand exhibited such overwhelming strength compared to everyone else that my unsettled awe turned into just plain fear. I decided to shift my gaze and focus on Damuel instead.

His fighting style was a lot more drab than everyone else's in the sense that there wasn't anything flashy about it: he simply thrust his sword into each feybeast, one after another. But it was clear that he had grown since last year. He wasn't having to rely on his stamina and strength to preserve mana, he wasn't gasping for air, and he wasn't anxiously scanning his surroundings. Instead, he was facing straight forward, fighting without any hesitation.

Having taken my advice seriously and incorporated it into his training, Damuel now knew how to vary the amount of mana he used in combat: he was using a little more when taking on the larger fetzes, and less when fighting the smaller ones.

"Damuel, it's been some time. Take a step back and drink a potion."

"There is no need, Lord Karstedt. I am doing just fine," Damuel said, shaking his head as he stabbed a zantze with his sword. Maybe it was due to him being positioned between two absolute powerhouses this year, but he was swinging with a lot more confidence and making sure to confirm each kill.

"There's no need to push yourself."

"I truly am fine," he replied quietly, not taking his eyes off the feybeasts for even a moment as he continued to swing his sword.

The battle continued for quite some time before Damuel eventually announced that he was falling back. This time, however, he was doing it on his own terms. Leaving the area he had been protecting to Karstedt and Ferdinand, he took a step back and leaned against the tree, downing a recovery potion. He would be resting until it took effect.

"Damuel, you're so much stronger now," I called down, leaning out the window of my Pandabus.

He looked up in surprise, then gave me a small smile. "Thank you."

A short while later, I noticed that he had closed his eyes. I could tell from his careful breathing that he was checking how much mana he had. When he opened them again, his gaze was immediately fixed on the feybeasts. He morphed his schtappe back into a sword, then leapt into battle once again. It seemed that his limits had increased enough to give him a newfound confidence, and now he was fighting with much more leeway than before.

He must have been taking his training really, really seriously.

I knew how much Damuel had wished to grow stronger, so seeing his hard work bear fruit filled me with pride like I was watching my own son. His recent growth was a powerful reminder of just how significant of a driving force love really was.

As I was admiring how much Damuel had grown and grinning about his love life, Justus suddenly called out to me. "Milady, it's time! I believe you should now pour your mana into the ruelle!"

After taking a deep breath, I leaned out of my Pandabus and reached for the ruelle fruit, which looked a lot like a purple crystal. Dyeing it with my mana was no easy task: all living things had an instinct to reject outside mana, so they violently resisted the process.

Damuel's Growth

I gripped the hard, smooth ruelle in my hands and started pouring in my mana all at once, visualizing myself smashing its resistance to pieces. The fact that I could feel slightly less resistance than last year likely meant that I had grown a little myself too.

I continued adding more and more mana, focusing my gaze on the ruelle as I steadily overcame its resistance. It wasn't long before it started turning from a translucent purple to a light yellow. Last year, it had felt as though my mana was being pushed back, but there wasn't anything like that now; my mana flow was fast and uninterrupted.

"Justus, will this do?" I asked, looking around just in time to see him cut down an eifinte on his way over.

Once the threat was eliminated, he flew up to the ruelle, staying on guard. "That was fast, milady... But yes, it's done. Upon removing it from the tree, please place it inside your bag at once."

The ruelle had now completely changed color. I held it in my left hand as I cut the stem attaching it to the tree with my magic knife, then trimmed away all the excess parts before putting it into my bag. It was a bag that blocked the flow of mana, so I didn't think I needed to worry about feybeasts snatching it away anymore.

"She's finished her gathering!" Justus called.

Karstedt responded with a firm nod. "Then we retreat!"

"Not yet!" I shouted back. "Wait just a little longer! Damuel needs a ruelle too!"

Ferdinand blasted a crowd of feybeasts to bits, then shot me a fierce glare. "What are you thinking, Rozemyne?!"

"Doesn't he need a sizable feystone for his proposal next summer? He won't have any opportunities to gather one himself while he's guarding me, so he might as well grab it now. I learned all about this from the knight stories," I said, proudly puffing out my chest.

Both Ferdinand and Karstedt smirked at my remark, almost as if to say, *"Look at this kid who can't even distinguish fiction from reality."* I couldn't help but blink in surprise.

"Did I misread them or something...?"

"No. However..." Ferdinand trailed off, then directed a meaningful glance at Brigitte. I immediately understood. You were obviously supposed to prepare the feystone stealthily, not in front of the very person you planned to propose to.

Gaaah! I thought I was being considerate, but was I actually just making things awkward for him?!

As I cradled my head in sheer horror, a wide grin spread across Karstedt's face. "Go get one, Damuel. You won't find feystones of a higher quality than those. They'll be perfect for your proposal," he said, continuing to cut down feybeasts all the while. Perhaps it was just my imagination, but I could have sworn I also heard him say, "Elvira really is looking forward to seeing what happens next."

Having the approval of the knight commander had sealed the deal, so both Eckhart and Ferdinand told Damuel to hurry up and get it over with. I peered over at Brigitte and saw that she was silently continuing to hunt feybeasts, intentionally not looking this way at all. It was a little hard to notice since it was dark and she was so far away, but it seemed that her ears had gone a bit red.

Sorry, Brigitte... I really didn't mean to embarrass you like this.

Damuel flew his highbeast up to a ruelle, then chanted "*messer*" to morph his schtappe into a knife. While I needed a high-quality feystone dyed completely with my own mana, Damuel needed a feystone meant for proposals. He wouldn't have to dye it with his own mana right at the tree like I did.

Damuel's Growth

He speedily chopped away some branches and gathered two nearby ruelles, one for the proposal, and one presumably for his own purposes. Then, with a pleased smile, he delicately placed them both in his own leather bag.

"This is my first time ever getting such a high-quality feystone," he said. "I'll bring it home and take my time filling it with my mana."

Upon returning to Dorvan's winter mansion, I slept as soundly as could be, filled with a mix of pride and satisfaction at having finally finished gathering all the materials I needed.

When morning came, I practically skipped down the hall toward Ferdinand's room. He had told me to come and see him after eating breakfast, presumably to continue the paperwork we hadn't finished the day before. I was planning to put my all into it so that we could start making the potion as soon as possible.

I'm going to be healthy soon! I'll get strong and everything. I'm finally going to be a normal girl. Eheheh... Eheheheh!

Damuel had headed to Ferdinand's room ahead of time, so I was currently being accompanied by Fran and Brigitte. I bounded along until we eventually arrived, at which point one of Ferdinand's attendants waiting outside opened the door to let us in.

"Good morning, Ferdinand! What do you need help with today?" I asked, greeting him in a bright and lively tone. But the atmosphere in the room was so heavy and serious that I hurriedly shut my mouth. Nobody was working—that is to say, everyone but the attendant waiting by the door had been cleared out, leaving nobody to do the work. It was just Karstedt, Ferdinand, and Eckhart, all regarding me with deep frowns, and Damuel, who met me with a pitiable stare like he was begging for help.

Um, Damuel...? What did you do?

"Brigitte, Fran. Leave."

I fought back the urge to cling to Brigitte and Fran as they sped out of the room, instead just blinking in utter bemusement. That gave Ferdinand ample opportunity to glare at me.

"I imagine you know why you are here, Rozemyne," he said. "What exactly did you do to Damuel?"

I honestly had no idea what he was talking about. Were they mad at me because I had treated Damuel wrongly as my guard knight? I desperately tried to recall everything that I had done recently.

"Um, um... What did I do to Damuel...? Do you mean when I suggested that he gather ruelles last night? Or when I gave him sweets while he was on guard duty the other day? Oh, but I gave those to Brigitte too, so—"

"No! Nothing like that at all. I am inferring that you are responsible for the unnaturally large increase in his mana capacity."

"...His mana capacity increased as the result of his own hard work. I did give him a little advice to help him out, but nothing would have happened without his rigorous training and dedication."

Upon finding out that this was simply about Damuel's recent growth, I let out a sigh, relieved that they weren't actually mad at me. But Karstedt looked down at me with a stern expression.

"What in the world was that advice you gave him, Rozemyne?" he asked. "His growth is outright abnormal. A laynoble like Damuel at the end of his growing period should not be displaying such a considerable increase. It's unprecedented."

"I just taught him my mana compression method with a visual example, in the same way that he used gewinnen pieces to help Angelica understand tactics," I said.

Karstedt and Eckhart frowned in confusion. Ferdinand, however, regarded me with angrily raised eyebrows. "Your mana compression method? I was not told of this."

"Hm? I mean, you've never asked me about it, Ferdinand. It hasn't really come up in conversation. Also, I developed it myself, so I don't even know whether it's a good thing for people to do. Maybe it just happened to work well with Damuel," I said thoughtfully, but Damuel slowly shook his head.

"I believe anyone going through puberty would see an exceptional increase in their mana capacity by using your mana compression method, Lady Rozemyne. I simply didn't report it because I did not want to return to being below average after finally getting more mana. Forgive me."

If everyone learned the same method and increased their mana capacities, then the average would rise with them, putting Damuel back at the bottom.

"I understand why you would want to hide it," Eckhart said. "It would make perfect sense to keep such a method a personal secret, or even have it passed down through one's family."

It seemed that Damuel wasn't getting scolded for keeping the technique a secret, but then why were we even here? I turned to look at Ferdinand, who was watching me quietly with his light-golden eyes.

"Rozemyne, it seems that, unlike Damuel, you did not intend to keep this a secret. Why, then, did you not think to spread this method throughout Ehrenfest, knowing that we are experiencing a mana shortage?"

"Well, I mean..."

It was true that Ehrenfest was currently suffering from a shortage of mana, and that most people probably took great interest in finding ways to help increase the amount of mana available. But I wasn't most people. I was wholly focused on spreading books, so it never really occurred to me that I should try to spread my method.

"Compressing my mana is something that I constantly needed to do to survive while living on the brink of death. I didn't really consider it something worth teaching to nobles with magic tools, and it's possibly a dangerous method that might actually kill people. I don't want to spread something that dangerous."

Karstedt gave an understanding nod, but Ferdinand pressed a finger against his temple. "Then why did you teach it to Damuel?" he asked.

"Damuel knows of my origins, so he understood the true meaning and weight behind me saying it was something that I did while on the verge of death."

Everyone else here also knew about my origins, and they all seemed to be wearing the same difficult frown.

"I see," Ferdinand eventually responded. "I understand your perspective, and why you did not feel motivated to make your technique more widely known. I will, however, ask you to spread it nonetheless. I wish for this mana compression method to be taught to other nobles in Ehrenfest. The mana shortage is a problem that must be solved as soon as possible, and nothing could be better for us than increasing the mana capacity of the children who shall support Ehrenfest in the future."

I could sense the slight urgency in his voice, but my understanding was that, for the past two years, Ehrenfest had managed to meet its mana quotas and yield bountiful enough harvests thanks to me performing Spring Prayer. As much as I could understand him wanting to increase the mana capacities of the blue priests who helped us to offer up mana, I didn't understand why he would so fervently want to increase the mana capacities of *all* nobles in general.

"It seems like you're in a big hurry to do this," I observed. "Is there a reason for that?"

"Not particularly. It is just one more way to prepare for Georgine using her position as Ahrensbach's first wife to harm Ehrenfest. Raising the average mana capacity of our nobles would aid us considerably."

If Ferdinand needed my help for some plan or another, then it would probably be wise for me to provide it. But my mana compression was hardly a reliable and safe process; I didn't want to just throw it out there in its current state.

"I don't mind spreading my method to help the duchy," I said. "But I do have some conditions."

Conditions for Compressing Mana

Eckhart and Karstedt inhaled with surprise, but Ferdinand simply raised an interested eyebrow. "Continue," he said.

"First, it must only be shown to those who have already learned the method taught in the Royal Academy," I explained. "This is a life-and-death technique, so I have absolutely no intention of showing it to people who can't already compress mana on their own."

Ferdinand, Eckhart, and Karstedt all nodded along slowly, as if my first condition were only natural. Damuel alone stood there awkwardly, clearly more concerned about whether or not he would be punished than what we were talking about now.

"Second, my technique may be taught only to those in the same faction as me. I have no intention of helping my opposition to get more mana."

It was purely because of my mana capacity that I had been accommodated as an apprentice blue shrine maiden and then adopted as the archduke's daughter, despite being a commoner. I wanted to preserve my superiority in that regard at least a little, and even I knew that it wouldn't be safe to aid my enemies like this.

"Restricting my technique so that only those in the Florencia faction increase their mana capacities would help to destabilize the Georgine faction, would it not?" I continued. "And with Sylvester set on Wilfried becoming the next archduke, this should be a good way of showing that he's firmly on our side."

Conditions for Compressing Mana

Georgine's supporters were desperate to absorb Wilfried into their faction, but having both him and the archduke deny these ties, as well as making it clear that Wilfried was a member of the Florencia faction, would cause any rumors about such an alliance to die out over time. The only reason such hearsay existed in the first place was because there was a lot of uncertainty in politics and Wilfried wasn't yet properly educated, so all we needed to do was tie him to his parents more.

"Would that not give you full control over the selection process?" Ferdinand asked. "I cannot say I would feel safe leaving such an important matter to your discretion."

"I'm still not all that familiar with noble politics myself, so I feel the same way."

I barely knew anything about which nobles had connections to which. It already took everything that I had to memorize the names of all the nobles related to my own family, and to put together a blacklist based on Bezewanst's letters. But neither group was necessarily set in stone, and the value of what was at stake would surely cause people to become desperate, so I didn't want to be in a position where it was solely my call whether or not any given noble was trustworthy.

"Instead," I continued, "I propose that nobles should need the approval of six different people: the archducal couple, as they hold the highest authority in Ehrenfest; you, Ferdinand, since you can use your wealth of knowledge to make rational decisions not influenced by emotion; Father, because he is the pillar of our military as knight commander; Mother, as she is the de facto leader of the Florencia faction; and lastly me, since I am the one providing the mana compression method."

Most of the people listed were quite simply my guardians; if someone had all of their approvals, then it was hard to imagine they would turn out to be one of my enemies. That was about as much insurance as I could ask for.

"Oh? That is quite a number of people. Is the archducal couple not enough for you?" Ferdinand asked with a slight, amused grin.

"I personally think Sylvester would prioritize his feelings as a father, freely giving away the information no matter what faction gets involved with Wilfried, and I similarly believe that Florencia's motherly affections would allow her heart to be swayed."

Karstedt gave a deep frown. "Rozemyne... are you saying that you don't trust the archducal couple?"

"I do trust them, but they are parents; I feel as though they'll put their children above all else. Just as my... Just as Mom and Dad did for me."

Perhaps due to having met my lower city parents before, Ferdinand seemed to instantly understand what I meant. A complex expression arose on his face—a mixture of reminiscence and bitterness. "So you base your expectations of parental emotions on them..." he said. "You will find that such a perspective does not hold water in noble society."

"Everyone has their own thoughts on parenthood, so I don't really care whether or not it holds water."

My personal opinions were rooted in my experiences with my Earth mother, who had given me all the books I could ever want, and my commoner parents, who stood up even to nobles to protect their children.

"Furthermore," I added, "no matter how thorough we are, our selection process won't matter if the method leaks to other duchies, will it? I was thinking of using a magic contract to prevent the people we teach from then passing it on to others, but do there exist magic contracts of a large enough scale to cover not just Ehrenfest, but the entire country?"

"...Such contracts do exist, though they are enormously expensive," Ferdinand replied. This was the man who referred to large golds as small change, so just how much could they be? I was honestly afraid to ask, but without a contract like that, there was no way for us to exclusively boost Ehrenfest's mana level.

"Money or mana—pick one. I intend for this method to be known only in Ehrenfest, and if you aren't willing to pay for magic contracts to ensure that, then consider this discussion over."

"The contracts can be arranged," Ferdinand replied carefully, wearing the same frown that he always wore when contemplating matters of money. "It will certainly be worth using a portion of Ehrenfest's budget."

"Ferdinand, could you make it such that not even married couples or siblings could teach the method to one another?"

"Naturally, since there would be individual contracts for each noble. But why?"

"I mainly don't want this knowledge spreading haphazardly. Mana compression is so dangerous that several professors are present while it's being taught, even in the Royal Academy, and accidents occur no matter how thorough the preparations are. Aren't you the one who mentioned this to me?"

I hadn't forgotten when Ferdinand asked how I was still alive, or when he mentioned that it was exceedingly rare for children to successfully learn their own style of mana compression. I didn't want something that dangerous to end up spreading like wildfire.

"This mana compression method is so effective that it allowed me to go from being an apprentice blue shrine maiden in the temple to the archduke's adopted daughter. I can imagine parents desperately forcing it on their mana-sparse children in a last-ditch effort to avoid them being sent to the temple, which I certainly wouldn't want to happen."

In noble society, children with less mana than was desired for their house's status were sent to the temple or given up to be adopted by other houses of lower status. There was a chance that parents wanting to avoid this fate might force my mana compression method on their children, which would result in a massive surge of pre-baptism deaths.

"Pre-baptism children are not considered to be people," Ferdinand responded.

"That's just from a political standpoint, though. Regardless of whether or not they're considered people by the duchy, they're still alive. And under no circumstances do I want real, living children to be put at risk like that. This is something that I simply will not tolerate, and I wholeheartedly refuse to concede on the matter."

As I made my position clear, Ferdinand tightly knitted his brow and lowered his gaze. When he looked up again, there was a piercing sharpness in his light-golden eyes that would permit neither weakness nor deception. "Would your opinion remain unchanged even if some children who could have become nobles were instead sent to the temple?" he asked, his voice lower than normal.

"I would much rather the eleven blue priests we have now than ten dead children and one noble," I said, meeting his gaze head-on. There was an enormous difference between joining the temple and living as a noble, but even knowing that, I wouldn't budge.

"I see." His eyes softened, then he placed a thoughtful hand on his chin. "As usual, I cannot understand why you would be so adamant about something that brings you absolutely no personal gain, but very well—I shall honor your wishes. Your mana compression

Conditions for Compressing Mana

method shall be taught only to those who meet your conditions, and they shall sign contracts that prevent them from sharing the technique among even their family members. Any other conditions?"

"I will charge a teaching fee as well. That much is reasonable, considering how valuable the information is, yes?"

"Hm... I did consider that myself, but would it not prevent laynobles from participating?" Ferdinand asked, tapping his temple and muttering some speculation about the optimal price. I could see Damuel pale out of the corner of my eye.

"If your goal is to evenly spread the increase of mana," I said, "why not charge laynobles less, raising the price more for each rank above that? Archnobles are born with enough mana that they can suffice without the method, so only those who feel there is value in the knowledge will need to buy it."

The color returned to Damuel's face, but now it was Karstedt who had gone pale. He began counting on his fingers, then started cradling his head. Perhaps I would need to implement a family discount.

"I shall accept your conditions. Now, Rozemyne—what is the principle behind your mana compression?" Ferdinand asked, a grin arising on his face.

But I merely smiled back at him and shook my head. "That can wait until you have signed your magic contract and paid your fee, Ferdinand."

"I see you've learned to be cautious."

"Anyone could guess that you're plotting something when you look at them with that villainous smirk of yours."

Ferdinand scoffed, then turned to look at Damuel, silently asking me what we should do with him. I directed my attention toward Damuel in turn; he looked like a criminal on trial and awaiting his sentence.

"I taught you of my own volition, so I will ask for no fee," I began. "*But*, I will have you sign a magic contract stating that you will not pass what you have learned on to anyone else, just like the others. Is that acceptable?"

"Of course," Damuel said, the smile on his face making it exceedingly clear that he was mostly just pleased about not needing to pay any money.

Karstedt sighed in relief. "With Ferdinand speaking to you so casually, it seems that I have nothing to worry about." And with our discussion about mana compression over, he began his return to Ehrenfest by highbeast.

Just how brutal does noble society have to be for my talks with Ferdinand to seem casual...? Or is Ferdinand the brutal one here? Honestly, I don't even want to think about it.

We took some time to rest after having seen Karstedt off, with plans to leave for Illgner the next day. We had at least this much leeway, since the province was relatively close to Dorvan.

"Rozemyne, as I am going to be accompanying you to Illgner, my own tax official will suffice. Justus shall be returning to Ehrenfest ahead of us. Do you have any issues with this?" Ferdinand asked.

"Not at all."

I could guess that Justus had been told to investigate the unsettling air around the Georgine faction Karstedt had mentioned, plus he probably wanted to start preparing for the mana compression stuff. Justus was one of Ferdinand's loyal retainers anyway, and not sending him to work at a time like this would be a waste of his talents.

"Excellent. I have much to do today, and it would be an inconvenience to have you wandering about the winter mansion causing problems, so I ask that you take this and spend the rest of the day reading in your room."

Conditions for Compressing Mana

"Understood! I won't leave my room at all!"

Yippee! A whole day of reading!

Hugging the bundle of papers that Ferdinand had given me to my chest, I giddily returned to my room. When I arrived, Fran pulled back a chair for me, which I eagerly hopped onto.

The papers were a dossier on the Georgine faction, containing the names of noble wives who attended tea parties hosted by its members, and descriptions of the almost-neutral laynobles who were friendly with them. As I leafed through it, I saw that entire family trees of the noble wives had been written out, and the last page concluded with the following lines: *"I hope this proves useful to you, Lord Ferdinand. Say hello to Rozemyne for me."*

"Mother..."

Elvira had evidently written out this dossier and gotten Karstedt to deliver it, warning us about the upcoming danger to help us avoid whatever might happen. I could feel the love of a mother in these pages, and tears started to well up in my eyes.

...I need to go over these and memorize all the names.

And so I gave the dossier a very thorough read-through. As expected, many of the people on my blacklist for being friendly with Bezewanst were listed here, so I knew more than half the names already. Trying to keep track of the complex family trees, however, was enough to make my head spin.

Illgner's Harvest Festival

As I was glaring at the lists, struggling to memorize them all, the flapping wings of an ordonnanz came into earshot. The bird flew into the room and landed on Brigitte's arm.

"You'll be arriving tomorrow evening? Got it. I'll discuss dinner plans with them later," it said in Giebe Illgner's voice. "Could you tell Lady Rozemyne that the Harvest Festival is scheduled for the day after tomorrow? Also, make sure you speak to her about what we discussed. I'm counting on you."

After repeating the message three times, the ordonnanz returned to the shape of a yellow feystone.

"My apologies, Lady Rozemyne. I informed my brother of our plans earlier, but I didn't expect him to respond while I was on duty."

"I don't mind. Contacting the giebe is part of your job. How are things in Illgner?"

Now that my gathering was complete, Illgner was next up on my list of worries. They had hurriedly begun educating their people in preparation for Ferdinand's visit, but I still wasn't sure how tomorrow would go.

"Things are starting to take shape. I'm told the gray priests have been working exceptionally hard."

"I see. That's good," I said quietly, letting out a small sigh of relief. "I… do apologize for all this. It never even crossed my mind before Ferdinand pointed it out…"

Brigitte blinked in confusion. "Lady Rozemyne?"

"I quite like how close the commoners are with the nobles in Illgner, and up until recently, I assumed it wouldn't be an issue so long as I handled things myself. I never thought that Ferdinand would personally travel there, or that other nobles would start visiting to observe the paper-making process."

Going forward, my discussions with giebes about expanding the printing and paper-making industries would be held at the archduke's castle. I had assumed that the Rozemyne Workshop in the temple would suffice for those who wanted to learn more about both industries, especially considering that Illgner was so far away, but the reality was that visiting the temple wasn't considered at all worthwhile from a noble's perspective.

The blood really had drained from my face when Ferdinand pointed out that no noble would want to visit the temple. Plus, even those who didn't mind going there wouldn't find it a meaningful reference, since the workshop there—ran directly by the archducal family—had unusual financing and labor arrangements.

"Please do not feel responsible for this, Lady Rozemyne. This is something that we should have understood on our own, without you or Lord Ferdinand pointing it out to us," Brigitte said. She then paused, hesitating for a moment before she continued. "Lady Rozemyne, there is something I wish to ask you. May I have a moment of your time?"

"I have been instructed to stay in my room for the entire day, so of course. It is rare for you to bring something up on your own, though."

After informing Damuel that she would be taking a temporary break from guard duty, Brigitte turned to face me; I assumed she wanted to talk about the *"what we discussed"* that the ordonnanz had mentioned. I straightened my back and looked at her, wondering what it could be.

"Lady Rozemyne..." Her amethyst eyes wandered uncomfortably as she seemed to question whether it was actually a good idea to ask me about this, her gaze eventually resting on the floor. "You mentioned at Hasse that gray priests are not permitted to marry. Is that true?"

"Yes. Gray priests are indeed not permitted to marry."

"I knew it..." Brigitte muttered, the disappointment clear on her face. I couldn't quite understand her reaction.

Why is she upset about that...? Hm... Wait, does Brigitte...? Oh no, Damuel! There was an ambush lying in wait, and we never saw it coming!

"Um, Brigitte... you don't happen to love a gray priest, do you?" I asked timidly. Both her and Damuel responded with a wide-eyed stare and a loud *"WHAT?!"*

"No! I'm not asking for myself!" Brigitte exclaimed, hurriedly shaking her head upon seeing how shocked Damuel was. "What are you even saying, Lady Rozemyne?!"

She had rejected the idea so firmly that both Damuel and I exhaled a relieved breath. "I just thought that might be the case, since you looked sad about gray priests being unable to marry," I explained.

"Both in terms of status and mana capacity, it is unthinkable for a noble to even consider marrying a gray priest. I am asking on behalf of a citizen in Illgner," Brigitte said, shooting a small glare my way before letting out a disappointed sigh.

I was relieved to hear that the townsfolk were still close with the nobles in Illgner, but the situation as a whole made me a little nervous. I tried to recall what I knew about gray priests.

"It's not an absolute impossibility... Giebe Illgner could purchase the gray priest in question and remove them from the temple's hierarchy, at which point he could permit the marriage himself," I suggested.

While I personally didn't feel right about people being bought and sold, it was exceedingly normal for nobles to buy gray priests and shrine maidens here—they were usually put to work as servants, clerks, and so on. I certainly didn't mind selling a gray priest if doing so meant he could get married and be happy, and I would gladly use my position as High Bishop to bless his marriage and reward him for all the work he had done.

"Lady Rozemyne, may I inform my brother of this immediately? Assuming he is indeed able to buy the priest and allow him to stay in the winter mansion this winter, then it would be best for them to participate in the upcoming marriage ceremony."

"...I will need to ask Ferdinand about this first. I've been told to speak to him before doing anything."

I asked Fran to pass a meeting request on to Ferdinand, only for him to return with a lecture. *"I believe I told you to stay in your room all day and read,"* the response had apparently been.

Having no other choice, I told Fran to go back with a new message: *"I will need an answer before we arrive at Illgner, but if you are too busy, I can simply handle this on my own."*

Ferdinand bitterly relented to a meeting at noon, during which I told him about the gray priest who wanted to get married. His response was the same as mine.

"That is perfectly acceptable so long as Giebe Illgner buys him. I assume he wishes to get married during the Harvest Festival the day after tomorrow, in which case prompt arrangements will need to be made. I shall prepare the— No, *you* shall prepare the documents in your room. I will prepare no more than the registration medal for you," Ferdinand said, swiftly ending the conversation by shooing me away.

And so I returned to my room, where, under Fran's supervision, I started writing up the documents required to purchase a gray priest. It was a depressing thought knowing that I was now personally involved in the buying and selling of people so long after Ferdinand had first mentioned it, but at the same time, I was glad that the gray priest would get to be happy and married.

"How are marriages celebrated, Fran?"

"I do not know. As far as I am aware, no gray priest has ever married before," he replied frankly before lowering his eyes and apologizing.

Sensing the conflicted emotions stirring inside him, I placed a hand on my cheek. "Do you want to get married too?"

"I do not. I am satisfied with my current life, and truthfully... I am not even certain what marriage truly is. Were I ever put in a situation where I was forced to marry, I would surely be deeply troubled," Fran said, knowing nothing except life in the temple.

His response made me a little concerned. "Do you think the woman in Illgner may be forcing the gray priest to marry her against his wishes?"

"That is not even worth thinking about; if the giebe decides to purchase the gray priest, then it is only natural that the gray priest be sold," Fran replied. His expression made it clear that he thought I was being too soft again.

There was no denying that the selling of gray priests to whichever nobles wished to buy them was common practice, but I wanted the gray priest to be as happy as possible; I couldn't help but hope that Giebe Illgner wasn't just exploiting him.

I arrived at Illgner the next day with worry in my heart.

Unlike during our last visit, the commoners didn't greet us with big waves, and there was no crowd waiting for us. Instead, they were all kneeling in wait, with Giebe Illgner at the front. Their positioning was a little clumsy, but it was minor enough to be forgiven, what with Illgner being a country province and all. It was clear from a glance that the gray priests had done all they could to train them, and the townsfolk had done all they could to learn.

"You must be tired after such a long journey. We can postpone dinner, so please use this time to rest at your leisure," Giebe Illgner said after we had exchanged our long noble greetings.

With that, Ferdinand and I were taken straight to our rooms; our attendants had arrived earlier by carriage to ensure that all the necessary preparations were complete.

"I shall be going to the side building once I am changed. Fran, please gather all of the gray priests," I said, promptly getting Monika and Nicola to help dress me for dinner. When I was ready, Monika stayed behind in my room while Nicola accompanied me.

I need to see things with my own eyes before speaking to the giebe... I'm the High Bishop, and I should know more about the situations my gray priests are in.

I hadn't at all predicted the possibility of Giebe Illgner or his people forcing a gray priest into marriage. My mind was so focused on preventing the gray shrine maidens from being forced to provide flower offerings—due in part to what had happened to Wilma—that the possibility of something like this happening hadn't even occurred to me. It wasn't until Fran had shared with me his own perspective that I realized gray priests didn't even have a strong conception of marriage, and now my heart was swirling with panic.

When I entered the side building, Fran was standing by the room normally used by blue priests. "This way, Lady Rozemyne," he said, gently opening the door for me. Inside, I could see Gil and four gray priests kneeling in wait.

"Gil, Nolte, Selim, Volk, Bartz—it is good to see you all again. Thank you for the hard work you have been doing. Brigitte and Giebe Illgner have told me much about your efforts."

"We are honored."

I sat in the chair that had been prepared for me and looked over the still-kneeling gray priests. "I will get straight to the point, for lack of time. An ordonnanz from Giebe Illgner informed me yesterday that one of you wishes to marry a citizen here. If this truly is the case, there are methods through which it can be accomplished. Which one of you might it be?"

All eyes fell on one person: Volk. He paled and hung his head.

"Do you wish to get married, Volk?"

"Forgive me, Lady Rozemyne."

"It is nothing to apologize for. Fran told me that he knows so little of marriage that, if put in a situation where he was forced to marry someone, he would be exceedingly troubled. Gray priests have very little power and are used to accommodating any demands given to them, so before anything else, Volk, I would simply like to confirm your feelings. Neither Giebe Illgner nor the woman in question are forcing your hand here, are they?"

Volk shot up his head and shook it from side to side. "No, nothing of the sort," he assured me.

I exhaled, relieved that my worst fears weren't true after all.

"In that case, do you desire this wedding yourself? Are you prepared to leave the temple and spend the rest of your life in Illgner? If you live here permanently rather than simply spending a season here as a guest, I imagine that your habits and way of thinking will conflict with those of the natives quite regularly. Plus, you will likely struggle in many ways to establish an equal marriage as opposed to a master-servant relationship. Do you still wish to stay here, despite all that?"

After a period of silence, Volk opened his mouth to speak. "I... have many fears. Just like Fran," he started, the words catching in his throat. "I do not truly understand what marriage entails... but even so... I wish to spend my life with her."

"I am relieved that you are not being forced into this. As you will not be able to marry while serving as a gray priest, I will arrange the necessary documentation for Giebe Illgner to buy you from the temple. Is this okay with you?"

"Yes. Thank you."

The tension drained from my shoulders. I now knew which gray priest wanted to get married, and that he wasn't being forced into it.

"I have a meeting with the giebe after dinner, so I must hurry back to my room," I said. "I shall listen to your full report on the workshop's results tomorrow."

With that, I exited the side building and started heading back to my room as fast as I could. My plan was to make it seem like I hadn't even left in the first place, but life wouldn't make things so easy for me.

"Lady Rozemyne! The High Priest is calling for you!" Monika exclaimed, having rushed over from the summer mansion. Ferdinand had apparently sent one of his attendants to my room with an urgent message, and the blood drained from my face as I realized that this meant he had learned of my absence.

"So, Fran... Do you think I'm going to get lectured?"

"Considering that you acted without his permission while in the midst of using potions to forcibly maintain your health, I imagine so."

Fran picked me up and we rushed to see Ferdinand. As expected, I was met with a sharp glare the second I stepped into his room.

"Why were you wandering about when you could collapse at any moment?" he asked.

"There was an urgent matter in the side building that I needed to address. I wanted to ask the gray priest planning to get married how he felt."

"...My matter is urgent as well. Fill this out before signing the sales contract with Giebe Illgner."

Ferdinand handed me back the contract that I had made under Fran's supervision. I could see that he had added some lines to it: there was now a section for listing Volk's abilities, and one for his experience in the workshop.

"He has knowledge of the paper-making process and is capable of teaching others about it. He also knows about printing and has experience printing things himself. And..."

I murmured to myself as I thought over Volk's abilities and wrote down everything that he could do. When I was done, Ferdinand looked over the filled-out columns and frowned as he counted the number of entries.

"Rozemyne, have you discussed a price with Giebe Illgner?"

"No. I only learned of this matter through an ordonnanz for Brigitte, so we haven't worked out any details yet. I thought we could just talk things over today."

Just a few days ago, a commoner had apparently pleaded with Giebe Illgner, saying that she didn't want to be separated from one of our gray priests. The giebe had been just as surprised as we were about the development, but so little had been said about it that I hadn't even known it was Volk the woman was referring to until I went to the side building myself.

According to the ordonnanz, Giebe Illgner had prepared some money for the purchase, but since I hadn't dealt with the sale of a gray priest before, I didn't really know what kind of price to expect.

"The average price of a gray priest would be around five small golds, but this varies significantly based on their individual capabilities," Ferdinand explained. "If we were to calculate a price using this table of skills and prices… he will certainly be quite expensive."

"Volk was originally trained to be an attendant, he has deep knowledge of the paper-making and printing industries, and he's skilled enough to have been sent to another region to establish a new business and actually succeed. Of course he would be expensive."

That much was common sense—after all, there was nothing that my magnificent gray priests couldn't do. I wouldn't have been able to sell them for cheap anyway, since then there wouldn't be anybody left to run the temple workshop. Now that would be a problem.

"Good. As long as you understand," Ferdinand replied. "Take care not to be emotionally manipulated into lowering the price. I must also note that, as the High Priest, it is my duty to manage the sale of gray priests. You may be providing final approval, but in general, it will not be your place to meddle here."

"I seem to recall the previous High Bishop forcing a contract with Dirk on his own terms," I pointed out, causing Ferdinand to grimace.

"Hence my warning. High Bishops are higher in status than High Priests, so it is not that you *cannot* manage contracts, but rather that doing so is supposed to be the High Priest's duty. Even your predecessor came to show me that contract with Dirk, though admittedly only once it had already been finalized. You may be a figurehead, but you are still the High Bishop, and I do not want you interrupting midway through the signing of Volk's contract. If you have any concerns, state them now."

"I've already confirmed Volk's feelings, so I have nothing more to say on the matter."

Sometime after meeting with Ferdinand, it was time for dinner with Giebe Illgner; we were having a meal in his mansion rather than an outside barbeque with everyone. Hugo had made the soup, but many of the other dishes were Illgner's specialties, made with plenty of local ingredients.

Ferdinand seemed to be satisfied with things, which prompted Giebe Illgner to ease up a little more.

"Today's soup is extraordinary. I would expect nothing less from your personal chef, Lady Rozemyne."

"Your praise warms my heart. I shall pass it along to the chef as well."

When the meal was over, we moved to the giebe's office to start sorting out the contract. My attendants and I entered to find Volk standing beside a young, honest-looking woman—no doubt his marriage partner.

Giebe Illgner regarded the couple with a soft smile that greatly resembled Brigitte's, and it was honestly a great relief to see how clearly he celebrated their union; while I knew that Volk wanted this marriage, deep down, I had still worried that he was being exploited.

Once Giebe Illgner had taken a seat, he promptly broached the subject. "Now then, High Bishop. About the sale contract for Volk..."

Before he could continue, however, I explained that the movement of priests was in fact under the purview of the High Priest. I gestured toward Ferdinand sitting beside me, who took the contract from one of his attendants, spread it out on the table, then pushed it over to the giebe.

"This is Volk's sale contract. I suggest that you look over it."

Giebe Illgner began reading at once, and an instant later, his eyes widened with shock. He looked between me, Ferdinand, and the contract multiple times, then over at Volk and the woman, before shutting his eyes tightly. "Is Volk truly this expensive...? The gray priest my father purchased a generation ago wasn't nearly so pricey. I believe he was only a single small gold."

"The value of a gray priest is determined by their abilities; that is the price of an apprentice capable of doing no more than simple serving work. Volk previously served as the attendant to a blue priest and has thus been trained to serve nobles. He is also deeply involved with the printing and paper-making industries directed by Rozemyne. Is it not obvious that he would be expensive?"

Volk and the woman stiffened, desperately looking to the giebe for help. He gazed back at the contract as they watched him, then lowered his eyes with an extraordinarily troubled expression.

"The price is so much higher than expected. I... I don't believe I can afford this."

"N-No way..." I heard the woman whisper.

"How much were you expecting?" I asked. Since he had been basing his estimate on his father's experience, I could assume that he had anticipated a price of a few small golds. But that wouldn't do at all—Volk was worth two large golds and two small golds.

"...I expected a high price due to his numerous talents, but I was thinking five to six small golds at most."

"You would have been right, were he not involved with the printing industry. But he is, and that constitutes the bulk of his worth," Ferdinand said, crossing his arms. Whoever purchased Volk would essentially be buying his knowledge of paper-making and printing as well, and considering the value that would bring them, it wasn't an option for us to lower the price.

"Lady Rozemyne..." Giebe Illgner looked my way, probably thinking that I would be more pliable than Ferdinand. But unfortunately for him, my financial negotiation skills came from Benno; I would probably be even harder to talk down.

Of course, I did want the marriage to happen and for love to be rewarded. I wanted to provide Volk with my support, since he was braving his fears to be together with this woman. But folding here would increase the likelihood of other nobles trying to get discounts as well. It was easy to imagine people accusing me of showing favoritism to Illgner, or holding faux marriages to manipulate my goodwill.

Benno had taught me to only lower prices after considering the consequences and determining whether I really wanted to take a loss, and so my only option here was to shake my head.

"I am afraid this is the end of our negotiations. No matter the circumstances, six small golds simply will not do," I concluded.

Giebe Illgner looked at the couple in question, the despair clear on his face. "But Lady Rozemyne. Volk and Carya are truly in love, and—"

"Giebe Illgner, I am unsure what you are struggling to understand here, but gray priests are not permitted to marry. As you cannot afford to buy him, you have no right to speak about his future. We are finished here."

"My... My sincerest apologies," Giebe Illgner said, kneeling before Ferdinand with a bitter expression. At the same time, I heard Carya give a pained choke, no longer able to bear her suffering in silence.

The air in the room was so awkward and heart-rending that I found myself tugging on Ferdinand's sleeve and whispering his name, hoping he could somehow resolve things.

"I am not the one who needs to act here," he scoffed, looking at me with a displeased grimace. "Think. What would *you* do if you didn't have the money for something?"

I immediately clapped my hands together. The solution was clear—Giebe Illgner would just need to earn the money to get what he wanted. Until then, I could keep Volk reserved, not selling him to anyone else.

"Giebe Illgner, I will grant you first purchase rights for Volk, so what do you say about spending one year earning the money that you need to buy him?" I suggested, but Giebe Illgner just hung his head sadly.

"It is unreasonable to earn that much money in a single year."

"Then you need only try harder," Ferdinand said, standing up from his chair. "Rozemyne, we are leaving."

I stood up as well, and together we exited the room. When I glanced back, I saw that Giebe Illgner was cradling his head, Carya had broken down in tears, and Volk was grimacing in pain, seemingly on the verge of crying himself.

If they try really hard, I honestly do think they'll be able to earn enough in a year.

Unlike before, Illgner now had newly developed paper. If they could find a niche that suited its quirks and then sell a ton, they would have more than enough to buy Volk. Lutz and I had made a ton of money super quickly when we first started making paper; they would simply need to do the same while there wasn't any competition. This was their only opportunity.

"Is it just me, or is Giebe Illgner rather unskilled when it comes to business matters?" I mused aloud.

"It seems to me that he has poor negotiation skills in general."

"Isn't that kind of a fatal flaw for a noble...?" Negotiating and laying the groundwork for plans were the basic fundamentals of noble life —Ferdinand had made sure to beat that into me.

"You are correct," Ferdinand replied with a nod, but then his expression became a difficult frown. He began to rub his temples while looking at me, seemingly searching for the right words, before finally opening his mouth again to speak. "Your business sense is quite abnormal for a noble, but putting that aside... you may give the giebe advice on how to earn money. Benno trained you in such matters, did he not?"

Whaaat?! Ferdinand showing other people compassion? That's certainly rare to see, I thought, looking up at him in shock. He seemed to read me in an instant, though, and flicked my forehead with a glare. *Ouchie!*

And so came the day of the Harvest Festival. Celebrations were due to begin in the afternoon, so the townsfolk spent the morning enthusiastically making all the necessary preparations. I wasn't usually exposed to this fervor, as things were normally ready by the time I arrived, but their excitement was infectious: it wasn't long before I could feel myself eagerly awaiting the festival as well.

Brigitte was asking for the day off, and while there wasn't much we could do with Ferdinand around, I did want her to enjoy the celebrations at home after being away for such a long time.

In the midst of all the bustle, I went to the side building with Fran and Damuel. Ferdinand was going to be taking care of the baptism ceremony and such, while the tax official he had brought with him would handle the province's Harvest Festival. Justus had already gone home, so I was basically just a visitor this time.

I entered a room in the side building to find Gil, Lutz, and Damian in wait, each holding boards and diptychs with their reports and notes written on them.

"Gil—it is good to see you well. Lutz—thank you for your work. And Damian—thank you for spending so much time on this trip," I began, praising the three for their work. "Now, what manner of paper have you created?"

Gil stepped forward first. "As a brief summary, we have made three new kinds of paper, namely from rinfin, nansebs, and effons. Schireis wood didn't work well with the tororo we got from degrova leaves, so we plan to bring the inner bark back to Ehrenfest with us and experiment using shram bugs and ediles instead."

"Three new kinds? That's splendid news," I said, earning me a happy smile from Gil.

"In the same way that trombe paper is fire-resistant, nanseb and effon paper might have special qualities of their own, given that they're made from feyplants. We haven't discovered what those are yet, though."

"Thank you, Gil. I suppose that is something we will simply need to keep in mind. Be sure to look for any special reactions while using them."

When Gil was done, Lutz stepped forward to give a report on the trauperles.

"Here is a white trauperle fruit. They are often gathered in Illgner at the start of autumn, but they're too bitter to be used as food. The juice from them produces firm, silky smooth paper, so we would like to bring a large quantity back to Ehrenfest with us to experiment with other kinds of wood."

"Paper made from trauperles might end up becoming an Illgner specialty," I commented.

Finally, Damian—who was now a lot more suntanned than before he had arrived here—came over to discuss the pricing with me. We eventually settled on a figure for the three kinds of paper, and I took care to ensure that the Plantin Company wasn't ripping me off.

"Now then," Damian said, "I will make the contract and return when it is ready."

With that, he exited the room. I looked around to confirm that Gil, Lutz, Fran, and Damuel were the only ones here, then smiled.

"Fran, could you stand watch outside the door for me?"

"...Please take care to keep your voices down," he said with a defeated sigh before leaving the room and shutting the door behind him.

I leapt into Lutz's arms at once. "Aaah, I was so lonely! There was nobody to hug me, I don't get any letters from home... It just sucks."

Lutz hugged me back, all the while shaking his head with blatant exasperation. Once my heart was sufficiently healed, I went and patted Gil on the head, saying that both he and Lutz had worked very hard.

"...So, how'd your gathering go?" Lutz asked.

"Eheheh. I've got all the ingredients now," I boasted. "Impressed with how hard I've been working?" But as I proudly puffed out my chest, Damuel muttered, "It was we guard knights who worked hard" behind me, causing Lutz and Gil to laugh.

I pouted, trying to explain that I'd worked hard too, but everyone was laughing too much to hear me. Soon enough, I was laughing along with them.

"Lutz! Lutz!" I chirped. "Now I'll finally get to be a normal girl!"

I could live my life normally, not having to worry about collapsing after running or getting too excited. But despite my excitement, Lutz just gave me a dubious look. He furrowed his brow and crossed his arms.

"You'll be healthy again, sure... but I don't know if you'll ever be a *normal* girl."

"And what do you mean by that, exactly?"

"I mean that once you get healthy, it'll be even harder to stop you from doing all sorts of crazy things, and you'll stick out like a weirdo even more."

"That's so mean!" I protested, but both Gil and Damuel voiced similar opinions.

Then, as things started to calm down, Lutz gave me a serious look. "Hey... Volk looked real depressed when I saw him earlier. Did things not turn out well?"

"...No, sadly. Giebe Illgner just couldn't afford to buy him, so negotiations broke down completely. The amount Volk can do means he's pretty expensive, and considering the future, I just can't afford to give him away for cheap."

Lutz narrowed his jade eyes and started running calculations in his head; he was being trained in the Plantin Company, and had long since become a better merchant than I would ever be.

"Yeah, I guess just knowing about printing stuff would cause him to shoot up in value, and that's not even including his attendant experience..." he conceded. "Can't really lower the price when the printing industry is going to be expanding so much, so... can't blame you here."

"I did tell Giebe Illgner that I'd give him first purchase rights for a full year, though. And with this much new paper, don't you think they'll be able to afford two large golds if they spend a whole year working like crazy to make as much as they can?"

"A whole year? Yeah. But that means Volk will need to keep working here in Illgner."

Gil raised his head. "Lady Rozemyne, could you allow me to give Volk some advice? Like, on how to make money and stuff. And could I reassure him that he'll be able to make enough so long as he tries his best? He was so happy yesterday about getting to marry Carya, but this morning he looked like he just wanted to die. I can't stand seeing him like this..."

I nodded. "Of course you can. I was actually wondering how to make that happen, since I don't exactly get many opportunities to speak to him. I think it would be most helpful if you and Volk speak to Giebe Illgner about this and ask that he request to borrow Volk from me for a bit."

"I'll see what I can do."

Everyone was watching the Harvest Festival with sparkling eyes: Gil, who had often been forced to stay back at the temple and run the workshop; Lutz, who had come to Hasse in the past on business but spent most of his time there in the monastery; and finally Damian and the gray priests, who were all seeing the celebration for the very first time.

"It certainly is interesting how they hold all the ceremonies at once," one gray priest commented.

"Indeed. There are too many people in Ehrenfest for that," added another.

Rather than sitting up on the stage like usual, I was among the participants with the Plantin Company and the gray priests. Ferdinand, meanwhile, was confidently standing on the stage and giving the blessings in his clear, resounding voice. I watched on, wondering whether that was how I looked when I was up there.

I always stand on something to boost my height, so surely people can see me when I'm on stage...

Once the ceremonies were over, it was time for the warf tournament. Lutz and Damian cheered fervently upon seeing the game for the first time, but the priests raised in the temple merely paled at how aggressive and chaotic everything was.

The variety of reactions brought a warm smile to my face—that is, until I spotted Volk in my peripheral vision. It looked as though there was something he wanted to say, so I glanced around, then gestured for him to come over.

"Volk, I do regret that negotiations broke down, but the price is non-negotiable. Considering the impact any concessions would have on future sales of gray priests to nobles, I cannot lower it for personal reasons."

He nodded sadly, clenched his teeth for a second, then looked at me head-on. "Lady Rozemyne, Gil informed me of what you said. Do you truly believe we can earn that much money in a single year...?"

"Yes. It will require a significant amount of work, of course, but now that Illgner has three new kinds of paper to call its own, it shouldn't be too difficult for you to earn two large golds. I made that much in about half a year when I initially started making plant paper with Lutz."

His face lit up with hope at my words. Unlike Gil and Lutz, Volk simply did his work as instructed without ever dealing with the financial side of things, so it was easy to guess that he didn't know how much plant paper and picture books were actually worth.

"I can lend you to Giebe Illgner if paid using the money you have earned up until now. My understanding is that the river here doesn't freeze during the winter, so you will have an entire year to work your hardest."

"Lady Rozemyne..."

"To tell you the truth, I am still worried about the prospect of a gray priest getting married. Living with someone who has entirely different values from you is a challenge, even among those of the same status with the same background. A gray priest from the temple and a citizen from Illgner will no doubt have contrasting perspectives, habits, and values. Your mindsets couldn't be further apart."

Volk lowered his gaze, knowing from experience just how true that was. But after a pause, he looked up and toward the group of people. I could assume he was gazing in the direction of the woman from before, though I couldn't see her from where I was.

"For the next year, dedicate yourself to making paper with her, and while you're saving money, do what you can to adjust to life here in Illgner," I said. "I would like for you to observe the lives of those outside the temple—to see other families and married couples—and work to learn everything about them. I pray that your relationship does not become one where Carya is constantly burdened; rather, I hope it becomes one where you struggle together, grow together, and care for one another."

Following the completion of the Harvest Festival, Giebe Illgner signed a contract with the Plantin Company, while I advised them on business matters and agreed to lend Volk to them for one year. And once all the discussions were over, I returned to Ehrenfest with all the people I had originally brought to Illgner. Volk and Carya saw us off, kneeling quietly and keeping their heads lowered the entire time.

My First-Ever Little Sister

Upon returning to Ehrenfest, I retrieved the small chalices from the blue priests who had traveled during the Harvest Festival, also receiving reports on the harvests and conditions in their respective provinces. I would need to collate these reports together in preparation for a meeting with the archduke at the castle.

And once this is done, we can get to work making my jureve. Let's do this!

Ferdinand and I arrived together at the castle, then went our separate ways, with me going to the northern building with Rihyarda.

"After you have delivered today's report to Aub Ehrenfest, milady, you are due to greet Lady Charlotte."

"Lady Charlotte...? That would be Wilfried's little sister, correct?"

"Yes. Her baptism ceremony is this winter, so a room and the like are being prepared for her as we speak."

Now that Rihyarda mentioned it, Elvira had actively ensured that my room in the northern building was ready for me to use right after my baptism ceremony. I hadn't exactly been in any position to help her with that, given that I was partway through having a noble upbringing hurriedly beaten into me at the time, but Charlotte was apparently learning to lead people by taking charge in how her room was arranged.

You know... it sounds like she's a lot more competent than Wilfried.

I considered that possibility as I entered the northern building and climbed the stairs. The door to the room beside mine was wide open, and I could see furniture being carried inside. A short girl about my size was observing the process.

She must have heard us come up the stairs as she immediately whirled around. Her dress fluttered, and her blonde, almost silver hair swept through the air behind her. Her face was so adorable that I could have mistaken her for a life-sized doll, and her lively indigo eyes blinked rapidly. When we locked gazes, she broke into a happy smile and immediately began walking over, her retainers following along with her.

"Rozemyne! Big Sister!"

Aah! She just called me "Big Sister"!

I was immediately overcome with emotion. Hearing that phrase from such a cute little girl with a big smile on her face was enough for me to embrace the idea entirely—I was Charlotte's older sister, and that was that.

"I haven't had my baptism ceremony yet, so I can't give an actual blessing... but may I give you a traditional greeting anyway?"

"Yes, of course."

Charlotte glanced up as she tried to remember the words of the prayer, then knelt and lowered her head. "May I pray for a blessing in appreciation of this serendipitous meeting, ordained by the fruitful days of Schutzaria the Goddess of Wind?"

"You may."

"May Schutzaria the Goddess of Wind bless you. I am Charlotte, daughter of Aub Ehrenfest. I pray that the threads of our fates be woven together."

My First-Ever Little Sister

Although Charlotte couldn't give actual blessings yet, she had the words memorized and recited them flawlessly. I knew all too well how nerve-racking it was to give that kind of greeting for the first time: back when I had given one to Elvira, I was so worried about messing up that my heart had started pounding.

As Charlotte knelt, I tried to roughly echo what Elvira had said to me in response. "I pray the same, Charlotte. I am your older sister."

She looked up at me with a relieved smile, and I couldn't help but smile back.

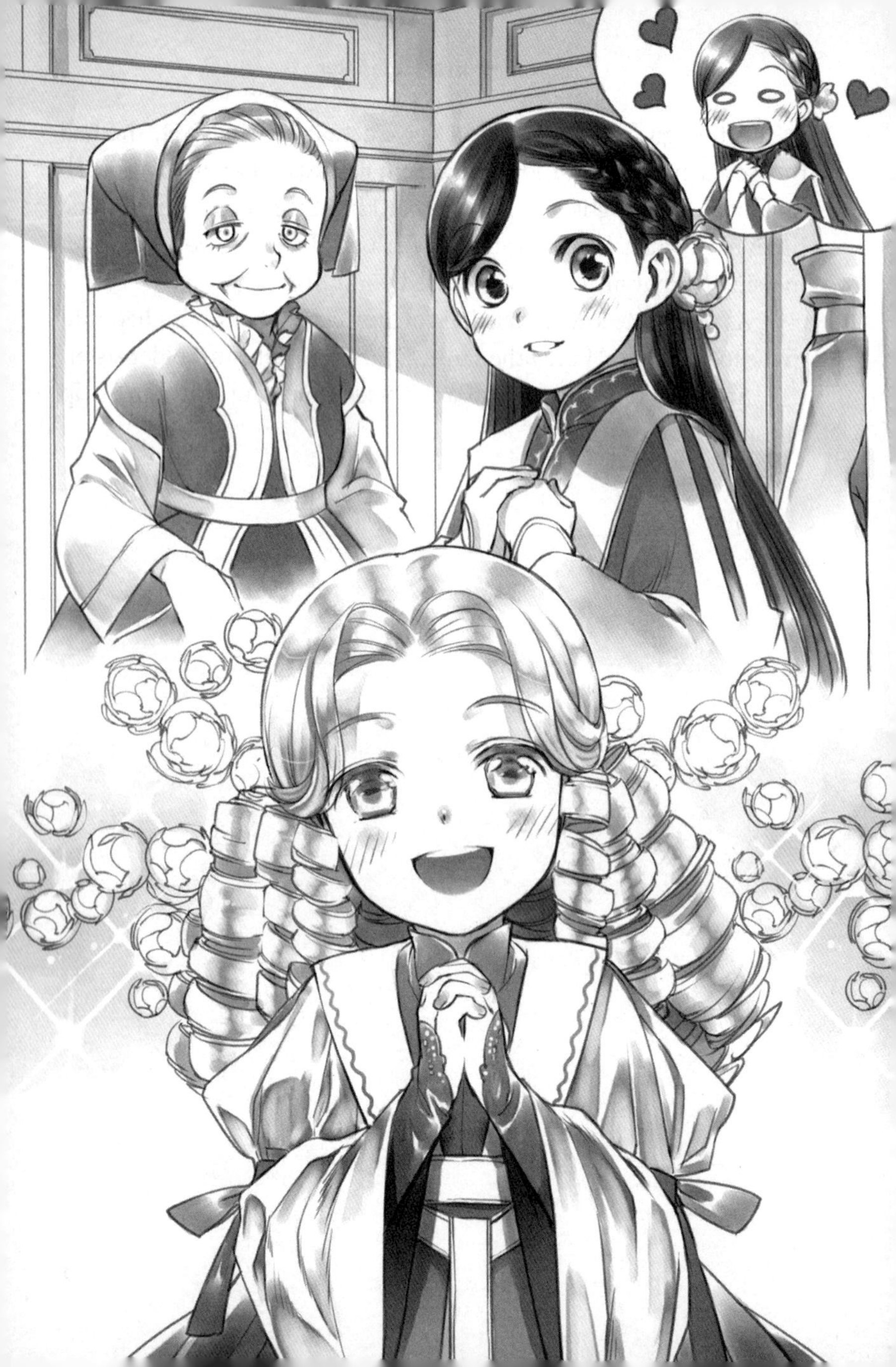

My First-Ever Little Sister

"You know your greetings very well," I said.

"I thank you ever so much. All of my other siblings are boys, and I've always wanted an older sister. I'm just so happy to see you."

"Me too. I always wanted a little sister!"

"I pray once again for our fates to be woven together."

Holy cow, Charlotte's super cute. She might even join Tuuli in my pantheon of angels.

An emotional sigh escaped me, at which point Charlotte tilted her head slightly. "Dear sister, you're the High Bishop, aren't you? Will you be giving me a blessing at my baptism ceremony?" she asked, her indigo eyes brimming with hope. I knew that look—she was giving me puppy-dog eyes.

So blessed! It's her first time begging me with puppy-dog eyes! Oh yes, I must grant her wish no matter what. It's my duty as her big sister!

"Oh, my cute little sister, I would love nothing more. So long as Ferdinand permits it, I shall bless your baptism... as your older sister."

"I am quite looking forward to it!" she said with a beaming smile. I gave a firm nod in response, and that was when Rihyarda took a step forward.

"Milady, it is about time for you to deliver your report. Would you like to hold a tea party when you return? Lady Charlotte certainly does love sweets."

The very thought was wonderful beyond words. I turned to Charlotte and saw that she was wearing the same smile that Wilfried always wore when presented with sweets. There was of course no denying that it looked much cuter on her.

"I believe I would. We can hold a tea party at fifth bell, when my report is complete. Ottilie, please instruct Ella to prepare sweets."

"As you wish."

After promising to hold a tea party with Charlotte, I sped to my room and got changed, then hastily made my way to the archduke's office by highbeast, Rihyarda urging me on all the while. When we arrived, Ferdinand was already there, and the scholars were all ready.

Sylvester straightened his back and looked at me. "Now then. Your report?"

"Charlotte is positively adorable," I said, starting with what I considered the most important point of discussion.

"Indeed. She certainly is," he replied with a nod.

"I have promised to perform her baptism for her."

"This is not what you are here for, fool!" Ferdinand barked, completing the comedy trifecta. "Give your report on the Harvest Festival!"

Out of respect for his righteous observation, I started giving my serious report. Every city in the Central District had produced a greater yield than last year—except of course Hasse—which was recognized as the result of my going everywhere for Spring Prayer.

"Seems like I'll want you to do the same next spring too," Sylvester said.

In all honesty, I found it really taxing to travel that much in such a short space of time, but that wouldn't be an issue, since I would have a healthy body by then. I nodded to show that I was fine with his suggestion.

Sylvester nodded in turn. "Everyone but Karstedt, Ferdinand, and Rozemyne—clear the room."

My plan had been to swiftly return to my room once my report was done, but it seemed this conversation wasn't over just yet. I sadly drooped my head, thinking about how much I would have rather been drinking tea with my cute little sister than talking with these three.

My First-Ever Little Sister

Once the last of the scholars and attendants were out, Sylvester cracked his neck and stretched, going from archduke mode to Sylvester mode.

"Sooo, Rozemyne... These two told me about your mana compression method, and I was wondering whether it worked on adults too. Does it let people fit more mana into their bodies even after their vessel for mana stops growing?"

"...I don't know, since I'm still a child. But it's very possible. Perhaps you should experiment?" I suggested, which made Sylvester lean across the table with shining eyes. He was positively overflowing with eagerness to try it out himself.

"Alright," he said. "We'll select individuals to learn it based on those who meet the criteria. That is: already knowing how to compress traditionally, belonging to the Florencia faction, and having the permission of the six of us. How about we start with your guardians and family? Seems like a good idea to me."

Sylvester, Florencia, Ferdinand, and Karstedt apparently all counted as my family here, and I got the impression that this would soon be expanding to our guard knights and attendants as well. Given how Sylvester was speaking like this was something that had already been decided, I could guess that he had settled on it in his head and was enthusiastically visualizing the results.

"If this does work for adults as well, then I might need to rethink how much I charge..."

I had been thinking of the cost as something like a children's education fee, but if my method worked on adults as well, then it would be applicable to a lot more people than I thought. This would, in turn, put a strain on people's family budgets, and I certainly didn't want to earn anybody's ire. We needed a perfect price that was accessible to everyone, while still remaining a considerable expense.

"Perhaps we could halve the fee for subsequent family members after the first purchase? Otherwise, buying the method for five people would prove expensive even for an archnoble, right, Father?"

Karstedt stroked his mustache. "That would certainly be a big help..." he said. I had specifically asked him because his family was the largest out of all those participating here.

"Rozemyne, getting more mana is extremely important to nobles. I want to spread news of this compression method during winter socializing, so the sooner we test this out, the better. What do you say?" Sylvester asked, now leaning completely over the table. He wasn't the only one, either—it looked like Karstedt and Ferdinand were both leaning forward a little too.

But despite their eagerness, preparing magic contracts for everyone would take some significant time.

"I promised to have a tea party with Charlotte today, and preparing the magic contracts for everyone would surely take quite some time. We can do this some other day."

"Guh?! Rozemyne, you—you're going to prioritize Charlotte over *me*, your adoptive father?!"

"Yes. She's much cuter than you are," I replied frankly.

"...Fair point. I'm one hot guy, sure, but I'm not as cute as her," he confessed with a groan, resting his head in his hands. I certainly had some thoughts on him calling himself "hot," but I ultimately decided to keep them to myself.

"Plus, I care more about my potion being made than spreading my mana compression method," I added. "I'll teach you all about it once my jureve is ready."

Despite us having gathered all the ingredients, we hadn't actually made the potion yet, since Ferdinand had told me to wait until after my report was done. I cared a lot more about finally getting healthy than other people having more mana.

My First-Ever Little Sister

Ferdinand narrowed his eyes slightly in thought. "Rozemyne, we can make the potion now, but you will want to wait before using it."

"Why is that?"

"The process of using a jureve puts one to sleep for days, months... or at times, even an entire season. You would do well not to use it if you wish to attend Charlotte's baptism ceremony."

In a shocking twist, my mana clumps had formed so long ago that it would take a significant amount of time for them to melt.

"Furthermore," Ferdinand continued, "although you said that you would perform the winter baptism ceremony yourself, there is much you will need to learn to make that possible. It will be much more complicated than the lower city's baptism ceremony—you will need to learn the blessing, the mana registration process, and the sequence of events leading up to the debut. That will not leave time to use the potion, no matter how much you wish to be healthy."

"I want to make the potion so that I can be healthy and have the strength for this kind of thing... but I have to push myself even more before I can use it? This is terrible."

But at the same time, I couldn't suddenly break my first promise to Charlotte—she would forever lose trust in me as her older sister. I wanted to be there for her baptism ceremony no matter what, even if that meant putting off using my jureve.

"Very well. Then I shall use the potion after Charlotte's baptism ceremony."

"No, because winter socializing begins after the baptism ceremony, and so too does the Dedication Ritual. Considering that we wish to keep your circumstances hidden from other nobles, it would be best to wait until Spring Prayer is over."

"Hold on a second. You really intend to make me wait another *half a year* before I can be healthy?! I want to be healthy *now*," I protested, but Ferdinand shook his head.

"We must not be hasty and misjudge the proper timing for using the potion," he said, but it honestly felt as though he was only pressuring me because he wanted to lessen his own burden. I was willing to postpone being healthy for Charlotte's sake, but I wasn't about to wait until spring for Ferdinand.

"Grr... If you want to delay me getting healthy for your own selfish reasons, I won't teach any of you the mana compression method until then! I'm going to become a normal girl and you can't stop me!"

Ferdinand frowned and tapped a finger against his temple, then widened his eyes in realization. "Rozemyne, what if you were to attend the winter baptism ceremony not as the High Bishop, but as her older sister? That would remove the need to learn all the processes at such short notice."

"That's not an option! I'm going to bless Charlotte as her older sister. I don't mind having a lot to learn in the slightest; I've spent years learning all sorts of things under time constraints."

There was no doubt in my mind that I would be granting the first request ever given to me by my darling little sister. Tuuli always did her best to do whatever I asked, and I wanted to be as great of an older sister to Charlotte as Tuuli was to me.

"Hm... I understand. You wish to play the part of a good older sister for your first little sister, correct?" Ferdinand asked, still tapping his temple.

I gave a big nod—that was exactly right. I wanted to show Charlotte my best side and become an older sister who she could respect.

"...In that case, would she not respect you even more if you performed not just the blessing at her baptism ceremony, but dedicated yourself to the duchy at the Dedication Ritual and Spring Prayer, too? Do you not think that is what a member of the archducal family should do?"

"I do!" I agreed, clenching my fists with fiery determination.

Ferdinand nodded, a smug look on his face. "Then work hard until Spring Prayer is complete."

"Right! I... Wait. What?"

I tilted my head in confusion, but before I could even process what had just happened, Sylvester pointed at the door. "Rozemyne, isn't it about time for your tea party? You can go now."

"I can?"

"Yep. Show my Charlotte lots of love."

"Of course!" I beamed, confidently tapping a fist against my chest before saying the traditional farewells. I then exited Sylvester's office, humming all the way back to my room.

At last, my tea party with Charlotte. Tralala, tralalalala.

It was a little before fifth bell and the tea party was ready, with Ella having finished preparing the sweets. Today we were having pie filled with seasonal fruits.

"Rozemyne, thank you ever so much for inviting me."

"Thank you for being here, Charlotte."

Charlotte sat in her chair looking a bit nervous, since this was her first time having a tea party with anyone outside her more immediate family. To be honest, I was a little anxious too, since this was my first tea party with my little sister.

"Wilfried praises you so much, Rozemyne, that I have been dying to meet you for so very long now," Charlotte began. She then told me how Wilfried had read picture bibles to her, and how she had lost to him in karuta and cards over and over again. She peppered all her stories with praise for me.

How could I ever convey the sheer strength of emotion I was feeling right now? Up until this point, my family had mostly just called me useless, but now I had a little sister who was praising me. The slight embarrassment aside, I was so happy that I wanted to roll around on the ground and squeal.

I owe you my life, Wilfried! It's thanks to you that my cute little sister has such a high opinion of me!

"You made those picture books, the karuta, and even Mother's hair stick, didn't you?" Charlotte continued. "The decorations on the hair stick look so much like real flowers; I simply love it."

"I designed them all, but craftswomen make them, not me. Would you like me to introduce you to the store which makes them?"

Hair sticks just like mine were currently all the rage in Florencia's faction—Brigitte wearing one during the Starbind Ceremony had made quite an impact, and the flowers were now being used both as hair ornaments and to decorate dresses. I could imagine that Tuuli and Mom had their hands full making them right now.

"You wouldn't mind? Would they be able to make one for me before my baptism ceremony, I wonder?"

"That might be difficult... I could lend you one of mine, assuming I have one that matches your outfit. Rihyarda, please bring me the hair sticks that incorporate the divine colors of winter."

"At once, milady."

Rihyarda promptly brought in the hair sticks, holding them up against Charlotte's hair one by one. As she discussed with her attendants which ones would look best on her, Damuel suddenly came into the room, having been guarding the door from outside.

My First-Ever Little Sister

"Lady Rozemyne, Lord Wilfried is requesting permission to enter. He wishes to speak with Lady Char—" he began, only for Wilfried to barge in from behind him. His attendants and guard knights were reaching out to grab him, telling him that he needed to wait until he had my permission, but he was actively ignoring them.

"I heard Charlotte was here."

"Wilfried, it's quite rude to enter a room before you have received permission," I said, implying that he should leave, but his eyebrows shot up with anger when he saw me.

"Shut up! Charlotte, you have to get out of here now. Don't let Rozemyne fool you!"

Excuse me...?

His exclamation came completely out of nowhere; I didn't at all understand what could have brought it on. Everyone stared at him in wide-eyed confusion, and as we froze with our mouths agape, Charlotte tilted her head and blinked.

"Whatever do you mean? Aren't you always praising Rozemyne?" she asked, and that was enough to snap me back to reality. I couldn't let him trash talk me in front of Charlotte like this. I needed to be an older sister she could respect.

"Wilfried, when have I ever deceived you? Please do not use such deceptive language."

"Just shut *up* already!"

With that, Wilfried raced toward me, moving so suddenly that Damuel yelped in surprise. Lamprecht stepped forward, shouting for him to stop, but Angelica—having been standing guard behind me the whole time—had already moved to intercept. She grabbed onto Wilfried's arm, twisted it behind his back, then forced him to the ground. He landed with a resounding crash.

"Ow! What're you doing, Angelica?!" he demanded.

"Please do not approach Lady Rozemyne before getting permission to enter."

"Who do you think you are?! Let go of me!"

"We are Lady Rozemyne's guard knights, so it's only natural that we would detain someone who barges into the room without first getting permission," Damuel said with a tense expression, moving forward and standing next to Angelica, who was still pinning Wilfried to the floor.

Lamprecht looked between Angelica and Wilfried, then over to me for help. I could hear his silent plea: Angelica was behaving as a guard knight should, but he still wanted her to let Wilfried go.

Just as I opened my mouth to give the order, however, Wilfried started flailing about. He shouted up at Angelica, trying to wriggle around to glare at her. "Rozemyne's the bad person here! Grandmother told me everything! Rozemyne and Ferdinand plotted grandmother's downfall! They're evil!"

Wilfried's grandmother... That would be Sylvester's mother, the former High Bishop's older sister, right? I'm pretty sure she's imprisoned somewhere you need the archduke's permission to enter, to stop her from escaping or meeting with any of her allies. How did Wilfried get authorization for a meeting like that, especially considering that he didn't even know she was imprisoned as a criminal when we said our farewells to Georgine?

"Wilfried, when and where did you have an opportunity to speak to your grandmother?" I asked.

Every retainer in earshot paled instantly. Rihyarda let out a quiet shriek and stiffened, while Lamprecht raced forward and shouted at Wilfried with such crazed intensity that spit actually flew from his mouth.

"When, Lord Wilfried?! When did you speak to Lady Veronica?!" he demanded.

"And *how* did you meet with her?!" another retainer added.

Judging by how panicked his retainers were, Wilfried had certainly not been granted permission to meet with the imprisoned Veronica. It was an extremely bad thing that he had met with her, too, such that this probably wasn't something that could be settled here and now.

"Rihyarda, please report this to Aub Ehrenfest. I believe that it would be best for him to come to us, with a carefully selected entourage."

"Understood, milady."

Wilfried's Actions

Rihyarda sped out of the room. Even she looked sick and pale; there was no doubting that Wilfried had done something absolutely unthinkable. A heavy silence fell over the room, and everyone stared at the floor with furrowed brows.

It was Wilfried himself, still pinned to the floor by Angelica, who eventually spoke. "Lamprecht! Are you not my guard knight?!" he exclaimed. "What are you doing?! Save me!"

Lamprecht gritted his teeth in frustration, then slowly shook his head. "Ever since autumn last year, you have ceased running away, and you have taken both your studies and training seriously. I was truly proud to see you dedicating yourself, becoming someone worthy enough to be the next archduke. And yet... why? Why would you do this?" he asked, speaking for all those who served Wilfried. They looked sad, frustrated, and filled with unbearable regret.

"Why and when did you do this? We cannot release you until we know."

"Wha?! Lamprecht, is me meeting with Grandmother truly that serious?" Wilfried asked, his eyes wide with disbelief. His gaze ran along his retainers as he remained pressed against the floor, and they all nodded with pained looks on their faces.

"...Yes."

Wilfried's Actions

Rihyarda soon returned with Sylvester, Karstedt, Ferdinand, and Eckhart, all of whom were wearing flat expressions that conveyed no emotion whatsoever. Sylvester looked between the still-restrained Wilfried and his ghostly pale retainers, then over at Charlotte and me, our tea party having been brought to an abrupt end.

"Tell me exactly what happened," he said. "Apologies, Rozemyne, but we're going to be using this room. Oswald, call all of Wilfried's retainers. Eckhart... take Rozemyne's and Charlotte's attendants to Wilfried's room and keep them there until this discussion is over. You stay though, Rihyarda."

Under Eckhart's directions, our attendants silently filed out of the room. Only my guard knights were allowed to stay, tasked with keeping watch. Damuel and Brigitte stood outside, while Cornelius remained inside with Angelica, who still had Wilfried pinned.

With her attendants gone and Sylvester looking so intense, Charlotte seemed incredibly scared. I gestured her over, and she gave a small nod before sidling up next to me. Meanwhile, Rihyarda was rushing around, making the necessary preparations for everyone to sit down and talk. I sighed as I watched our tea party turn into a meeting area for a serious discussion.

What a waste of a good tea party.

"Excuse me."

Just as Rihyarda was finishing her preparations, Florencia arrived, having probably been busy with some other work. She silently looked at Wilfried on the floor, then at Sylvester.

"Rozemyne, milady, here is your seat. Lady Charlotte, here is yours," Rihyarda said, guiding us to our chairs around the round table.

Ferdinand, Sylvester, and Florencia sat in that order, with me being on Ferdinand's left and Charlotte on Florencia's right. There was another seat between Charlotte and me, a bit farther apart than the others were. It was probably for Wilfried, but he was still restrained.

"We have arrived at Oswald's urgent summons. This is the place, correct?" Wilfried's other retainers asked as they all entered the room. Their eyes widened at the sight of their master being pinned to the ground, and they promptly moved to kneel by the table, swallowing hard at how serious the archducal couple looked. I could feel the tension in the air getting heavier with each new person who arrived.

Once Oswald had confirmed that everyone was present, Sylvester, having been carefully staring at Wilfried this entire time, turned his gaze to me. "Rozemyne, could you have Wilfried released? I need to speak to him."

As requested, I ordered Angelica to let him go. She obliged with a small nod, then moved to the door to continue her guard duty.

"Wilfried, sit," Sylvester commanded.

Wilfried stood up slowly, nodded, and then sat in the chair Rihyarda had pulled out for him. He looked annoyed.

For a few seconds, silence once again dominated the room, accompanied by a prickling sense of unease. I clenched my fists tightly on my lap, and that was when Ferdinand spoke.

"All those involved in an event see things from their own unique perspectives. One must make these perspectives clear before coming to a judgment. Know that stating falsehoods is a sin."

Sylvester leisurely scanned Wilfried's lined-up attendants and guard knights. His eyes stopped at the end of the line, where the head attendant Oswald was kneeling.

"Oswald, it has been quite some time since I last received a report about Wilfried running away to avoid his duties. When did you lose sight of him?"

"Not once have we lost sight of Lord Wilfried while on duty. For the past year, he has dedicated himself to his work with admirable diligence. Our reports were all true," Oswald replied, raising his head to look Sylvester in the eyes while his fellow attendants all nodded in agreement. "In fact, I am the one who is truly curious here. Just how *did* Lord Wilfried deceive us?"

"I didn't deceive anyone!" Wilfried yelled angrily, prompting Sylvester to look at him with furrowed brows.

"If you have deceived no one and done no wrong, Wilfried, then you can answer honestly regarding your actions. When did you meet with your grandmother?"

"During the hunting tournament, Father," Wilfried replied eagerly.

Everyone's expressions changed in an instant, but I wasn't following. Why was that so shocking?

"Um, what's the hunting tournament?" I asked. "I'm unfamiliar with it."

"You are likely unaware since you spend that time traveling the duchy for the Harvest Festival," Ferdinand began. "As the name implies, nobles gather to hunt in the castle's forest. It is a large-scale tournament held before winter socializing. The hunted prey become food for the winter, and awards are given to those who hunt the most, so it is the most important time of the year for knights in the Noble's Quarter who wish to distinguish themselves."

It was an event held at the same time as the Harvest Festival, functioning as a way for the castle to restock its food reserves before winter. Knights, scholars, and attendants could all join in, with those who participated competing to hunt the most feybeasts. In the meantime, women (excluding the female knights) and children would provide their support while enjoying a calm, graceful tea party.

This was probably the hunting that Sylvester had said was *"way too boring"* back when he had disguised himself as a blue priest.

"Were you not with Florencia during the hunting tournament?" Sylvester asked.

"I was, but some of my friends from the winter playroom came over halfway through, so we went off to play."

"I believe you were with Oswald then. I instructed him not to let you out of his sight," Florencia said, eyeing the attendant carefully.

"Nothing abnormal happened while I was there," Oswald responded, "and I stayed with him until Linhardt came to relieve me."

Linhardt had desperately run around trying to keep up with Wilfried and his friends, but at one point, he tripped over and fell hard enough to hurt his legs. While Linhardt was being treated, Wilfried was looked after by his friends' attendants.

"We played hide-and-seek while Linhardt was being healed, sneaking out of the tea party's plaza and hiding under tables so the adults wouldn't find us. While we were passing under one, we heard nobles talking about things. They said that Grandmother and Great Uncle had been arrested because of Rozemyne and Ferdinand."

"Who said that?"

"Everyone there. The men, the women—everyone."

Ferdinand, who was briskly taking note of everything mentioned at the meeting, muttered to himself. "It seems the children brought him there deliberately, rather than them simply happening upon a gathering of former Veronica faction nobles..."

I lowered my eyes, recalling the time Rihyarda had warned me about parents acting through their children. It was unbelievable that kids were expected to be mindful of political plots even when playing tag or hide-and-seek with their friends. In fact, I was certain that I would have fallen for the same trick myself had I been in

Wilfried's Actions

Wilfried's position. Never would it have occurred to me that all the adults there might be part of the same former faction, and I probably would have believed what they were saying, if only because so many of them were saying it.

In another world, I'd be the one sitting where Wilfried is right now...

The only reason I hadn't made a mistake like this yet was because I spent most of my time in the temple and seldom engaged with castle affairs. Had I needed to learn serious noble relations like Wilfried, I certainly would have messed up too.

"Wilfried, despite my order that no nobles from other duchies be allowed into the city, your great uncle spurred your grandmother into using my official seal without my permission to grant one such noble entry. She was punished for forging official documents and disobeying my direct orders. I explained this to you before. Were you not listening to me?" Sylvester asked with a frown. He was checking whether Wilfried had trusted other nobles over his own father, but Wilfried shook his head hard in response.

"I jumped out from under the table and told them what you told me, but... they said that while it was true Grandmother had committed the crime, it was Rozemyne's fault it had happened in the first place. Then they said that Ferdinand was pulling the strings from the shadows. They told me Rozemyne and Ferdinand were trying to take over Ehrenfest..."

With so many unfamiliar nobles crowding him, I could understand why Wilfried might have been nervous. He probably would have protested if they had called Sylvester a liar, but instead, they agreed with him, simply seeming to provide more information on the situation. Their words had no doubt slid straight into his mind without him ever considering whether or not they were true.

To complicate matters further, not everything those nobles said was untrue. It was fair to say I was the reason Veronica had broken the law, since her specific intention had been to sell me to Count Bindewald, and an argument certainly could have been made that Ferdinand was pulling the strings from the shadows, since he had long been working to remove the High Bishop. From Bezewanst's perspective, he had set out to commit one simple crime, only to have Ferdinand dump a huge list of violations onto him—violations so small that even Bezewanst himself had forgotten about them. It would be harder to think Ferdinand *hadn't* lured him into a trap.

"Then one of them said that I could just speak to Grandmother myself and ask her who's right," Wilfried continued.

Sylvester squeezed his eyes shut. The plot was fairly devious, if you asked me: Wilfried had essentially been raised by his grandmother since birth, so it only made sense that he would love her more and consider her more trustworthy than his actual mother, who had only recently been given the opportunity to regularly interact with him. Veronica had his unconditional trust, and it stood to reason that he would welcome her guidance in a situation like this.

"One of the men said Grandmother was imprisoned in the Ivory Tower, and when I asked where that was, a woman gave us directions and suggested we go see it for ourselves. We only went to scout it out."

Wilfried had followed the directions with his friends, saying over and over again that he was just checking to see if the tower was really there. And in the end, they actually found it.

A man standing at the entrance had informed them that only the archduke and his children could open the door to go inside. Everyone else tried and failed, then looked over at Wilfried with hopeful eyes. He eventually opened it, just out of curiosity.

"Nobody else could open the door, but I could. It opened for me the second I touched it."

"Not surprising. So, did you enter the tower? Did anyone else go in with you?" Sylvester asked lifelessly, drained of energy. He was simply asking for the record: everyone knew that Wilfried had gone inside, otherwise he wouldn't have been saying that his grandmother had told him things.

"I went in alone; they said that nobody else could enter, in the same way that nobody else could open the door. Grandmother really was in the tower. She told me everything. The truth," Wilfried said, glaring at Ferdinand and me. "Grandmother is locked in the tower, suffering, all because of Rozemyne and Ferdinand."

Florencia tightly closed her eyes, a pained look on her face.

"Father, please," Wilfried continued. "You have to save Grandmo—"

"*Silence*! Do *not* finish that sentence!" Sylvester shouted, slamming a fist against the table. "Protesting my decision is nothing less than treason against the archduke!"

Wilfried's eyes widened at how violently he had been interrupted. "Father...?"

"*I* am the one who discovered your grandmother's crimes and sentenced her to be imprisoned. Not Rozemyne. Not Ferdinand. *Me*. Aub Ehrenfest."

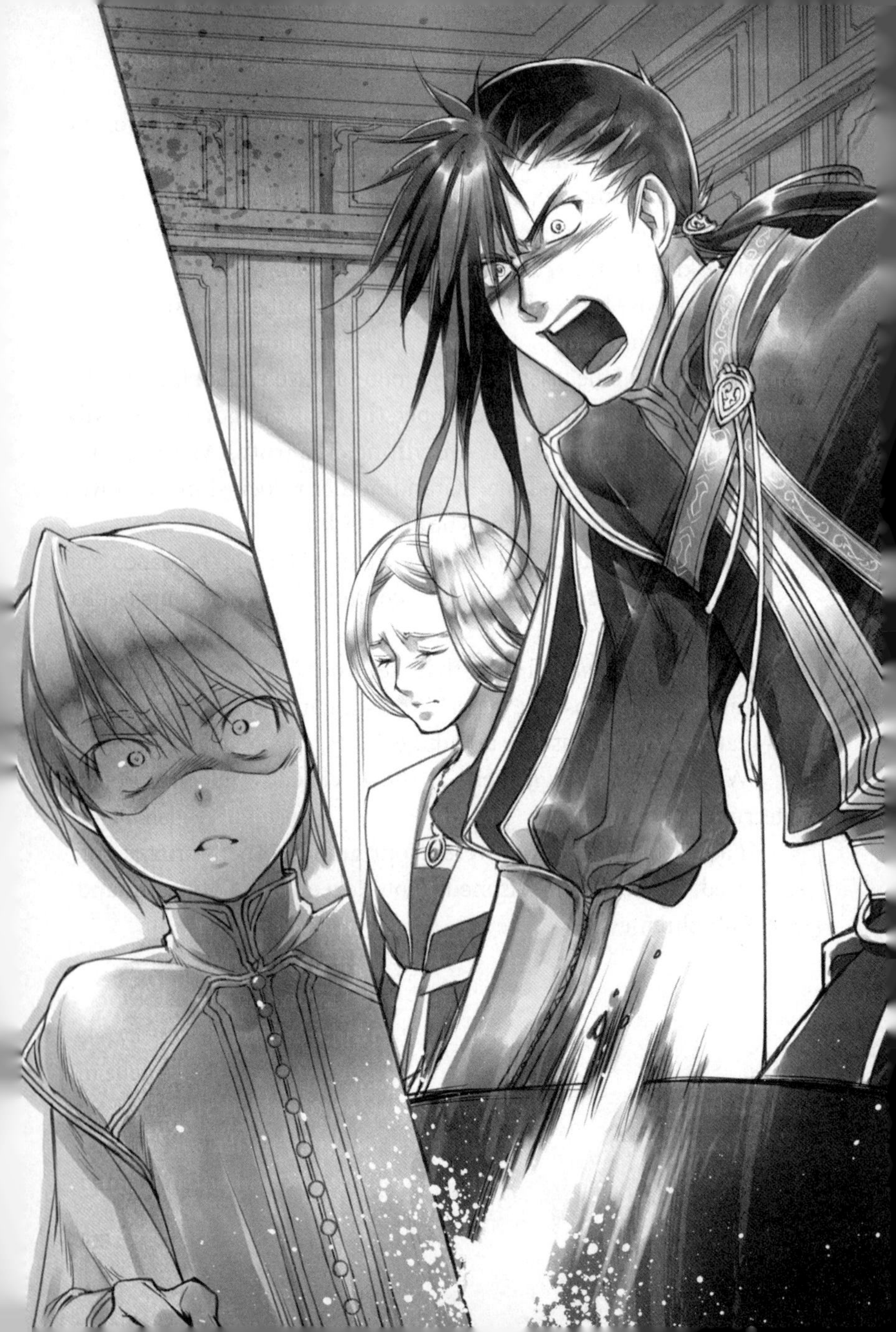

Wilfried's Actions

Wilfried recoiled in shock, having already spent so much time echoing his grandmother by accusing Ferdinand and me. It looked entirely as though he had known she had been imprisoned for committing a crime, but not that his father had sentenced her himself. He probably thought that Ferdinand and I had done it ourselves, given that she kept blaming us.

"Do you wish to join the rebel faction, opposing both me and your mother Florencia?" Sylvester asked with a stern expression.

Wilfried hurriedly shook his head, his expression overcome with anxiety. "I'm not trying to oppose either of you!"

"But that is how it comes across when you defend your grandmother and speak against my decisions. You must watch what you say. How many times have I told you to think before you speak...?"

"But..." Wilfried trailed off, glaring at Ferdinand and me while frustratedly biting his lip.

It was at this point that Florencia rose from her chair and walked over to Wilfried, stroking his cheek with a sad smile. "You were told what your grandmother Lady Veronica believes to be true, but there is no singular truth in this world. As Ferdinand said, everyone has their own perspective. The truth I know is that Rozemyne was a victim in all this—it was not her, but Lady Veronica who laid out plots and brought chaos to the duchy."

"What are you saying, Mother?!" Wilfried shouted in disbelief, shaking his head as if to push her words from his mind.

Florencia embraced him, her voice trembling. "Lady Veronica stole you away from me right after you were born. I was not permitted to touch or even hug you. And now, not even satisfied by that, she has guided you into committing such a grave crime. That is the truth from my perspective."

Wilfried froze, blinking in surprise as he looked up at Florencia, who was on the verge of tears. "I committed a crime...?" he asked.

"You did," Sylvester answered. "That is a tower for imprisoning members of the archducal family who have committed unforgivable crimes. Those who enter it without my permission as aub are considered traitors, either plotting rebellion or attempting to free the prisoners within."

"What...? Nobody there said anything like that..." Wilfried said weakly, paling as he realized how grave his situation really was. The blood drained from my face as well; I hadn't realized that Veronica was imprisoned somewhere so important. I had assumed she was merely stuck in some mansion or another, and that speaking to her wouldn't be that serious of a crime.

"This was the plot of those who brought you to the tower, but you are still the one who committed the crime," Florencia explained. "Simply passing around rumors and telling you the location of the tower are not things that nobles can be truly charged for."

All they had done was gossip at a tea party.

All they had done was answer the questions they were asked.

All they had done was play with Wilfried, harmlessly joining him on an adventure.

And when they had discovered that the tower really was there, all they had done was ask him to open the door. None of this would have happened had Wilfried not gone inside. The others hadn't forced him in, nor had they entered themselves.

"Out of all those involved, only you can be charged with a crime, Wilfried. And if you are found guilty of abetting the escape of a major criminal imprisoned by the archduke, you will not only be disinherited... you will once again be taken away from me, even though we are finally together..." Florencia whispered, tears dripping from her eyes.

Wilfried's Actions

I looked over at Sylvester. It was clear that he was desperately trying to think of a way to help, but Wilfried had admitted to his own wrongdoing. With his crimes already this set in stone, it would not be easy to protect him.

"Good grief... What a pain. Is this not why I said to disinherit him ahead of time?" Ferdinand said dryly.

Wilfried flinched at the remark. "But, but... Rozemyne plotted everything..."

Ferdinand ceased writing and looked up. "There are as many truths as there are people. Rozemyne, tell Wilfried *your* truth. You lost a great deal because of his grandmother, did you not?"

He gasped and looked my way. "Rozemyne's truth? No... No, Rozemyne plotted everything..."

"That is not how I experienced things, Wilfried."

Though I wasn't really sure what Ferdinand was thinking here, I went ahead and told Wilfried my fake backstory. I explained that I was secretly raised in the temple; that the former High Bishop had mistaken me for a commoner and spread false rumors among the nobility; that he had asked his older sister Veronica to sneak a foreign noble into Ehrenfest with the intention of selling me; that my guard knights and attendants had gotten hurt while protecting me; and, finally, that I had been adopted by Sylvester to keep me safe from the foreign nobles who were after my mana.

Wilfried was visibly shocked. He knew that his grandmother had committed a crime, but he hadn't truly known how I was involved with it all. "S-So, what did you lose then, Rozemyne?" he stammered.

My family, I answered silently, lowering my gaze.

"I lost my freedom, Wilfried. Before then, I was making books with people in the lower city. But now I cannot visit the lower city, and I cannot speak freely with commoners. I also have to undergo a strict upbringing so that I do not bring shame to the archducal family. I was thrust into the position of High Bishop immediately after my baptism to make up for a mana shortage. You understand how draining of a job that is, yes?"

"But... that's not what Grandmother said at all..." Wilfried murmured, biting his lip and looking down at the floor. He was an honest and sincere person at heart. He really was. Despite him having said over and over again that I was an evil plotter, he was actually listening to me and trying to understand the situation.

Florencia watched on sadly, tenderly stroking her son's hair. "Rozemyne has suffered much because of the crime Lady Veronica committed. Even now, would you say that your grandmother is not at fault? Rozemyne did all she could to help you when you were at risk of being disinherited, did she not? Is that not your truth?"

Wilfried gasped again, gazing back at me. "Forgive me, Rozemyne. I, er... I'm an idiot. You did so much for me, and I just..." His face was reddening with shame before my very eyes.

"It's quite alright. I am not particularly fond of Lady Veronica, given the crime she committed at Bezewanst's request, but I have never met her before—in fact, it was only recently that I even learned her name. But to you, she is a precious family member. It is only natural that you would trust her more than you do me."

Had I needed to decide between trusting Wilfried or Tuuli, I would have picked Tuuli without a second thought. I would have stubbornly supported my family no matter what anyone said, refusing to listen to others or reconsider my beliefs as Wilfried was doing right now. His sincerity was genuinely impressive.

"And yet, you believed your grandmother, scorned Rozemyne, and entered the forbidden tower," Ferdinand interjected dismissively. "I would hope you are prepared to receive your punishment."

"Punishment..."

"A fitting punishment would be disinheriting you and sending you to the temple, or alternatively, locking you in the tower alongside your grandmother."

Florencia had said basically the same thing, but while she spoke as a mother concerned for her son's future, Ferdinand's voice was cold and lacking emotion.

"Sylvester, is Wilfried going to be charged with a crime?" I asked. "He was blatantly tricked into doing this, and while he did enter the tower, he didn't do anything bad while he was inside."

Sylvester didn't answer, instead glancing over at Ferdinand. While he personally didn't want to charge his son with a crime, he wouldn't have a choice if pressured from the outside. He needed to convince Ferdinand before doing anything else, and I was willing to do what I could to help.

"Wilfried was a victim of entrapment," I continued. "Had I been in Wilfried's position, I may have done the very same thing. Because, I mean... Lady Veronica is his precious grandmother. His *family...*"

I knew that *"I might have done the same thing"* was a dumb defense that wouldn't hold much water, but I didn't think it was right to persecute him over this. My feelings for my own family made me vulnerable in exactly the same way.

Ferdinand gave a thoroughly displeased grimace. "You truly are soft," he muttered, his brows drawn together, before looking over at Wilfried. "You have now learned three separate truths: one from your Grandmother, the former first wife; one from your father, Aub Ehrenfest; and one from Rozemyne. I wish to know what you think and feel with this knowledge in mind."

Wilfried lowered his eyes a little, resting a hand on his chin as he organized his thoughts beneath Ferdinand's gaze. Then, after thinking for a bit, he slowly raised his head and looked at Ferdinand head-on.

Wilfried's Punishment

"...I thought it was strange that Grandmother's truth was the only one that didn't match what everyone else said. Assuming they're all telling the truth, then she's the odd one out. I love her, but... if the question is whether she's right or wrong here, I think she's wrong now," Wilfried said plainly.

Ferdinand watched him calmly before prompting him to continue. "I see. And...?"

"...And I need to apologize. I'm sorry for everything I said, Ferdinand."

Ferdinand widened his eyes slightly at the apology, then tightly furrowed his brow, carefully looking over Wilfried as though he were dissecting him.

"Wh-Why are you so mad at me? I apologized, didn't I...?" Wilfried stammered, flinching back. With Ferdinand now watching him with an even harsher gaze, he was almost on the verge of tears.

"Don't worry," I said reassuringly. "You're doing fine."

"What's fine about this?!" he yelped. I had an explanation at the ready, though; it was a bit hard to understand, but Ferdinand wasn't mad at all.

"It may look as though Ferdinand got mad after you apologized, but this intense expression actually means he's now putting his all into listening to you. All your words will reach him as you intend them to."

"...R-Really?" Wilfried glanced between Ferdinand and me, and then at Florencia beside him, who was tightly holding his hand.

"Rozemyne," Ferdinand interjected, "keep your irrelevant observations to yourself."

"They're not irrelevant; they're important. And you really should have accepted Wilfried's apology before getting all serious like that."

He scoffed. "I did not say anything because I have not yet forgiven him," he said, speaking like a big meanie before looking back at Wilfried. "Tell me what you think about the nobles who were at the tea party."

"They... answered my questions kindly. But they tricked me into committing a crime, so they weren't actually being kind at all. I understand now what Oswald meant when he said that not everyone who approaches me with a smile is my friend. He was talking about people like them."

It was a lesson that he hadn't understood until experiencing it for himself. Oswald grimaced in regret; he was surely thinking that this whole situation could have been avoided if only he'd helped Wilfried to fully grasp it sooner.

Ferdinand nodded, acknowledging that this was an important thing for Wilfried to recognize. "And that is why you were taught not to speak with nobles you do not know, and why watching what you say was so thoroughly beaten into you. Your head attendant hand-selects those allowed to meet with you to minimize dangers such as this."

"So there was a point to all those rules..."

As a child of the archduke, Wilfried had a mountain of rules and restrictions piled onto him: don't do this, don't do that, you mustn't *ever* do this... Without him understanding why these rules were there in the first place, it was little wonder that he would continuously break them.

"We would not restrict your actions without good reason," Ferdinand said. "There is a point to everything in your education."

"...I know that thanks to my reading, math, and harspiel practice."

"I see. Do you have any other thoughts about all this?"

"The crime Grandmother committed comes off entirely differently depending on who's talking about it. It's important to get lots of perspectives on things."

Ferdinand knitted his brow even tighter at this remark, appearing to have fallen into thought.

I clenched my fists, wanting to push things in the best possible direction for Wilfried. He had certainly done something shockingly careless in committing a crime, but he was growing in the right direction—he was learning from his mistake. It wasn't that he was a failure, but rather that his education up until this point had been insufficient. This incident would no doubt prove to be a huge step for him. I had learned a lot from it, too.

"Under normal circumstances, you would be sent to the temple or imprisoned alongside your grandmother as punishment," Ferdinand eventually said. "But matters here are not so simple."

"What are your thoughts?" Sylvester asked Ferdinand, his expression making it clear he was just as intensely focused.

"We do not know the goals of our enemies. In the same way that those involved in an event can have their own particular truths, those working together in a plot may have their own particular goals. There are simply too many people involved for us to say anything for certain," Ferdinand said bitterly as he looked over the notes he had written. "We are dealing with someone who knows both where the tower is and who is capable of opening its door. They must have also known, then, that once the door is open, anyone can enter. And yet they did not rescue Veronica."

"Anyone can go inside?!" Wilfried yelped in surprise, having simply believed the other nobles when they said that they couldn't enter.

"You were with them, so yes, they could have gone in as well. The most likely reason they did not was to avoid committing a crime themselves, though it is also possible that whoever provided them with the information did not intend to rescue Veronica, and thus falsely told them they would not be able to enter."

The schemes that nobles came up with were so convoluted that I really couldn't keep up. "I-I see... So, um... who exactly can open the door, then?" I asked, trying to organize the information at hand.

"It can be opened only by those capable of interacting with the foundation's magic," Sylvester explained. "That would be me, Florencia, Bonifatius, Ferdinand, you, and Wilfried."

"The question is how they discovered the tower," Ferdinand said. "The door's barrier means there are no guards stationed there, and it is largely hidden by the surrounding trees. Few people know about its existence, let alone its function."

"And yet someone brought it up at the tea party. Can we narrow down who laid the trap based on that information? Was Grandfather the one standing by the tower?" I asked, tilting my head curiously.

Wilfried angrily raised his eyebrows. "I would have recognized Bonifatius! If the person were someone I knew, I would have said their name."

"Plus, Bonifatius was rampaging around during the hunting festival, trying to compete with me and win despite his age," Sylvester added. "People would have found it strange if they heard he was quietly playing with children by the tower."

Grandfather was rampaging around in competition with Sylvester...? I haven't really spoken to him much, but I guess that's how he normally acts when he's not around me.

Ferdinand tapped a finger against his temple. "It is my belief that the former Veronica faction wishes to reunite under Wilfried, in which case it would be a very effective psychological attack to drive a wedge between him, Rozemyne, and his parents. And the reality is that they accomplished just that, albeit only temporarily."

Wilfried and I were two core members of the Florencia faction, and pitting us against one another would force our parents to pick a side, only destabilizing things further.

"Perhaps they wish to create an archduke faction and a rebel faction, but as things stand, any such rebel faction would die out before it even began. Wilfried is on track to be disinherited or executed, neither of which would make him an ideal figurehead," Ferdinand continued. "Having him enter the tower was such a blatantly hostile move that I consider it much more likely that their goal is not to make him a leader of sorts, but rather to eliminate him entirely."

"But that doesn't make sense either. If they wanted him gone permanently, they could have achieved that the moment they got him away from the tea party," Sylvester said with a raised eyebrow.

Wilfried trembled at the reminder of just how much danger he had been in. The establishment of an opposing faction was bad enough, but the thought that he actually could have been killed was so terrifying that it sent a shiver down his spine.

Ferdinand nodded in agreement with Sylvester. "Indeed. Had they wished to eliminate Wilfried, that would have been a most fortunate opportunity. But instead, they let him go."

"In other words, getting rid of him isn't their goal here?" I asked.

"It seems to me that they simply do not care what happens as a result of all this. It is possible they did not know how insufficient Wilfried's education was and thus incorrectly predicted how he would react to the situation, but regardless, there is no doubting that they accounted for this unexpectedness in their plans."

It seemed that with so many people involved, the plotters would never have made a plan so susceptible to chance.

Ferdinand frowned, tapping the paper on the table with his pen. "To speak honestly, it may be that Wilfried was not their target at all. If we read more deeply into this and presume that hurting him was merely a preamble to their true plot, it becomes even harder to determine their goals and who they are after."

"Hm... Yeah. What in the world is their endgame?" Sylvester asked thoughtfully.

Ferdinand briefly glanced my way, as if silently suggesting that *I* was their true target. A heavy sigh escaped me; I was exhausted from all the malice that surrounded us as it was.

"I guess this was all just harassment..." I murmured.

"Harassment?"

"Yes. They wanted Wilfried to see the state his grandmother is in to damage his familial relationships, and to make both you and Florencia struggle over how to punish your child. No matter what you do here, some nobles are going to be unhappy, right? And while the mana shortage means we can't afford to simply execute every noble involved, it would be equally dangerous to leave them alive. Every option here hurts Ehrenfest in some way or another. What else could it be but some outsiders harassing us?"

Sylvester's eyes widened. "I was so focused on the factions here that I never even considered that... Good point. You're surprisingly smart, Rozemyne."

"What do you mean '*surprisingly* smart'?!" I snarled, but he ignored my question and instead gave me a fairly serious look.

"Alright, Rozemyne—I've got a question for you and all your wits. Let's say this *was* harassment from the outside. If they hold a grudge against me and want to see me suffer, what could I do here to displease them most?"

"Nothing at all, of course. Just keep things the way they are. What could frustrate them more than seeing that their attempt to stir things up hasn't had even the slightest impact?" I said. Trying to harass someone but getting no response would probably disappoint them to no end.

Sylvester grimaced. "Keep things as they are, huh? But there is no denying that Wilfried committed a crime; we need to do something about it."

"...So you say, but the person in question is admitting to their crime, and we have all the evidence we need. Why does the punishment need to happen immediately? I would say it can wait until we've figured out who pushed him into this and what their goals are. What would you say to postponing the punishment—or rather, simply keeping things as they are—until we have more information?"

Sylvester seemed convinced, but Ferdinand flatly shot down the idea. "No. That manner of response would greatly undermine the position of the archduke, which is exactly what the enemy wants."

"If that's their goal, then it's going to happen whether Wilfried is punished or not. And if they're hoping to reduce the amount of mana Ehrenfest has available, then eliminating Wilfried or getting us to execute all the nobles involved would only please them. We should keep things as they are and gather more information before deciding whether or not to punish anyone," I suggested, but Ferdinand obstinately shook his head.

"He cannot get away from this without facing the consequences. Wilfried must receive some form of punishment, and that is non-negotiable."

"In that case, we could make it seem as though we're punishing him, when in reality we're not doing anything at all."

"Do you have any ideas, Rozemyne?" Charlotte asked, breaking her tearful silence to look up at me with her eyes shining hopefully. "Are you going to save Wilfried?" I could tell that she was praying for me to rescue him.

Okay, I need to make sure I look good in front of Charlotte. I want to seem cool, but I don't actually have any good ideas! Aaah! Aaaaaah!

I flailed about internally as I desperately tried to piece something together, putting my so frequently mocked brain on full throttle in an attempt to remember as much as I could about the treatment of criminals.

"If one of our priorities here is figuring out who we're dealing with and what their goals are, we should use the magic tool for peering into memories," I suggested.

There were apparently so many people involved in this scheme that Wilfried couldn't remember all their faces, and since he had interrupted their gossip without going through any introductions, he didn't know their names either. But if we peered into his memories with the tool, then as far as I was aware, it would be easy to determine their identities.

"He was of course tricked into it, but Wilfried is now a criminal who committed a grave crime," I added. "We should therefore use the magic tool reserved for grave criminals to identify our enemies. That way, people will understand that we have punished Wilfried, *and* we will greatly increase our knowledge of the situation. If we proceed to maintain the status quo afterward, won't it seem like we are making a calculated political decision based on information that only we have?"

I truly had put my heart into my suggestion. Ferdinand was thinking it over carefully, lightly tapping his temple with a stern expression. Charlotte, meanwhile, continued to watch me with hopeful eyes, spurring me to continue.

"It will serve as a meaningful punishment for Wilfried, since all his embarrassing memories will be revealed, and if Sylvester is the one who uses the tool, he can see what problems have been holding his son back."

"We certainly would be able to identify a significant swathe of dangerous nobles in the duchy that way..." Ferdinand mused. "Very well. We shall use these memories as a base on which to punish the nobles involved, and remove the guarantee that Wilfried will be the next archduke. How does that sound, Sylvester? Do recall that Wilfried is being targeted because you proclaimed him to be the next archduke."

Sylvester grinned with relief, then turned to Wilfried. "As mentioned, you are to be treated as a grave criminal, and your memories will be searched with a magic tool. In turn, your position as the next archduke will no longer be guaranteed. This is your punishment. Take care not to behave so carelessly again, and *never* leave the sight of your attendants and guard knights."

"Yes, Father."

With the decision made that Wilfried would only receive a light punishment, the mood eased considerably. I even noticed Charlotte place a hand on her chest and let out a quiet, "Thank goodness."

"Truly..." Florencia agreed, wiping the tears from her eyes and hugging Wilfried close. "I could ask for nothing more than to avoid my beloved son being taken away from me again. Rozemyne, I thank you ever so much."

I responded to her kind words with a smile.

Wilfried, who was wriggling awkwardly in his mother's arms, called out to me next. "I love my Grandmother, but now I understand that she was wrong. I'm... sorry for doubting you. Really."

"Think nothing of it, dear brother."

Wilfried's Punishment

With that, Charlotte leapt down from her chair and raced over to me. "Rozemyne, you're so amazing! I'm so proud to have a big sister like you!"

"You saying that makes this all worthwhile, Charlotte."

Woohoo! I did it! I'm a respectable older sister now!

Charlotte and I joined hands and jumped for joy while both Sylvester and Karstedt also praised me for my suggestion. Out of the corner of my eye, I spotted Wilfried wiggling out of Florencia's arms and going over to his attendants, asking them to stick with him. Lamprecht gave a big nod in reply.

Ferdinand, having been watching us all, rose from his chair and strode over to Wilfried, who tensed up in fear of what he was about to be told.

"It will not be easy to overcome this stain on your reputation. If you continue to work hard and focus on the future, however, you will surely continue to grow," Ferdinand said. "Sincerity such as yours is a hard virtue to acquire."

For a moment, Wilfried simply looked up, his mouth agape in confused disbelief. But his expression soon turned into a happy—albeit somewhat conflicted—smile. "I'll do my best," he said, kneeling down. "I'll do my best not to waste the opportunity given to me. Thank you, Ferd— No, thank you, Uncle."

With that, Ferdinand swiftly exited the room, seemingly having nothing else to say to Wilfried. I wasn't sure if anyone else had noticed, but he had walked away a little faster than usual.

The Jureve and Mana Compression

Several days after Wilfried's fate had been decided, Ferdinand summoned me from my temple chambers, having received news from Justus. I had just recently seen Tuuli for the first time in ages—she had come by with the Gilberta Company to deliver a new hairpin—and I was so excited to have received a letter from my family that I practically skipped into his hidden room, only to be scolded when I asked what this was all about.

"Do you not remember the very reason we were gathering information? We discussed this only a few days ago."

"I can't spend all my time living in the past, you know. A few days ago is ancient history."

Forgetting about things days after they stopped being relevant to me was just in my nature. I was the same way back on Earth, too—I would pass a test, then forget everything on the syllabus that I didn't think was important. In other words, I had a very short and selective memory. There were just so many other, more substantial things that I wanted to focus on: the new paper, the new ink, my letter from Tuuli, my next toy for Kamil... I simply didn't have enough free time to dwell on stuff that had already happened.

"This is not a matter of the past," Ferdinand said. "The incident before was simply an information-gathering exercise for our enemies. In fact, I would say the true attack has yet to come."

The Jureve and Mana Compression

His unexpected revelation sent me reeling with shock. If that had all just been them gathering information, what in the world was going to happen now? I truly had no idea what went on in the minds of nobles; I could never predict what they were about to do next.

"Based on the information gathered, we have concluded that they were prodding us to see how we would react."

"And that's why they were so passive?"

"Indeed. We believe they were testing a variety of things: whose opinion Wilfried would trust most, how Sylvester would deal with one of his children committing a crime, how those around him would react, how the nobles within Ehrenfest would move, and so on."

They had used Wilfried, a child, to harass Ehrenfest, all so they could sit back and see what happened. This was one nasty plot.

"Have you determined who it was that pulled such a baffling scheme?"

"We are referring to someone who knows not just the location of the tower, but also how to open it. Someone who does not care to save Veronica. Someone who was targeting Wilfried, but cared not whether he was disinherited or executed so long as it caused problems in Ehrenfest. Only the head of one faction in particular would do this."

It appeared that Ferdinand had managed to identify our enemies: there was a serious gleam in his light-golden eyes.

"I wish to solidify Ehrenfest's defenses sooner rather than later. To this end, Rozemyne, I ask that you teach me your mana compression method as soon as possible."

"Like I said before, that can wait until my potion is ready. If everyone else gets a power boost while I'm stuck in this weak body, then I'll be the only one in danger, won't I? My health comes before the mana compression technique."

Ferdinand stood up, shaking his head in defeat. "Very well. We shall brew the potion tomorrow morning in place of your usual duties."

Tomorrow...? It certainly seems like he's in a rush.

And so it was decided that we would make my potion tomorrow, from third to fourth bell. Ferdinand would normally make his plans at least three days in advance, but here he was, willing to disregard standard working hours and at such short notice. It was probably a testament to just how much danger we were really in.

The next day, I was taken straight into Ferdinand's hidden room, just as we had arranged. I spoke to his back as he took out various ingredients and checked his instruments.

"Ferdinand, could it be that you're in a really big rush to learn about my mana compression technique?"

He turned around to face me, looking completely stunned, as though he couldn't believe what I had asked. Then, his expression shifted into a grimace. "How long does it take for your mana compression method to show results?"

"I have no idea. I used it subconsciously to keep myself alive. Damuel learned it at the end of spring, but to my understanding, his mana was continuing to grow around that time anyway. This is going to be the first time that an adult who's no longer growing uses it, so I genuinely can't say for sure whether it will even have an effect."

"As I thought..." Ferdinand replied. "Those of us in your inner circle will experiment to see whether or not the method increases our mana capacities. In the case that it does, we shall have members of our faction try it as well, and from there we will teach it to those who join our faction in hopes of getting more mana. But if our wider goal is to increase Ehrenfest's overall mana capacity, just how many years might that take? I would like to have made at least some progress before Georgine arrives for her visit next summer."

The Jureve and Mana Compression

It had taken Damuel half a year to increase his mana capacity enough for those around him to notice, but he was an unusual case. Ferdinand wanted to see if the method worked on adults whose capacities *weren't* still naturally growing and how quickly it would show results. But if we wanted to do these tests before Georgine's visit next summer, then we really didn't have much time.

"I see why you're rushing now…"

If Georgine was the kind of person to cause this much trouble just to see how we would react, then who knew what would happen if she got serious.

"This is why I would like to postpone the brewing of your jureve, if possible."

"No! Absolutely not!" I yelled, shaking my head hard. "First you said you'd make it when we'd gathered the ingredients, then you said after Charlotte's baptism—or really, after the Dedication Ritual and Spring Prayer—and *now* you're saying we should postpone it until after Georgine's visit? Just how long do you intend to make me wait? The potion brewing comes first, *then* we can do the mana compression."

Caving here wasn't an option: I knew that Ferdinand would just keep postponing it forever otherwise, and I wanted to get healthy again as soon as possible.

"How stubborn…" he muttered.

That goes for the both of us, bub. Say whatever you want, I'm not budging on this.

"I understand that you want to spread my compression technique out of concern that something might happen, but that is the very same reason I want to get healthy. As I am now, I wouldn't even be able to run from danger! I'd just pass out!"

I cared more about my own well-being than expanding other people's mana capacities. Ferdinand himself had said that we didn't know who exactly was being targeted here, and if we wanted to address our weak points first, then my health was an obvious priority.

"I see... You do have a point," Ferdinand said with a nod, my desperate ranting having finally gotten through to him. He picked up a large box and started making his way out of the hidden room. "We need space to brew your potion, so we shall first create a hidden room in your High Bishop's chambers."

"Hm? Why not just do it here?" I asked, looking around his material-and-instrument-filled room. He turned back to me and did the same.

"...Because there is not enough space in which to work, no?"

Stored in the room were several large instruments intended for experiments, stacks of parchment and boards covered with research notes, and so many materials that every single shelf was completely full. Ferdinand had a point—there was simply too much stuff. Plus, unlike my current hidden room, only those with a certain level of mana could enter. This meant cleaning attendants were unable to go inside, which was unideal since Ferdinand's hidden room always ended up a huge mess like this whenever he had a breakthrough with his research or discovered some new material.

"In any case, you will need a hidden room to sleep in when you consume the potion. It does not even require that much effort to create a hidden room large enough for our purposes, so I would rather you simply get it over with."

I apparently needed a hidden room with a barrier of my own for safety's sake, since we knew that using the jureve would put me to sleep for a lengthy period of time.

The Jureve and Mana Compression

"How big does the room need to be?" I asked.

"One as large as your room will do. Only you and I will register our mana with it; we need at least one person capable of entering your room while you are asleep."

And so I made a hidden room in my High Bishop's chambers. It wasn't a very nerve-wracking experience, given that I had already done the same thing in the orphanage and the monastery. I placed my left hand—the one on which I wore my magic ring—on the feystone built into the door leading inside and poured my mana into it.

Once the door had my mana, a magic circle shining with pale-blue light arose above it. I poured more mana in, registering it with the feystone, at which point a red light began to streak through the magic circle. The same red light circled my wrist, forming various complex patterns and letters.

I'll never get tired of seeing all this fantasy-esque stuff. It really gets my heart racing.

I excitedly watched as the mana coursed through the magic circle, at which point Ferdinand placed his hand onto mine and began pouring his mana in as well. Only then did I remember him mentioning that we would both be registering ourselves this time. The red light streaking through the magic circle shone brighter, perhaps due to the additional mana.

Actually... how does registering two people's mana at once even work?

As I tilted my head, Ferdinand gripped his schtappe with his right hand while standing behind me and said, "*stylo.*" His schtappe turned into a pen, which he then touched against the magic circle. The letters written in red started to disappear and reappear, moving all around as though they were dancing. Some letters jumped away from the magic circle, bursting in the air like small explosions. He was using his schtappe to manipulate them and gradually rewrite the magic circle, and the sight was so strangely beautiful that I was desperate to try it out myself.

"Ferdinand, it's incredible how you can manipulate the letters like that. Could you teach me to write magic circles too?"

"That will have to wait until you get a schtappe of your own."

"Aww…"

I slumped my shoulders sadly; it seemed that my days of writing cool magic circles in the air wouldn't come anytime soon.

Ferdinand gave a nod. "That should do."

With everything completed, he handed out brooches with feystones in them for his attendants to wear. These were apparently magic tools signifying that the wearers had permission to enter the High Bishop's hidden room, and the attendants who had put them on busily started moving boxes packed with materials and such inside.

"Line that box up against the wall," Ferdinand said, giving his attendants instructions while spreading out a large cloth in the center of the room. At a glance, the magic circle on it resembled the teleportation circles that tax officials used during the Harvest Festival.

"Ferdinand, is this a teleportation circle? It looks a lot like the ones used for taxes."

"Yes, it is something similar. Step back."

Ferdinand moved me away from the circle, then poured mana into it. It seemed that while the magic circle used for taxes was for sending items to the castle, this one was for retrieving items from elsewhere. He stuck his hand inside and began pulling out various things.

Wowee! He's like the English nanny from those popular children's books!

Out came a box large enough to be a stone bathtub, a cauldron big enough to hold my entire body, a long metal stick resembling an oar, a large table, and several more boxes. Ferdinand's attendants carried away each item as it appeared.

"This is supposed to be my hidden room, but it almost looks like it's turning into a second workshop for you, Ferdinand."

"Actually, this is *your* workshop. You will need one for when you enter the Royal Academy regardless, so I saw little harm in establishing it now."

Just hearing that I now had a workshop was enough to get me pumped. My dreams of the future swelled as I thought about adding bookshelves to fill with documents, or even going one step further and adding beautiful, beautiful high-density mobile shelving like all the fancy libraries had now.

"Rozemyne, return from whatever fantasies you are caught up in and put the seasonal ingredients that you collected into the mixing cauldron," Ferdinand said, interrupting my elaborate planning of my future workshop to point at the large cauldron. I would apparently be mixing the ingredients with my mana.

"That's one large cauldron. I could easily fit inside it."

"What, would you like me to boil you?" Ferdinand asked, an actually serious look in his eyes. I hurriedly shook my head.

"No! I wouldn't be edible, no matter how much you cooked me!"

"I have no intention of eating you and suffering the enormous stomachache you would no doubt give me. Rather, I was thinking about the high-quality mana I could harvest from you."

"That's even scarier!"

Eyeing Ferdinand cautiously, I undid the decorative cord on my sash and set it aside. I then wrapped my sleeves up so they wouldn't get in the way, and stepped onto a wooden box to increase my height. In front of me was the large cauldron, and in my hand was an oar-like spatula; all I needed was a bandana on my head and I would have looked just like a school lunch lady.

"Put the feystones you gathered into the cauldron one by one, starting with the spring ingredient and then continuing in chronological order," Ferdinand explained. "Wait until each feystone melts before placing the next one in."

I followed his instructions, placing the green feystone I had made from rairein nectar into the cauldron before beginning to stir the contents. I could already feel the large spatula absorbing my mana.

"Could it be that brewing a potion actually requires a lot of mana?" I asked.

"Yes, depending on the quality of the potion and the quantity produced," Ferdinand replied curtly, using balance scales to measure the non-feystone ingredients. I could only see him side-on, but it was still clear that he didn't want me bothering him: there was a rare sparkle in his eyes as he measured the ingredients, making it apparent just how much fun he was having with this experiment. There were no two ways about it—he was completely absorbed in his hobby.

I, on the other hand, had already grown tired of making the potion; I was quite literally just standing atop a box and stirring the cauldron. It was boring. Aside from the feystone making clinking noises as it moved about inside, nothing was happening at all.

How long do I have to do this...?

The Jureve and Mana Compression

My thoughts began to wander, and that was when the feystone abruptly started to melt. It drooped like molten metal, sticking to the bottom of the cauldron.

"Aah! Ferdinand! The feystone melted!"

"Put the next one in and continue to stir."

I did exactly that, dropping in the blue feystone that I had made from the riesefalke egg. It didn't make any noise due to the melted green feystone covering the cauldron, which also made it harder to move the spatula.

Stir, stir, stir...

Stir, stir, stir...

Perhaps due to the green feystone having melted, the blue feystone started melting sooner than I expected. Once it had broken down, I added the ruelle feystone, and then finally the schnesturm feystone.

Stir, stir, stir...

Stir, stir, stir...

"Ferdinand, my arms hurt..."

"Endure it. You are the one who wished to make the jureve as soon as possible."

Ferdinand dismissed my complaints without a second thought as he peered into the cauldron, tossing in various ingredients that I had never seen before one after another. They had been chopped into tiny bits so that they would mix together better, which made this whole experience feel a lot more like cooking. Given how methodical and precise Ferdinand was being here, perhaps he had it in him to be quite the excellent chef.

Stir, stir, stir...

Stir, stir, stir...

"...I would like to rest for a little while," I said.

"No. It is almost done," Ferdinand replied, taking a small jar out from a box and pouring the thick black liquid inside into the cauldron.

I was surprised to see him adding something so dark into the vibrant four-colored mixture, but it didn't seem to change the potion by even a shade. I took a closer look, wondering why this was the case, when the liquid in the cauldron started to rapidly expand out of nowhere.

"Eep! It's going to spill out!"

"Do you truly think I would add enough for that to happen? Do not get so surprised over every step of the process."

"But the potion's gone from just barely covering the bottom to taking up like eighty percent of the cauldron, all in mere moments! That'd surprise anyone! I mean, there's no way I can drink this much!" I yelled, pointing wildly at the concoction. I had assumed that we'd be making a little extra for a reserve potion, but I certainly didn't need this much.

Ferdinand gave a casual shrug. "You will drink half a glass or so, but a jureve is generally not something that you consume—rather, it is something that you immerse yourself in," he said, gesturing over to the ivory-colored stone box. The completed potion would apparently be poured into it, and then I was supposed to sleep inside.

This was certainly an unexpected development. Every potion I had encountered up to this point simply needed to be consumed, and with Ferdinand carrying a reserve jureve on his belt as we spoke, I had assumed this would be no different.

"...I won't drown?"

"You have nothing to fear; I have never heard of anyone drowning while using a jureve. More importantly, though, you have stopped mixing. We are just adding the finishing touches, so you must not slacken here."

As I got back to stirring the cauldron, Ferdinand added a drop of some other potion. It plopped into the middle of the concoction, which flashed brightly and then turned light blue.

"There, it is complete. Now it can be used at any time."

With that, Ferdinand put a lid on the cauldron. He then covered it with a cloth that had a magic circle on it, which would apparently stop the potion from spoiling or reducing in quality. He sure had a lot of strange yet convenient tools lying around; I wanted to see a complete list of everything he had at some point.

"Ferdinand, how long am I going to be asleep after I use the jureve?"

"For you, I expect anywhere from a month to a season, but no exact prediction can be made. That is why I recommend you get your affairs in order ahead of time, such that even a long rest will not interfere with your business."

"My affairs...? Like, write letters to my family and give instructions to my attendants?"

"Correct. As your guardian, I shall be taking over all printing industry-related matters while you are asleep. Contact Benno to ensure that this will not introduce any problems."

My family would no doubt be shocked to learn that I was going to be asleep for maybe even a full season. I would need to give Lutz a letter describing the whole situation before I used the jureve.

Wilma could manage the orphanage on her own, while Fran and Zahm would surely be able to take care of all the attendant-related matters. It was leaving the workshop that I was most concerned about, but I doubted the industry would expand much while I was asleep; Gil and Fritz would simply be preparing stories to be printed, so I couldn't imagine they would come across any problems.

While I was counting on my fingers everything that I would need to prepare before using the jureve next spring, as we had previously arranged, Ferdinand gave me an annoyed glare. "I have finished your jureve as promised, and that will have to be enough for you," he said. "We are going to the castle tomorrow."

"Are the contracts all prepared?"

"Yes. Just because your own planning and forward-thinking skills are poor, do not assume that mine are as well."

And so, urged on by Ferdinand, I went straight to teaching everyone my mana compression method during the afternoon the next day. Sylvester's office was cleared of everyone but those who would be learning the technique, and multiple boxes, capes, bags, and irons had been prepared just as I requested. There were ten of us in total: me, Ferdinand, the archducal couple, Karstedt's family, and finally Damuel, since he also needed to sign a magic contract.

"Now then. Please sign your contracts."

While everyone signed the contracts agreeing not to become my enemy or teach the mana compression method to anyone else, I started collecting their money. Archnobles were charged two large golds each, with my future plan being to charge mednobles eight small golds and laynobles two small golds. These prices would of course be halved from the second purchase onward in each family.

When I told Sylvester that half of whatever I made would go straight to Ehrenfest—in part to pay for the magic contracts—he practically wept with joy. Damuel didn't need to pay, so he was simply signing a contract as a guarantee that he wouldn't spread my technique.

Once that was all done, I began my explanation.

"If you would be so kind as to help, Damuel, it would be much appreciated."

The Jureve and Mana Compression

I demonstrated my mana compression method the same way I had with Damuel: stuffing a spread-out cape into a box, making it as compact as I could, and calling that the traditional method; then showing that they could fit even more into the box by folding the cape, and explaining that this was how they should go about compressing their mana.

"I see. Your visual example sure makes it easy to understand, and I feel like it'll make it easier to compress mana too," Sylvester said, closing his eyes and trying it for himself.

"Do you think it will also allow adults who have already passed their growth period to increase their mana capacity?" I asked.

"Seems like it," he replied, the excitement clear in his voice. Sylvester had never actually folded a cape before, but after visually demonstrating the process and helping him to imagine it, he found it surprisingly easy to compress his mana. Karstedt and Elvira had their eyes closed and were focusing on doing the same.

"I am told that if you compress your mana too rapidly, you will essentially become drunk on it and feel sick," I said, "so please don't push yourselves."

It was important to compress just a little bit of mana to free up some space, and then compress the new mana that flowed into that space. Repeating this process would increase your overall mana capacity.

That said, Damuel had mentioned that boosting the density of mana in your body too rapidly would make you sick. I was unwell and collapsed so often that it was hard to tell whether or not I also experienced mana sickness, but it was undoubtedly the case that compressing mana wasn't good for the body. Damuel had pushed himself especially hard since he needed more mana by next summer, but under normal circumstances, one would want to gradually increase their mana density to give their body time to adjust.

"It seems like even I will be able to increase my mana capacity with this," Eckhart commented.

"Wow! *Wow!*" Lamprecht exclaimed. "Seems like I had a lot more space than I thought!"

"I'm going to use this to get a ton more mana than the both of you," Cornelius added.

The three of them wore stunned expressions as they moved about their mana. They were all rich archnoble children with attendants, meaning they too had never folded their own capes before. Forceful stuffing was the only mental image they had known, which meant my compression method would work especially well for them.

While everyone else reacted to the new mana compression technique with pleasant surprise, Ferdinand alone shook his head with a frown. "Unfortunately, it does not seem to be having much of an effect for me."

As it turned out, he had already been using a similar mental image to compress his mana—exactly what I would have expected from someone so serious and methodical. It seemed that, during his stay in the Royal Academy, he had experimented extensively to increase his mana capacity as much as possible.

"In that case, I shall teach you the next step," I said, the knowledge that Ferdinand hadn't expected there to be more bringing a grin to my face.

I placed several of the folded capes into a bag, climbing onto it and crushing the capes down. Ferdinand's eyes widened as he watched the bag compress to less than half its former size.

"So, Ferdinand? What do you think? This is the Rozemyne Mana Compression Method."

"Hm… I shall try it."

The Jureve and Mana Compression

With that, Ferdinand closed his eyes and began compressing his mana. Then, after a period of focus intense enough for beads of sweat to have formed along his brow, he suddenly reached for a potion on his belt and started drinking it. No sooner was it all gone than he closed his eyes again and resumed focusing.

"What did you drink, Ferdinand?"

"A mana restoration potion. I can hardly compress my mana without first completely filling the space," he said, speaking as though it were obvious.

My cheeks twitched. "Isn't that, like, super terrible for your body?! I *just* said that compressing your mana too much would make you feel sick, so why are you doing something so dangerous?! In fact, why would you *ever* do something like that after I specifically put *so* many conditions in the magic contracts to make things safer?!"

Even Damuel had gotten mana sickness from the method, subsequently having to wait for his mana to recover naturally. What was Ferdinand thinking, using potions to recover on the spot?

Despite my obvious frustration, Ferdinand merely waved a dismissive hand in my direction. "I will stop if I feel there is any danger. There is nothing to worry about," he said, immediately focusing himself again.

I had so little to do while everyone was compressing their mana that I started ironing the capes I had previously stuffed into the boxes. Ferdinand opened his eyes around the time I had finished ironing my third one, letting out a slow sigh while looking at me with a conflicted expression.

"...You are quite strong, Rozemyne. Mentally speaking."

"What do you mean?"

"It requires backbreaking effort to compress mana as much as you do," he said, scratching his hair frustratedly. When I examined his face more closely, I realized that he actually looked a little sick, though it was rather subtle. I furrowed my brow, at which point he started tapping his temple.

"These are just my personal observations, but I believe one's mental fortitude will largely determine how much mana can be compressed through this method," he continued. "For one, it will not necessarily result in change—knowing the method will mean nothing if you do not have the mental fortitude to execute it. Furthermore, due to it rapidly changing the density of your mana, it would be best to gradually increase the density over a longer period. Doubling the density with the Rozemyne Method in such a short time span is quite a sickening experience; it will require an extensive amount of time for one to grow accustomed to."

For a moment, I couldn't tell whether Ferdinand was actually being serious, but the look on his face told me that he was.

My eyebrows shot up in anger. "Didn't I say pretty much all of that before we started?! Do you just not listen when people speak to you, Ferdinand?! Are you actually a fool yourself?!"

Someone please *give me a harisen right now!*

It would be some time before the results became apparent, but nonetheless, the core leaders of Ehrenfest all continued to compress their mana.

Charlotte's Baptism Ceremony

On top of my usual yearly duties—handling winter preparations for the orphanage and my chambers, arranging winter handiwork, and making the necessary printing arrangements—I now had to rigorously study winter socializing under Ferdinand, teach my mana compression method to the archducal family's guard knights and a part of the Knight's Order, and study baptismal practices day and night to grant Charlotte's first wish.

I was absolutely pooped.

Ferdinand was going to handle the mana registration medals and speak from the bible, but noble baptism ceremonies were a lot more involved than lower city ones. Not to mention, this was a baptism being held during winter socializing, when all the nobles in Ehrenfest were gathered together. I was becoming more tense by the day, determined not to fail.

And in the end, I managed to learn everything that I needed to.

I had worked so, so very hard, to the point that my head was now a complete mess. But I had no intention of letting Charlotte know how much this had drained me. Why? Because I wanted to act all cool and casual about it. I wanted her to be like, *"Wow! You're so cool, big sister!"*

Autumn ended with me nearly having worked myself to death, and then came winter.

The lower city's winter baptism was held amid the falling snow. It was then that I genuinely started to believe the gods of this world were real, because wow, they sure were rewarding me for working so hard. Despite the cold weather, my family had come to the doors of the temple. They peered inside with worried expressions, a warmly wrapped Kamil wobbling about around them.

W-Wow! Look, everyone! My little brother is adorable! In fact, he's so cute that I'm worried someone might kidnap him. Because, I mean, I want to kidnap him! I'm the kidnapper! It's me! Look at those precious little cheeks! Praise be to the gods!

A single glance at Kamil wiped away all of my exhaustion. He even looked up at me and waved his hand about. Tuuli had probably gotten him to do that, but I didn't care; he was waving me goodbye.

Aah, geez! What should I do?! I'm so excited, I don't even think I'll make it back to my room!

As I trembled atop the staircase shrine, overcome with emotion, some gray priests mercilessly shut the doors. But even then, I could still see my little brother's overwhelming cuteness when I closed my eyes.

"Rozemyne, do not stand there in a daze. Return to your chambers."

"Oh, Ferdinand... All this excitement is making my head spin. I'll need a moment to rest."

I leaned against the podium on which the bible was usually placed and felt the pleasant chill of the ivory stonework. As it cooled me down, I shut my eyes and started to digest just how adorable my little brother was.

"You are too excited to move?" Ferdinand asked incredulously. "How much of a fool are you?"

Charlotte's Baptism Ceremony

He was the last person I wanted a lecture from right now; he looked as though he was suffering from a serious mana hangover, no doubt having used my compression method too much. Either way though, I was serious about not being able to move.

"If you wish to rest, drink a potion and return to your chambers. At this rate, you will not recover in time for Charlotte's baptism ceremony."

"Well, we don't want that."

I opened my eyes again, only to see a scary-looking Ferdinand right in front of me. He picked me up so suddenly that I jerked in surprise, then he climbed down the staircase and handed me over to Fran, who was worriedly waiting at the bottom.

"Fran, ensure that she recovers before it is time to depart for the castle."

"As you wish," Fran replied with a diligent nod, walking away with me in his arms.

As soon as we were back in my chambers, I was made to drink a potion and then sent to bed with a collection of wooden boards, all of which contained essential details about the baptism ceremony.

"There is also reading material available, so rest in bed at your leisure until it is time to leave."

"O-Okay..."

I picked up one of the wooden boards and started to read; it was impossible to defy Fran when he wore such a chilly smile.

And so days passed with me doing nothing but studying for the baptism ceremony and giving instructions to people. Before I knew it, it was time for us to leave for the castle.

This year, we were going to arrive the day before the baptism ceremony. Fran had mentioned that this was due to Ferdinand delaying our departure for as long as possible, since he imagined that I would find it easier to relax in the temple than the castle. Thanks to him, I could take on Charlotte's baptism ceremony at full strength.

Rihyarda and Ottilie changed me into my ceremonial High Bishop robes first thing in the morning. Then, after making sure my new hair stick from Tuuli was properly in place, I exited my room.

I arrived at the grand hall even earlier than last year, making sure I was there before Charlotte, and was promptly taken to a waiting room. Cornelius was serving as my guard knight, wearing his Royal Academy cape and brooch.

The front gate to the castle's main building was visible through the waiting room window, and I could see carriage after carriage starting to arrive. Nobles and their families would step out of one carriage, with their attendants alighting from another close behind. Some of these attendants—presumably the music teachers—were carrying instruments.

"There certainly are a lot of people..." I murmured.

"This sudden influx is only natural, since all the nobles in Ehrenfest gather on the first and last days," Cornelius said with a small smile as he, too, looked out the window. Highbeasts were swooping down from the sky and landing as well, making things even more crowded. I could imagine the grand hall was already filled with people.

"I see you've arrived, Rozemyne."

Ferdinand entered the room, also wearing his ceremonial robes. There was a brief period of waiting before a scholar came to get us, announcing that it was time for our appearance in the grand hall.

When I entered with Ferdinand, everything was set up the same way as the year before, with the altar at the middle of the stage. The audience was again divided down the middle: on the left facing the stage were the archducal couple and their retainers; on the right were the musicians with harspiels and the families of the kids to be baptized with their magic rings.

Charlotte's Baptism Ceremony

The two of us walked down the center of the grand hall, Ferdinand taking a single step for every three or four of mine. We climbed up the stage and sat down, at which point he grumbled something about how slow I was. It was a bit late for him to be complaining about that, though.

Sylvester the archduke climbed up the stage once we were seated.

"Once again, Ewigeliebe the God of Life has hidden away Geduldh the Goddess of Earth. We must all pray for the return of spring," he announced, marking the beginning of winter socializing. The nobles held up their shining schtappes and prayed for the Goddess of Spring to heal as soon as possible.

Sylvester then discussed the incident during autumn's hunting tournament and the resulting punishments. He announced that Wilfried was no longer guaranteed to become the next aub, that his memories had been searched, and that the guilty nobles had been punished.

The punishments themselves weren't particularly severe, since the nobles had acted within a legal gray area without committing any substantial crimes. There was a demotion here, a pay drop and a fine there... But they were being revealed as criminals to all of noble society, and everyone knew this would erase their chances of receiving important positions or promotions henceforth.

That would serve as their true punishment.

Once the detailed reports were over, it was finally time for the baptism ceremony and winter debuts. The archduke returned to the audience, while I moved to the center of the stage and stepped up onto the box prepared for me, taking care not to tread on my robes.

Ferdinand then came up next to me. "We welcome the new children of Ehrenfest," he said, his voice resounding through the grand hall.

The musicians all started to play at once, then the main doors slowly opened and the children lined up behind them started walking inside. Charlotte, as the daughter of the archduke, was at the very front. I could see her expression stiffen as she noticed all the eyes on her.

Charlotte was wearing what one would expect for a winter baptism: warm, fluffy white clothes, the decorations and embroidery of which were red, the divine color of winter. Her red collar made of wool and the red flowers on the hair stick I had lent her made her blonde, almost silver hair stand out even more than usual.

Her worried indigo eyes fell on me, and I returned a small smile.
Do your best, Charlotte. I'll be doing my best, too.

The children briefly stopped in front of the stage. I gestured for them to climb up, maintaining eye contact with Charlotte as they all formed a line.

Eleven children had their baptism ceremonies this year, five of whom were being baptized now. The process was largely the same as last year, the main difference being that I was performing the ceremony as High Bishop.

Ferdinand's voice resounded clearly throughout the grand hall as he regaled the audience with tales from the bible. When he was done, I called the children over one at a time, starting with the laynobles and ending with my dear little sister.

"Charlotte," I said, and she approached with a happy smile.

I pinched the mana-detecting magic tool between thin pieces of mana-blocking leather and held it out. She gripped it, and the watching nobles applauded as it began to shine. I then took out a medal, pressing the magic tool against it like a stamp to register her mana to it.

Charlotte's Baptism Ceremony

"Five gods have granted you their divine protection: Light, Water, Fire, Wind, and Earth. If you dedicate yourself to becoming worthy of this protection, you will surely receive many more blessings."

Once the mana registration was complete, Ferdinand briskly took the medal and placed it in the organized box. At the same time, Sylvester climbed up onto the stage carrying a magic ring used for emitting mana. He slid it onto Charlotte's finger with a gentle smile, no doubt overjoyed at how much his beloved daughter had grown.

"I grant this ring to you, Charlotte, now that you have been recognized by the gods and the people as my daughter. Congratulations."

"I thank you ever so much, Father."

Charlotte happily stroked the red feystone ring that was now on her left middle finger. Sylvester raised his head, his eyes signaling for me to continue, so I nodded and gave Charlotte a blessing.

"May Geduldh the Goddess of Earth bless you, Charlotte."

With that, the red light of a blessing shot from my ring and onto her. In truth, these blessings had proven harder than anything else I had needed to practice for this baptism ceremony, since it was extremely difficult for me to adjust how much mana I put into them.

According to Ferdinand, my emotions had a considerable impact on my blessings, for better or worse. Had I not restrained myself, then I would have subconsciously given Charlotte a much larger blessing than the other noble children. Such favoritism wouldn't be acceptable for the High Bishop at a baptism ceremony, so I had been forced to spend a ton of time learning to exercise more control.

My training had evidently been successful though, as I ended up giving her a blessing that was pretty much equivalent to the ones everyone else received. I internally let out a sigh of relief.

This time, Charlotte poured mana into her own ring, and the floaty red light flew my way as she thanked me for the blessing. The crowd of nobles clapped at the spectacle, and thus ended my little sister's baptism ceremony.

"Now then, we shall offer our prayers to the gods and dedicate our music to them."

The winter debut followed the baptism ceremony. We would be rejoicing over the baptized children entering noble society, praying for the gods to continue providing their divine protection, and playing harspiel while singing in dedication to them.

A chair was placed in the middle of the stage, and just like last year, the laynoble children were the first to perform. I would call a name, and the summoned child would nervously come and sit down. Their music teacher would then bring up their harspiel and hand it to them with brief words of encouragement.

At the end of each performance, I would give the same response: "You have done well. The gods are surely rejoicing." I would then call up the next child, all the while sweating at the thought of accidentally mixing up their names or the order in which they were to perform.

"Charlotte," I eventually called. As the archduke's daughter, her performance came last. She sat in the chair, accepted her harspiel, then got into position.

Ooh, she's good. That's my little sister for you!

Unlike Wilfried, who had just barely scraped by after skipping out on years of practice, Charlotte had clearly taken her studies as a child of the archduke quite seriously. Her playing was exceptionally beautiful, and as her older sister, I would need to continue practicing myself so that I didn't fall behind.

Charlotte's Baptism Ceremony

"You have done very well," I said. "The gods are surely rejoicing."

"Thank you."

With that, Charlotte descended the stage, thus ending the winter debut. Ferdinand delivered the closing words, then the two of us exited the grand hall together.

"Ferdinand. Milady. We must get you both changed during the gifting ceremony," Rihyarda said.

Our work was done as High Bishop and High Priest, but now we needed to participate in society as nobles. The gifting ceremony had nothing to do with us, since it was simply when the archduke gave capes and brooches to the new students going to the Royal Academy, which meant it was an ideal opportunity for us to get ready.

After the ceremony, they would announce when the students were due to leave for the Royal Academy, so Damuel and Brigitte were currently serving as my guard knights.

"Hurry, everyone!" Rihyarda barked while briskly walking forward, compelling Damuel and Brigitte to start jogging down the hall. I made Lessy move faster as well to keep up with them.

We entered the room and found Ottilie waiting with my clothes ready. She and Rihyarda took me out of my High Bishop robes, then changed me into an outfit that was predominantly red.

"Come now, milady. You must hurry."

Once my hair had been smoothed down and my hair stick was put back in, Rihyarda practically drove me out of the room. I got into my highbeast and sped to the dining hall where lunch was being prepared.

"You did wonderfully as the High Bishop. Lady Charlotte is surely overjoyed," Rihyarda praised. And so I entered the dining hall with a goofy grin on my face. The gifting ceremony was complete, and everyone was waiting for my arrival.

"My apologies for the wait," I said as I took my seat.

"Worry not, Rozemyne. It was Charlotte who so desperately begged for you to be the one to bless her during her baptism. Preparing in time was quite the ordeal, was it not?" Florencia asked with a kind smile, commending my efforts.

"Not at all. I would do anything to grant the request of my darling little sister," I replied with an elegant smile and a shake of my head.

In reality, it really had been an ordeal—so much so, in fact, that I had felt half dead while performing the ceremony. But I put my all into it nonetheless, entirely so that I could secure the praise and respect of my cute little sister.

"You were an excellent High Bishop, Rozemyne. And so lovely," Charlotte said, her indigo eyes sparkling with admiration. "I hope to be just like you one day."

Yes! This is what I wanted! My hard work has been rewarded!

After lunch, we returned to the grand hall to begin socializing. This was when we exchanged greetings with the adults.

I had missed out on the socializing last year: granting a huge blessing during my debut had resulted in lunch and the gifting ceremony being swapped around, and then I was promptly scooted out before the nobles could greet me. This year, however, my attendance was mandatory; we three children of the archduke needed to travel the hall together to show the other nobles that, despite the issues Wilfried had caused, there were absolutely no problems between us.

I looked around to see all the nobles laughing in conversation, then hurriedly clutched my stomach. It wasn't that I had eaten too much during lunch; rather, it was hurting from the stress of thinking about what was coming next.

Just how many people in here are my enemies...? Mother's list couldn't have covered them all, and enemies I don't know about are absolutely the scariest.

While I had memorized every name on the list that Elvira had given me, I hadn't yet paired them with faces. Wilfried and Charlotte had also been given lists covering the former members of the Veronica faction, but it was unlikely they had managed to memorize all the names in such a short space of time.

"Lady Rozemyne, Lord Wilfried, Lady Charlotte—I wish you all a good afternoon."

We started off greeting members of the Florencia faction and making casual conversation, so the pain in my stomach eased a little. It helped that I was putting my all into this; as Charlotte's older sister, I needed to be her guide into women's society.

But after we had finished speaking to those in the Florencia faction and started talking to the nobles prodding for information about the hunting tournament incident, well... my stomach was in constant agony.

Nobles would approach Wilfried with wide grins spread across their faces, but I would step forward to block them, shielding him and Charlotte behind my back while giving the standard formal greetings. I didn't fail to keep up my elegant smile, even when I knew those we were speaking to were on the blacklist.

"We are anxious that a soft cloth has drifted to the Ivory Tower," the nobles would say, to which I would reply, *"Schutzaria the Goddess of Wind protected him such that he would not leap out from beneath the lion. Isn't that right, Wilfried?"* This prompted them to leave with a bemused, *"Ah, I see,"* but the thought of more conversations like that coming one after another made me feel sick.

"Rozemyne, what was that noble saying?" Wilfried asked me quietly, despite having nodded along in agreement just a second ago. I looked around to make sure that our guard knights were surrounding us before whispering back.

"They're wondering if you meeting with Lady Veronica in the Ivory Tower is a sign that you joined the former Veronica faction."

"What did you tell them, dear sister?" Charlotte asked.

"That there was obviously no chance Wilfried would ever leave Aub Ehrenfest."

Wilfried simply blinked at me. "That's confusing... Why do you know euphemisms like that, Rozemyne?"

"Because Ferdinand beat them into my head specifically for today."

He had told me to stand in the line of fire, since Wilfried didn't understand the euphemisms and Charlotte had no prior experience speaking with nobles due to having only just been baptized. It was my job to handle these interactions in their place, which meant learning all sorts of subtle insults and ironic expressions that those here would most likely be using to refer to the incident.

"All because of my mistake..." Wilfried murmured, visibly frustrated. "Forgive me."

"Um, Rozemyne... Did my request perhaps put you in a difficult situation?" Charlotte asked.

"Oh, don't worry about that," I replied to Charlotte. "This was all something I needed to learn sooner or later as the High Bishop."

Despite my attendants and guardians surrounding us, the socializing continued to be painfully stressful. But it eventually came to an end, and as we were enjoying the delicious-looking food that was lined up in the grand hall, seventh bell mercilessly rang.

Charlotte's Baptism Ceremony

"We should be taking our leave. It is now time for the adults to converse."

"Yeah. Father, Mother—please excuse us."

"Good job today. May you sleep well with Schlaftraum's blessing."

After exchanging the noble form of "goodnight" with the archducal couple, we started heading toward the doors leading out of the grand hall, all the while performing the same greeting with those we passed. We happened upon Bonifatius on the way, so I called out to him.

"Good evening, Lord Bonifatius."

"May you sleep well with Schlaftraum's blessing."

"Thank you."

The three of us continued saying goodnight to those we knew, until we eventually exited the grand hall. We had one attendant and four guard knights each, and I felt my heart lighten just from knowing that nobody was staring at us anymore.

"I'm glad that ended safely," I said. "That should be the most time we spend around adults for a good while."

"Right. Tomorrow's karuta in the playroom," Wilfried added. "I'll show you how much I've improved after a whole year of training."

"I've improved too, and so has everyone else, dear brother."

I explained to Charlotte what the playroom was like as we walked through the main building and started making our way to the northern building. But when we were between the two, something caught my eye. I could have sworn that I saw a window move slightly.

"Oh?"

"What is it, Lady Rozemyne?" Damuel asked.

"I believe that window just moved. Would you take a closer look for me?"

"As you wish."

"I'm sure it was just my imagination," I reassured Charlotte, but I had Damuel check things out just in case.

"It's unlocked..." he muttered. But no sooner had the words escaped him than the window was flung open. Ten adults covered entirely in black cloth leapt into the castle, weapons in hand.

"Eep!"

"Who are these people?!"

The guard knights moved at once to protect their charges, turning their schtappes into weapons and encircling the attackers to block them in. They glared at the intruders, who glowered back in turn.

Charlotte and I were on the side closer to the northern building, while Wilfried was closer to the main building. We were separated.

"Leave this to us! Half attack, half defend!"

Damuel and Brigitte joined with two of the guard knights protecting Charlotte and two protecting Wilfried, then they all charged the attackers with their weapons drawn, starting a chaotic brawl.

"Wilfried! Run to the main building and call for help!" I yelled. "Lamprecht, hurry!"

In an instant, Oswald picked up Wilfried and rushed toward the main building. Lamprecht and another guard followed after them, weapons in hand.

"Rozemyne, we should hurry to the northern building! There is a barrier there!"

I hurriedly turned around and saw two of Charlotte's guard knights running to the northern building with her, having no doubt been trained to flee there in times of danger. But right now, we didn't have any knights who could respond to new attackers.

Sweat trickled down my cheeks. I undid my seat belt and leaned out the window of my Pandabus to yell again. "Charlotte, wait! It's dangerous!"

Moments before Charlotte reached the hall to the northern building, three more attackers clad in black leapt through another window. The two guard knights defending her responded instantly, but there was no one to stop the third attacker from picking her up and leaping back out the window.

"Charlotte!"

"Kyaaah!"

There was a loud flapping noise; then a winged horse came into view just outside the window. I swallowed hard, taken aback by the sudden appearance of a highbeast. This meant we were dealing with nobles.

The kidnapper holding Charlotte got his highbeast to spread its wings wide, and then they shot up into the dark, wintry sky.

Kidnapped Daughter

Charlotte's white clothes and the flying horse stood out against the dark night sky through the flung-open window, and I watched them shrink into the distance with wide-open eyes. In an instant, anger coursed through my body, and I could feel the mana exploding in my veins. It was so hot that it felt as though my blood was on fire, but my mind was calm with an icy disposition.

"How dare they touch my cute little sister... How dare they!"

Crushing the attacker would have been an ideal move, but he was too far away, and the Crushing required eye contact to work. Determined to get Charlotte back at once, I allowed my anger to consume me. I sat back in my seat, gripped the steering wheel tight, and practically started flooding Lessy with my mana.

Unforgivable! I don't care what anyone says; I'm going to make them pay!

"Wait, master of my master!"

"Lady Rozemyne! I will accompany you! Excuse me!"

I blinked in surprise as Stenluke the Magic Blade called out in Ferdinand's voice—something that I still wasn't used to. Then, half a second later, something struck Lessy's roof, shaking my one-person Pandabus. Two hands reached out and gripped the side windows from above, at which point I realized Angelica had leapt on top. My eyes widened at her completely unexpected maneuver.

"Angelica! That's dangerous!"

"I don't want to waste mana on my own highbeast," she shot back. "This is fine! Hurry!"

"Get a move on, else they will escape!"

Urged on by Angelica's sharp voice and Stenluke's Ferdinand-esque warning, I reflexively slammed down the accelerator as far as it would go, causing Lessy to lurch forward in a mad dash for the window.

"Stop! You're being reckless, you two!" Cornelius cried as he ran after us from behind, but it was too late. In my fury, I had poured a torrent of mana into my Pandabus, and we had already leapt into the night sky to chase the shrinking highbeast.

Lessy beelined through the chilly night air with Angelica still clinging to the roof. The brightly shining moon made our targets shine with a radiant white light.

"Give Charlotte back!"

"Sister?!"

Charlotte, still caught in her kidnapper's arms, turned to see my Pandabus. She reached out a desperate hand toward me, her face stiff and her indigo eyes wet with tears.

How dare you make my dear Charlotte cry!

I needed to reach her hand. I was going to save my little sister no matter what. My eyes fixed on the white horse, I poured even more mana into Lessy.

The black-clad kidnapper turned around. His face was almost entirely covered, but his eyes revealed a sickening sneer, as though he was mocking Charlotte's cries for help. But upon seeing me, he jerked in surprise.

"Wh-What in the…?! That wingless grun, flying?! But how?!" he yelled, the panic clear in his voice. The confident sneer from just moments ago had now been replaced with pure shock.

It seemed that he hadn't known my Pandabus could fly just like a normal highbeast. Whether this was because he had only ever seen me using it in the castle halls or because he had received his information from the castle scholars, I wasn't sure. But either way, this was a sure sign that he didn't have much to do with the archducal family retainers who spent time in the northern building.

"You'll suffer for this!" I shouted in a rage, blasting Lessy ever forward. The man tried to speed up his highbeast as much as possible to escape me, so I sped up as well. I was getting closer and closer.

"Sister! Help me!"

The man looked back to check where I was, his eyes now overcome with fear. He turned his head again and again, looking between Charlotte and me as I rapidly closed the distance.

But before I could catch up, he clicked his tongue. After quickly adjusting his grip on Charlotte, he tossed her to the side and into the air, before turning slightly and shooting away in the opposite direction.

Charlotte's indigo eyes widened in shock, her white clothes fluttering as she sailed through the air. It had happened to me so many times now that I knew exactly what she was feeling—the unusual sensation of weightlessness, and the suddenly overwhelming fear. I immediately turned Lessy's steering wheel, aiming straight for her.

"Charlotte!"

Rescuing her was my priority. The black-clad man would get away, but that didn't matter; capturing him was a job for the knights. I darted at full speed toward my little sister, only for Stenluke to cry out a warning.

"No, master of my master! You will crash into her!"

"Bwuh?!"

I hurriedly slammed my foot down on the brake upon realizing that Stenluke was right. Lessy's fur shot up as he came to an abrupt halt, the entire Pandabus lurching forward from the sudden stop. An instant later, Angelica leapt from the roof.

"Wha?! Angelica?!"

"Don't worry! I'm using physical enhancement right now!"

She twisted her body, tackling Charlotte in midair and hugging her tightly. Charlotte immediately wrapped her arms around her savior's back, desperately clinging to her.

"Target secured!" Angelica cried.

The relief of not having slammed my highbeast into Charlotte, the joy of my little sister having been safely rescued, and my gratitude for Angelica's expert moves all stirred within my heart like a maelstrom.

"Angelica! That was incredible!" I yelled, waving both my hands in gratitude. But before my very eyes, the two of them continued with the same momentum, moving away from me and toward the trees below.

"What is the plan, master?" Stenluke asked Angelica. "As we are now, we will fall to the ground with the young woman."

"I don't know!" she responded.

And there went my joy. The blood drained from my face in an instant.

"You didn't plan ahead, Angelica?!" I cried.

"Not at all!" came her lively response as she continued to plummet. It seemed that her only thought had been to secure Charlotte's person.

"Um... I... Someone, help!"

I leaned out the window to see how far they had fallen, ready to dive down in Lessy to try and grab them. But before I could, a wolf-like highbeast sped right beneath me.

"I'll make it!" Cornelius cried as he shot past, having caught up to us on his highbeast. He charged straight toward the rapidly falling Angelica and Charlotte.

"Cornelius! You can do it!"

I watched with sweaty palms as he quickly caught up to them at max speed. He flew next to them, grabbing Angelica by the cape and swinging her and Charlotte onto his highbeast. Having stopped their fall, he then made sure they were both sitting securely behind him.

"Aah! Cornelius! You're so cool!"

Abruptly stopping in the middle of such a rapid descent would have been dangerous, so Cornelius kept moving toward the ground while gradually shifting his highbeast about. He then made a big loop before rising back up and heading my way. His flying appeared to have stabilized, which meant that everyone was finally safe.

"Yes! Yes! Amazing!"

I clapped my hands in joy, when Lessy suddenly lurched forward again. I wasn't touching the steering wheel, nor had I pushed down on the accelerator, but he nonetheless started to tilt backward.

"What…?"

I was knocked back into my seat, having no idea what was going on. It was like my Pandabus was being dragged down by something. I blinked in confusion and grabbed the steering wheel, stepping on the accelerator in an attempt to get Lessy back to normal.

"What? Hello? What's happening?!"

His feet started to move, but then they abruptly stopped again as though something had wrapped around them. We were being pulled down and away against our will.

"Wait, wait, what?! We're going down! Eeeeeek!"

"Rozemyne!" Cornelius yelled in surprise as he saw my Pandabus start plummeting toward the forest surrounding the castle. Charlotte and Angelica were screaming behind him.

I screamed too, desperately clutching the steering wheel. But just before I reached the forest, the moon illuminated a thin net of light that was covering my highbeast. Goosebumps rose on my skin the second I realized that this wasn't my Pandabus breaking down—a malicious actor had captured me.

Looking around in a panic, I saw someone in the shadows of the trees pulling the mana net. It was one of the kidnapper's allies. I couldn't quite make him out, but his dark hands were visible thanks to the illuminated web.

I have to escape, I thought. But at that moment, the net was pulled even harder than before, jerking both Lessy and me down hard. We smacked into a bunch of trees before finally slamming into the ground with a huge crash.

"Ow…"

The impact was weaker than I thought, but I was launched up into the air and thrown all over the inside of my Pandabus. I really should have fastened my seatbelt, and I was starting to realize just how much I would need to invest in an airbag. But those thoughts only distracted me from the pain for a brief moment.

I pulled myself up to stand inside Lessy, who had fallen on his side, which naturally meant that my upper half stuck up out of the window.

"Eep?!"

The moment I was on my feet, bands of light shot out and wrapped around me. I could trace them back to another black-clad man, this one wielding a schtappe. Thoughts of when Ferdinand had used similar bands to restrain Bezewanst and to grab me during the schnesturm hunt flashed through my mind, and in an instant, my assailant yanked me to him like a snagged fish.

He pulled so violently that I practically flew through the air. I could see Lessy return to a feystone out of the corner of my eye, either due to my focus and mana connection with him having broken, or these bands being made from someone else's mana.

"Ngh!"

The man didn't catch me like Ferdinand would have, instead just allowing me to slam against the solid ground. I bounced, then slid across the dirt.

"Finally caught you. An apprentice shrine maiden being adopted by the archduke brought shame to our whole duchy. But I know someone who'll be very glad to have you in her possession."

The black-clad man looked down at me, his merciless gray eyes narrowed. While they were the only part of his face that I could see, they were enough for me to understand—he viewed me as an object, not caring how I thought or felt in the slightest. His was the gaze of a noble looking at a commoner.

I was used to that look, though it had been an entire year since I saw it last. Thoughts of all the dangerous nobles I had encountered ran through my mind—Bezewanst, Shikza, Count Bindewald... I didn't have any good memories with people who wore that expression.

A shiver ran down my spine as I frantically poured mana into my ring...

"O Goddess of Wind Schutzaria, prote— Guh!"

But the moment I started to chant, the man stomped on my stomach. I wiggled about, trying to escape the agonizing pressure, but he just leaned forward and put more weight on me.

"Ah yes, I do remember the Saint of Ehrenfest being able to use blessings..." he said with a sneer before pulling out a potion bottle and popping it open. I couldn't imagine its contents were anything less than terrible. "How about you just drink this?"

I struggled desperately, but with his foot still pressing into my abdomen, I was as helpless as a mouse stuck beneath a cat's paw. He grabbed my jaw and forced the potion into my mouth, the bitter liquid overwhelming my senses. I tried blocking it with my tongue and coughing it out, but the man noticed my struggling and pinched my nose. When I ran out of oxygen and started gasping for breath, it finally went down my throat, pouring straight into my lungs.

"Ngh! Gh— Gah!"

"Shut it," the man said curtly, holding my mouth shut as I started to choke and looking around cautiously.

I started to lose all feeling everywhere the potion had touched. I was unable to move my lips and tongue, the sensation similar to the numbing before a dental procedure. I shuddered in fear, desperately trying to move my arms and legs.

"Rozemyne! Rozemyne!"

Cornelius had descended into the forest and was searching for me, but his shouts were echoing from some distance away. I wanted to scream to him, but I had now lost the ability to move my mouth or speak at all. It was almost certainly the potion. The only noise I could make was a weak exhalation, and my blood went cold with dread as I realized that I could neither cry for help nor pray for a shield of Wind. My limbs were getting increasingly heavy too, such that I couldn't move them properly anymore.

"Seems like the potion's working..."

The man removed the bands of light with what I could only assume was a grin, but my body was already so numb that I couldn't move. I tried to at least Crush him, given that I could see his face, but my terror must have been surpassing my anger, as I was struggling to move my mana about.

I'm scared...

The black-clad man took me over to two men waiting by two horses, instructed them to transport me to a carriage, then disappeared into the shadows of the trees. The two men were dressed somewhat like servants, and since they weren't clad in black, I looked them all over in an attempt to memorize as much of their appearances as possible. But they soon put me in a bag as though I were luggage, blocking my vision with a layer of cloth.

So scared...

I could feel someone pick me up and then tie me into place. They must have laid me over one of the horses, and an instant later, it started galloping away. My body shook, each bounce causing me to land hard on my stomach. But due to the numbing potion, the impacts didn't hurt at all; they just felt kind of weird. My senses being this messed up only made me even more terrified.

So, so scared...

"Rozemyne!"

I heard Cornelius rushing this way, probably having heard the galloping of the horses, but it wasn't easy to use a highbeast with wings in a place with so many trees. I could hear his panicked cries growing increasingly distant.

Help me! Cornelius. Angelica. Damuel. Brigitte. Ferdinand. Father. Sylvester. Dad. Lutz...

Their faces ran through my mind, and I cried out in a silent voice. *Someone, help me!*

Rescue

The horse I was tied to was galloping at an incredible speed, and I could feel the rough impact of every single jolt. I was enveloped by the cloth bag and still couldn't see anything, so all I knew was that I was being taken somewhere.

Huh? I can't move my eyelids anymore...?

I could no longer even blink, my eyes only opening and closing due to the force of each bounce, and a chill ran through me as I realized that I couldn't move a single part of my body. The anxiety-inducing thought that I might just lose all of my senses and die here started to feel more and more likely as time went on, and it was all I could do to force it from my mind.

No, no, no... That black-clad man said to carry me to a carriage, and that someone would be happy to have me. He wouldn't have made me drink a potion that would kill me... right?

It was a little strange to be analyzing the words of an enemy, but with the feeling that I was about to die growing stronger and stronger, I was grasping at whatever straws I could. They weren't planning to kill me; they had simply disabled me so that I couldn't resist. The man's eyes had been cold and lacking in human sympathy, but there were no traces of murderous intent. Had he wanted me dead, it would have been easiest to kill me then and there.

I kept telling myself that everything would be fine, but just as I was starting to calm down, a terrible realization hit me.

What if the dose was safe for most people, but not for me...?

That seemed extremely possible, but I desperately tried to shake the thought away. We were still within the castle grounds; so long as Wilfried and his retainers reported the attack, then reinforcements would surely be coming soon.

They'll go to the northern building where the attack happened, get brought up to speed, and then they'll come straight here.

I broke out in a cold sweat as I wondered what the reinforcements might do. Would they actually reach me? Would they notice the horse running through the dark trees and underbrush? Would they make it before the potion made me stop breathing?

Maybe Ferdinand can help...

A mad scientist like him who knew all about potions would surely be able to do something about the poison. I just needed to put my faith in his extreme talents.

Save me, Ferdinand!

Then, out of nowhere, I heard a massive explosion.

The horse that had just moments ago been running in a steady line neighed and reared. I was only raised into the air a little since I was tied onto its back like luggage, but the man riding beside me let out a scream that made him sound just as terrified. This must have frightened the horse even more, as it suddenly sped up to a furious pace.

The other horse that had been riding next to us had presumably also lost its mind, since I could hear it running in another direction.

"Calm down! Stop!"

The horse being frightened only made the bouncing worse, and I could hear the man yelping for it to stop. My vision remained blocked by the wall of cloth, but the nighttime forest that had previously been enveloped in a silence broken only by hoofbeats was now teeming with life. I could hear nearby birds and animals letting out surprised noises as they fled.

"ARE YOU THE FOOL WHO KIDNAPPED MY ONLY GRANDDAUGHTEEER?!"

And then came a bellowing voice so loud that my body actually started to tremble. It was perfectly audible even with the cloth bag over my head, and my heart clenched despite all of my senses being messed up by the poison.

The words and the ferocity with which they were spoken told me exactly who was coming to my rescue.

G-Grandfather?!

Bonifatius's shout was filled with seething anger. It rang out even louder than the explosion, to the point that the horse kicked its legs again before stopping entirely.

What...? The horse stopped running?

All of a sudden, I could feel it start tipping over to one side, and it was then that I started to panic more than ever. Given that I was tied over it, there was a chance I would be crushed depending on which direction it fell.

Um, wait... Wait!

I let out a silent scream, but the ropes binding me to the horse were suddenly cut, and I felt someone speedily pick me up.

"Rozemyne, are you in there?!" came Bonifatius's unmistakable voice as he raised the bag I was in high into the air, crudely shaking it to investigate. But the poison had numbed me into silence, and I could neither respond nor complain.

Grandfather, I'm upside down! I can't feel anything, but the blood is going to rush to my head! Stop! Don't shake me!

"No matter how much I shake her, she isn't responding! Don't tell me she's dead?! Rozemyne, I'm getting you out of there right now!" he yelled, and for a brief moment, he stopped shaking me to hold me sideways.

But my relief didn't last very long at all. He gripped the edge of the sack, then hefted me up in the air again. I could tell that he was about to swing it around to get me out, and so I started silently screaming in a desperate attempt to stop him. If Grandfather swung as hard as he could, then my small body would undoubtedly be sent flying.

Wait, wait, stop! Someone, please stop him! I'll die!

My cries of course reached nobody, and Bonifatius swung the bag in an attempt to free me as quickly as possible. I was instantly launched out, flying into the air exactly as expected while spinning as fast as a high-speed drill.

Hyaaaaaah!

"Gwah?! Rozemyne is flying?!"

I heard Bonifatius let out a panicked cry, but then someone else caught me with a grunt.

"Bonifatius! Did Karstedt not tell you to stay away from Rozemyne so as to not accidentally kill her? Good grief... I understand your concern, but doing that would have proven fatal even for a healthy person. Are you alright, Rozemyne?"

Ferdinand... I owe you my life.

He prodded my cheek to check whether I was conscious, but considering what Bonifatius had just done, even that felt supremely kind and gentle. I had nothing but gratitude for Karstedt having kept Bonifatius away from me up until now.

"She's not dead, is she...?" Bonifatius asked, sounding a little dejected after his scolding.

"I can hardly say she is doing well, given that she is utterly unresponsive, but she does have a pulse," Ferdinand replied, briskly giving me a checkup. He measured my temperature and pulse, then leaned forward, putting his face so close to mine that I could feel his breath. "I smell a potion. This is... not good."

Rescue

I heard a rustling noise, then something like a scrap of paper was stuffed into my mouth. There was a pause before Ferdinand muttered again, his voice tinged with anger this time.

"To think they would use *that* of all things..."

"What is it, Ferdinand?"

"Rozemyne will die if we do not give her an antidote as soon as possible."

"What?!"

Both Bonifatius and I screamed at the same time, though my voice never actually left my throat. I had considered the possibility that I might die like this, but with Ferdinand now saying it as well, there was no longer any doubt in my mind.

I heard some clinking metal, followed by a strong smell. I quickly concluded that Ferdinand had opened one of the potions hanging from his belt, at which point he abruptly pulled open my jaw and stuck a liquid-soaked cloth into my mouth. It was wrapped around his pointer finger, and he rubbed it against my teeth and gums like he was brushing my teeth.

Urghghghghgh!

Ferdinand then removed his finger, leaving the cloth stuck in my mouth. "That was a potion to dull the effects of the poison, but it will do little more than buy us time. I must hurry to my workshop and get the antidote at once. I will take her back to the temple now to begin the process."

"What?! The temple?! That's no place to heal Rozemyne...!"

The temple was not a place that nobles visited by choice, so it was understandable that Bonifatius would not approve of taking me there to recover. But I trusted my attendants in the temple a lot more than those in the castle, and nothing would have made me feel safer than being right by Ferdinand's workshop and the jureve we had made.

"I understand Rozemyne's ill health and her potion tolerance more than anyone. Being at the temple will also make it harder for other nobles to approach her and interrupt us. Even this conversation is wasting time, so if you'll excuse me..."

Ferdinand wrapped my body in a cloth, but unlike the nobles who had thrown me into a bag like I was an object, he adjusted my head and left space for my face so that I could breathe. He was treating me like a person, and once I was securely wrapped, he picked me up.

"Ferdinand, wait! I'll look after her in my estate!"

"I am the only one who can save Rozemyne right now! *Do not interfere!*" Ferdinand roared, dropping his polite act entirely and squeezing his arms around me tighter. The raw anger in his voice sent a shiver down my spine; I would die for certain if they started arguing here.

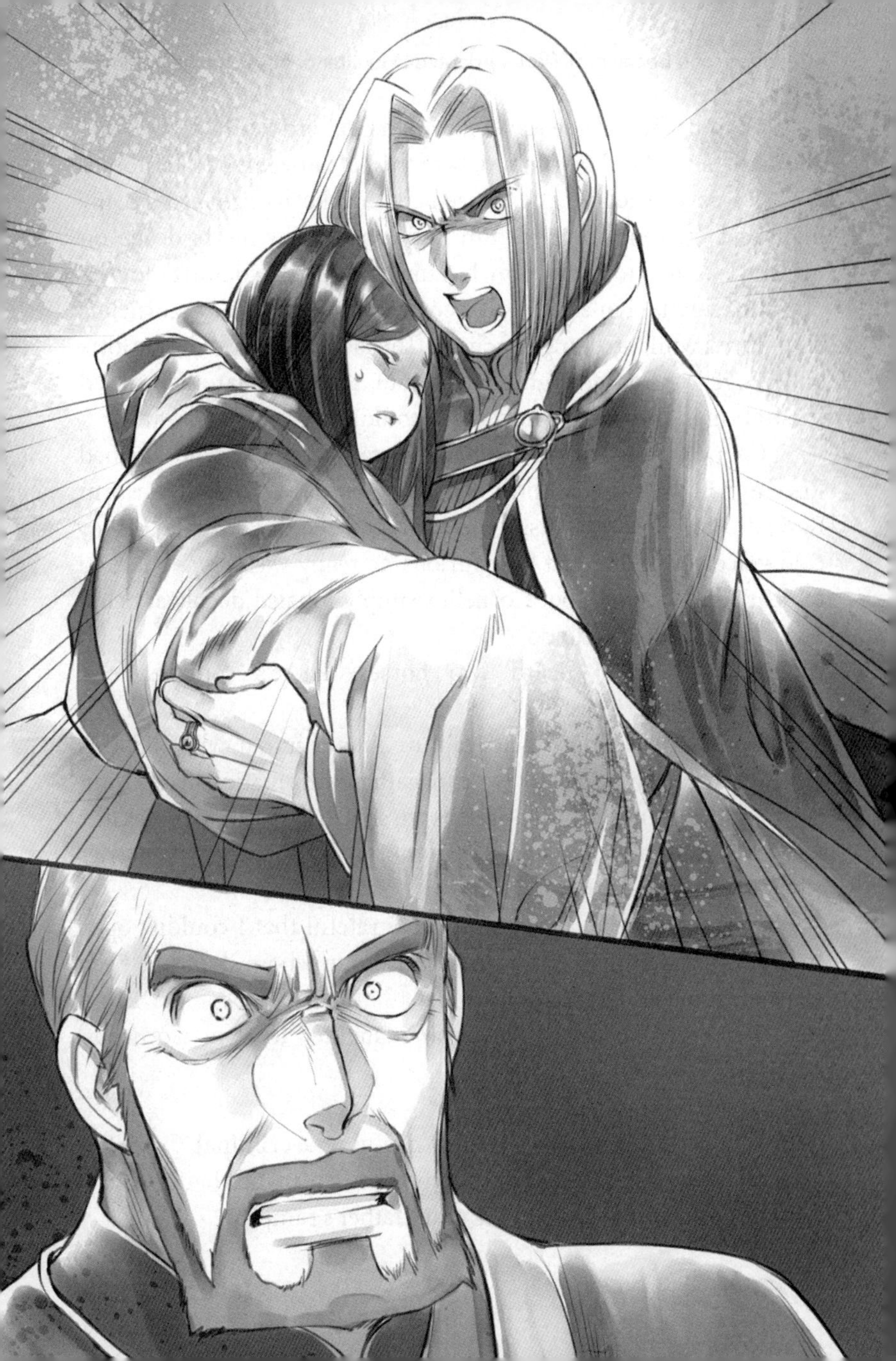

"Grandfather, please leave Rozemyne to Lord Ferdinand," came another voice. "Lord Ferdinand, take this! It's Rozemyne's feystone."

It was Cornelius, and it seemed that he had picked up my highbeast feystone. I heard him put it back into the birdcage on my hip. I wanted to thank him, but my mouth still wouldn't move.

"Rozemyne, I'm sorry that I couldn't protect you..." Cornelius murmured while stroking my cheek. The fact he had saved Charlotte and Angelica was enough for me, but I could hear the pained frustration in his voice. It hurt that I couldn't tell him it was fine.

"Cornelius, if you are truly sorry, capture those who harmed Rozemyne. We are dealing with nobles here, and the worm Bonifatius crushed was just a mere servant," Ferdinand said, his icy cold voice conveying just how furious he really was. I was shocked to hear him so angry, but Cornelius simply inhaled deeply at being given a job he needed to do.

"Grandfather, I heard two horses. There's someone else somewhere in the forest."

"Bonifatius, I ask you to capture the criminal who did this to Rozemyne alive so that we can gather information from him," Ferdinand continued. "Take care not to smash his head to pieces like you did with that other man; we cannot investigate their memories when they no longer have a brain."

At that moment, I was genuinely grateful that I couldn't open my eyes. I certainly didn't want to see a man whose skull had been crushed to bits by Bonifatius.

"Very well. I entrust my granddaughter to you. Cornelius! Follow me!"

"Yes, Grandfather."

With that, Bonifatius ran off to capture the criminal. Cornelius hurried after him, having been warned by Ferdinand that it was his job as a grandson to contain his grandfather's rampage.

Rescue

"Rozemyne, I will save you no matter what," Ferdinand whispered. "So please, fight the poison for as long as you can."

I bobbed a little, likely due to Ferdinand adjusting his grip on me, and then I heard the flapping of wings as he summoned his highbeast. I could tell that he was blasting to the temple at a terrifying speed, judging by the way the cloth was flapping in my mouth. There was no doubt in my mind that he was moving much faster than anyone else in the duchy could hope to keep up with, and soon enough, we came to a stop.

Sharp footsteps echoed out as Ferdinand started striding along, and the scent filling the air assured me that we truly had arrived at the temple.

It was already past seventh bell, so all was silent apart from Ferdinand's continued footsteps. I couldn't feel the presence of anyone else.

"Open it," came Ferdinand's voice, followed by someone gasping and hurriedly opening a door. I then heard him say "Fran," so I could guess we had arrived at my High Bishop's chambers.

"High Priest, what bri— Lady Rozemyne?!"

Fran had evidently been staying up late for work or something of the sort, and he let out a surprised yell upon seeing me. Ferdinand gave a brief explanation of the circumstances while handing me to him.

"She was poisoned. I am going to fetch the antidote. Change her clothes into something white while I obtain the potion from my workshop. Do not remove the cloth in her mouth; it is soaked with a potion delaying the spread of the poison."

"Understood."

While still carrying me, Fran used his free hand to ring the bell for summoning attendants. I heard various footsteps as they quickly gathered around us.

205

"Nicola, Monika—please get Lady Rozemyne changed into white clothes at once. Zahm, Fritz, Gil—adjust the light and temperature of the room."

"Understood!"

It was impossible for just Monika and Nicola to change my clothes when I was entirely limp, so Fran held me up as they undid the buttons on my back and removed my hair stick.

"Stay strong, Lady Rozemyne."

"Fran, is she okay?"

It was clear from their voices that Nicola and Monika were quite concerned about my total lack of movement.

"The High Priest is here," Fran replied in a hard voice. I could feel his hands trembling slightly as he held me up.

"I'm coming in," Ferdinand announced, entering before my attendants could even respond. I then heard him set something onto a table.

Despite my supposed lack of consciousness, it was unthinkable for Ferdinand to enter a room while its resident was in the middle of being changed. It just went to show how much my life was in danger, and I could feel my heartbeat quickening in fear.

"Leave her in those underclothes. Simply wrap her in a blanket for warmth. We do not have any time to waste, and she shall be using the jureve after the antidote is applied regardless," Ferdinand said, and a moment later, I could feel a blanket wrap around me. "Give her to me, Fran."

I was promptly handed over to Ferdinand, who seemed to be sitting in a chair. He removed the cloth from my mouth and stuck a slender tube in its place. It seemed to be a syringe of some sort, and while a potion was being dripped into my mouth little by little, I couldn't taste anything at all.

Rescue

Is it that the potion has no flavor, or have I just lost my sense of taste as well…?

Ferdinand checked my pulse once he was done giving me the antidote, then let out a light sigh. "I believe I made it in time. Fran, continue holding her in this position until the antidote begins taking effect. Take care to watch the position of her tongue, as it may prevent her from breathing."

"Understood."

Fran took me once again, supporting me while carefully watching the position of my head and body.

"I shall go and prepare the jureve," Ferdinand announced. I heard his footsteps moving away from us, then sensed multiple people moving closer as I remained slumped against Fran.

"Fran, will Lady Rozemyne be okay?"

"Of course she will. The High Priest said that he was able to act in time," Fran replied, his voice soft with relief due to his utter faith in Ferdinand. And since everyone had just as much faith in Fran, the despair in the air slowly began to fade.

"I'll read a book to you," Gil said next, "so please get better soon, Lady Rozemyne."

A warmth flowed through my heart as he started reading aloud, and as I continued to listen, Ferdinand's potion began to take effect. I could now move my lips a little.

"Ah! Lady Rozemyne is smiling! It seems that she can hear you, Gil!" Nicola said happily, motivating him to read louder. I heard some relieved sighs, then the sounds of Nicola and Monika clearing away my clothes and hair stick.

By the time Gil had finished the first picture book, I could move my mouth and tense my eyelids a little. Then, after several attempts, I finally opened my eyes.

"Lady Rozemyne!"

The faces of my attendants all lit up with smiles as they gathered in front of me. I could still barely move my lips, but I tried talking anyway.

"Sorry... for... worrying..."

"Please do not force yourself. The potion should be finished soon."

I was happy to be surrounded by attendants who cared so much for me, no longer in that dangerous forest alone with the cold-eyed noble. The feeling slowly returned to more and more places.

"I think I can talk a little now..."

"If you still cannot move, please wait as you are for a bit longer."

"Okay..." I replied, still drooped against Fran. I didn't risk nodding, since I wasn't sure I would be able to lift my head back up on my own. "So, Fran... I'm about to use my jureve potion, right?"

"I imagine so, given that the High Priest said that you would be."

Ferdinand had mentioned that using the jureve would cause me to lose consciousness for a while, so it would probably be best for me to give what instructions I could before using it.

"In that case, please deliver the letter I prepared to Lutz. Furthermore, ask Ferdinand to return my personnel in the castle to the temple. As for temple affairs... continue as you would if I were simply staying at the castle for a long time. You are all very skilled, so I imagine things will continue running smoothly even while I am using the jureve, but please do your best."

"You may count on us."

I gave as many pointers as I could remember, then decided to trust them with the rest.

"Fran, I would like to go to the hidden room. Would you kindly carry me there? You should be able to enter if you're with me."

He picked me up, and I reached out a trembling hand to touch the feystone on the door. I could feel my mana flowing in bit by bit, but things were far from normal; it seemed that despite the antidote bringing movement back to my limbs, the mana inside my body was still barely moving. I was hardly an expert on the subject, but that didn't seem like a good thing to me.

"High Priest, Lady Rozemyne has awoken."

I somehow managed to open the door, and inside I found Ferdinand pouring the jureve into the ivory box, which might as well have been a bathtub or a coffin.

"Ferdinand, I can move again, but my mana feels kind of stuck," I said. "It's like it's all hardened."

"Drink this jureve at once," he replied, his expression darkening in an instant. He poured some of the jureve into a cup and then handed it to Fran.

I raised the jureve to my lips, barely able to move my hands, then slowly drank it with Fran's support. The fact that it tasted a little sweet told me that my senses were coming back.

The entire time I was drinking from the cup, Ferdinand continued pouring the jureve from a pitcher into the bathtub. The pitcher itself wasn't that large, but the jureve was flowing from it non-stop. And despite him not even touching the cauldron, it seemed that the jureve within it was slowly draining.

"It's almost like the pitcher and cauldron are connected..."

"Not almost—they are. Now... that should be enough," Ferdinand said, setting aside the pitcher. He then hefted me up and placed me in the ivory bathtub filled with the jureve. A magic circle was inside, and the instant I sat down, the mana lines on my body surfaced and reddened.

"The magic circle seems to be functioning properly. Your mana, however, is..."

Ferdinand trailed off, mumbling to himself and checking the mana flow in my arms and neck. My eyelids began to droop as he looked me over.

"I feel kind of tired, Ferdinand..."

"Yes, that is due to the potion. You may allow yourself to fall asleep where you are. Rest well, Rozemyne."

"Night night, Ferdinand. I entrust the rest to you..."

"Indeed. I shall eliminate all those who threaten to disturb your sleep. You have nothing to fear," Ferdinand said, covering my eyes with his large hand.

My vision darkened, and I felt my consciousness drifting away as the jureve gradually seeped into me. My entire body was floating in the swaying liquid, and the feeling was so nostalgic, so comforting...

And So, the Future

I was in a soft, fluffy world made of pink. But despite the floor being so soft, when I tried to go anywhere, I was met with heaps of sizable rocks. All the paths were blocked off no matter how much I wanted to go down them.

What should I do about this...?

As I fell into thought, an ivory watering can suddenly popped into my hand. When I tipped it, some liquid began pouring out.

A closer look revealed that the watering can's liquid was making the giant rocks break down a little. I started swinging the watering can around and dissolving the hard rocks like they were made of sugar. The really hard places didn't want to give at all, but when I focused the water on them, they started to dissolve anyway. I kicked some of them experimentally, and they shattered into pieces.

Okay. I can pass through now.

There were some parts that didn't entirely dissolve, but, well... my only concern was getting down the path. I moved on to the next pile of rocks, and then the next one, breaking them all apart one after another.

The watering can would occasionally run dry, but then it would replenish itself after a short while. I focused on dissolving the rocks and just kept pouring the liquid everywhere.

I've done so much with just a single watering can. Somebody praise me. I think I deserve it.

With an immense sense of satisfaction filling my chest, I slowly opened my eyes. I saw someone's silhouette within my wavering vision, and an instant later, two large hands thrust themselves toward me. My head was lifted up, and I was halfway forced into a sitting position.

"Eugh! Gahh!"

Air rushed into my mouth and nose the instant I was pulled up, and I started blinking in confusion as the unexpected development sent me into a coughing fit.

I'm going to drown in air!

As I desperately flapped my mouth, I was struck hard on the back. Some liquid that had been deep in my lungs flew out of my mouth, instantly making it easier to breathe, but my back still tingled. I glared up at the person who had hit me with tearful eyes.

"That hurt, Ferdinand..."

As it turned out, the silhouette belonged to Ferdinand. We were in my hidden room, and I was sitting inside the ivory bathtub filled with the jureve. Ferdinand had tightly furrowed his brow, and everything looked the same as it had before I went to sleep.

"Finally awake, I see. I cannot believe you slept that long..." Ferdinand said as he touched my cheek, measured my pulse, and did some other checks. Once he was done, he let out a slow sigh. "You seem to be fine."

I blinked several times, then tried wiggling my fingers. I couldn't quite get them moving right.

"Am I really healthy now?" I asked.

I could move my mana properly again, which hadn't been the case before I slept, but it hardly felt as though I was any healthier. Maybe my muscles had atrophied while I was asleep.

And So, the Future

As I continued to wiggle my hands in the jureve, Ferdinand grimaced uncomfortably. "Erm, Rozemyne... I have an exceedingly unfortunate announcement to make."

"What is it?"

"Your mana has not... entirely dissolved."

It felt as though time had suddenly frozen. I thought of the year I had spent struggling to gather ingredients, and all the difficulties involved with the jureve, then looked up at Ferdinand with utter disbelief.

"WHAAAAAAAAAT?! Hold on. Why? Why has it not dissolved?! Is it because of those few times with the watering can?! Was slacking off that bad of an idea?!"

"I did not slack whatsoever," Ferdinand said with a frown. I hurriedly tried to shake my head, but the feeling hadn't yet returned, so it just slumped forward. Had he not reached out and held my forehead up, I would have sunk right back into the jureve.

"I'm not talking about you, Ferdinand. I mean what I did in my dream," I explained. "Ngh... My head feels all fuzzy."

Ferdinand pressed a finger against his temple and let out a heavy, heavy sigh. "You give me headaches whether you are asleep or awake," he muttered with a glare, causing me to falter.

"Okay, the dream talk can wait for now... Why hasn't my mana dissolved yet?"

Ferdinand continued to tap his temple as he explained what had happened. "To put it simply, your mana had already hardened too much. The jureve was necessary to dissolve the mana hardened by the poison you consumed as well, and it was not enough to dissolve all of your already hardened mana on top of that. Let us say that your initially hardened mana was ten units. I made a jureve that was of a high enough quality to dissolve fifteen, just to be safe. But right before the time came to use it, your mana hardened to a state of twenty units. Since the jureve was only capable of dissolving fifteen, we have our current situation."

"So I'm at least healthier than I was before...?" I asked, looking down at the mana lines covering my arms. It was beyond me to tell whether they had changed at all.

Ferdinand also looked down at me and nodded. "Indeed. Your mana has not completely dissolved, but you should be much healthier than you were before."

"Well, I guess that's good enough for me. It's certainly better than dying..."

Deciding to consider this a meaningful step forward nonetheless, I stretched my neck and looked around me. There was a wooden box right next to the ivory one I was in, and I could see five books stacked atop it. They were bound in the same way Rozemyne Workshop books were bound, but I didn't recognize any of them.

"Ferdinand, what are these?"

"They are books that one of your attendants brought. Gil, I believe his name is. He said that you might wake up sooner with books stacked next to you, and thus with every new one they published, they brought a copy here."

In a shocking twist, it seemed that Gil had stacked up all the newly printed books for me.

"Yay! New books!"

I excitedly reached out to take one, but then I noticed that my hand was still soaked with the jureve. Ferdinand glared at me like I was an idiot.

"You will ruin them if you touch them with those hands."

And So, the Future

"I figured..."

"I asked for a bath to be prepared, as I noticed that you were about to awaken. It should be ready soon."

"Okaaay. Wait. Hold on a moment..." I had been asleep long enough for five new books to have been printed—that thought alone took me a moment to fully process. "Ferdinand... Just how long was I asleep?"

"Roughly two years."

My eyes widened in disbelief. "Excuse me...?"

"A new record, I believe. But either way, I am just glad you have awakened in time to attend the Royal Academy."

"W-Wait. How old am I right now?"

"This is the autumn of your tenth year—the Harvest Festival has just ended. In the winter, you shall be enrolling in the Royal Academy," Ferdinand explained.

I immediately started to panic. I had gone into the jureve during the winter of my eighth year, but now it was the autumn of my tenth. It seemed that I had skipped over my ninth year entirely.

"N-No way! Where did my ninth year go?!"

Noooooo! I screamed silently, cradling my head. But Ferdinand merely shrugged.

"You experienced your seventh year twice, so this merely equalizes things, does it not?"

Repeating my seventh year had certainly been unexpected, but skipping over an entire year was something I had expected even less.

"This certainly doesn't equalize things!" I complained. "Also, you say that I'm ten years old now, but I don't feel like I've changed at all." My hands, for one, didn't look any bigger. It was hard to believe that two years had passed when I was still this small.

"Your bodily functions barely operate while in the jureve, as all of your energy is directed toward dissolving the mana. It is similar to being half dead, so unfortunately... you do not grow while under its effects," Ferdinand explained, avoiding eye contact with me.

"WHAAAT?! But you said I'd be healthy! Ferdinand, you liar!"

I was a bit healthier than before, sure, but this was at the cost of losing my entire ninth year and having to attend the Royal Academy without having grown at all.

Epilogue

For several days, Rozemyne had been opening her unfocused eyes while soaking in the jureve and looking around aimlessly before closing them again. Ferdinand, who had been observing her closely, knew that this meant she would be waking up soon, but her body still hadn't risen out of the liquid. It remained submerged.

Even during the Harvest Festival, Ferdinand raced back to the temple almost every night to check on her, but progress was frustratingly slow. It took forever, but finally, her eyes began to focus. And after rapidly blinking a few times, she rose out of the jureve as if to say that any further healing was impossible.

Ferdinand sighed in relief, sticking his hands in to help Rozemyne sit up and patting her on the back to help her breathe. She seemed to feel much better upon spitting out the jureve that was stuck in her lungs, and while she spent some time coughing, her breathing soon sounded normal again.

"That hurt, Ferdinand…"

Rozemyne looked up at him with an angry glare and complained, but Ferdinand had no idea what he had done to deserve that. She knew nothing of the struggles he had gone through, and the fact that she did nothing but grumble upon waking up was surely a sign that she lacked any gratitude whatsoever.

"Tell me when you have finished bathing. There is much for us to discuss regarding what happened while you slept. If you have any questions, save them for then."

Ferdinand entrusted Rozemyne to her attendants, then returned to his chambers, where his own attendants were waiting with smiles.

"The High Bishop has awoken, then? I imagine that is her handprint," one of them said, pointing at a wet mark on Ferdinand's robes where Rozemyne had grabbed him. His robes were a wet mess in general though, owing to him having stuck his hands into the jureve to help Rozemyne sit up and then having carried her out.

"I shall arrange a change of clothes," the attendant continued.

"Indeed."

"This news comes as a considerable relief to us all. We were worried about when the High Bishop would finally awaken," the priest said with a smile as he returned with the change of clothes. Such small talk was rare for Ferdinand's attendants; they truly had all been waiting for Rozemyne to wake up.

Because now that Rozemyne is awake, we will not be disturbed by those messages any longer... Ferdinand thought with a sigh, turning to look at the corner of his desk where a bunch of yellow feystones had piled up.

They were mostly ordonnanzes from Bonifatius, containing messages wherein he roared, "WHEN IS ROZEMYNE WAKING UP, FERDINAND?!" They had arrived all too often over the past half a year, to the point that every single person in the High Priest's chambers was dead tired of them.

Good grief... I was already frustrated at how long it was taking Rozemyne's mana to dissolve. How many times did I need to refrain from barking back that I was the one who wanted to know when she was going to wake up more than anyone?

"High Priest, now that the High Bishop has finally awoken, you can spend today resting at last."

Epilogue

"No, not yet. Once Rozemyne has been cleaned up, I shall visit her chambers to explain what happened over the past two years. Allow her attendants in, if any arrive."

"Understood."

Ferdinand finished changing and moved to his desk, where he tapped each of the yellow feystones one by one with his schtappe and poured mana into them. He transformed all twenty-something into ordonnanzes at once, filling the room with ivory birds in an instant. He then faced them and spoke.

"Rozemyne has awoken. If she is in good health, I will bring her to the castle at third bell three days from now. Do *not* come to the temple, as she is still recovering from her sleep."

With that, Ferdinand swung his schtappe, and the ordonnanzes all flew away at once. Incidentally, over half of the twenty-something ordonnanzes were replies to messages from Bonifatius, and since each one repeated its message three times, he would soon be hearing the news thirty to forty times. Just the idea brought Ferdinand a small amount of satisfaction; it was his small revenge for having been forced to listen to Bonifatius bark about Rozemyne almost every single day for months now.

However, Ferdinand's satisfaction was short-lived: as he began organizing a study guide covering what Rozemyne needed to memorize before leaving for the Royal Academy, an ordonnanz returned with an excessively joyful message.

"HURRAAAAAAH! ROZEMYNE! SHE'S AWAKE?!"

The yells echoed through the temple three times as Ferdinand could do nothing but listen and rub his temples. As it turned out, Bonifatius was a pain even when Rozemyne was awake. Ferdinand really didn't want to deal with him any longer, so when the ordonnanz turned back into a yellow feystone, he simply left it there and continued with his work.

Will things truly go well...?

Although Ferdinand was greatly relieved that Rozemyne had finally awoken, he also felt some unease. She had not grown at all, meaning her appearance was exactly the same as it had been two years ago—though this was expected, given that she had been soaking in the jureve the entire time. Her understanding of the world and her memories were also all exactly as they had been before her long slumber.

Ferdinand recalled what had happened when he retrieved Rozemyne from the jureve and handed her to Fran. Her attendants had all eagerly rushed forward to see her after such a long time, but her eyes had merely widened in shock when she saw how much they had all grown. Fran hadn't changed much, since he had already come of age, but all her apprentice attendants had come of age while she slept.

Rozemyne had ended up stiffening and looking up at Ferdinand, clutching his robe with a terribly anxious look on her face despite the happy smiles of her attendants. She would now need to adjust to how the world had progressed without her, and that would not be an easy task.

That said, I am glad she awoke before the start of winter socializing...

Ferdinand had been agonizing over whether she would wake up in time to attend the Royal Academy at the proper age, but it seemed things would indeed work out as he had hoped. It would have been possible to delay her enrollment for a year, but such a thing was considered a black mark in noble society, which would have led to undue pressure and potential rumors.

Epilogue

That would have been terrible, given that Rozemyne already has so many weaknesses that run the risk of being spread through other duchies as rumors.

As Ferdinand organized what Rozemyne needed to learn to enter the Royal Academy, an attendant called out to him.

"High Priest, it seems the High Bishop is ready."

Grandfather on the Day of the Baptism

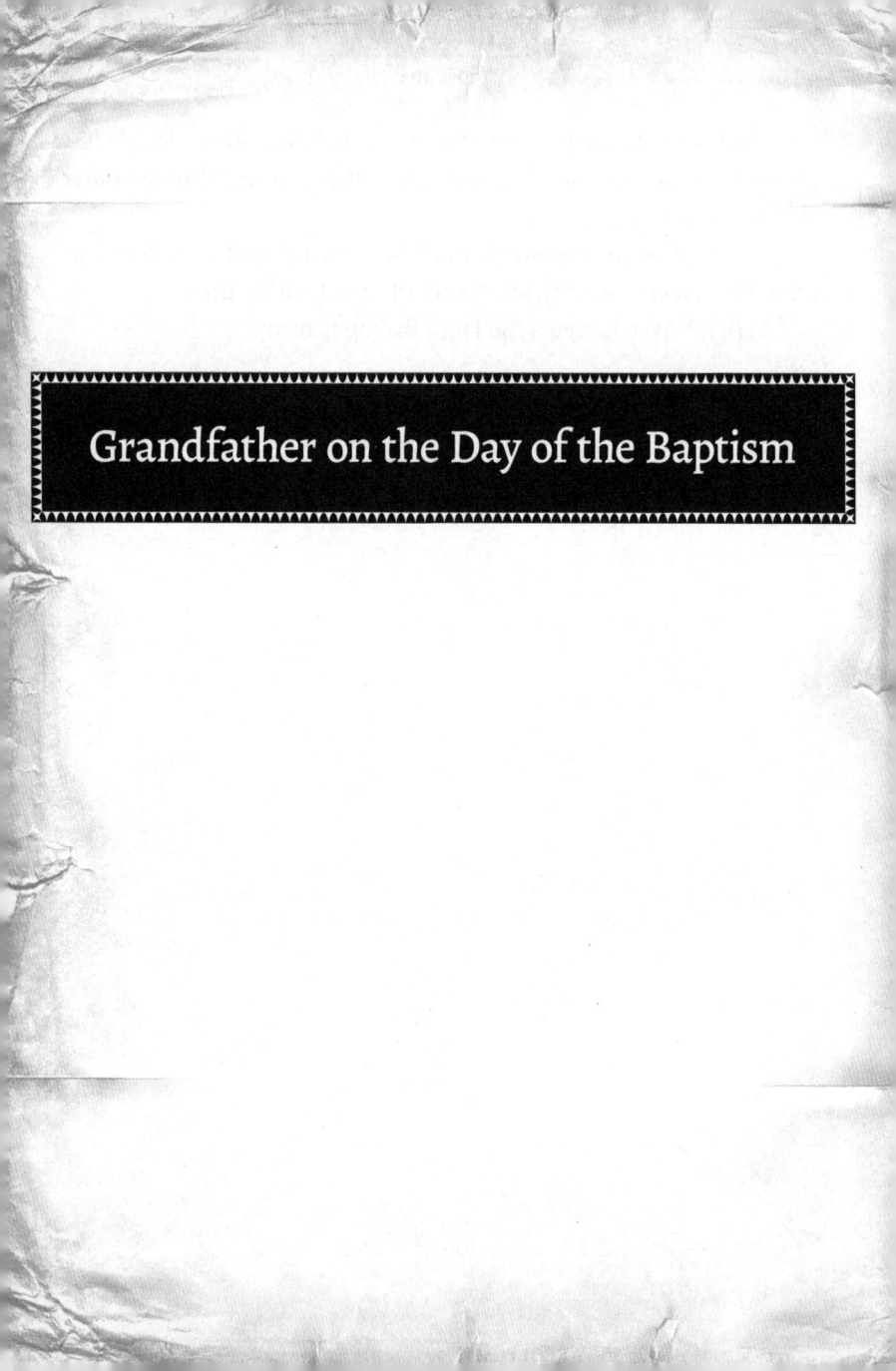

My emotions were a violent storm. Why? Because my granddaughter Rozemyne was much too cute and talented. She had performed the baptism ceremony brilliantly despite her tiny, fragile body and the huge crowd of nobles watching her, and now she was heroically protecting Sylvester's child.

Splendid work, Rozemyne! That's my granddaughter for you! To think those nobles would dare bring such petty complaints to you about Wilfried... Had Karstedt and Elvira not told me to keep my distance to avoid accidentally endangering your life, and to avoid interfering with the baptism ceremony you've dedicated your all to for Lady Charlotte's sake, I'd have stepped forth as your grandfather and demolished those hateful mednobles with a single bark!

Elvira had said it would be an issue for Rozemyne to start relying on her strength to solve all her problems like I did, since she had enough mana for that to actually be dangerous. That was just a pain though, as far as I was concerned. It was only natural that those who had power should be free to use it, so I didn't see what all the fuss was about.

My son Karstedt maintained that this way of thinking was the reason I had been denied the position of archduke, but the reality was that I had intentionally avoided it—not because I wasn't skilled enough to take on the role, of course, but because that whole business just seemed bothersome to me.

Still, who would have guessed that a child weak enough to have been knocked unconscious by a few snowballs would have enough mana to provide such enormous support to Ehrenfest...

Last winter, I'd stood watch with a large squadron of knights as the children threw snowballs at each other. It truly was a heartwarming sight—that is, until Rozemyne was targeted while trying to make a snowball herself. A few consecutive shots was all it took to knock her out, which terrified not only the knights watching but Wilfried and his friends (who had thrown the snowballs) as well.

After witnessing that shocking display of weakness, I was afraid of getting anywhere near Rozemyne.

Those pitifully small snowballs were enough to knock her unconscious! So much as a touch from me would probably kill her, just as Karstedt fears.

At seventh bell, Rozemyne began leaving the grand hall, saying her farewells to the archducal couple and those close to her along the way. I swiftly moved to the door that she and the children were heading toward, determined to have her speak to me as well.

"Good evening, Lord Bonifatius."

"May you sleep well with Schlaftraum's blessing."

Indeed... My granddaughter truly is the cutest. It's very frustrating that she can't call me "Grandfather" in a formal setting like this, but oh well.

The only times Rozemyne had ever called me "Grandfather" were when we first met at her baptism ceremony and during the spring Archduke Conference when she had helped with the Mana Replenishment. Wilfried had never had enough strength to thank me after performing the Replenishment, but Rozemyne would always say, *"Grandfather, thank you ever so much,"* with that perfect smile on her face.

Grandfather on the Day of the Baptism

In retrospect, I hadn't appreciated how precious my time spent with Rozemyne outside the influence of the public eye really was.

Aah, the next Archduke Conference can't come soon enough. I hope it lasts longer than usual, too.

While I was deep in thought, one of Wilfried's attendants rushed back into the grand hall with the boy in his arms, despite them having left just a moment ago. Lamprecht—my grandson and one of Wilfried's guard knights—was also with them.

Their panic was a sure sign of danger. I instantly scanned the room while using enhancement magic to strengthen my eyesight; nobody I saw seemed to know what was going on.

"There has been an attack in the hall leading to the northern building! The guard knights are currently engaged in battle. At least one of the attackers was wielding a schtappe. Lady Charlotte and Lady Rozemyne are currently isolated on the northern building's side. We request reinforcements at once!"

"Knight squadrons one through four, go!" Karstedt barked as the knight commander without missing a beat. "Everyone else, seal off the grand hall! Consider all nobles not here potential suspects!"

The knights present immediately started moving to secure the grand hall.

"Karstedt, I'm going to rescue Rozemyne!" I shouted.

Not only was I the son of the archduke from two generations ago, but I had also once served in the Knight's Order. It was for those reasons that I continued to assist the archduke even during my retirement. I had admittedly used to avoid work, but now I was actively taking on as many duties as possible, all to ensure Rozemyne's safety as best I could. She would almost certainly say, *"Thank you, Grandfather. I love you!"* in response to all my help, and I wouldn't allow anyone to take that away from me.

"Father?!" Karstedt cried in a panic, but Sylvester shouted out before he could even try to stop me.

"Go with him, Ferdinand! Stop Bonifatius from going too far!"

Ferdinand sighed. "You would ask the impossible of me...?"

I ignored the conversation going on behind me, bursting through the doors of the grand hall as they were still being sealed and sprinting to the northern building. I used magical enhancement to strengthen my legs, blasting past the knights who had rushed to provide support ahead of me.

I may be sixty years old, but those young'uns won't outdo me yet! I'll arrive there before anyone else!

It was quite some distance from the grand hall to the northern building. As I sprinted down the halls with my enhanced legs, the thought crossed my mind that I could have moved even faster with a highbeast like Rozemyne's.

"Rozemyne! Where are you?!" I shouted as I turned corner after corner.

Soon enough, I came across the knights fighting against black-clad enemies. I enhanced my eyesight at once, but I couldn't see Rozemyne or Charlotte no matter where I looked. The other guard knights had most likely taken them to the northern building, but I wasn't going to leave until I had confirmed their safety myself.

"ARE YOU SAFE, ROZEMYYYNE?!" I roared, leaping onto one of the black-clad attackers' backs and crushing his skull with a single swing of my enhanced arm. He fell to the ground with a thump, and then his entire body blew into pieces. "Ngh?! What?! He exploded on his own!"

Blood and organs sprayed across the hall along with shreds of the attacker's black clothes, the shock waves of the blast sending both the other assailants and the knights falling to the ground.

Some knights started to throw up as they were smacked in the face with chunks of meat, the foul stench of blood overwhelming their senses. I noticed their faltering out of the corner of my eye and instantly barked out an order.

"Don't let your guards down, you idiots!"

My shout willed them back to their feet, but no sooner had they regained their footing than the remaining black-clad attackers started to explode one by one in a chain reaction of sorts. I was used to my enemies exploding when I punched them or struck them with weapons, but this was my first time seeing them blow up by themselves.

"What's happening here...? I don't understand it, but I won't protest our enemies dying on their own. You there. Is Rozemyne safe?"

"...I don't know. Lady Charlotte was kidnapped, and the last thing I saw was Lady Rozemyne chasing after her on her highbeast."

"You useless idiot!"

I scolded the guard knight, then raced toward the flung-open window. There was no point in staying now that the enemies had self-destructed; my job wasn't to gather information to pin down the culprits, but to rescue Rozemyne.

I reached the window just as Rozemyne's guard knight Angelica returned, carrying a very pale Charlotte.

"Aah! It is good to see you safe, Charlotte. Where is Rozemyne?"

"She was kidnapped by someone. She used her own guard knights to save me, and..." Charlotte trailed off, her eyes welling up with tears.

I turned to Angelica with a wide-eyed stare. As a guard knight, she promptly explained the situation in practical terms.

"Cornelius is chasing after them now. I plan to join him once Lady Charlotte's safety is assured. Lord Bonifatius, please take care of her for me."

Angelica tried handing Charlotte to me, but I ignored her. It was somewhat of a struggle even with my enhanced eyes, but I could see Cornelius descending into the forest way off in the distance.

"Rozemyne is my granddaughter. I will go in your place!"

I pushed Angelica aside and leapt out the window into the night sky, creating my highbeast in midair and landing on its back. Having it flap its wings would create too much noise, so I glided through the night air while moving them as little as possible.

I focused carefully, trying to pick up every sound that I could. The forest spread so far that it completely hid the movement of servants, but I heard the hoofbeats of horses rushing toward the front gate some distance away from where Cornelius had landed.

There!

My eyes widened as I soared through the air, no longer concerned about making noise as my highbeast flapped its wings hard. I poured an immense amount of mana into it so that I could move at maximum speed, the cold night air whipping past me as I raced toward my destination.

As I closed in on the kidnappers, I started filling my schtappe with mana to prevent them from escaping any farther. White-hot sparks flashed at its tip as more and more mana accumulated within.

By the time the ball of mana was bigger than my head, I had gotten close enough to see the running horse without even needing to enhance my eyesight. I swung my schtappe down, aiming in its path.

The ball of mana soared through the night sky with a tail of white light, then sank into the trees. A moment later, a loud explosion resounded through the air.

Grandfather on the Day of the Baptism

The forest was suddenly abuzz with the cries of animals and birds, all scattering away from the freshly formed crater among the trees. The horse began a mad dash as well, no doubt terrified by the sudden explosion.

"ARE YOU THE FOOL WHO KIDNAPPED MY ONLY GRANDDAUGHTEEER?!"

I dove down on my highbeast toward the horse, all the while unleashing a wave of mana. It froze in place, unable to move as it took my Crushing head-on, then started frothing at the mouth.

The man who had been gripping onto the horse's reins was thrown from its back. I crushed his skull in anger and started searching for Rozemyne.

And then I spotted it—a bag tied to the side of the horse.

I cut the rope in an instant, then used my enhanced leg to kick away the horse as it fell toward me. It soared through the air before hitting a tree.

"Rozemyne, are you in there?!"

The bag was so light that I struggled to believe a child could be inside. But after shaking it about a little, there was no doubt in my mind.

"No matter how much I shake her, she isn't responding! Don't tell me she's dead?! Rozemyne, I'm getting you out of there right now!"

Although I strained my ears, she gave no response at all. The blood draining from my face, I hurriedly grabbed the edge of the bag and shook it hard, desperate to get her out. The weight inside shifted around, then the bag began to open.

By the time I realized what would happen next, it was too late. The bag ripped open and Rozemyne was thrown into the air, rapidly spinning in a direction that I hadn't anticipated at all. I reached out, but she was already too far away.

"Gwah?! Rozemyne is flying?!"

An instant later, Ferdinand—who had evidently been following me—caught Rozemyne in midair moments before she slammed into a tree. She was safe now thanks to him, but my heart had leapt so suddenly into my throat that I'd half expected it to shoot out my mouth.

Ferdinand determined that she had been forced to consume a strange potion that was lethally poisonous to her, then departed for the temple with her to prepare an antidote. In all honesty, I didn't want to entrust my cute granddaughter to the temple; in fact, I didn't want to entrust her to another man either, whether he was her guardian or not.

But even if I had taken her to my estate, I wouldn't have known how much of the antidote to give her, and the castle was no doubt in such a state of confusion right now that her treatment would have been delayed for who knew how long. It was also true that, as my son Karstedt had warned, I might accidentally kill Rozemyne just by touching her.

That sure was dangerous a moment ago...

I wiped the sweat from my brow as the image of Rozemyne flying toward the tree flashed through my mind. The most I could do for her now was search for the other horse with Cornelius and identify the culprit.

"Cornelius! Follow me!"

"Yes, Grandfather."

The other horse had gone berserk as well, so we were able to pin the criminal down quickly enough. But this man was also a servant, not a schtappe-wielding noble. Given that Cornelius had seen a mana net ensnare Rozemyne, there had to be a noble among them.

"Who ordered you to do this?" I asked.

"I do not know. A noble dressed in black told me to do as he said, and so I obeyed."

I probed the area for the presence of others, but I couldn't sense anyone. For now, we had no choice but to take this servant with us.

As we tied him up, the red light of a knight requesting assistance flew into the air. I exchanged a look with Cornelius, then hefted the servant over my shoulder and raced deeper into the forest on my highbeast.

Upon reaching where the rott had been launched, we found that Angelica had tied up a black-clad noble.

"Lord Bonifatius, he's too heavy for me to carry. Could I ask for your assistance?"

"Excellent work, Angelica. Just leave it to me. Now... what fool dared to lay a hand on my granddaughter?"

I gripped the cloth covering the criminal's face and forcefully tore it off. He let out a sudden yelp of pain; apparently, I had managed to grab a chunk of his flesh as well. The man looked up at me with a pitiful expression. I recognized him.

"Viscount Joisontak..."

"Lord Bonifatius, I—!"

"Silence!" I barked.

Viscount Joisontak was related to Karstedt's late third wife, Rozemary. We were the most distant of relatives, but the sight of someone connected to my family participating in this crime made the blood rush to my head. I gritted my teeth and tightly gripped my schtappe, stabbing it around to disperse the anger compelling me to beat this man to death. He shuddered with fear the moment I looked down at him.

"State your excuses to Aub Ehrenfest; I have no desire to hear them. I am just barely resisting the urge to rip your head from your shoulders and smash it into pieces."

I bound Viscount Joisontak with magic, tied him to the servant, then brought the two of them back to the castle.

"Cornelius, report this to Aub Ehrenfest. I will keep watch so that this fool cannot escape. Angelica, stay with me. Not even I can risk moving alone."

"Understood."

Upon arriving at the prison, I tossed Viscount Joisontak into a cell made for holding criminal nobles and placed schtappe-sealing bracelets onto his wrists. Then, after listening to the basics of his story, I gagged him and finished locking him away.

"Angelica, we will be standing watch until Aub Ehrenfest summons him," I said, dropping down into a nearby chair. She looked between our prisoners and me, then sadly slouched her shoulders.

"You're so strong, Lord Bonifatius... I was using physical enhancements, but Lady Rozemyne was still kidnapped from right in front of me."

"You rescued Charlotte though, right? From what I understand of the situation, Rozemyne is the most at fault for ignoring Cornelius and flying off on her own. She was too reckless for someone who knows not how to protect herself. It's very possible that Charlotte would have died if not for your skill with your enhancements. You did well."

Angelica was fairly strong for a mednoble, and she used physical enhancement magic at a higher level than most others. Her current technique was certainly wasteful, as she needed to fill her entire body with mana to strengthen it, but even then, she was doing very well for someone her age.

Her face clouded over at my praise. "Is that really true? When I dedicate my mana to enhancements, I rarely have enough left over for anything else. And even when I do, I can't do any

Grandfather on the Day of the Baptism

other magic at the same time. If only I were able to summon my highbeast while using enhancements... Then I could have saved Lady Charlotte on my own, and Cornelius could have dedicated his efforts to protecting Lady Rozemyne," she lamented, biting her lip and regretfully lowering her blue eyes.

"Had you failed to do something that was within your capabilities, then that would absolutely be worth reflecting on. But there's no use bemoaning something that you knew you couldn't do from the very beginning, since no amount of thinking will change that fact."

As a member of the archducal family, I had a greater mana capacity than most. On top of that, my many years of using enhancements had made me skilled enough to focus them, strengthening only the parts that I needed to. This now came as naturally as breathing to me, but using enhancements as a whole wasn't easy. One could of course train to be more efficient, using the smallest amount of mana possible to enhance themselves, but it otherwise required one to have an enormous capacity.

Mastering enhancements was a staggering challenge, and so few archnobles bothered to use them, much less mednobles.

"If there's something you cannot do, all you need to worry about is learning how to do it. The fastest route to improving enhancements is to increase your mana capacity, but that is an eternal struggle in itself..."

Angelica had more mana than the average mednoble, but it would be hard for her to increase her capacity any further than she already had. I grumbled to myself, trying to think of a solution, when she slowly began to shake her head.

"I'm currently increasing my mana capacity using the Rozemyne Compression Method. It hasn't helped much yet, but it will in the future."

"The Rozemyne Compression Method?! What in the world is that?!"

I balked as Angelica gave me an explanation; it seemed that Rozemyne had thought up a new method of compressing mana. A short while before winter socializing had begun, the guard knights of all those in the archducal family except Wilfried were taught it, in addition to a portion of the Knight's Order. Wilfried's guard knights weren't yet included, since the Ivory Tower incident had occurred so recently and nobody knew what exactly was going to happen next.

"I haven't heard anything about this mana compression method!"

"I really don't think you need any more mana, Lord Bonifatius…"

"Shut up. As Rozemyne's grandfather, it is absolutely necessary that I learn about this before others do. What manner of compression method is it?"

Angelica placed a hand on her cheek and tilted her head. "I'm bound by a magic contract not to tell anyone, so you'll have to petition the archducal couple for Lady Rozemyne to teach you directly. She's the only one who can answer your questions."

Internally rejoicing over this new excuse to meet Rozemyne, I carved *"Have Rozemyne teach me her mana compression method"* into my mental schedule. Then, I began to stroke my beard.

"Alright, Angelica—if your mana capacity is going to increase, I'll train you myself. I'll spare no effort to ensure that Rozemyne's guard knights can protect her well."

"Really?" Angelica asked eagerly, her blue eyes shining with anticipation. "That makes me so happy, Lord Bonifatius. Please do!"

We exchanged a firm handshake, and just like that, I had acquired a new disciple.

"Since you can already do a full-body enhancement, how about you try using partial ones? It's important to be able to focus your mana into a specific part of your body to minimize waste."

"I see," came an unexpected but familiar voice. "I would benefit greatly from my master conserving her mana, but is there a certain trick to doing these partial enhancements?"

For some reason, when I began to teach Angelica about enhancements, it was her sword who replied—and in Ferdinand's voice, too. I couldn't help but stare at it.

"What is that...?"

"Stenluke. He can speak now, thanks to Lady Rozemyne gracing me with her mana."

It seemed that Angelica had obtained a talking manablade after Rozemyne had contributed to it. It could even memorize what it heard.

"Angelica, I would like that sword."

"I cannot give it to you. Stenluke is my precious manablade, and I worked hard for Lady Rozemyne to donate her mana to him. Would you be so willing to give away a gift that you yourself received from her, Lord Bonifatius?"

"...Good point. My mistake."

I understood how she felt in an instant; I would never be able to give away a present from my darling granddaughter.

That said, I would like a gift from Rozemyne as well. Perhaps I should raise a manablade myself and likewise have her pour some mana into it. Though I would much rather it speak in her voice than Ferdinand's...

Just as I was starting to seriously consider building my own manablade, Cornelius came in to get us. "Grandfather, the interrogation room has been prepared."

"Give your report first. What's the situation?"

"Sir! Since the culprit has been captured, the aub has allowed the nobles in the grand hall to return home, acknowledging that they all have alibis. They got into their carriages and promptly left while the Knight's Order kept watch for any suspicious movement. As for the nobles not in the grand hall... most were attendants serving the archducal family. They were all interrogated nonetheless, but as they were serving in the archducal couple's chambers and looking after the archduke's children, their alibis were quickly confirmed as well," Cornelius reported. "I must also announce that Lord Ferdinand has just returned from the temple."

"Angelica, enhance only your arm as best you can and carry this," I said, standing up and handing her the bound servant. "Follow me."

"Yes, Teacher!" she replied, accepting the man with a big nod. She tried enhancing just her arm, and while the mana still flowed throughout her entire body, it seemed to accumulate more in her arm than anywhere else. I considered that a success, at least to some degree.

"Teacher...?" Cornelius repeated, looking between us.

Angelica proudly puffed out her chest while carrying the criminal. "Lord Bonifatius has accepted me as a disciple. He'll be training me from now on."

"You're training under him of all people? I can't believe this. Are you insane?" Cornelius asked, completely aghast.

"Silence, weakling! You would dare say that when you always run from my training like a coward?!"

Cornelius faltered, then narrowed his eyes at me in annoyance. "On the contrary, I haven't run from your training even once, Grandfather. In fact, have you ever *allowed* me to run away?"

"Hmph! Of course not. Ah, Cornelius. I will train you as well. Rozemyne has no need for guard knights who are incapable of protecting her."

Grandfather on the Day of the Baptism

I wanted to protect Rozemyne myself, but being the son of the archduke from two generations ago meant that I was a member of the archducal family. My status did not allow me to serve as my granddaughter's guard knight, so all I could do to help protect her was train her guard knights.

"Grandfather, does this mean you also intend to train Damuel and Brigitte?"

"Of course. The more strong knights Rozemyne has, the better."

I thought about it for a short while, then realized that if Charlotte were kidnapped and Rozemyne's newly trained guard knights went to her rescue, then Rozemyne herself would once again end up unguarded. That completely defeated the point.

Perhaps I should just retrain every single guard knight serving the archducal family...

I pondered how best to train them on my way to the archduke's office, dragging the noble culprit behind me all the while. We soon reached a staircase, and he yelped in pain as his head beat against every single step. It was annoyingly loud, but I ignored him; I needed to focus on planning out a training regimen.

Rozemyne, I'm going to do all I can to make the guard knights serving the archducal family stronger.

When we reached the archduke's office, a guard knight standing outside opened the door for us. "Lord Bonifatius has arrived," he announced. Cornelius stepped in first, then me with Viscount Joisontak, then Angelica with the servant.

In the room were the brains of Ehrenfest: the archducal couple; Ferdinand; and Rozemyne's parents, who were standing by the back wall. Along the right wall were five higher-ups of the Knight's Order and one guard knight from each member of the archducal family, and along the left were Norbert and Rihyarda—the two managers of the castle's attendants—plus the archducal couple's scholar-officials.

I looked around at everyone gathered, noting that their eyes were all drawn to Viscount Joisontak. I gave Sylvester a nod.

"At your orders, Aub Ehrenfest, I have arrived."

"Good work, Bonifatius," Sylvester replied.

I looked toward Ferdinand. "Before the interrogation begins, allow me to ask... Is Rozemyne well?"

"Her life is no longer in danger, but I think it best that we refrain from discussing any details until the room has been cleared; there is no need for us to share undue information with a criminal."

Ferdinand made it sound as though he were referring to Viscount Joisontak, but his eyes made it clear that he was actually suggesting someone gathered here might be involved with the criminals. Sensing that, I had no choice but to postpone asking about Rozemyne.

"Now then, Bonifatius—tell us what happened after you rushed out of the grand hall," Sylvester said. And so began the interrogation.

I explained what had happened after I exited the grand hall, detailing how I had arrived at the battle before the other reinforcements due to my enhancements, crushed the skull of an enemy with a single punch, rescued Rozemyne, captured the servant, and then followed a rott to where Angelica had captured Viscount Joisontak.

"The servant appears to have only been following orders given to him by a black-clad noble. He knows only that he was to take a bag to a crestless carriage nearest to where he and the other servants work."

"Aub, there were indeed such carriages located there, just as Lord Bonifatius says," confirmed the knights who had observed the nobles going home.

Grandfather on the Day of the Baptism

Crestless carriages were for transporting attendants and servants. There were particular marks left on them so that the servants could still identify which carriage was theirs, but those marks were decided on an individual level, so outsider nobles wouldn't be able to identify them.

"Once all the nobles in the grand hall were gone, only Joisontak's crested carriage and three carriages without crests remained," one knight continued. "We expect that he brought the black-clad attackers along with his attendants and servants."

"...However, one of those crestless carriages was far removed from the others," another added. "Even if he had successfully kidnapped Lady Rozemyne, it would have been quite noticeable."

The knights all spoke as though Joisontak's guilt was already confirmed. That was understandable, given that he had been the only noble absent out of all those in the grand hall. The viscount, however, was shaking his head hard with tears in his eyes, unable to speak due to his gag but nonetheless trying to protest their claims.

There was no denying that Joisontak was guilty of a kidnapping, but something about his desperation caught my attention. I looked at Sylvester. He seemed to share my confusion, and waved a hand to silence the knights.

"Wait. I would like to hear Viscount Joisontak's perspective as well."

No sooner was his gag removed than Joisontak frantically cried out. "Aub Ehrenfest, I have but one crested carriage and two crestless carriages. I know nothing about the carriage that was far removed from the others. Furthermore, I did not kidnap Lady Rozemyne. Is it not true that I only kidnapped Lady Charlotte?"

Viscount Joisontak was adamant that he was not involved in Rozemyne's kidnapping whatsoever. In fact, he was so desperate to make that point clear that he spoke openly about everything he had actually done.

"Thoughts, Angelica?"

"It's true. Viscount Joisontak kidnapped Lady Charlotte, not Lady Rozemyne. After he tossed her away, he escaped to the east, putting him a considerable distance away from the south where Lady Rozemyne was rescued. I believe it is unreasonable to say that he is responsible for both."

A buzz ran through the room at Angelica's words, and Sylvester's expression hardened.

"In other words, there is another criminal among the nobility?"

"I suppose it would *technically* be possible that he turned south after fleeing to the east, captured Lady Rozemyne's highbeast, forced her to drink the potion, handed her over to the servant, then immediately fled back east to the management building..." Angelica stated with a serious expression, but everyone there knew that was something no normal human would be capable of.

I thought back to where Viscount Joisontak had been captured. It certainly was far away from where Cornelius had descended into the forest. Given how difficult it was to use a highbeast with so many trees blocking its wings, it was impossible for Viscount Joisontak to have committed both kidnappings.

Perhaps I would have just barely been able to pull off something like that, assuming I used my enhancements to their maximum ability and sprinted at full speed, but it was flat-out impossible for Viscount Joisontak. Were he capable of that level of enhancement, he never would have been captured by Angelica.

"Viscount Joisontak, who did you work with?" Sylvester asked, lightly drumming his fingers against his desk as he turned his gaze from Angelica to him.

"I worked alone," the viscount replied. "Considering the risk of someone else leaking the plan, I deemed that more reliable."

So he said, but it was clear he had been manipulated into doing this by someone else. Viscount Joisontak simply did not have it in him to think up and execute such a large-scale plan.

"In that case, Viscount Joisontak, explain in detail all that you have done."

The account that Joisontak proceeded to give was ridiculous enough to induce a room-wide headache. His thoughts were so foolish that even I, as someone who was not really known for thinking things through, found myself at a complete loss for words. It was no wonder then that Ferdinand, a person who actually specialized in concocting detailed plots whenever he wanted something done, had frozen in place with his hands pressed against his temples.

To summarize, Viscount Joisontak had planned to kidnap one of the archduke's children and hide them in the management building he had discovered in the forest during the hunting tournament. After capturing Wilfried or Charlotte, he would have told Rozemyne about the building and joined her in rescuing them to earn her favor. In the case that he kidnapped Rozemyne herself, he would have arrived to free her before anyone else, thereby earning her gratitude.

It was unbelievable.

How did he intend to tell Rozemyne where they were when he hasn't even been permitted to speak to her? And if she herself were kidnapped, I obviously would have arrived to rescue her before anyone else. What an idiot.

He had used black-clad Devouring servants to stall the guard knights, assuming that his involvement would go entirely undetected as he had hidden them in crestless carriages and planned to blow them up once he had escaped. It was a thoughtless, dead-end plan filled with more holes than I could count.

On top of that, this fool spent very little time in the Noble's Quarter, so he hadn't known that Rozemyne's highbeast could fly through the air. Her chasing after him was something that he hadn't even considered, so he threw Charlotte aside and fled in an attempt to avoid getting caught. But Angelica was able to apprehend him—another thing that he hadn't predicted at all.

In the end, Joisontak really hadn't thought that Rozemyne would love her adoptive sister enough to risk her life trying to rescue her, given that the two had only just met during the baptism ceremony.

My head ached as he described how the basic premise of his plot had been turned upside down. He had been stupid and reckless beyond words. With an imbecile like this rampaging about, the man who had kidnapped Rozemyne must have had an easy time hiding his momentary involvement.

Elvira let out a thoroughly exasperated sigh. "Rozemyne is the Saint of Ehrenfest—a compassionate young woman who shows kindness even to orphans. Did you not know that, despite proclaiming to be her family?"

"Lady Rozemyne is the daughter of my little sister Rozemary, which makes her my nie—"

"You are mistaken, Viscount Joisontak," Elvira interrupted with an icy cold smile, her near-black eyes trained on him in a quiet stare. "You are not her family. Rozemyne is *my* daughter. I attended her baptism ceremony as her mother, and she respects me as such."

Newborns were only recognized as noble children at their baptism ceremony, and those who interacted with them during it were firmly established as their mother and father. It wasn't rare for an especially skilled and mana-rich child of a concubine to be baptized as the child of a first wife, for example, but the lack of a blood relation meant it *was* rare for them to develop a positive relationship.

"I am truly glad that Rozemyne was born with no connection to you whatsoever; it would simply be too sad for her to be related to someone who kidnaps and poisons her despite believing himself to be her uncle," Elvira remarked. "She has no need for self-proclaimed family members who do nothing but harm her. Surely you understand how I feel as her mother?"

I could see the deep frustration lurking beneath Elvira's composed smile as she firmly cut all remaining ties with Rozemary's side of the family. Now that she had a just cause, she would no doubt eliminate them without mercy. Elvira had long suffered due to Karstedt's third wife; I knew this for a fact, since she had often come to me to discuss matters while Karstedt was away.

Of course, I also had no intention of showing mercy to those who had endangered my cute granddaughter's life. I was barely able to hold back from crushing the man's skull to bits as we spoke. The sooner he was dead, the better.

"Given that you poisoned the adopted daughter of the archduke, I imagine you will be executed posthaste," Elvira continued.

"I did not poison her, Lady Elvira! Why would I ever bring harm to Lady Rozemyne?! She is my niece!"

"She is nothing to you. Furthermore, regardless of whether or not you harmed Rozemyne, you attacked the castle and brought harm to Lady Charlotte, did you not?"

The viscount hung his head; his crimes were clear enough that having him executed was simply a matter of course. But we still did not know which noble had manipulated him from the shadows and harmed Rozemyne directly.

"Karstedt, did you confirm the identity of every noble in the grand hall after it was sealed?" I asked. As the commander of the Knight's Order, he had most likely managed the knights there while I was gone.

He gave a serious nod. "Yes. Everyone was checked, including those who returned from the bathroom. Nobody else was outside."

The knights lined up along the wall all nodded in agreement; the Knight's Order had checked over every noble in the grand hall to confirm their alibis.

Sylvester fixed Joisontak with a piercing gaze that made it clear no lies would go undetected. "Viscount Joisontak, did you consciously work with any co-conspirators?"

"...No, my lord, I did not."

It was then that Ferdinand slowly began to speak. He had been listening silently up until this point with a finger pressed against his temple. "What I am curious about are those who attacked the castle near the northern building. Were they truly your personal soldiers?"

"Lord Ferdinand, may I request permission to speak?" came a voice. It was Damuel, one of Lady Rozemyne's guard knights, looking up with steeled resolve.

It was rare for layknights to even ask for permission to speak in a meeting like this, but Ferdinand immediately allowed it.

"There is no doubt in my mind that they were Count Bindewald's personal soldiers," Damuel explained. "I checked their rings in the middle of the battle, and while my word alone may not be enough, they are the same ones I saw at the temple."

Count Bindewald was the criminal archnoble from Ahrensbach who had used forged documents from Veronica to enter the city without the archduke's permission. He then attacked the archduke's secretly adopted child, Rozemyne, and his half-brother, Ferdinand.

A stir ran through the room.

"Count Bindewald's? Surely you must be joking..." a knight murmured, bemused.

"He is not," Karstedt said, speaking up in support. "Damuel has served as Rozemyne's guard knight since before her baptism. He was there when Count Bindewald attempted to kidnap her."

Ferdinand nodded. "Did anyone else notice the rings?"

Some of the guard knights who had participated in the brawl did notice the rings on the black-clad attackers, but none had noticed the crest. What's more, according to the knights who had gathered evidence at the scene of the crime, no rings had survived the explosions. The observation of a single laynoble in the heat of battle was hardly strong evidence, but it seemed to be enough for Ferdinand.

"Viscount Joisontak, where did you get those soldiers? Why were they in your possession? Given their rings, they should belong to Count Bindewald."

"I-I have no idea. Giebe Gerlach gave them to me some time ago, saying that he no longer had a need for them. That's all. I had no idea they were connected to a criminal from another duchy..."

Viscount Joisontak's eyes were wide open in shock—he truly had just been a puppet manipulated into this. If we wanted any more worthwhile information from him, there was not much more we could do other than investigate his memories directly.

"...That is enough. We are done here. As you laid your hands on a member of the archducal family, your execution will not be up for debate," Sylvester said. He gestured for Viscount Joisontak to be taken away, and two knights stepped forward at once to remove him. "Summon Giebe Gerlach to me tomorrow."

"Yes, sir!"

Giebe Gerlach oversaw a province located next to that of Count Leisegang—the home province of my wife. I knew through her that the Gerlachs and the Leisegangs had been embroiled in an intense conflict for many years. I dug through my memories, searching for any other worthwhile information.

Now that I think about it, I remember my wife mentioning that Giebe Gerlach's wife had invited Georgine to a tea party...

Giebe Gerlach was summoned for questioning the next day. Unlike the night before, there were considerably fewer people in the room: the archducal couple, Ferdinand, Karstedt, myself, and five higher-ups in the Knight's Order.

"Now then, Giebe Gerlach—I have a question for you."

"Yes, my lord?" Gerlach replied. While he seemed confident and at ease, I could see his slightly soft belly tremble slightly. He was no well-trained knight.

He's a good height, though. He could be quite the fighter if only he trained a little. Good grief... What a waste of good youth. Take inspiration from my abs, young man!

As I placed a hand on my well-trained abs, considering whether the scholars needed to participate in my training as well, Giebe Gerlach blinked as though he didn't at all understand why he had been summoned.

"Why were you in possession of Count Bindewald's soldiers?" Sylvester asked.

"I do not recall having ownership of any such things."

"You are aware of the attack near the northern building last night, correct? The soldiers used once belonged to Count Bindewald."

"May I ask what that has to do with me?" the viscount asked, crossing his arms with a peaceful smile as though to say that he didn't understand the line of questioning at all. He intended to play dumb for as long as possible.

Sylvester returned a smile of his own. "We captured the criminal responsible for the attack, and he said that he received the soldiers from you, Giebe Gerlach. It is only natural that I would call you over to be questioned. And I do believe that your province is on good terms with Count Bindewald, is it not?"

Grandfather on the Day of the Baptism

"Oho, did he now...? I must say that I am quite the victim here," Giebe Gerlach replied, blinking dramatically. He then shook his head, looking around the room for sympathy. "It is true that I was on good terms with Count Bindewald and received soldiers from him, but at no point did I own them myself."

"Oh? Continue."

"As you wish. At the time, Count Bindewald had supposedly been permitted to enter the city, but it would have been improper for him to bring so many soldiers, so he decided to leave them in my province before his departure. He then committed a crime, as you know, and was imprisoned. Those related to him in Ahrensbach must have been punished somehow, as they stopped contacting me entirely."

"And?"

"Feeding and housing his soldiers was a strain on my expenses, but I could not simply cancel their contracts while Count Bindewald still lived. And so, I offered them to Viscount Joisontak, informing him that they would still be fine servants even if their contracts limited their value. I did not even consider that he would use them to cause trouble within the castle."

Ah. This man is a culprit as well...

The thought struck me out of nowhere. I couldn't explain why, but my gut was telling me he was guilty. Beneath his peaceful-looking smile was something more malicious—a nasty smugness that filled me with extreme disgust. I could have alleviated that feeling by beating his head in, but I had spent my entire life being warned again and again not to act purely on instinct. It was important to first have some justification that would be deemed acceptable by noble society.

"It is true that I gave Viscount Joisontak the soldiers, but I have nothing to do with this incident. As the Knight's Order has confirmed, I was in the grand hall. I knew nothing of the plan, nor that it would be executed last night," Giebe Gerlach said confidently.

The knights had indeed verified that he was present in the grand hall during the attack. There was no doubting he had caused trouble by giving the black-clad soldiers away, but that alone wasn't enough to accuse him of directly harming the archduke's children.

An infuriating arrogance burned in Giebe Gerlach's eyes, as though the matter were already settled. Everyone here surely had a bad feeling about him, but his alibi was genuine, so nobody here could challenge him further.

I knew he was the criminal, but how could I prove it...? I desperately tried to figure out how he could have been responsible for Rozemyne's poisoning without compromising his alibi. Thinking like this wasn't normally my job, but there had to have been some way for him to do it.

What would I have done if I weren't capable of enhancing magic...?

I crossed my arms, trying to consider as much as possible: the grand hall being sealed, the viscount's alibi, where I had saved Rozemyne, where Cornelius had initially entered the forest... In the meantime, the interrogation continued as I thought.

"Giebe Gerlach, was Viscount Joisontak the only person you gave Count Bindewald's soldiers to?" Ferdinand asked.

The giebe replied with an immediate nod. "Yes, he is the only one."

"So you no longer have any of his soldiers?" Ferdinand continued, deeply furrowing his brow.

"Of course. I no longer have any of the count's soldiers in my possession," he replied, his smile broadening and his eyes gleaming with a notable nastiness. Ferdinand gave a thin smile in return.

"That will do," Sylvester interjected. He then jutted his chin toward the door. "You may leave," he said to Giebe Gerlach.

The giebe gave a humble bow and then exited. Only once the door was completely shut did I turn to Sylvester.

"Aub Ehrenfest," I said, my eyes flitting to the tapestry behind him. Through it was the Mana Replenishment hall; I was trying to signal that I wanted to discuss something with him that could be known only to members of the archducal family.

Sylvester noticed my gesture and stood up with a small nod. "I am going to enter the Mana Replenishment hall with Bonifatius. Karstedt, guard the office in my absence. Everyone else, please wait until we return."

And so Sylvester and I entered the Mana Replenishment hall. The feystone containing the divine colors of the gods turned in the midst of the pure-white space. The moment we were inside, Sylvester dropped his solemn archduke expression and allowed his exhaustion to show on his face. I too dropped my formal airs, relaxing my shoulders.

"What've you got for me, Uncle?"

"You said that the grand hall was sealed, yes? Was the entire hall sealed?"

Sylvester, probably remembering Giebe Gerlach's attitude from earlier, gave a frustrated nod. "Yeah, the Knight's Order sealed off the entire hall. What're you getting at here?" he asked, knitting his brow. There was a mix of emotions in his dark-green eyes—annoyance at being doubted, but also hope at the thought I might have noticed something important.

"Including the passages for servants and the secret exit known only to archdukes and their successors?"

Sylvester widened his eyes with shock, then looked up slightly as he tried to recall exactly what had transpired in the grand hall. "The servant passageways were sealed off, as I remember, but not the secret exit."

Secret exits were generally known only to the archduke; they were such critical escape routes that not even the Knight's Order was informed of their existence. As such, it was hard to imagine that any guards had been posted on either end of the passageway in the grand hall: while they had been ordered to secure it, they couldn't seal off something that was unknown to them.

"I found Rozemyne around the area of the forest frequented by servants, but Cornelius had descended before me and found the feystone for her highbeast much farther away. If we operate under the assumption Giebe Gerlach handed Rozemyne to the servants and then had them leave by horse, he must have at one point been around where Cornelius descended."

Once I explained precisely where Cornelius had entered the forest, a look of complete disbelief arose on Sylvester's face. I continued.

"These are ancient memories, so I cannot be too sure of them, but... my father once told me there is a passageway leading from the grand hall to that area of the forest. Is this true?"

"It is. But isn't that passageway supposed to be known only to archdukes?" Sylvester asked with a frown, admitting its existence while giving me a look that demanded an explanation.

"I'm a bit older than your father, remember? I too received a full archduke's education."

It had happened back when my little brother—Sylvester's father who would later become the archduke—was still young. My father, the reigning archduke, had become critically ill, and while he did eventually recover after a hard-fought battle, I had received a full archduke's education to preserve the line of succession in the case that he died before my little brother came of age.

"Is there any chance that Georgine leaked the information to the viscount? This is only a gut feeling, but it certainly could have happened..."

"Impossible! Georgine, knowing the existence of the passageway? Do you not remember how much she agonized over losing the archducal seat because of me?" Sylvester asked, his confusion clear on his face. It was then that I realized his understanding of the situation wasn't quite the same as everyone else's.

Sylvester seemed to think that Georgine had been married to another duchy instead of becoming the archduchess, much like many unremarkable members of the archducal family were. But to those who knew her from birth, she was a highly skilled woman who had been trained to take the archducal seat from the very beginning.

Georgine had only been wed to another duchy because she was so obsessed with becoming the next archduchess that the archducal couple at the time determined she would never work well with Sylvester, and so sent her to Ahrensbach.

At the time, they had hoped she would support Sylvester and use her abilities for the sake of Ehrenfest, just as I had done for my little brother. It was likely the previous archducal couple had such naive hopes because I hadn't much cared about taking the seat, despite having received an archduke's education myself.

"Sylvester, you knew Georgine for only a few years, after you were moved to the northern building. But before then—before you were baptized—she received an archduchess's education right up until she came of age. It is safe to say that everything you know, she knows too."

Sylvester squeezed his eyes shut, then nodded. "Do you have any proof that Georgine was involved? Or Giebe Gerlach? If so, I can—"

"As I said, this is only a gut feeling. I am certain he's involved, though. I'd recommend discussing this with Ferdinand. Have him scrounge up some evidence or lay out a trap of sorts. I'm not good at this kind of detailed work; my expertise only reaches as far as identifying enemies and crushing them. But rest assured, once you give me permission, his skull will be in pieces."

"Come on, that's not making it easy for me... But I have to admit, Uncle, your animal instincts are always too on the money for me to ignore. I'll assume that Giebe Gerlach is indeed the culprit and have Ferdinand investigate him. He'll probably complain about the extra work, but..." Sylvester trailed off, stroking his chin with a frown as he started to work things through in his head.

"Good. It's best to leave the thinking to Ferdinand. This isn't something that either of us should be taking into our own hands, obviously."

If Sylvester made any moves, our enemies would figure everything out in an instant. It was best to leave this kind of work to Ferdinand and his pet scholars.

"That said, now you can safely refuse Georgine's visit," I continued. "Wilfried invited her back, but he's now being punished, and the soldiers who rampaged in the castle belonged to an Ahrensbach noble. We have plenty of reasons to refuse her return on the grounds of security. Should buy us a few years, don't you think?"

"You're right. I'll need to turn her down and buy us enough time to get Ehrenfest back on its feet."

Sylvester needed to close the border to Ahrensbach nobles, who had now repeatedly exposed the archducal family to danger. He would then use that time to strengthen his retainers and Florencia's faction, all while weakening the lingering Veronica faction.

"This is what it means to be the archduke. Do your job. I'll beat some sense into the archducal family's guard knights and do what I can to strengthen the Knight's Order."

"Thank you, Uncle." Sylvester's eyes gleamed as he looked toward the future.

I exited the Mana Replenishment chamber with newfound motivation, but when Ferdinand told me that the poison would put Rozemyne to sleep for at least a year, I barely resisted the urge to chase Giebe Gerlach down and smash his face into a wall.

"You'll let me hit him at least once out of anger for denying me a year's worth of time with my granddaughter, right?" I asked with a completely serious expression.

Sylvester's eyebrows shot up in anger. "If you want permission for that, come to me with evidence! Your instincts aren't enough! Until you've done that, then no!"

It's beyond obvious to me that he's a culprit, but I suppose real life isn't always that simple...

In the end, it took not one year for Rozemyne to awaken, but nearly two. I had been denied entry to the temple despite wanting to check up on her, and so I repeatedly sent ordonnanzes to Ferdinand requesting updates, venting my worry and unease by training the archducal family's guard knights as mercilessly as I could.

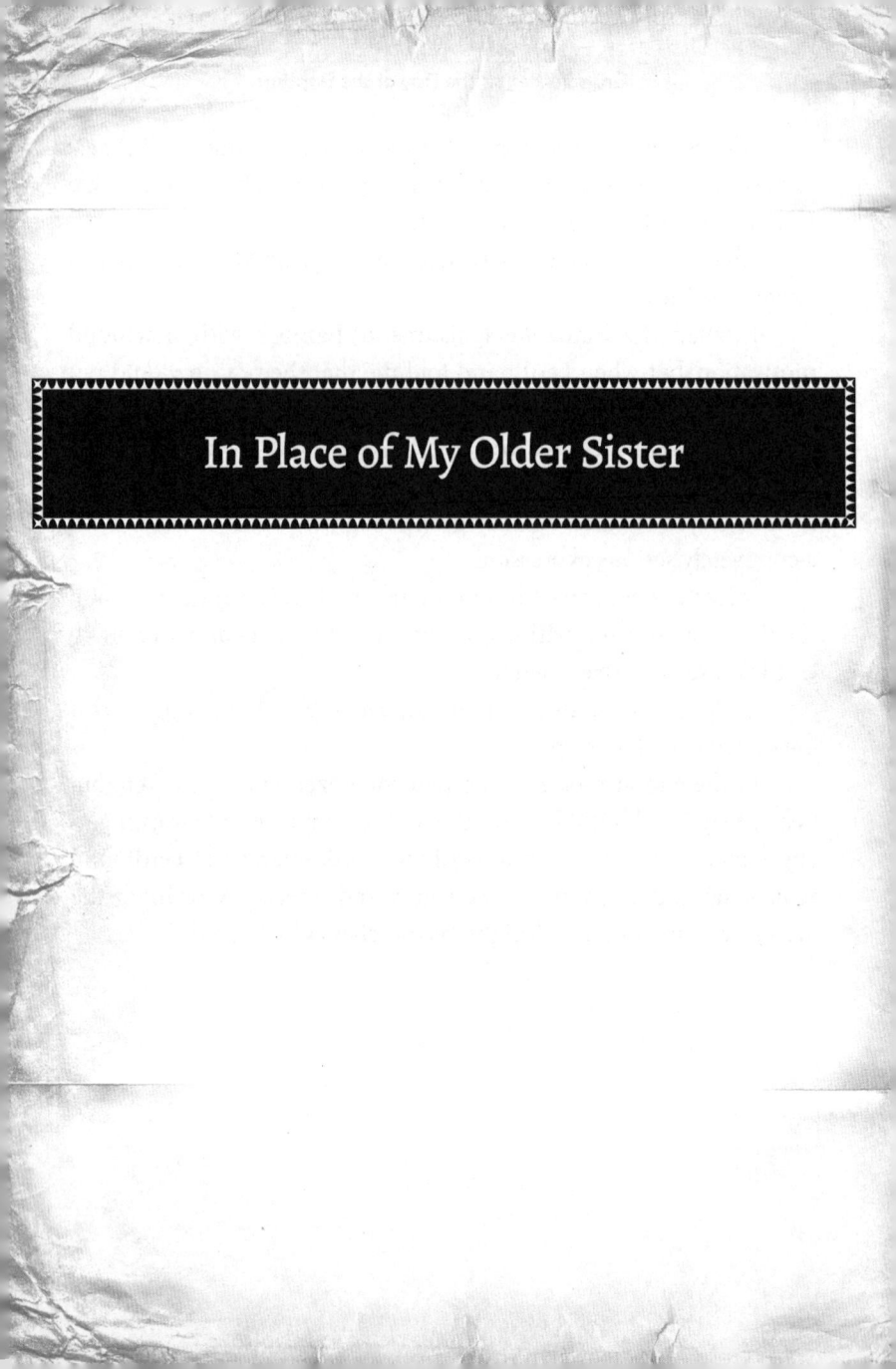

In Place of My Older Sister

This morning, right after breakfast, Father, Mother, and Uncle Ferdinand visited the northern building. I was called to my older brother's room as well, where I was told the details of last night's attack.

They had caught one of the culprits, but it was likely that even more people were involved behind the scenes. My older sister Rozemyne had almost died after being poisoned, and to dissolve her hardened mana, she would need to use a potion called a jureve and sleep for over a year.

My older sister, who had used her own guard knights to save me, putting her own safety on the line...

I started to sob, only for my uncle to scold me for wasting my strength. "There is no use crying when you could be working to repay her," he said with a stern expression. "Crying is easy, and to be frank, it is a waste. I would much rather you dedicate your time and energy to filling the hole created by Rozemyne's absence."

Father warned Uncle Ferdinand that he was being too harsh, while Mother told me that Rozemyne would certainly not be happy to know that she was the reason for my tears.

I dried my eyes and looked up, at which point Uncle Ferdinand asked Wilfried and me to lead the winter playroom in Rozemyne's place.

If he wants me to repay her, then I'll do everything I can to take on her duties while she's gone.

"As for the upcoming Spring Prayer, I would like to request Wilfried's assistance," Uncle Ferdinand continued. "He performed Mana Replenishment during the Archduke Conference, and Charlotte cannot help due to her inexperience controlling mana."

This was no laughing matter; I was being removed from Spring Prayer right after steeling my resolve to repay Rozemyne. What else could I do now that I was being denied my best opportunity to repay her?

"Uncle, I *can* help! If all I need to do is get used to controlling mana, then I can practice during the winter, just as Wilfried practiced during the Archduke Conference. I too am a child of the archduke; please allow me to do what I can to make up for the absence of my sister, who was only poisoned because of what she did for my sake."

My teachers had all said that I was more skilled than Wilfried, given how often he ran from his studies. By working hard, I could surely make up for Rozemyne's absence.

"Charlotte, controlling mana is not easy," Father said. "Learning will be a painful, arduous process. If that's fine with you, then do as you wish. Being able to control mana and see with your own eyes what Rozemyne has been doing will surely be good for your growth."

"Yes, Father."

"I'll go to Spring Prayer too!" Wilfried declared to Uncle Ferdinand with tightly clenched fists. "I can't just let Rozemyne keep saving me without helping her in return!"

I stared at my brother, my eyes wide with surprise. This was not the Wilfried I knew—the Wilfried who was kind but lazy.

"Very well, you two. Practice controlling your mana by pouring it into the foundational magic over the winter. You will be supported by Bonifatius and the archducal couple."

"Ferdinand..." Father began with a grimace, but my uncle simply grinned and gave him a diligent bow.

"May you assign them their duties for Spring Prayer, Aub Ehrenfest."

After asking Father to take care of our mana practice and assign us to our duties for Spring Prayer, Uncle Ferdinand gave both Wilfried and me letters.

"These are from Rozemyne," he said. "Written in them are schedules and plans for the winter playroom. I do not expect you to lead it as well as Rozemyne did, but please do what you can."

"Right!"

And so came our first goal: leading the winter playroom. I hugged Rozemyne's letter to my chest as I headed there with Wilfried. To make what was written a reality, my brother and I needed to work together.

Uncle Ferdinand had said that he would be sending Rozemyne's head attendant and guard knights to the playroom, but her personnel were returning to the temple. He wanted us to use our own personnel well, and to take in the advice of those around us as we progressed.

Uncle said he didn't think we could lead the playroom as well as Rozemyne, but she managed to do it when she was my age. I'll show him that I can do just as good a job!

"Good evening, everyone."

Since I had been told to get help from as many people as possible, I called over all of Rozemyne's guard knights and attendants to show them the letters, starting with her teacher Moritz. The letters described having students of the Royal Academy gather information on duchies and take extensive notes during lectures to abet the creation of study guides. They would be rewarded for their work depending on the quality of the information and how detailed their notes were.

"What will they be receiving as payment, exactly?" one of the guard knights asked.

"Money, though I do not understand where Lady Rozemyne's comes from," Cornelius answered. "What are your budgets, Lord Wilfried and Lady Charlotte? Do they come from your head attendants, or would we need to speak with Aub Ehrenfest?"

I moved to explain my budget to Rozemyne's apprentice guard knights, but before I could, another guard knight waved his hand in the air.

"Lady Rozemyne's budget is handled by her guardian, Lord Ferdinand, as she often traveled between the castle and temple," he explained. "She will determine the value of the information, so I think we should start by paying a small fee to all those who provide any. Lady Rozemyne can then pay them in full when she awakens."

"I see. In that case, I would like for you and Brigitte to manage the information and handle the payments, Damuel. I'll get the students at the Royal Academy to begin gathering the information and making their study guides."

Rozemyne's guard knights swiftly distributed the work between themselves. But for some reason, Angelica, who had shown such splendid initiative when rescuing me, seemed to be keeping her distance from the conversation.

"Can we expect the help of Lord Wilfried's and your retainers at the Royal Academy, Lady Charlotte?" Cornelius asked.

"Why of course. Ernesta, I trust you to help them."

"You may count on me, Lady Charlotte."

Wilfried's and my apprentice guard knights gave a firm nod as well, agreeing to fulfill Cornelius's request.

In Place of My Older Sister

"Lady Charlotte, I do believe that Cornelius and the others will handle this Royal Academy business just fine. What instructions did Lady Rozemyne leave regarding the winter playroom?" Rozemyne's head attendant Rihyarda asked. I knew her well, since she had previously served as Father's head attendant, so I could show her the letter without worry.

It said to continue having the children read and write based on their individual ability, since new picture books were coming soon; to increase the number of digits in their multiplication and division exercises; and to recover the picture books and toys lent out the previous year before going through the rental process again.

"Professor Moritz, will we be able to accomplish what Rozemyne did last year?" I asked.

"I will ensure that we do," he said with a deliberate nod. "Last year, Lady Rozemyne handled the children with expert dexterity and motivated them to study through various means. I myself am a professor here—a teacher. I will use Lady Rozemyne's methods as a reference to make it through the winter."

"Yeah, I'll help make up for Rozemyne's absence too!" Wilfried declared, having experienced last year's winter playroom firsthand.

Rihyarda fell into thought, then raised a hand to swiftly interrupt the discussion. "I hate to say this when you're all so motivated, but once everyone has greeted Lady Charlotte, it would be best to explain Lady Rozemyne's absence, simply state our plans for the playroom this year, and then conclude things for today."

"Oh my, but why?" I asked. "I can do as the letter says just fine."

"Everything requires preparation. Lady Rozemyne prepared sweets as a reward for the children who won last year, but could you ask the same of your chefs?"

I hadn't planned for that kind of thing at all. As I faltered in surprise, Rihyarda looked up a little, as if recalling what Rozemyne had done.

"Lady Rozemyne had her personal musician help with harspiel practice, selected books for the children to transcribe based on their particular skill levels, organized the children into groups for karuta and card tournaments, and prepared sweets and the like to reward the winners. You would be hard-pressed to do the same so abruptly, especially considering that you did not see Lady Rozemyne work last year. It would be best if you instead spent today distributing the workloads and preparing for tomorrow."

None of what Rihyarda had explained was mentioned in the letters.

"That's easy to say, but we still don't know what to do," Wilfried interjected. "Do you, Rihyarda?"

"Oh yes, Wilfried, my boy. I certainly do."

At Rihyarda's direction, Professor Moritz prepared tests to measure the abilities of those in the playroom, while we organized the workloads of our personal musicians and the like. Wilfried's guard knights would work alongside the Knight's Order to start training the children.

As I watched the others busily moving about, I received my first greetings from the children. I had been informed ahead of time which ones had tricked Wilfried during the autumn hunting tournament, and I needed to memorize their faces well. One of the challenges awaiting me this winter was carefully choosing how I interacted with them.

"Lady Charlotte, I was told that Lady Rozemyne would be resting for a very long time. May I ask just how long that will be?" a laynoble named Philine asked quietly, having been at the end of the line waiting to greet me. I could sense her worry about my sister in her wavering grass-green eyes.

In Place of My Older Sister

"I am truly sorry, but I do not know the exact details either."

"Lady Rozemyne said during the winter playroom last year that she would turn my mother's stories into a book. This year, I worked hard and wrote the stories out myself instead of simply speaking them aloud for her to transcribe. I was hoping she would like to see them..." Philine explained before sadly lowering her gaze.

I was not capable of making a book for her; it was my very first day and I was already failing. My pride and self-confidence had swelled over my years of working hard to be worthy of my status, all the while being told that I was more competent than my brother, but now that assurance was starting to crack.

Our challenge began the next day. We started measuring the children's knowledge using the tests that Professor Moritz had diligently written up overnight. Meanwhile, Wilfried relied on memory to put last year's teams back together and set up games with the karuta and playing cards.

And we actually have sweets prepared today...

During the games, I was entrusted with looking over the group of newly baptized children. I needed to secure as many wins as I could here to establish myself as an unbeatable wall, just as my sister had done the year before.

Unfortunately, my resolve was shattered to pieces in the blink of an eye. The children had practiced karuta and cards with their siblings over the year, and they were now so good that I had no chance of winning. In comparison, I had only ever been able to practice during Wilfried's occasional visits, so the children promptly demolished me.

As infinitely frustrating as it was, I couldn't simply give up and accept defeat. But as I prepared for a second round, a guard knight named Damuel quietly called out to me. He wished to see my sister's letters so that they could handle the study materials currently being returned.

"What exactly do you mean when you refer to returning study materials?" I asked.

"Lady Rozemyne lent out study materials in exchange for stories, for the sake of laynobles who could not afford them. Ah, yes—the list of borrowers is right here."

The list of names that I hadn't understood the purpose of turned out to be those who had borrowed study materials and the stories they had offered. Damuel requested that I summon them all together.

I called for the laynobles to return their study materials, and they promptly gathered with them in hand. A guard knight named Brigitte delicately put the materials into a wooden box while Damuel marked their names off on the list. As I watched their perfect teamwork, the games of karuta that the older children had been playing came to an end.

"The winners shall now be given sweets," I announced.

"Yesss!" came the excited cries. "I've been waiting all year for this!"

With that, I distributed the sweets among the children who had won. They rejoiced and immediately began to devour them, but then their expressions changed. For the briefest moment, they looked at their rewards with a frown, then forced a smile back onto their faces and politely commented, "These are delicious."

I tilted my head in confusion, at which point Wilfried stepped in. "Sorry, everyone... Rozemyne is sick this year, so her personal chefs aren't here. They won't be the same sweets as last year."

It was then that I remembered the sweets I had eaten during my first tea party with Rozemyne and understood everything. They were all delicacies I had never eaten before, each one more delicious than the last. None of my personal chefs were capable of making them.

I sadly lowered my eyes, but as the sorrow swept over me, Philine quietly took my hands. "There is no need for you to feel so down, Lady Charlotte. The fact that there is a reward at all is more than enough," she said. "I don't get to eat sweets often at home, so I'm delighted to be rewarded with them."

"That's right, Charlotte. My personal chefs wouldn't be able to make any of those sweets either," Wilfried reassured me. "Rozemyne came up with them herself, so they're special. Her attendants told me all about it."

It seemed that Rozemyne had not only been making picture books, but sweets as well.

Will I truly be able to fill the hole that my sister left behind…?

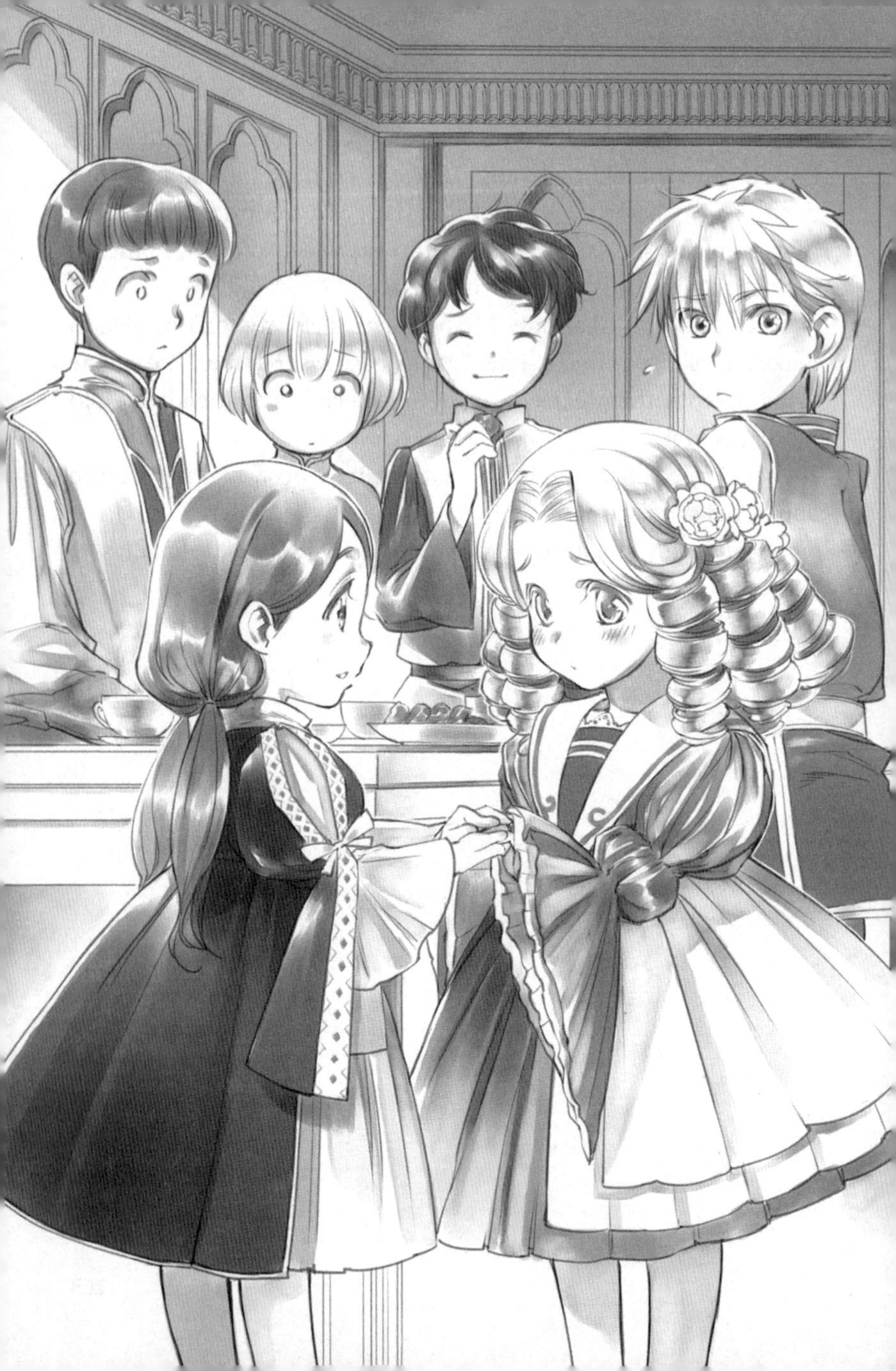

In Place of My Older Sister

Supper came and went with me having failed to do anything right, and then began my first magic lesson.

I registered my mana in Father's office, then entered the Mana Replenishment hall for the first time. It was a strange room with a massive magic tool, which I would be providing with mana—not my own, mind you, but mana that was already stored in feystones. Wilfried was going to be supported by Bonifatius, while I was being supported by Mother.

"Place your hand on top of the feystone like so, then visualize your mana flowing deep, deep into it," Mother explained while placing her hand atop mine. I gripped the feystone firmly, determined to succeed this time.

"I am one who offers prayer and gratitude to the gods who have created the world," Father began.

As he prayed, I could feel the mana in the feystone start flowing into me. Having someone else's mana trying to enter me was a gross sensation, so I hurriedly pushed for it to flow out the opposite side of the feystone. It required an immense amount of strength to fight against the flow, and despite trying my best to focus, I could feel my head getting increasingly fuzzy.

"That's enough," Father said, at which point Mother took the feystone out of my hand. The pressure I had been so desperately resisting went away all at once, allowing a wave of exhaustion to wash over me. I ended up crumpling down onto the floor; I didn't have the energy to move at all.

But while I was so exhausted that I could barely even move my mouth to speak, Wilfried stood up normally and said, "Whew! Glad that's over."

"You sure seem energetic, Wilfried…"

"He was as exhausted as you the first time he did it, Charlotte. He sure has grown," Father said with a chuckle.

Wilfried gave a big nod. "I think I got used to it when we were offering mana every day throughout spring. Rozemyne used her own mana for this, not relying on the feystones, but even then she was totally fine. She said that she was already used to doing it because of the Dedication Ritual. She collapses if she so much as runs, sure, but Mana Replenishment is nothing to her."

Wilfried tried to console me by saying I would get used to it, but hearing those words only brought tears to my eyes.

"Charlotte, are you okay?! Was it so hard that it's making you cry?!"

"No, Wilfried. It's just... Never in my wildest dreams did I think I would be so useless. I cannot fill the hole left by Rozemyne at all."

I had visualized myself doing so much better. Rozemyne had fallen into a long sleep because of me, so I at least wanted to do an excellent job of repaying her. I had hoped that I could contribute enough to make her proud of what I had done, but instead, I was failing at everything.

"Charlotte, don't compare yourself to Rozemyne," Father said. "It is her abundance of both knowledge and mana that led to her becoming known as the Saint of Ehrenfest—one worthy of being adopted by the archduke. There's no need for you to completely fill the hole she left. Just do what you can and put your all into it. You're doing very well."

He tried to console me as well, but I was still frustrated with myself. I had never thought there would be such a huge gap between us, especially considering that she was only one year older than me. Taking her place during her absence was the only thing I could do to repay her for what she had done, but I just couldn't manage it.

My day ended with me feeling miserable and defeated.

In Place of My Older Sister

Once the students had departed for the Royal Academy, it was time to focus on the children's studies for real. We needed to alternate between writing and math lessons, schedule different musicians for harspiel practice, organize groups for karuta and cards based on their skill levels, prepare sweets as their rewards, take on the roles of unbeatable rivals to motivate them to grow, and manage the stories that the children brought us.

We encountered many problems here as well, but each time one arose, Wilfried and I asked those around us what Rozemyne had done. We were doing our best to lead the winter playroom as smoothly as possible.

"Did Rozemyne really do all this on her own...?" I whispered in semi-disbelief.

Professor Moritz sighed and shrugged his shoulders. "I do recall Lady Rozemyne giving me various suggestions before class started each day, but I never would have guessed that she micromanaged things so carefully. She sometimes participated in the games, but it had seemed to me that she otherwise only ever read books or wrote out stories."

It seemed that Rozemyne had been carefully observing the expressions of the children while writing down the stories for her picture books, and when they grew restless, she would suggest switching over to math. Only now did Professor Moritz realize the importance of doing this. What's more, it was a lot easier to lose track of time when teaching a large group of children compared to a single student.

As Wilfried and I spent our days struggling to lead the winter playroom as described, Uncle Ferdinand arrived with a new task for us to complete. He had delivered us each a sizable stack of boards, saying that we needed to memorize them all before Spring Prayer.

There were three boards' worth of prayers and traditional greetings that we had to learn as a bare minimum, five boards we would really want to have memorized, and two boards of extra content for us to memorize if we wanted to do exactly what our dedicated sister had done.

"Seems like Rozemyne really memorized all of these; her temple attendants told me about it. Well... I'm just gonna go with these three for now. It won't be much, but I won't make any mistakes this way."

As much as I wanted to say that I would memorize all ten to better make up for Rozemyne's absence, I no longer had the confidence that I could do exactly what she had done. My pride had been shattered to pieces, and so I took only three boards, just like my brother.

"...Rozemyne sure is incredible, isn't she?" I muttered weakly as I looked over the rows upon rows of densely packed words constituting all the prayers I needed to learn.

"Yep," Wilfried agreed. "Rozemyne's incredible. That's why we need to catch up as much as we can while she's asleep."

I was genuinely impressed that Wilfried had the motivation to work so hard when his goal was to catch up to Rozemyne. My heart had grown dark with thoughts that she was too special and forever beyond my reach, but his sincerity seemed to be shining a bright light on me that chased the shadows away.

"I'll catch up to both you and her, Wilfried!"

We competed with each other to learn as many of the prayers as possible, and even if we couldn't do everything that Rozemyne had done, we had gotten a respectable grip on leading the playroom properly by the time spring was around the corner.

Goodness, time passes by so quickly, doesn't it?

I sighed in relief at our busy winter finally coming to a close, at which point Philine came walking over. "Lady Charlotte, will you be lending out and selling study materials this year as well?" she asked.

In Place of My Older Sister

Only then did I remember that the Plantin Company had sold learning goods last year. I paled at the realization that I hadn't planned for that at all.

How could I forget?! It was right there in Rozemyne's letters! What do I do?!

The one who saved me from my floundering was none other than Damuel. He was so skilled when it came to planning and other administrative duties that I genuinely questioned whether he was a scholar instead of a knight. After I told him the problem, barely holding back my tears, he instantly sent an ordonnanz to Uncle Ferdinand, who then got permission from Father to use the playroom for business and scheduled for the Plantin Company to visit at the end of winter.

"Thank you for your help, Damuel."

"This is nothing compared to being dragged around by Lady Rozemyne, trying to realize her crazy ideas," he replied with a peaceful smile. And then it hit me—serving someone special like my sister was so difficult that even the knights had to do the work of scholars to keep up.

Of course I can't do exactly what Rozemyne does... She's special. One of a kind.

I had started to make peace with myself when springtime came. For Spring Prayer, both Wilfried and I would be leaving the city of Ehrenfest for the first time and traveling across the Central District. It would be a journey that lasted half a month, which meant we needed to prepare three carriages and quite a significant amount of luggage.

Our attendants in the castle knew little about religious affairs, so Wilfried was being served by one of Uncle Ferdinand's attendants, while I was being served by Fran, one of my sister's temple attendants.

"It is an honor to serve you, Lady Charlotte."

"The honor is mine as well, Fran. Would you kindly tell me more about my sister?"

"If you have a question that you wish for me to answer, please do not hesitate to ask."

We first headed to Hasse, our carriage rattling along as we went. On the way there, Fran explained what relationship my sister had with the city: she had saved its citizens by negotiating with Uncle Ferdinand after they committed treason, educated them, and overall acted just as one would expect a saint to act.

"Lady Rozemyne despises death far more than one would ever expect. She persistently searches for resolutions where nobody has to die, and I feel that she often experiences great difficulty as a result. This value she places on human life is the reason she treats even orphans and gray priests such as myself with care and respect," he said, a small, proud smile forming on his face.

I started to worry a little, wondering whether my own attendants and guard knights admired me so sincerely. I had been taught that nobles needed to use their subordinates well, but it was only upon seeing how respected Rozemyne was that I myself wanted to become someone who my retainers could look up to.

"Fran, is there anything that my sister especially likes? I would like to give her a gift when she awakens, to thank her for saving me."

"Lady Rozemyne loves books to such an extent that no other answer comes to mind. All her temple attendants know this, and so we are all working hard to create as many new books for her as possible."

When we arrived at Hasse, we were welcomed by its people with an almost manic fervor. To them, this was no normal Spring Prayer, but a special one that showed the archduke had forgiven them after an entire year of grueling perseverance.

In Place of My Older Sister

The stage for Spring Prayer had already been set up. Fran went up first to put the chalice—a divine instrument—into place and lead into the ceremony. Meanwhile, I was changed into ceremonial robes in the carriage, with both the white High Bishop robes and the spring hair stick that I was due to wear belonging to Rozemyne.

Incidentally, Wilfried had brought the ceremonial blue robes that had previously been made for Rozemyne, albeit with a few minor modifications so they would fit him. We had no other choice, since having underage children perform these ceremonies was usually unheard of, and the only child-sized ceremonial robes available belonged to her.

"I'm ready."

"You risk dirtying your robes, Lady Charlotte. Please allow me."

As I attempted to descend the carriage's steps, Fran picked me up and began walking me to the stage. I had never been carried like this in the castle, and Fran gave a bit of an uncomfortable smile as he saw my eyes widen in surprise.

"Lady Rozemyne walks at an exceptionally leisurely pace and often comes close to tripping over her robes, so I carry her when we are at farming towns. I understand that this must be unusual and perhaps even unpleasant for you, Lady Charlotte, but please forgive my rudeness; the ground is wet and slippery."

Fran climbed onto the stage and set me down behind the podium with the divine instrument on it. There were more people gathered before me than all the nobles who had attended my debut, and I could feel their eyes boring holes into me. Their fervent, desperate looks were so intense that I was struck with the urge to simply flee the stage in fear.

I was conscious that I was even more nervous than I had been during my baptismal debut, in part because seeing Rozemyne's reassuring smiles and hearing her voice had been enough to ease my fears about my performance. Only a single season had passed since then, yet it already felt like forever ago.

What if I fail? Everyone will surely be disappointed that I couldn't do what my sister could...

As I anxiously tensed up, the town chiefs who would be receiving the blessings came up onto the stage with large buckets. They all had hopeful looks in their eyes as they approached me, and I could feel my throat drying up.

As my mind swam with thoughts of failure, Fran stepped forward and handed me a single feystone dyed a light yellow. "Lady Charlotte, this is the feystone you will be using for this blessing. I am told it is filled with Lady Rozemyne's mana," he explained. "Please deliver her mana to the people she has shown so much concern for. This is something that only you can do. You practiced extensively for this day, correct? Please pray and offer up Lady Rozemyne's mana."

Only I can deliver my sister's mana to Hasse...

I had declared that I would fill the void left by my sister, so this was something that I absolutely had to do without fail. After a few deep breaths, I touched the feystone filled with Rozemyne's mana against the feystone on the divine instrument. Then, I slowly opened my mouth.

"O Goddess of Water Flutrane, bringer of healing and change. O twelve goddesses who serve by her side. The Goddess of Earth Geduldh has been freed from the God of Life Ewigeliebe. I pray that you grant your younger sister the power to birth new life."

In Place of My Older Sister

I forcefully pushed my mana against the feystone so that its mana would flow into the chalice, which made it start glowing a bright yellow. The gathered citizens let out cries of awe and excitement, but I kept my eyes lowered and continued the prayer.

"I offer to you our joy and songs of glee. I offer to you our prayers and gratitude, so that we may be blessed with your purifying protection. I ask that you fill the thousand lives upon the wide mortal realm with your divine color."

When I was done, Fran deftly took the chalice and poured the glowing green liquid within into the lined-up buckets.

I was a little more used to controlling mana than before, but performing my first divine ritual in front of this many people was surprisingly exhausting. In a somewhat embarrassing display, I collapsed into a sitting position atop the stage, lacking the strength to move.

"You did excellently, Lady Charlotte. Please take this, a potion for rejuvenating one's mana, as a token of the High Priest's appreciation of your efforts," Fran said, holding out a potion with a smile.

"Thank you."

I gratefully took the potion and opened it, only to be struck with a painfully foul odor. I instinctively looked up at Fran, wondering whether this was a cruel prank of some kind.

"Fran, the potion seems to smell quite horrible... Is this truly for drinking?"

"Lady Rozemyne said something similar when she was first given one, but yes, it is indeed a potion for you to drink. The High Priest uses these when he needs to recover Lady Rozemyne's health in as short of a period as possible. The smell and taste are both terrible, but it is very effective."

I drank the potion, swallowing desperately as I tried to hold back the tears and stop myself from throwing up. The taste was so terrible that my tongue tingled and the tears broke through, streaming down my cheeks, but my exhaustion faded in an instant and I could move again. Even then, though, it wasn't a potion that I wanted to drink again in my life.

"Lady Rozemyne used these potions to recover her mana and strength while performing the ceremonies, drinking one whenever she ran out of mana or energy so that she was ready for the next. Each of her Spring Prayers and Harvest Festivals have been similar. If necessary, please do not hesitate to ask for another; the High Priest has given me many potions for this occasion, and Spring Prayer is far from over."

Rozemyne performed ceremony after ceremony while drinking these potions, all so she could offer up her mana for the sake of Ehrenfest? She sounds less like a saint and more like an outright goddess...

No longer did I feel any surprise, shock, awe, or envy toward Rozemyne. Those feelings had vanished, and all that remained was the urge to worship her.

Two Marriages

Three years had somehow passed since I inherited the position of Viscount Illgner.

Since the death of my father and my becoming the giebe, it was safe to say I had encountered a storm of problems. Brigitte had canceled her engagement in a fury after learning that her former fiancé Hassheit and his family sought to take my life, forcing us to band together as a family to endure the hostilities that followed. The nobles in Illgner subsequently left our province to move elsewhere, and my little sister had proven unable to find a new partner before graduating from the Royal Academy. The fact that I had needed to escort her to the stage during her graduation ceremony in place of a partner remained a painful memory for us all.

After her graduation, Brigitte had entered the Knight's Order, diligently working to establish new connections to lessen the abuse Illgner was suffering as much as possible. She had even agreed to go to the temple and lower city, which had enabled her to secure a position as the guard knight of Lady Rozemyne, the newly adopted daughter of the archduke.

I had tried to stop her out of consideration for her honor, but Brigitte was determined to be useful to Illgner in any way she could—and her efforts had borne fruit, in that her position as guard knight dramatically lessened the abuse that our province received. We finally had a little room to breathe again.

Two Marriages

The plan had then been to obtain Lady Rozemyne's official protection. We expressed our hopes of such, and she graciously allowed us the opportunity to develop the printing industry before the other provinces. It was the very best we could have hoped for, but it wasn't long after starting that we ran into a string of problems: visitors from Ehrenfest revealed our shortcomings one after another, and the arrival of high-ranking nobles such as Lord Ferdinand meant that my resolve and pride as a noble, as well as my attitude toward my citizens, was constantly called into question.

There were times when I regretted my choice to accept Lady Rozemyne's offer—never had I expected it would demand this much change and place such a heavy burden on my people. But there was no going back now; to further its advance forward, Illgner needed to continue developing its paper-making industry.

"We finished, milord! Check out these papers!" Carya exclaimed one summer afternoon, having burst into my office with a broad smile across her face. Volk followed close behind, regarding me with a polite bow before scolding his overenthusiastic partner.

"Carya, you need to be more polite to Giebe Illgner."

"S-Sorry. I was just a little excited..."

After her apology, Carya exited the room and re-entered. It was a remnant of how the gray priests had trained the servants in the mansion during their stay last year.

With Lady Rozemyne currently sleeping in a jureve for recovery purposes, it seemed that Lord Ferdinand was rebuffing nobles who expressed an interest in the printing and paper-making industries. This would not last forever, though; there would soon be nobles visiting Illgner to examine our workshops, so it was necessary for the servants in the mansion to know and observe proper etiquette.

"So you have finished, Volk?" I asked.

"Yes, Giebe Illgner. We have reached our paper production goal." He held out several sheets of completed paper, wearing an overjoyed smile. As someone who generally masked his emotions with a peaceful, unassuming expression, it was a rare sight to see.

I took the sheets of paper and took inventory of them based on type. In all honesty, I hadn't expected that they would actually succeed, but Volk and Carya had placed their faith in Lady Rozemyne's words and poured their all into their work. Their long days of toiling in the cold river until their hands turned bright red had finally been rewarded, and their bright, satisfied smiles were like two dazzling suns.

"So you have. I must soon leave for the Noble's Quarter to participate in this year's Starbind Ceremony. While I am there, I will sell the paper to the Plantin Company and arrange for your purchase, Volk."

"Giebe Illgner. If possible, I would much appreciate you taking the time to ask the High Priest how Lady Rozemyne is doing."

"Certainly."

I sent an ordonnanz to Brigitte, asking her to arrange a meeting with Lord Ferdinand, then left for the Noble's Quarter by highbeast. As I was the only one coming from Illgner to attend the Starbind Ceremony, this method of travel was ideal: the province was far enough away that I wanted to minimize carriage use as much as possible. There was of course the matter of transporting the paper, but I had simply tied it onto my highbeast. It wasn't the most respectable approach by any means, but it achieved the desired results nonetheless.

When I arrived at the Noble's Quarter, my head attendant stationed at my winter mansion greeted me with surprise. "You are here sooner than expected, my lord."

"Benefits of traveling light and alone."

"That is a fair bit more luggage than I would expect from someone traveling light…"

While my head attendant looked at me with narrowed eyes, I glanced to the servants taking my luggage inside. "Could you have the boxes taken straight to my office?" I asked. "They're important products for Illgner."

"As you wish. However, my lord, might I ask that you act a little more like a proper noble while you are in the Noble's Quarter?"

"You're right. I shall try."

On the day of my meeting with Lord Ferdinand, I departed for the temple in a carriage carrying our precious boxes of paper. My attendants grimaced upon hearing that we were heading to the temple, but I myself wasn't particularly bothered; I had already heard so much about the place from Volk and Brigitte.

I had planned my departure such that I would arrive just in time, but even then I was the last to arrive. Already in the High Priest's chambers were Benno and Damian from the Plantin Company, Gil, Rozemyne's head attendant, and Lord Ferdinand himself.

"Welcome, Giebe Illgner."

Beneath the High Priest's watchful eye, I announced the progress Illgner had made with the paper-making industry and sold the products we had developed. The sale itself went shockingly well; perhaps this was largely due to us having signed documents regarding the transaction ahead of time, but the establishment of a Plant Paper Guild and a set amount for the paper meant that the merchants did not even attempt to negotiate the price down.

"Giebe Illgner, I am exceptionally pleased to have purchased such high-quality paper," Benno said. "I look forward to doing further business with you."

"Of course. I feel the same."

When Benno had voiced his intention to fix the price of paper with a magic contract, I had quite promptly assumed he was wasting his money on something trivial. But with how smoothly our meeting had gone thus far, I had to admit it was mighty convenient. My opinion of doing business with merchants had certainly improved a little.

With the transaction complete and the Plantin Company having exited the office, it was time for me to purchase Volk. Lord Ferdinand confirmed that the money we had earned from the Plantin Company was indeed enough, then signed the contract.

"And with that, the contract is complete," Lord Ferdinand announced. "I must say though, this has happened much faster than Rozemyne predicted..."

"Indeed. Volk took his work very seriously. He believed in Lady Rozemyne's assurance that this was possible and poured his all into making paper."

"I see. Has he adjusted to life in Illgner?"

The sudden inquiry made me blink in surprise. As rude as it sounded, I had genuinely never expected Lord Ferdinand to care about the well-being of a gray priest. He must have read my expression, as he followed up with a dismissive scoff.

"Rozemyne and her attendants were exceptionally concerned about the gray priest they had left in Illgner," he continued. "They often expressed their worries about this Volk, and while I personally see no point in fretting about someone who has chosen to follow their own path, not everyone finds that so easy."

With that, Lord Ferdinand glanced at Lady Rozemyne's nearby servants with a sardonic smile. Among them was Gil, who had made paper in Illgner with the others. I could understand why he would worry so much about Volk, and his purple eyes implored me to answer.

"Volk is doing his best to adapt to the unfamiliar environment. He is adjusting to Illgner's customs as best he can, and with the servants in the mansion learning temple customs from him in turn, I would like to believe we are both influencing each other in a positive direction," I replied to Lord Ferdinand.

Gil gave a small sigh of relief, his expression softening now that he knew Volk was well. His reaction brought a smile to my face, reminding me that Volk had expressed concerns about those at the temple as well.

"Lord Ferdinand... might I be permitted to ask whether Lady Rozemyne has awoken yet?"

"She shows no sign of awakening," he replied, turning back to me after handing his copy of the contract to an attendant. "Why do you ask? I believe she will remain asleep for one more year."

I noticed that his sharp golden eyes were now closely examining me, and so I quickly explained that Volk had been worrying about her.

"I also thought that he and his partner might like to receive Lady Rozemyne's blessing at their marriage ceremony..." I added.

"If such is their desire, they need only wait until she awakens. Whether or not they choose to do so is up to them; now that Volk is no longer a gray priest, they may do as they please," Lord Ferdinand replied.

I could imagine that Volk would readily wait however long it took for Lady Rozemyne to awaken, but whether Carya could match his patience was another matter entirely.

Back when the Plantin Company had departed from Illgner, I had given Volk a room in my mansion where the single servants stayed. It would have been inconvenient for him to be the only one using the side building, and Lady Rozemyne had told me to treat him as much like any other servant as possible. As a result, he went from being one strange guest among many to standing out terribly among the other servants.

Volk was a peaceful fellow, and on a good day he would exude and move with even more grace than I could as the giebe—though this was in part because I was so accustomed to running around a heavily forested and mountainous province. Nonetheless, his experience serving nobles had instilled into him a certain humility.

It did not take long at all for the single women to be drawn to Volk, no doubt attracted to how different he was from the other men in Illgner. They used all manner of excuses to be near him, putting Carya in such a panic that she was trying to marry him as soon as possible.

"I imagine they shall marry at the end of autumn—the woman Volk is taking as his wife will not want to wait."

"I intend to visit Illgner this autumn to see firsthand the progress of the paper-making industry," Lord Ferdinand explained. "I will inform Rozemyne of the Starbinding and how their relationship is faring when she awakens."

"You have my thanks," I replied, crossing my arms in front of my chest.

Lord Ferdinand paused for a moment, as if debating whether or not to continue, then opened his mouth again to speak. "Giebe Illgner, this may come as unwelcome advice, but you are simply too direct and honest. Your virtuousness will only lead to you being easily exploited in noble society. I advise that you learn more about noble methods, whether you enjoy doing so or not." His furrowed brow made him appear displeased, but his tone of voice was more relaxed than anything.

There were few people willing to give me such warnings now that I was a giebe, and so I considered his advice beyond valuable.

"I shall take your generous advice to heart, my lord."

I returned to my winter estate with my copy of the contract and the small amount left over from my purchase. Volk was now a true resident of Illgner. He would likely work as an educator for the mansion's servants while continuing his operation of the papermaking workshops.

I may wish to have him advise me on these matters as well...

My behavior was certainly more appropriate in the Noble's Quarter, but when in Illgner, I couldn't help but relax. It would likely be a good idea to have Volk point out whenever I started to slip.

"Welcome home, Brother."

"Ah, Brigitte. You're home? Do you not have training today?"

I returned to my estate to find Brigitte, who would normally be in the knight dorms, sitting around at ease.

It had come to my attention that Lord Bonifatius, uncle of the current archduke and former commander of the Knight's Order, was thoroughly training the knights serving the archducal family, improving them one by one. His training sessions were known for being excruciatingly intense, such that Brigitte had once complained that the knights would be dead in mere moments were there ever an enemy attack right after one.

"None at all," Brigitte answered. "That doesn't mean I've spent the whole day relaxing though; Lady Elvira invited me to a tea party this morning. More importantly... how did your business go?"

"Lady Rozemyne was right: they were able to save up enough money. I just finished buying Volk and getting all that in order."

"That's good to hear. Now he and Carya can finally be happy together. Should we get them a gift of some kind?"

I sat down in the chair opposite Brigitte and showed her my copy of the contract. A smile crept onto her lips as though it were her own marriage on the horizon, and she began to ponder what she could give them. Carya was her childhood friend, and it was heartwarming to see her so pleased about her finding happiness.

"While I am of course happy for Carya, I'm worried about your own Starbinding…" I said.

Last year, Brigitte had attended the Starbind Ceremony wearing a dress that Lady Rozemyne had designed for her. While there, she was approached by none other than Hassheit. It was clear that he only wanted Lady Rozemyne's support for himself—he hounded her about giving him another chance to restore her honor, stating that none would show interest in a woman who had canceled an engagement in the past. She could not even rebuke his claims, as it was true that no other men had approached her, but she had managed to endure nonetheless without accepting his hand.

It was then that her fellow guard knight, Damuel, came to her unexpected rescue. He and his friends stood up for Brigitte, with Damuel defending her honor by asking for her hand in marriage. There was a considerable gap between their mana capacities, but he had accounted for this by stating that he would grow his by next year's Starbind Ceremony and request to marry her again.

One year had passed since then, and with the Starbind Ceremony fast approaching once again, I was eager to see his progress.

"Brigitte, can I ask what your plans are here?"

"I'm not sure what you mean…" she replied, grabbing a nearby cushion and hugging it to her chest. She lowered her gaze briefly, then looked up at me with puppy-dog eyes. "What do you think of Damuel, Brother?"

It seemed that she had fallen for him. She hadn't taken his last proposal seriously, claiming that it was merely to protect her honor, but a lot had apparently changed over the past year. I was glad to see her excited about the prospect of marriage after having given up on it for so long.

Two Marriages

I thought back to how Damuel had behaved when visiting Illgner. It was clear that he cared a lot about Brigitte, and it was hard to find fault with his considerate personality. He also seemed to take no issue with Illgner being a country province, and Lady Rozemyne had placed much faith in him.

"He seems like a fine man to me, but what of your mana?" I asked. "Damuel claimed he would be able to increase his capacity by this coming Starbind Ceremony, but is it not unlikely that it grew enough for you to marry one another?"

Damuel was a laynoble, while Brigitte was a mednoble. Their capacities last year had just barely been close enough for them to bear children, so a marriage certainly wasn't impossible, but the others in her family would no doubt rather she pick a better partner for the sake of their future children—and of course, any outsider would laugh their union off as ridiculous. It was for precisely these reasons that Damuel was getting teased, as nobody had taken his proposal as anything more than a gracious effort to protect Brigitte's honor. No matter how hard a laynoble tried to increase their mana capacity, there was only so much progress they could make.

"Has his capacity grown since last year?" I asked.

"Yes, by quite a shocking amount. I still have more than him, but we're almost equals now," Brigitte replied somewhat shyly, the look on her face making it clear she had already decided to marry him.

My eyes widened in surprise; never had I thought it possible for a laynoble to increase their capacity to such an extent. "Was he just a late bloomer to begin with?"

Most people searched for marriage partners in the Royal Academy before their graduation, which meant those whose capacities developed slightly later on in their lives struggled greatly. As he was now, however, it was possible that Damuel would continue to grow further still.

"That very well might be the case, given how dramatic his growth has been, but I think the biggest contributing factor is the mana compression method that Lady Rozemyne taught him. It works even on adults, though its effectiveness depends on the person."

"To think the rumors were true..."

Word of a new compression method invented to grant Ehrenfest more mana had been floating around during last year's winter socializing. Its source was unknown, but with every noble alive wanting to increase their capacity, it had sparked quite a buzz.

"As of right now, it has only been taught to a select few people: the archducal couple; the knight commander and his family; Lord Ferdinand; the guard knights of the archducal family, excluding those serving Lord Wilfried; a portion of the Knight's Order; and Lord Justus. Their plan is to gradually spread the method to others they can trust once Lady Rozemyne awakens. As for Damuel, well, um... he was taught after explaining to Lady Rozemyne that he wished to marry me."

Lady Rozemyne teaching Damuel her new mana compression method was surely a testament to just how much she trusted him, so his marriage to Brigitte would no doubt prove beneficial for Illgner. And with Lady Rozemyne being such a deeply compassionate person—as shown through the advice she had so willingly given to Volk—I could imagine she would continue to associate with Brigitte even if she quit being her guard knight after getting married. Now that Illgner was changing so dramatically, we truly needed that continued support.

"As long as your mana capacities are compatible, I'll leave this decision to you, Brigitte. If this will make you happy and you think it will be good for Illgner, that's enough for me; I approve your marriage with Damuel, both as your brother, and as Giebe Illgner."

Brigitte's amethyst eyes glimmered with joy, and she regarded me with a beaming smile as gentle as a bouquet of newly picked flowers. "Thank you, Brother. Speaking of which... Lady Elvira asked me something similar during her tea party. She wanted to know whether I intended to accept Damuel's proposal. It was terribly embarrassing. The party itself was rather small, but the first wife of Ehrenfest herself was in attendance, so she listened as my love life was being dug into..." Her lips were pursed, but the fact that her delighted smile still shone through suggested to me that she had quite enjoyed it after all.

"What did you say?"

"I said that I intend to accept and return to Illgner with him."

"You intend to return to Illgner?" I repeated, blinking in surprise. Her response had caught me completely off guard.

"What, do you not want me to? Is it not the duty of a married woman to start raising children? I want to raise mine in my home province."

With neither her nor Damuel being the heads of their respective houses, they could only remain in Ehrenfest by purchasing a home in the Noble's Quarter. This would mean having to stay in a cramped house with no garden, rearing their children in a place she had never before lived while participating in society as a laynoble. That was why she instead wanted to start a family in the large province of Illgner, giving their children the same upbringing she had received—running across the open fields and through the mountains, not along the ivory paving of a dense city.

"What has Damuel said about that?"

"Hm...? His family doesn't own any land, so I don't think he'll care too much about where we live. He said that he liked Illgner, and Lady Elvira praised my attachment to my hometown, so she said this would be a good opportunity to test his love for me."

"I see..."

Brigitte was straightforward to a fault. Knowing that canceling her engagement had put Illgner in perilous waters, she had asked to serve as Lady Rozemyne's guard knight, even willing to endure going to the temple and the lower city. She had been desperate to acquire any support she could from the higher classes, and as admirable as that was, being so driven by one's love for their hometown was not proper for a knight—prioritizing the protection of one's province and people was the expected mindset of a land-owning noble. Brigitte hadn't changed at all, even now that she was serving as a guard knight for the archducal family.

She is not dedicated solely to her charge, and that is the problem here.

A sigh escaped me. Lady Elvira had almost certainly expressed support for Brigitte's feelings and permitted her to return to Illgner because she had determined that she was unfit to continue serving as Lady Rozemyne's guard knight. And with that settled, Lady Elvira planned to exploit her removal to test Damuel as well—not to see whether he truly loved Brigitte, but to see whether he would remain loyal to Lady Rozemyne no matter what happened.

Were Damuel not a guard knight serving the archducal family, it certainly would have been possible for him to move to Illgner. It was an exceedingly rare opportunity for a laynoble to marry the little sister of Giebe Illgner, but he was a knight who had been raised in the Noble's Quarter, assigned to his position of guarding Lady Rozemyne so that he could atone for a previous failure. It was very unlikely that he was considering this an opportunity to move to Illgner; in fact, him doing so was unthinkable.

"...Brigitte, what will you do if Damuel refuses to move? Would you consider staying in the Noble's Quarter and marrying there?"

Her eyes widened. She thought for a moment, then shook her head. "Never. Retiring as a guard knight and living in the Noble's Quarter won't help Illgner, and I can't even imagine life as a laynoble. It is thanks to Lady Rozemyne's observations that I am able to see what Illgner lacks—I was able to see my hometown from the perspective of an outsider. I wish to use this opportunity to improve the province while leaving its good parts intact."

She truly would do anything for the sake of Illgner, from visiting the temple and lower city to even accepting a marriage she personally didn't want. There was no denying she would make the ideal daughter of a land-owning noble: she was willing to accept Damuel as her husband, despite his lower status as the second son of a laynoble, all so that she could remain in her home province.

"Brigitte, I understand now just how deeply you care about Illgner, but please remember that you are the one choosing to stand so firm on this matter. Do not resent or curse Damuel should he choose the path of a guard knight over a future with you."

"Brother, what do you mean by that?" Brigitte demanded, throwing aside the cushion and abruptly jumping to her feet.

"Damuel is not like we land-owning nobles: he was raised in the Noble's Quarter and assigned as Lady Rozemyne's guard knight to atone for a past mistake," I said quietly, attempting to calm her. "With his charge being a member of the archducal family, I cannot imagine he is able to leave her side, though I will of course welcome him with open arms should he ultimately come to Illgner."

She sat back down, shocked into silence, once again pressing a cushion to her chest. Tears started to well up in her eyes as she thought carefully about her situation, but I merely stood up. Even as her older brother, it was not my place to interject on this matter; what she did next was entirely up to her.

And so came the night of the Starbind Ceremony. Brigitte was in the grand hall wearing the same outfit as last year, though it was no longer quite so unique: many women now had dresses of a similar style, while others wore hair sticks decorated with flower ornaments much like Lady Rozemyne's. Not everyone had taken such direct inspiration from Brigitte, however—some were dressed in attire that was rare to see in this day and age. This in particular was a rare sight to behold, considering that the ceremony was normally dominated only by whatever was the most popular fashion at the time.

The presence of other women wearing similar dresses meant that Brigitte wasn't drawing as much attention as last year, but many still watched her with anticipation, eager to see the next chapter in her love story. Wives particularly interested in romantic rumors were eyeing her constantly.

As for Damuel, his knight friends were slapping him on the back and jabbing him in the sides with their elbows, going on about how jealous they were and demanding to know how he had increased his mana capacity to such an extent.

Once Lord Ferdinand had performed the Starbinding, it was time for the unwed to begin searching for partners. Yet again the young folks set out, though only a small portion of single men and women ended up crowded with suitors. Everyone else was either focusing on closing the distance between a coworker they had a crush on or introducing their family to others in preparation for next year.

"Brigitte."

Damuel stepped forward, steeling his resolve as a crowd gathered in anticipation of what was about to come. He knelt down before her and held out a stunningly radiant purple feystone.

Two Marriages

"My fate crossed yours at the guidance of the King and Queen gods, who rule the heavens far above," he began, reciting the first line in the traditional proposal. "I feel that I will only continue to grow if you are by my side. I wish for you to be my Goddess of Light."

As everyone watched on with bated breath, Brigitte returned an elated smile, then pressed her lips tightly together. "Damuel, my light shines only within Illgner. Will you accompany me there...?"

His eyes widened in shock as he looked up at her, unable to believe his ears. He remained on his knees, wavering slightly as she quietly awaited his answer. The two were completely still, frozen in the moment as though Dregarnuhr the Goddess of Time was playing a trick on them.

Each beat that passed felt like an eternity. Damuel, upon seeing the immovable determination in Brigitte's gaze, squeezed his eyes shut. He then looked downward, his brow drawn into a pained frown, and slowly shook his head.

"...I cannot go to Illgner. I am Lady Rozemyne's guard knight."

"I... I see," Brigitte whispered. Tears streamed down her cheeks, landing upon the feystone that was just as amethyst as her eyes.

"It is bittersweet, but there remains beauty even in love that fate has denied," sighed a voice from behind me. I swiftly turned around.

"Lady Elvira..."

I took a reflexive step back upon seeing the graceful archnoble wife before me, regarding me with a calm expression and wearing a hair stick very similar to Lady Rozemyne's. When I attempted to kneel, she waved to stop me, placing her hand on her cheek and narrowing her dark-brown eyes into a smile. I straightened my back, realizing that she was judging me as a potential enemy.

"I too wish for Brigitte's happiness, Giebe Illgner, much like Rozemyne does. I was truly moved by her determination to return home to Illgner, and the kindness she holds for her people. For the sake of her future happiness, I will find a suitable marriage partner for her—one willing to dedicate themselves to Illgner's future."

Brigitte had chosen her home over a life with Damuel in the Noble's Quarter, leaving me with no avenue by which to refuse an offer from an archnoble like Lady Elvira. But above all else, Illgner needed Lady Rozemyne's support to survive, which meant maintaining a positive relationship with her mother was absolutely necessary. As Giebe Illgner, I had only one answer I could possibly give.

"I am honored by your kind consideration, and graciously entrust finding a good husband for my little sister to you."

No Rest for Us

Snow had just started to fall when Gil stopped me on my way out of the workshop, handing me a few letters with a dark, clouded expression. He stressed that I needed to be extremely careful with them, and that I should only read them in the presence of people who were "in the know."

He didn't need to explain what he meant by that; Gil only ever became this emotional over things to do with Myne, which was why I always went straight to her place when he gave me letters like these. I raced all the way to the stairs to her home and up to the front door, all the while wondering what they might say.

"Hey. It's Lutz. Is everyone home?"

"Uh huh. Oh, wait... Is this...?"

I nodded at Tuuli, who had answered the door, and showed her the letters in my bag. Her blue eyes instantly lit up, her braid swishing behind her as she spun around to those inside the house. "We have letters!" she cried, the excitement clear in her voice.

To nobody's surprise, Gunther was the first one to react. He burst out of the bedroom, still wearing his bedclothes and looking a little sleepy—he had probably just gotten into bed for a nap before his night shift. Meanwhile, Effa wiped her hands, having finished up something in the kitchen, before coming to join us.

Seeing everyone gathered around the kitchen table, Kamil reached out his arms and went, "Up! Uuup!" I waited for Effa to heft him up before spreading out the letters for everyone to read.

The letter for me started with, *"I'm going to use the potion that'll make me healthy, which I think will put me to sleep for about a season. Take care of the workshop and the Gutenbergs for me."* It was written in a very casual, Myne-like tone, and went on to give some more detailed instructions for the Gutenbergs.

There was also a letter for her family, which opened with a message addressing them all: *"I've made a potion that'll make me better, which means I'll finally be a normal girl. I'm going to be asleep for a while, but don't worry—everything's going to be okay."* Below it were more personalized notes, one for each of them.

"So she's finally gonna be healthy, huh?" Gunther said.

"I can hardly believe it…" Effa added.

"Lutz, what's with this other letter?" Tuuli asked. "It's written by Fran, and while I can read the words, I don't really get what they mean…"

Fran's letters were always so rife with noble euphemisms that it was little wonder Tuuli was struggling. Meanwhile, I studied noble euphemisms in the store, and my recent trip to Illgner had given me some valuable experience, so I could understand them better than most. I took the letter and started to read it.

"No way…"

"What is it…?" Tuuli asked, tilting her head quietly. Gunther, in contrast, must have noticed my expression stiffen, as he leapt up from his chair with a tense look on his face.

"What happened to Myne?!"

"She was attacked by someone at the castle and poisoned…" I explained. "The High Priest thinks she'll survive, but now the potion will put her to sleep for over a year…"

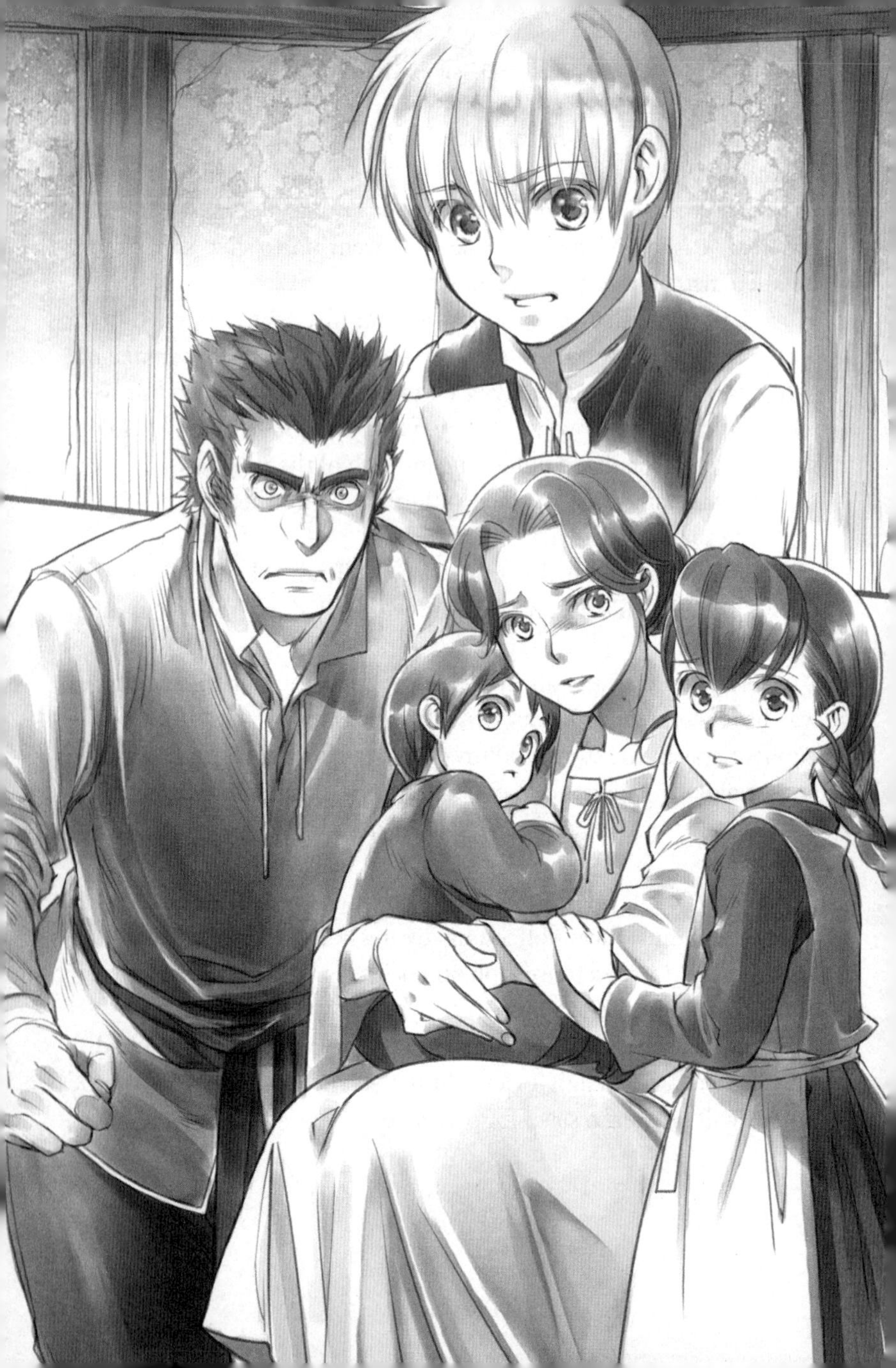

No Rest for Us

The letter also asked us to tell Master Benno, but that wasn't important right now.

As I sat there in silence, Gunther snatched the letter from my hands. It seemed that he wanted to confirm things for himself, but he couldn't read it either. He slammed it back onto the table, his brow furrowed, then forced out a long sigh as he thumped a fist against his forehead over and over again. He was most likely trying to vent the anger building up inside him.

"She'll be asleep longer, but her life's not in danger..." I tried to reassure him. "It could be worse."

Tuuli was starting to look concerned. "Will Myne really be okay...?"

"She's a strong girl. She'll be fine. I'm sure she'll be fine," Effa replied, repeating the words with a forced smile. "Whenever she was sick and bedridden in the past, I always worried that she wouldn't make it through. But she always did in the end, didn't she? This'll be just like that. All we can do is believe and wait. She'll be just fine..."

I could tell that she wanted to go and check on Myne, but that of course wasn't an option. She couldn't even ask for updates. It made perfect sense that she was overcome with worry.

Kamil looked fearful as well; he didn't understand why everyone was wearing such grim expressions. Our eyes met, and he reached an uncertain hand toward me. "Lutz, Lutz... Toy...?"

"Sorry Kamil, I don't have any toys for you today. Your big sister's sick in bed and can't make any new ones right now," I said, giving him a pat on the head. I folded up my letter, putting it back in my bag to show Master Benno tomorrow, then turned to the others still gathered around the table. "I'll ask Gil for more details when I see him next. That's all I can do, but—"

"You're doing more than we could ever ask for," Effa said, cutting me off. "You should head on home; it's getting late. And here, as thanks."

I accepted a pork sausage from her and then left Myne's, running down the stairs, through the plaza with the well, and up the stairs to my house.

"Welcome home, Lutz. You're back late today."

"Hey. Had to drop by Myne's for something. Here, this is from Mrs. Effa."

I handed over the sausage I had just been given, which Mom took with a small smile. "It's been two whole years since Myne died, but you still call it Myne's place. Weird, that, ain't it?"

"Old habits die hard... It'll take some time to adjust. Anyway, I'm hungry. Boil that sausage for me if there's no food left."

"I saved some for you, don't worry. Go put your stuff away," Mom said, chuckling at my awkward attempt to change the subject. But what else could I have done? The words had come out of my mouth without me even realizing.

I went into the bedroom. It was cramped and uncomfortable, since four growing boys had to share it. The one sliver of good news was that Zasha had found someone to marry, which meant he would soon be leaving to live in his own home. That was the only thing keeping me going.

That said, I've got enough money that I could leave right now, if I really wanted to.

I had enough saved up that I could rent a room on my own and even hire a servant to handle chores for me; in fact, I could even rent a bigger place for my whole family to move into. But doing that would make it harder to deliver letters to Myne's family, and since I was a leherl, I would be moving into Master Benno's place when I turned ten anyway. I was going to stick with my family until then, and that resolve had only grown stronger after seeing Myne be ripped away from hers.

After setting my bag down, I headed to the table for supper. Ralph gave me an annoyed look the moment I sat down; he had already eaten but was staying seated solely to complain at me. I already knew what he was going to say.

"You went to Tuuli's again, didn't you?"

"Yeah, 'cause I had to deliver something from the workshop," I answered casually, pulling a bowl of soup in front of me and starting to eat.

Ralph had been grumbling about my relationship with Tuuli a lot lately. He looked at me like he had more to say, then started rapping the table with frustration. It was honestly pretty annoying. I just wanted to enjoy my meal.

"Y'know, Ralph... If you care that much, why don't you just go ask her to hang out?"

"It ain't that friggin' easy!"

Tuuli had turned ten and signed a contract to be a leherl for the Gilberta Company. She was a rising star, having moved up shockingly high in the world for someone born in the poor side of the city. In other words, she was such a beauty that nobody else here could even hope to compare. More than enough boys had set their sights on her now that they were turning ten and thinking about the future, Ralph included.

"Even when I ask her to hang out in the forest on Earthdays, she just turns me down most of the time," he continued.

Ralph had fallen head over heels for Tuuli; she was getting better at sewing and became prettier by the day, not to mention she actually kept herself clean. He probably wanted to use his position as her childhood friend to stay close to her, but they had to work every day except Earthdays now that they were both ten, so meeting up wasn't easy.

"I mean, she doesn't have the time to go to the forest..." I explained.

"Why not?"

Myne's family didn't have to pay for medicine now that she was out of the house, and as a leherl for the Gilberta Company, Tuuli was receiving special hair stick orders from the archduke's adopted daughter herself, so they were no longer so poor that they needed to go out of their way to gather in the forest. Their new financial situation meant they even had the money to move to a better area if they so wished, but they had decided to stay for the sake of stability and to preserve their memories of Myne.

Not that any of this mattered to Ralph, of course.

"Tuuli's working hard and putting her all into becoming a first-rate seamstress. She's even going to the Gilberta Company on her days off to learn from Corinna, so she's real busy right now."

"Gaaah! I know it's just because of work, but it really ticks me off that you know more about her than I do!"

"What, want me to stop talking about her?"

"...No. Tell me everything you know. *Everything.*"

I gave the pouting Ralph a brief explanation of what Tuuli had been up to lately. There wasn't all that much I could say though, given that we worked at different stores now.

"Oh, right... If you really want to ask her out, Ralph, you don't have much time left."

"Whaddaya mean by that?!"

"She's a leherl, remember? She's commuting from home 'cause the Plantin Company split from the Gilberta Company last summer, but once spring comes, she'll be moving to live up north."

When the Plantin Company had gone independent, it started moving locations to another store—albeit one that was still close to the Gilberta Company. The move was being done gradually day by day, and enough progress had now been made that Master Benno and Mark could finally start living on the second floor of the new building, with winter preparations and the like now all completed.

Once all their remaining belongings were put away, Corinna's family would relocate from the third floor to the second. I had heard they were planning to do this move during the winter, while they were locked inside anyway due to the snow. Tuuli would be given a room as a leherl apprentice come spring when they were done with that.

"Just wait for me, Tuuli!" Ralph shouted into the wind as I continued eating my soup. Boys in love sure were a pain.

I do kinda want to support Ralph, given that he's my brother and all, but I really doubt Tuuli's going to marry anyone from around here when she has the favor of the archduke's adopted daughter.

The next day, I headed to the Plantin Company for work.

"Good morning, Mark. I wish to speak to Master Benno regarding the High Bishop."

Mark nodded and instantly sent word to Master Benno, who told me to come to his office. As always, I was impressed by the speed and precision with which Mark worked. I wanted to learn by his example, but his talent was still way beyond me.

Master Benno cleared the room of everyone except Mark and me, at which point I told him that Myne was expected to be asleep for over a year.

"But she's not going to die or anything, right?"

"No. According to the letter, the High Priest expects her to be asleep for over a year. It's all written here."

Master Benno read the letter with Mark, then muttered, "I see."

"I suppose there won't be any new businesses established for quite some time then," Mark said.

"Yep. This is good timing if you ask me," Master Benno agreed, relaxing a little.

I grimaced. Myne was going to be asleep for a whole year, and the only thing he had to say about it was that it was *good timing*? That was just messed up.

My thoughts were suddenly disrupted as Master Benno flicked me on the forehead. "It's way too easy to guess what you're feeling from the look on your face. You know as well as I do that Rozemyne tries to move things along at an unreasonable pace. She's sown the seeds for more than enough big new things, and they need time to settle. We all know she's gonna start another rampage the moment she wakes up, so we should use this time to stabilize the work we've already started."

I had assumed we would continue expanding the industry in her absence, but that apparently wasn't the case.

"We've gotta study the things from Illgner, develop new ink, proliferate the hand pumps, and introduce new kinds of books. Go and tell the Gutenbergs that we're gonna be focusing on what we've already got on our plates instead of expanding out more. I'll get the lehanges up to date."

I responded with a big nod, then got to work writing out letters of invitation to the Gutenbergs, having the new lehanges who had just joined the store deliver them.

"Hey, Johann. You sure this is the Plantin Company?"

"Uh huh, this is the place. Excuse me! Can we talk to Lutz? Huh...? I'm Johann. The, er... The Gutenberg..."

On the day of my meeting with the other Gutenbergs, I heard two familiar voices coming from near the Plantin Company entrance and rushed out to welcome them.

"Johann, Zack—thanks for coming despite the heavy snow. Right this way."

We had all assembled in a meeting room. There were Johann and Zack, the smiths; Ingo, the foreman of a carpentry workshop; Heidi and Josef, the ink craftspeople; Gil and Fritz, representatives of the Rozemyne Workshop; and finally the three of us from the Plantin Company. Only now that we were all together did I realize just how many Gutenbergs there were now. It felt like an eternity ago that Myne and I were struggling to make paper by ourselves.

Now that I think about it, I could really do with some buttered potatoffels right about now...

As I remembered how extra tasty they were during the cold seasons, I offered seats to Johann and Zack, then sat down myself.

"I've got some bad news for everyone. It's about Lady Rozemyne..." Master Benno began, going on to explain that she had entered a long period of recovery. Once he was done, I read out the letter I had received from her.

"...So basically, she wants us to keep up the printing and invent some ink that goes with the new paper," I summarized. "Ingo, she wants you to make the bookshelf she talked about before. Johann and Zack, she wants you to make more metal letter types and circulate those hand pumps as best you can."

The moment Heidi understood the meaning of the euphemism-laden letter, she stood up and started pumping her fist in the air. "Yesss! Time to make new ink! I love Lady Rozemyne *sooo muuuch*!"

"Good gods, Heidi! Calm down! Learn to read the room!"

Josef desperately tried to contain his wife, whose eyes were positively glowing with excitement. He forced her back into her chair before awkwardly scanning the room, suddenly noticing that Johann was staring forward with wide-open eyes.

"Lutz... Aren't the letter types and hand pumps both *my* thing? Am I going to be the only busy one here? What's Zack going to be doing?!"

Maybe he had a point. It was Johann's job to handle all the precision stuff, so he was usually the one who had to make the things Myne ordered. But before I could agree, Zack grimaced, digging a finger in his ear as he shot Johann a glare.

"Listen up, pal—I've gotta think up how to make mattresses with springs in them, and she's asked me to make carriages less rocky. I've got tons to design, and unlike you, Lady Rozemyne's not my only patron. I've got plenty of other work to get on with, so how about you stop complaining and just be grateful you've been given something to do? If you don't like it, get some new customers."

Only a patron interested in extreme precision work like Myne would understand Johann's value, so he didn't have much choice here except to give up and handle the work.

"Look, if you really hate making the same thing over and over again, why not train a successor to take your place?" Zack continued. "Lady Rozemyne's gonna have tons of new orders for you when she wakes up."

Johann paled, his body starting to tremble. "N-No way... She won't... No way..." he repeated in a desperate attempt to reassure himself. But Zack made a good point—Myne was adamant that she would wake up healthier than ever, and without the risk of collapsing keeping her at bay, there wouldn't be anything to stop her from going on an endless rampage.

Bleh... Just thinking about it gives me a headache.

As I cradled my aching head, Master Benno looked over to Ingo. "What was that about a bookshelf? Another new invention?"

"Yup. It's a real crazy one, too—there are wheels on the bottom so it can be moved around. There's also this 'high-density mobile shelving' thing she was talking about. She sent a ton of concepts my way, so my plan's to finish those up alongside my other jobs. Her rough designs mention a few metal parts, so I might be asking for your help Johann, but…" He shot the poor boy an awkward look; Johann was only looking sicker and sicker. "Eh, what can I say? We're in this together."

"Wait, wait…" Johann murmured weakly. "Doesn't that mean… I'll have even more work?"

"Congrats. Looks like you won't just be making letter types," Zack said with a grin.

Heidi enthusiastically chimed in as well. "New work is so much fun, right?! Let's all work hard together!"

"I HATE THIIIS!" Johann yelled, tears welling up in his eyes.

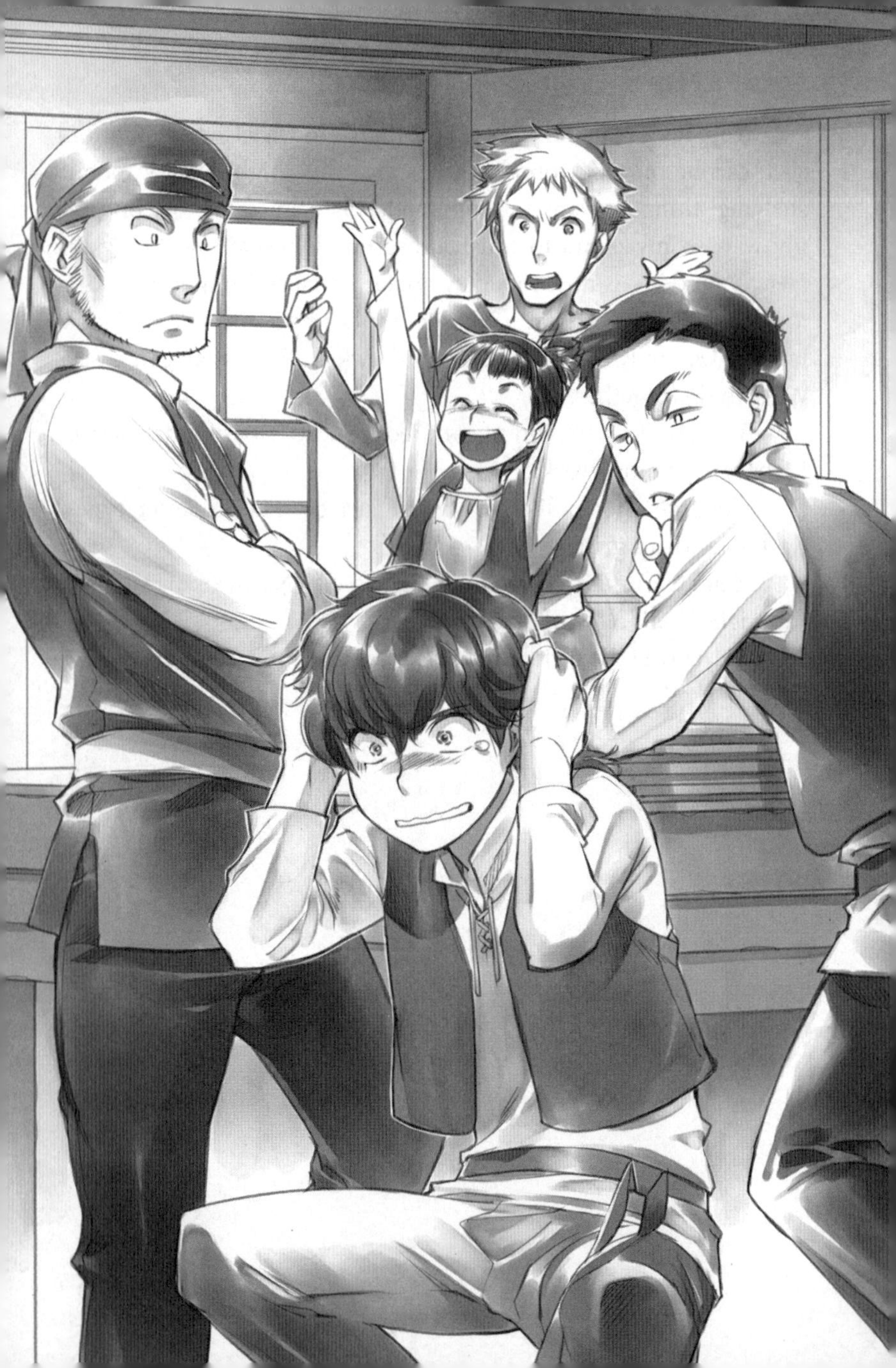

The room was soon awash with laughter, and with that, Master Benno brought the meeting to a close. "So yeah—everyone, get your work done before Lady Rozemyne wakes up. The High Priest is handling her funds for now, and we're always ready to pay, so just keep doing what you're doing."

"Right!"

The blizzards lasted longer this winter than the last, but spring still came around eventually. It was halfway through the new season that Gil came to me to discuss something—they had nearly gone through all the stories Myne had prepared for them to print.

"I spoke to Fran about this as well," he explained. "He got the High Priest to give us the stories she got from the noble children at the castle, but they're all written how a kid would talk, so they're pretty hard to read. Seems like Lady Rozemyne was fixing up the text to make them readable enough to print, but, er... I don't really know how to do that..."

Their problem sure was a tough one: we couldn't print books without stories to put in them. Our main products were picture books for nobles, and we had even started selling them to rich merchants, who had started to express interest purely because the nobles had them. Stopping printing now wasn't an option.

"...Pretty sure she gave Tuuli a handwritten book. I'll ask if we can borrow it."

"Alright. Thanks. If we make a lot of new books, Lady Rozemyne might actually wake up faster to read them. That's why I want us to print as many as we can for her."

"Makes sense. She might just leap out of that thing if there's a stack right next to her."

After my talk with Gil, I went to the Gilberta Company where Tuuli now lived to ask her about borrowing the book.

"I don't mind, since I know Gil and the others will treat it with care, but... Myne wrote it specially for us, her family; I don't think it'll make a good product," she said, taking out a book titled *Mom's Stories*. It was a compilation of all the tales Myne had written onto clay tablets way back when.

I flipped through them and recognized several as the stories she had told me on the road to the forest. The nostalgia hit me so hard that I wanted to cry. I missed those days so much.

"You're right that these are a lot different from the other picture books," I agreed, "but can I borrow it anyway?"

"I don't mind. But will you do something for me too?"

It was rare for Tuuli to ask for a favor in return. I started to blink in surprise as she steeled her resolve and looked up at me, her blue eyes now brimming with determination.

"I want to learn proper etiquette. You've been doing *so* much better ever since you learned from the gray priests in Illgner, and now you can even read letters with complicated noble euphemisms in them, right? Mrs. Corinna said that she'll start taking me to noble estates once I've learned proper etiquette, but I don't know how to do that on my own. So how about this: I'll lend you the book if you introduce me to a gray priest who will teach me."

The gray priests had trained me alongside the servants in the Illgner mansion. I personally hadn't noticed myself getting that much better, but both Master Benno and Mark had praised my improvement, and my movements were apparently so much more elegant now that even Tuuli had taken notice. Given that she was born as poor as me, I understood why she was so concerned.

Before Myne had entered the temple and started her workshop, both Tuuli and I had looked down on the gray priests and shrine maidens for being orphans, somewhere deep inside of us.

Myne of course had started to respect them purely because they let her into the book room, but she was a natural exception—I could guess that everyone in the lower city would feel the same way about the priests as we originally had. Once you really got to know them, however, it became apparent that they had learned extreme etiquette to be presentable to nobles, and they were all well-educated. They knew things that we could never hope to learn without their help, no matter how much money we had.

"Alright. I'll speak to Gil and Fritz about this."

The Rozemyne Workshop's focus on printing meant it now worked with the Plantin Company rather than the Gilberta Company, so Tuuli—a leherl working for a clothing store—couldn't enter the temple without an invitation from Myne the High Bishop. We would need to send word ahead of time before she could come.

When I next went to the workshop, I handed Gil the book I had borrowed from Tuuli and told him what she wanted.

"So yeah, could you help Tuuli out with her etiquette somehow? C'mon, Gil..."

"Uh... If she wants to learn, she'll need a shrine maiden to teach her, not a priest. I'll ask Fran and Wilma about it. Tuuli's been a big help, so I do wanna pay her back."

Tuuli had been breaking her back to help the children in the orphanage, going out of her way to teach them how to sew and cook, not to mention traveling with them to the forest. She was used to spending time in the orphanage too, since she had visited the temple classroom several times over the winter.

Fran and Wilma were both quick to agree to help her out, as thanks for everything she had done for them. The only condition was that she needed to stay with me when she was coming to the temple; she couldn't be here alone.

Since I was going to be with Tuuli anyway, I decided to learn alongside her. There was no denying that my time in Illgner had taught me all sorts of things, but there was still a huge gap between my skills and those of an attendant like Gil. I needed to work harder too.

"And that's what happened, Master Benno. I'll be going to the orphanage every Earthday to work on my etiquette," I explained.

"Just you two? We can't send anyone else along with you?"

It seemed that Master Benno wanted to use this opportunity to have leherls at the Plantin and Gilberta Companies learn etiquette as well, but with Myne asleep and unable to give her permission, I doubted anyone else was going to be allowed in.

"I don't think so. Fran and Wilma are making a special exception here as thanks for how much Tuuli has done for the orphanage."

"Hah. Can't believe I'm saying this, but I sure wish that rampaging little gremlin was awake..." Benno sighed. His expression then turned serious. "Lutz, learn everything you can while you're there. It may not last forever, but right now you've got a tight connection with the archduke's adopted daughter. That's a once-in-a-lifetime opportunity; don't hesitate to milk it for everything it's worth."

"Yes, sir!"

"Also, Rozemyne mentioned this before, but..."

Master Benno went on to give me a list of warnings, then granted me his permission to buy a few things. Once he was done, I went to Corinna's workshop to deliver the letter of invitation from Master Benno and call Tuuli over.

"Tuuli, they said okay. They'll teach you etiquette."

"Thanks, Lutz! I'm gonna do my best and learn everything I can!" she exclaimed, clenching her fists and giving me an enthusiastic smile. Myne had taught her how to handle certain situations in the past, but she didn't have anything resembling a full education.

What's more, the etiquette Corinna had taught her was the bare minimum to stop her sticking out in the workshop; her main focus was, of course, teaching the apprentices about sewing.

"Alright, let's go shopping. You'll need some clothes with big sleeves, used or not. They're going to be important for when you're learning to carry yourself properly."

"Whaaat?! I don't have the money for that!"

Tuuli had a guild card as an employee of the Gilberta Company, and due to her being a leherl working for the archduke's adopted daughter, she earned a lot more than other girls her age. But even so, she didn't have enough to just casually buy clothes with big, fluttering sleeves made for the daughters of rich families.

I looked at my own guild card. I had enough money to cover the costs myself, and the fact that I'd been too busy to go out and buy anything lately meant it was only piling up.

"I'll pay for them this time."

"I couldn't ask you to do that."

"Don't sweat it. When Myne wakes up, I'll just subtract it from her old savings," I said, waving a dismissive hand as Tuuli predictably tried to refuse my offer.

"Her old savings...?"

"The same money I've been using to buy the rest of your clothes. Myne was saving up before her death so that her family could use it. What's important here is you getting a proper education, and developing the skills you need to meet Lady Rozemyne without having to depend on anyone else, right? Myne won't complain about us using the money to buy the study materials you need."

"Study materials...? But clothes with big sleeves are expensive, aren't they? This isn't like paper. They're a waste of money," Tuuli replied, shaking her head and then fixing me with a glare. But they weren't a waste of money.

"You won't get a proper feel for things without the sleeves. They're necessary. If you think they're a waste of money, you should just give up on learning etiquette entirely. You're lucky enough that the orphanage is willing to teach you this stuff; under normal circumstances, you'd need to shell out a ton of money and hope there's a teacher willing to educate you, y'know?"

"...You're right. Let's go buy the clothes, then."

Tuuli and I went to buy the frilly clothes needed for our practice. I took this opportunity to also get her a few normal outfits to wear at the sewing workshop, and she let out a shriek upon seeing the mountainous pile of girls' clothes.

"I don't need this much, Lutz!"

"There are a lot of rich apprentices at both Corinna's workshop and the Plantin Company, right? Myne was worried about the two of us sticking out, so she always butted in to tell me what clothes to get and when. Master Benno pointed out that I need to worry about these things myself now that Myne's gone, so... yeah. This is my share."

I added my clothes onto the pile as well. I wouldn't have given what I wore any consideration either had Master Benno not mentioned it, so I needed to be careful as well.

"I had no idea..." Tuuli murmured, now looking at the clothes in a whole new light. She gave a small smile, then reached for them with tearful eyes. "Myne always said she was buying the clothes to reward us for helping her shop for her attendants, but she was actually looking out for us as well... How was I supposed to know that? You have to say that kind of thing out loud. In fact, she was always so busy with things that I sometimes wondered if she'd forgotten about us... I feel so dumb now."

"You guys may not realize this, since you can't speak to her directly, but it's crazy how much love you all show for each other.

No Rest for Us

She loves you as much as you love her. Gotta say, my family aren't at each other's throats or anything, but I don't have the same thing with my brothers at all."

Just like that, I was using my Earthdays off work to go to the orphanage with Tuuli and improve my etiquette. Fritz taught me, while Wilma taught Tuuli. This, of course, meant that Tuuli and I were spending all our days off together, which earned me even dirtier looks from Ralph. Nothing I said ever helped my situation either, so I decided to at least test the water with Tuuli, for his sake.

"Out of curiosity, have you been thinking about love and getting into a relationship at all? The girls you know are getting into those things, aren't they?"

"They are, but my hands are honestly too full right now. I'm so busy trying to catch up to Myne that I'm just like, 'Don't get in my way with this love junk. I have stuff to do.'"

In other words, she knew that she was of the age where most girls started to get excited about romance, but she wasn't very interested herself. She didn't want other people wasting her time with it, either.

"Yeaaah, I know how you feel. I'm too busy for that stuff as well, so..."

There had been plenty of country girls in Illgner, but there was so much on my plate right now that, like Tuuli, I just didn't want to pursue any sort of relationship.

Sorry, Ralph. Seems like nobody has a chance with Tuuli right now.

It was near the end of autumn, about a year after Myne had gone to sleep, when Master Benno hurriedly summoned the Gutenbergs together for an emergency meeting. Everyone seemed to be varying levels of annoyed about being called over in the midst of winter prep, but they all straightened their backs after seeing the serious look on his face.

"Lady Elvira—that is, Lady Rozemyne's mother—wants to establish her own printing workshop. Her side of the family, the Haldenzels, are making a big move to establish the industry in their province. The High Priest said they'll be constructing a paper-making workshop, a private ink workshop, and a printing workshop. Seems like she's saying it's her duty as Lady Rozemyne's mother to spread the industry as much as she can."

Heidi tilted her head to one side. "So, um... what does that mean for us?"

"All of you are gonna be participating in a large-scale operation planned to last from next spring until autumn. Spend this winter making sure your workshops and stores will continue functioning without you, and send word to your respective guilds. I'll deal with the guildmaster of the Merchant's Guild."

Every expression in the room changed in an instant—nobody had expected such a huge workload to be pushed onto them out of nowhere.

"Isn't this all too sudden?!"

"The original plan was for us to start now, so you should thank me that you have as long as you do. I managed to delay things until spring, since we don't have any connections with the workshops in Haldenzel to help us out, and the rivers being frozen over means we wouldn't have been able to make paper anyway."

As it turned out, he had managed to buy us an extra season of prep time by agreeing to do their printing in the Rozemyne Workshop during the winter. That was Master Benno for you.

"Lady Elvira is a natural-born archnoble. Unlike Lady Rozemyne, she wasn't raised in the temple, and she doesn't care at all about our commoner circumstances. To make matters worse, the only person who can stop her is currently comatose. Get ready to leave the moment spring comes around."

No Rest for Us

Myne was asleep, but now her family was going on a rampage in her place—a family of archnobles we commoners had no way of stopping. We burst out of the meeting room in a panic and with pale faces; it seemed we Gutenbergs would never get any rest after all.

Meanwhile at the Temple

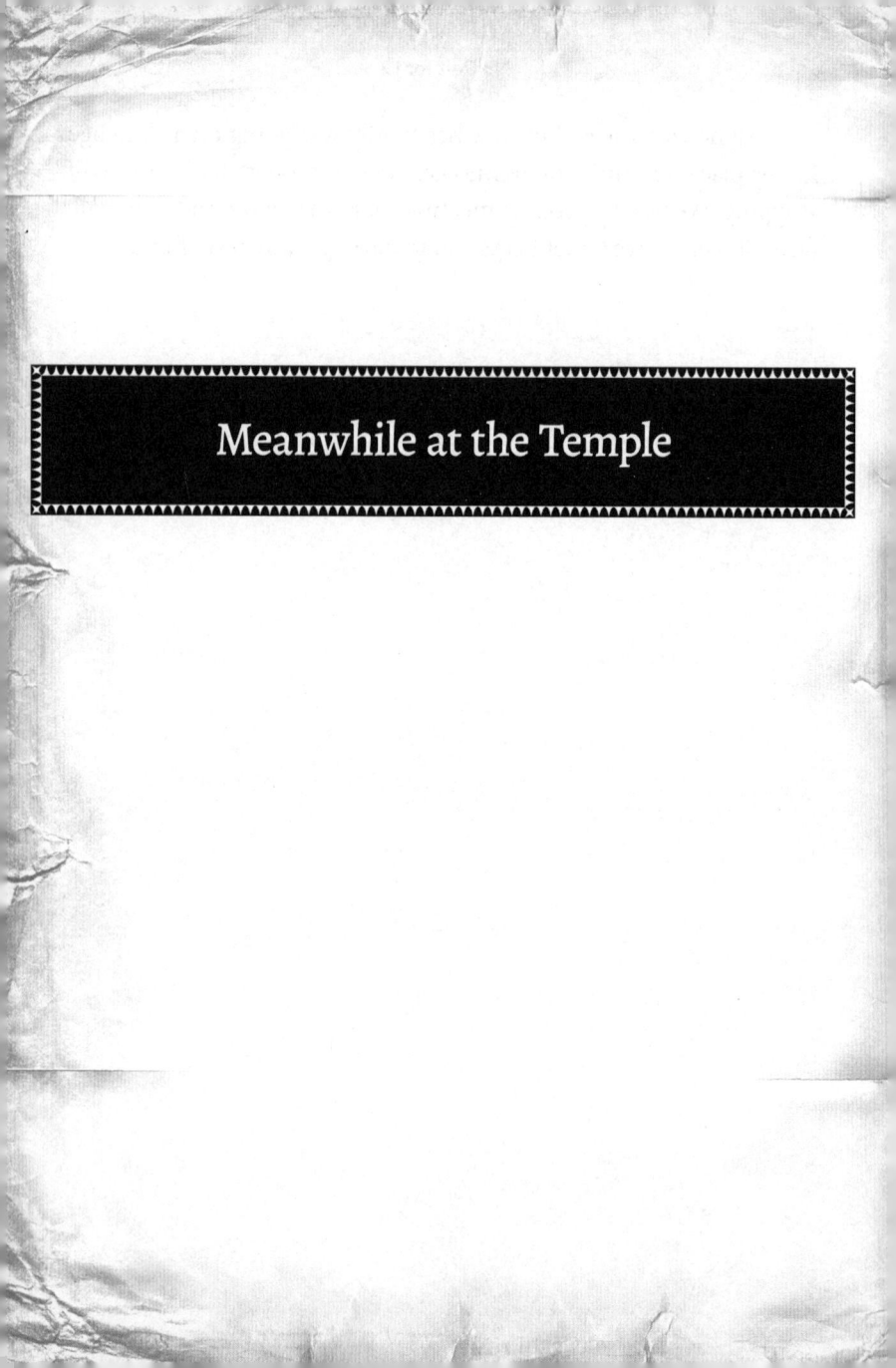

Before me was Lady Rozemyne, silently floating in a box containing a light-blue potion, bright-red lines streaked across her body. The High Priest removed his hands from the concoction, the small ripples on its surface making her hair sway ever so slightly.

He wiped his hands on a towel as he stood up, handed the towel to me, then opened the door. I couldn't enter or leave this workshop on my own, so I hurriedly followed him out. He glanced back a single time at the box in which Lady Rozemyne was sleeping, then quietly closed the door.

"And now, only I can enter this room," the High Priest said. "Rozemyne is safe."

Even if attackers came to the temple, there was nothing they could do to reach her. Only once the High Priest knew that she was safe did his expression return to normal. He now looked as he usually did while at work.

"Fran, if you have any of the letters or memos Rozemyne left behind, show them to me. I wish to establish what plans she had for this winter."

"As you wish."

I promptly went to Lady Rozemyne's work desk and took out the letters she had written to people. I also gathered the notes she had made for herself; she always copied them from her diptych onto proper paper so as to not forget them, which meant we would not have any issues identifying her immediate plans. It was initially a shock to see her using such expensive paper for mere notes, whether it was ripped or not, but I had since grown used to it. Lady Rozemyne felt most at home writing on plant paper, not wooden boards.

As I was organizing the letters into those for her noble associates, her temple associates, and her lower city associates, an ordonnanz flew into the room. It announced that the criminal had been caught, then returned to its yellow feystone form. The High Priest replied, "Very well. I shall return at once," then sent the ordonnanz back.

"Fran, there is work for me to do at the castle," he announced. "I will not return until it is time for the Dedication Ritual. I entrust the temple to you and my attendants. Use the blue priests as needed to finish the necessary preparations."

The High Priest took the letters for Lady Rozemyne's noble associates at once, then strode briskly out of the room. Once he was gone, the other attendants—who were supposed to have retired to their rooms for the day—returned to the High Bishop's chambers.

"Fran, what did the High Priest say? Is Lady Rozemyne going to be okay?" Monika asked, looking up at me with worry. Nicola and Gil waited just as expectantly for my answer; they were all worried about Lady Rozemyne being rushed to her workshop so quickly.

"He said it is likely she will remain asleep for over a year. The poison she was given has put an unexpected strain on her body."

"No way..."

Everyone looked to be on the verge of tears, but it would be a long time before Lady Rozemyne awakened; there was no point in rushing things.

"I will provide more details tomorrow. It is late, and you all need rest."

Meanwhile at the Temple

The apprentices returned to their rooms, still unable to accept what had happened, while I alone stayed behind. It was my turn on night duty, and so I organized the room before writing a letter for Lutz, who could explain the circumstances to both Lady Rozemyne's lower city family and the Plantin Company.

I spent the following day having to explain Lady Rozemyne's situation again and again. The apprentices were up early, having been unable to sleep out of worry, so I gave them the explanatory letter I had written to Lutz and went for a much-needed nap.

Fourth bell rang before I knew it, and when I sat down for lunch, everyone demanded yet more explanations. The High Priest had not given me very precise details in the first place, so despite all their questions, there was not much I could say.

"As Lady Rozemyne said previously, please think of this as her staying at the castle for an extended period of time. We have no choice but to continue as if she were simply away. Please resume what you have been doing so that she does not encounter any complications upon her awakening."

After finishing lunch, Zahm and I organized documents relating to Rozemyne's work before leaving for the High Priest's room. He would need to handle her High Bishop work while she was gone.

"Will the High Priest not collapse at this rate?" I asked, worriedly eyeing the mountain of documents before us. Zahm paused for a moment, then shook his head.

"I assume he will survive, thanks largely to him taking Lady Rozemyne's advice and training other blue priests to help him. I shudder to imagine a world in which he had not done so. Even if she had done nothing else, this fact alone would have earned her my utmost gratitude. Praise be to the gods!"

Zahm had once served the same blue priest as Fritz, so he had quickly come to appreciate both the High Priest's competence and the ease of working beneath him. He had been praising Lady Rozemyne for her skill ever since she was an apprentice blue shrine maiden, thankful for her ability to help the High Priest with his work.

When the time had come to choose one of the High Priest's attendants to leave and serve Lady Rozemyne, Zahm had volunteered sooner than anyone. The food in the High Bishop's chambers was of a higher quality, and the greater workload for each attendant made one's contributions feel that much more meaningful—not to mention that Lady Rozemyne taking on more work would ultimately relieve the burden on the High Priest.

"Now then, shall we go? The High Priest's attendants will need matters explained to them as well."

With that, Zahm and I carried the box of documents from the High Bishop's chambers to the High Priest's chambers.

"Fran, Zahm—we have been waiting for your arrival," one of the attendants said. "This shelf has been cleared for you."

The High Priest must have made arrangements ahead of time, as space had already been cleared for the documents we brought with us. Everyone worked together to organize them and collect information on the events of the previous night, agreeing to do our best to minimize the High Priest's burden and select what jobs could be entrusted to the blue priests.

"Zahm, might I ask you to explain the situation to Brothers Kampfer and Frietack?" I said once the documents were organized. I then headed for the orphanage, and Wilma came rushing over the moment I arrived.

Meanwhile at the Temple

"Fran, I heard from Monika that Lady Rozemyne is going to be asleep for a long time. What will happen to the orphanage?" she asked, so worried that her face was sickly pale. All those who knew how terrible the orphanage had been before Lady Rozemyne became the orphanage director were deathly afraid of her giving up the position, as this introduced the possibility of things returning to the way they had been before.

"Everything is going to be fine. Authority over the temple will shift to the High Priest while Lady Rozemyne is asleep, but I have been instructed to continue overseeing things as I have been. As for the budget, we cannot use Lady Rozemyne's guild card, but the High Priest is managing the High Bishop's payments and the money she is given for being the archduke's child, so we will surely not lack in that regard. As winter preparations are complete, we will be able to last until spring without issue, so long as we are not wasteful."

"...That is true," Wilma murmured with an understanding nod. I also took it upon myself to assure the worried orphans that we would not run out of money while the workshop continued to operate.

I hadn't mentioned this to anyone, but Lady Rozemyne had a locked box—her "under the mattress bank," as she called it—which also contained a considerable sum. Those funds would serve as a safety net, hopefully preventing our circumstances from ever becoming too dire.

"Wilma, those in positions of authority must show neither worry nor panic. Please calm yourself. Lady Rozemyne is going to be fine."

"...Forgive me."

"I will now announce the goals Lady Rozemyne wishes to be completed over the winter."

The task Lady Rozemyne had entrusted the orphanage with last year was for everyone to learn the alphabet, as well as single-digit math. Everyone must have remembered the additional meat they had previously been rewarded with for succeeding, as their concerned gazes soon hardened.

"This year's task is for everyone to learn the basic knowledge required of an attendant before reaching ten years of age. Gray priests who have served as attendants will work as teachers."

Having learned from the situation with Volk, Lady Rozemyne wished to increase the value of all the gray priests. She would rather they be sold as skilled attendants than lowly servants, since their treatment would vary dramatically based on their position, and servants that were more capable went for more money.

"Delia, Lady Rozemyne was worried about Dirk," I continued. "Please contact me at once should he begin to show any abnormalities. The High Priest is exceedingly busy, so his treatment could otherwise be delayed."

"Understood."

My final task was to go to the workshop, but it became clear pretty soon after I arrived that Gil was putting his all into making books, convinced that they would encourage Lady Rozemyne to wake up faster. He did not seem to need my help, and so I simply handed him the letter for Lutz and left.

The next day, Lady Rozemyne's personnel returned to the temple. Without her there to protect them, staying in the castle not only ran the risk of their recipes being leaked, but also of those with authority forcibly stealing them away to serve someone else. Lady Rozemyne had specifically asked that Ella and Rosina not be left there, since they were both especially vulnerable as young women.

Meanwhile at the Temple

The personnel were informed that Lady Rozemyne would remain asleep for over a year; then they were given their instructions.

"Ella, Hugo—please continue preparing food for the attendants and the orphanage, as you have been. Lady Rozemyne also wishes for Nicola to be given an opportunity to advance her dreams of becoming a chef, so please accept her services and guide her as an assistant. You are to assist with the completion of the recipe book, on which little progress has been made due to how busy things have been, and should you have any spare time once that is done, she suggests that you start trying to invent new recipes of your own."

"Understood."

Nicola wrote down on her diptych everything that needed to be done in the kitchen with a broad smile across her face. She would be handling all the writing, as neither Ella nor Hugo could read, which was also likely a contributing factor toward the recipe book having progressed so little.

"Rosina, please teach the orphanage children to play music. Lady Rozemyne has said that you may recognize some of them as having musical talent, even if they do not see it themselves. She believes that affording them an opportunity for their skills to blossom may change their futures for the better."

"In other words, I need only teach them as Lady Christine taught me? Very well. I will do what I can."

Upon hearing that Lady Rozemyne wished to improve the value of the orphans to secure better workplaces for them, Rosina—who had been purchased to serve as a personal musician once herself—smiled softly and nodded.

So began life in the temple without Lady Rozemyne. Nicola assisted the chefs while working as an attendant, while Gil and Fritz continued their duties in the workshop and in the orphanage over the winter. Zahm, Monika, and I generally spent our days working in the High Priest's chambers, taking breaks only to eat and sleep.

"Preparations for the Dedication Ritual are complete."

"Does that mean the firewood is also ready? Brother Kampfer, have you decided on an order for the priests?"

"Brother Frietack, please send word to the other blue priests."

We were able to finish preparing for the Dedication Ritual before the High Priest returned, just as we had the previous year. The work was completed without any considerable issues; not only was this the second time Brothers Kampfer and Frietack were being entrusted with the preparations, there were also more blue priests willing to help.

"Is everything ready?" the High Priest asked upon his return. He checked to make sure the preparations were properly completed, then praised the blue priests for their work. "Well done. You may now rest until the Dedication Ritual in two days' time."

He had the blue priests leave the room, then went into his hidden room to retrieve a bag of feystones. Once he had it, the two of us headed to the hidden room in which Lady Rozemyne was still asleep. She looked just as she had on that fateful night, though the blue in the potion was darker than before and the red lines on her skin seemed to be glowing.

"I left her alone for too long..." the High Priest muttered, his brow furrowed and the frustration clear in his voice.

He instructed me to put the feystones into the potion, and so I promptly obliged. There were black feystones and clear feystones; I took them out of the bag and dropped them into the potion one by one. They started to absorb Lady Rozemyne's mana, causing the potion's color to fade before my very eyes.

Meanwhile at the Temple

"This fool compressed her mana far too much," the High Priest sighed, taking Lady Rozemyne's hand and glaring at the red lines on her skin. "These feystones won't suffice at all. She is fortunate it is time for the Dedication Ritual."

I then heard him murmur that the process would take longer than he had expected.

While the High Priest recorded something about Lady Rozemyne's health on a board, I removed the feystones that were now filled with her mana, delicately wiped them, and then carefully put them back in the bag.

"That should do for today," the High Priest said.

It became a daily job for me to take the feystones the priests had emptied during the Dedication Ritual and put them back into Lady Rozemyne's potion to refill them. It was thanks to her mana that the Dedication Ritual concluded without issue, but even afterward, we needed to continue storing mana in preparation for Spring Prayer.

The High Priest and I entered the workshop once again. It certainly was a relief seeing Lady Rozemyne each time, but the fact that she appeared completely unchanged was disheartening.

Please wake up soon, Lady Rozemyne...

With the Dedication Ritual complete, the High Priest focused his efforts on the paperwork that had accumulated. Despite the increase in workload, both Lord Damuel and Lord Eckhart were busy receiving special training with the Knight's Order, so the High Priest was once again supporting his lifestyle with potions, such that his attendants would murmur about how often they saw him reach for them.

It was easy to see that he was being buried under an avalanche of work—not just his own as the High Priest and from the castle, but also Lady Rozemyne's High Bishop work and her duties with the orphanage, the workshop, the Plantin Company, and the like. Despite having invested much time training blue priests to assist with his work, they were not capable of managing the orphanage, nor could they do business with the Plantin Company.

"It is rare for members of the Plantin Company to visit during the winter, and the orphanage likewise spends most of that time in hibernation, so I do not foresee any problems," I said.

"Indeed. Rozemyne already has her attendants handling the workshop and orphanage, and I would like for them to handle some measure of the work."

Once spring came, however, it was necessary to sell the winter handiwork and start making paper, which inevitably meant dealing with money and taking on duties that could not be put off. The High Priest had work being loaded onto him from the castle as well, despite his numerous temple duties, so there was nothing he could do but give a bitter frown and pick up another potion.

"There is nothing I would like less than to ask *him* for help, but I suppose I have no other choice..."

The High Priest sent an ordonnanz, and after what was no more than a brief wait, we saw a highbeast racing toward the temple at immense speed. In mere moments, Lord Justus, who had no reservations about visiting the lower city and understood Lady Rozemyne's predicament, was kneeling before the High Priest with sparkling eyes.

"Lord Ferdinand, I have arrived at your summons. You may count on me to manage the workshop and handle business with the merchants."

"Fritz, take Justus to the workshop and explain to him the finances of our business with the Plantin Company. Justus, I am too busy to deal with you causing problems. Contain yourself. Is that understood?"

"As you wish. Now then, Fritz—let us depart."

"Fritz, report to me the moment something happens. I shall not hesitate to beat Justus down in an instant, if necessary."

Lord Justus, not even trying to hide his excitement, practically dragged Fritz out of the room with him. I was terribly concerned about this; had calling for him truly been a good idea?

"High Priest..."

"Fear not, Fran. Justus has a love for gathering information, but he does not disclose his secrets lightly. Furthermore, he is my retainer; his eccentric nature belies his competence."

As the High Priest predicted, Lord Justus quickly grew accustomed to the workshop. He wasn't the kind of person to lord his status over others, and according to Fritz he was exceptionally skilled when it came to fitting in with groups and working with others.

After many more visits to the workshop, Lord Justus asked me about the general workflow prior to Lady Rozemyne's situation. I started preparing the relevant documents from the High Bishop's chambers, in the meantime deciding to ask him what he thought about his time there so far.

"Lord Justus, how has the workshop been?"

"Very stimulating. Everything is so interesting there, as I would expect from something overseen by Lady Rozemyne. She has trained quite fascinating subordinates; they even allowed me to swish the water when I first visited."

It was neither proper nor acceptable for a noble to perform manual labor, so I could easily imagine how conflicted the workshop workers must have been when Lord Justus asked to do such a thing. Fritz must not have had an easy time.

"But the second I touched the paper on the boards," Lord Justus continued, "one of the leherls from the Plantin Company yelled at me. 'What're you doing, you idiot?!' he shouted, loud enough for everyone to hear."

Lutz, why in the world would you do that?! And Fritz, how could you allow that to happen?!

But as the blood drained from my face, Lord Justus continued with an endlessly amused expression. Silence had apparently fallen over the entire workshop after Lutz's outburst, with even Lutz himself realizing he said something that he shouldn't have. Before anyone else could speak up, however, Fritz had protectively stepped forward wearing the kind of cold smile one would normally expect from Lord Ferdinand, immediately giving Lord Justus a strict lecture that he recalled verbatim.

"I did not expect the High Priest to send us someone so incompetent that they would not understand the time and money lost from damaged paper, even after having the entire process explained to them. He surely must have made an error in judgment due to being so busy. A manager who destroys products cannot take Lady Rozemyne's place, and so I will report this to the High Priest at once. We do not need someone who fails to understand the importance of our work."

"...A-And what did you do then, Lord Justus?"

"I obviously didn't want to be called useless and kicked out on my first day, especially knowing that Lord Ferdinand was desperate enough to have actually requested my help, so I gave them enough to cover the cost of the paper and a little extra to keep them quiet. Whew... It sure was close. I need to use this opportunity to show off my talents and regain my honor. I've got to admit, I expected nothing less from Lady Rozemyne's subordinates, considering how she herself always stands up to Lord Ferdinand, lecturing him about his reliance on potions being unhealthy and all that."

Meanwhile at the Temple

That was probably not how most nobles would have reacted, but in any case, I kept my silence; he had evidently deemed it necessary to pay them off, and with the incident already over, I saw no reason to question his decision. There was equally no need to trouble the High Priest with such a matter, so I took Fritz's lead and spoke not a word about it.

Lord Justus did not come to the temple particularly often, no doubt busy with his own matters, but he was just as skilled as the High Priest had said: each time he arrived, he finished up multiple days of work all at once. While here, he would report to the High Priest on both the workshop and some other duty he had been given before returning to the Noble's Quarter with yet more work pushed onto him. From the snippets of conversation I had managed to catch, it seemed that he was gathering information on the culprit who had harmed Lady Rozemyne.

The midpoint of spring approached, and so began preparations for Spring Prayer. It seemed that the archduke's children would be taking Lady Rozemyne's place this year, traveling the Central District with feystones in hand. Their plan was to divide the journey threefold to shorten the overall process, much like Lady Rozemyne and the High Priest had done, except this time while borrowing two important people from the archduke. It was truly heartrending that the High Priest was enduring such an overwhelming workload that he was forced to use any means available to him to get things done.

As I knew more about the ceremonies than Lady Rozemyne's other attendants, I accompanied Lady Charlotte as a guide. The High Priest gave me special instructions while we were preparing.

"Fran, use this opportunity to create a new saint. Tell a moving story to all those you can: 'Saint Rozemyne was poisoned protecting the archduke's children, both of whom have declared their wish to offer blessings in the place of their sister to repay her noble deed.' If they are showered with praise for being as compassionate and extraordinary as Lady Rozemyne, then it will become easier for us to use them next year as well."

After the High Priest had explained how to lay this groundwork, he handed me a considerable number of the improved-flavor rejuvenation potions. He seemed to have noticed my hesitation to exploit the still-young children of the archduke, as he then gave me a dismissive scoff.

"If Charlotte and Wilfried do not finish Spring Prayer feeling confident in their own abilities, and subsequently refuse to also take Rozemyne's place for the Harvest Festival, it is the orphanage that will suffer first due to the lack of food that would have been paid to Rozemyne for the winter," he noted.

His message was clear: I had no choice but to accept the duty of establishing the legend of Saint Charlotte. The past few years had taught me all about the importance of money; this Spring Prayer needed to go well no matter what, or the temple and orphanage would suffer.

As it was not traditional for underage apprentices to perform religious ceremonies, the only child-sized ceremonial clothes available to us belonged to Lady Rozemyne. We gave Lady Charlotte her white High Bishop robes, which required no alterations whatsoever, and Lord Wilfried her blue ceremonial robes, which did need some alterations to accommodate his marginally greater height. These adjustments did not take long at all though, thanks to Corinna of the Gilberta Company having accounted for Lady Rozemyne growing when she made the outfit.

Meanwhile at the Temple

We requested the usual carriages from the Plantin Company and prepared to bring back Achim and Egon, who had been staying in Hasse's winter mansion. We also had knights accompanying us at the High Priest's request—twice as many as usual to guard against a potential attack by members of the nobility.

Lady Charlotte did not have a highbeast, as she had yet to enter the Royal Academy, so I traveled in a carriage for the first time in quite a while. She seemed to have great respect for Lady Rozemyne, as she rejoiced when I told her about her sister's experiences in the temple. In return, I was graced with stories of Lady Rozemyne's time in the castle, so it was a very productive journey overall.

When Richt first spotted Lady Charlotte upon our arrival in Hasse, he mistakenly thought they hadn't been forgiven after all. Following my explanation that Saint Charlotte was dedicating herself to bless the land in her sister's absence, however, he welcomed her with tears of gratitude.

Lady Charlotte was notably tense about performing her first ceremony, but she took the feystone with Lady Rozemyne's mana and completed it brilliantly. We reunited with Achim and Egon before moving to the monastery, where I first checked to see that everything was in order, then had Lady Charlotte award the soldiers with their payment.

"Fran, may I ask how the High Bishop is?" Gunther asked upon receiving his money, his expression clouded over.

"It seems the burden on her body was even greater than the High Priest expected, and her sleep will most likely continue for longer still."

"I see..."

While we were on the road, Lady Charlotte used far fewer potions than Lady Rozemyne, and when Spring Prayer came to an end, she had used only a small portion of all those we had brought. I couldn't help but sigh at how unhealthy and weak Lady Rozemyne truly was, that she had needed to use the bulk of our potions just to survive to the end.

Upon returning from Spring Prayer, Gil came to me for advice, wanting to know how we should proceed with the printing. My understanding was that Lady Rozemyne had gathered stories from the noble children while at the castle, and after discussing matters with the High Priest, he delivered to me the stories collected in the winter playroom. I promptly gave them to Gil, but he merely scratched his ear uncomfortably and shook his head.

"I can't print these. They're written the way kids talk, so they need to be fixed up to read more like a book. Do you know anyone who can do that?"

"I can say with all certainty that nobody has the time to do such a thing at the moment."

With that said, Lady Rozemyne had managed to write her manuscripts alongside assisting the High Priest, memorizing the procedures for many ceremonies, and heading to the castle to play her role as a noble daughter. Despite all the time we had spent together, I still found myself stunned by her love for books and her obsession with making them.

Several days later, Gil came to say that Tuuli wanted us to teach her proper etiquette. She would pay us with a book of collected short stories that Lady Rozemyne had made for her and her family. The text was already edited to be readable, and Gil wanted to have it printed next after the collection of knight stories.

Meanwhile at the Temple

Tuuli was Lady Rozemyne's true sister, and she had provided much help to those in the orphanage. The High Priest therefore granted her his permission, determining that this would be a good opportunity to repay her for all she had done. There were no better people for this task than Rosina and Wilma, since they had been strictly trained in the way of proper etiquette beneath Sister Christine, and so I asked for their assistance. It seemed that Lutz would be learning alongside Tuuli as well.

I came by to see how the lessons were going for a short while. The sight of their struggles made me a little nostalgic for when Lady Rozemyne had continuously gotten her long sleeves caught in everything she possibly could.

While I was there, Wilma mentioned that Tuuli was offering advice on how to raise Dirk. The orphanage had lost all of the gray shrine maidens who had given birth themselves, so nobody was quite sure how to raise a toddler. Lady Rozemyne had provided some guidance, but Wilma and Delia wished to know all they could, and so they were endlessly grateful for Tuuli's wisdom; she had learned much from helping raise her younger brother, who was a similar age to Dirk.

Nicola came of age at the end of spring. We held a small celebration just as we had for Rosina, but she largely just wailed about how Lady Rozemyne wasn't there to teach her new recipes as she had expected. This outburst was somewhat short-lived though, as a smile returned to her face the instant Ella brought out some sweets and mentioned that Lady Rozemyne could simply teach her the recipes when she eventually awoke.

The Italian restaurant came asking for new recipes around the same time as Nicola's coming-of-age ceremony, but we simply said they would need to come up with some themselves, as it was due to be another year before Lady Rozemyne woke up. This somehow turned into Hugo and Leise sharing information about their original creations, which in turn fired up the kitchen staff. They spoke as though their pride as chefs was on the line, determined to produce food that was worthy of Lady Rozemyne's name.

Halfway through summer, sometime after the Starbind Ceremony, Lady Rozemyne's guard knight Lady Brigitte was relieved of duty and returned to her home province of Illgner. It seemed that she was preparing to get married.

Lord Damuel seemed to be exceedingly depressed, so I could imagine things had not gone well between them. I could not say I was surprised, though: the High Priest had mentioned that a relationship would be trying for them, given their different classes and circumstances. I did not understand marriage much myself, but I could at the very least pray to the gods that he would see more success in his duties as a knight than he had trying to procure a wife.

Hugo and Ella walked up to me, passing by Lord Damuel as he continued to mope.

"What is this important announcement you spoke of?" I asked.

The two exchanged a look, bright grins creeping onto their faces. "We're getting married," Hugo announced. "Both of our parents approved."

I could see Damuel covering his ears out of the corner of my eye; this evidently wasn't something that he wanted to hear about right now.

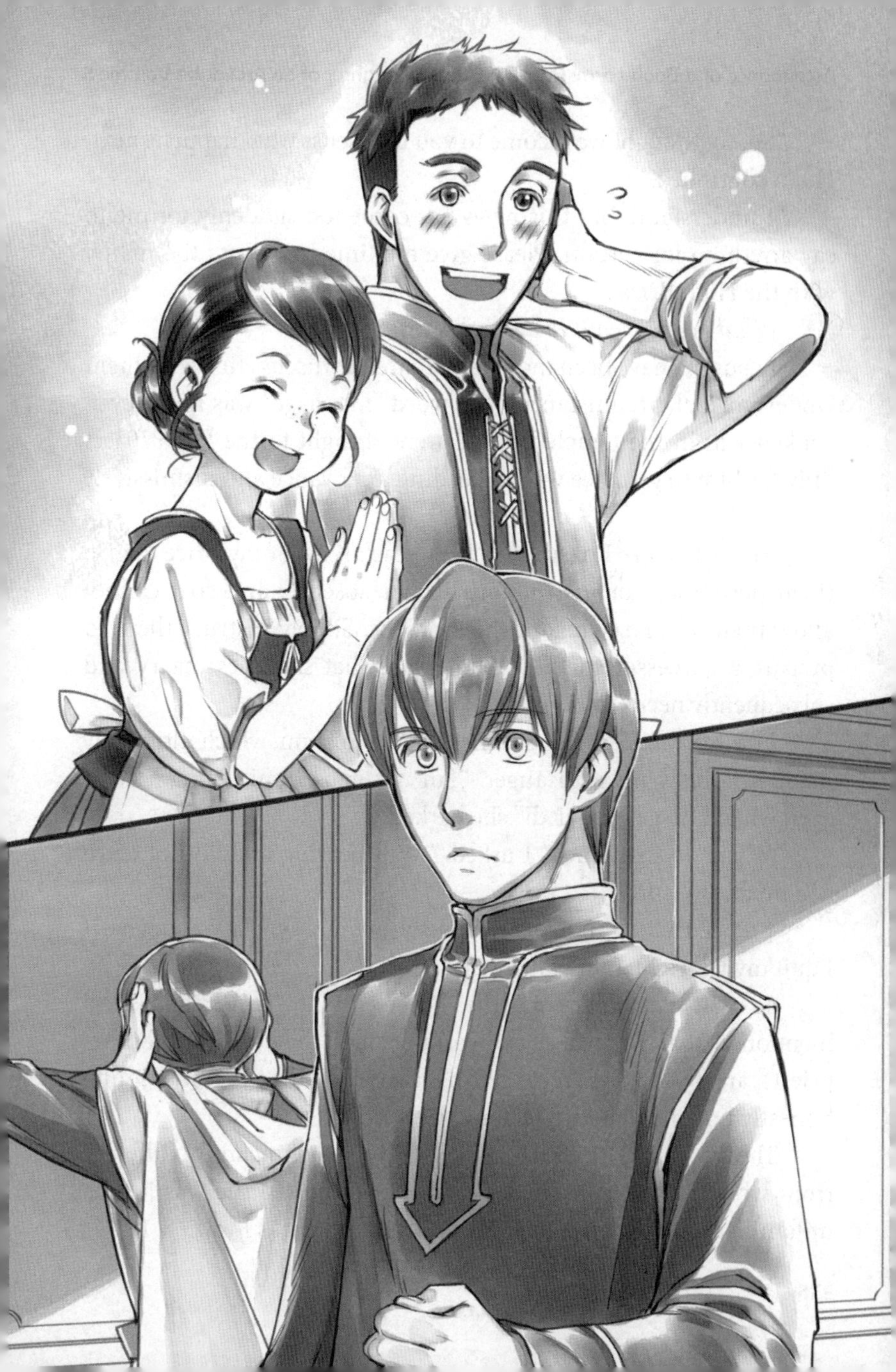

"So, we thought we'd come to you to discuss what happens next," Hugo continued.

"I understand, but this news has come too suddenly for me to say anything for certain. Please give me time to discuss the matter with the High Priest."

What is one meant to do in this situation...?

I couldn't have been more unprepared to discuss this with them. Under normal circumstances, the word "marriage" was never even spoken within the temple walls. I went straight to the High Priest, only for him to grimace with exceeding annoyance and dismissively wave his hand.

"Those two are Rozemyne's personnel. It is not my place to give them permission or instructions in her absence, and so I cannot allow them to marry before she awakens. Simply instruct them to prepare a successor for Ella in the case that she does marry and subsequently needs to resign."

I passed the High Priest's message on to them, which ultimately made Ella blow up with anger. "I'm not gonna quit being a cook, even when I do get married!" she barked.

"What? Is that true?" I asked. "Will bearing a child not leave you unable to work?"

"I'd need a little time off, obviously, but how would we survive if I quit my job right after getting married?!"

"Is that customary in the lower city...? The High Priest mentioned that women cease working once they are wed, but as priests are forbidden from getting married, this subject is quite honestly not one that I understand."

The married life Ella spoke of was significantly different from what the High Priest had said. It seemed that he was just as unfamiliar with the circumstances of commoners as I was.

Meanwhile at the Temple

"Nobles are a lot different from us commoners. I plan on working even after getting married, but if that's new to you guys, I guess I'll need to wait until Lady Rozemyne wakes up for sure. Oh well," Ella said, seeming to give up relatively quickly. Hugo, on the other hand, was not so understanding.

"Hold it, Ella. Don't give up that easily!"

"Hm? I'm not giving up. There's no getting around the fact we've gotta wait though, is there?"

"But waiting means not being the stars of next year's Star Festival, right? Right?!"

"Who can say? It all depends on Lady Rozemyne," I said, earning me a sharp glare from Hugo.

"Gah! Am I fated to never get married?! I can get girlfriends, but not wives?! Is that how it is, Fran?!" he exclaimed, grabbing me by the shoulders and shaking me about. There was no answer I could give him, though; this matter truly was beyond me.

Summer ended and development of the new ink was completed, which meant the Rozemyne Workshop could now start printing higher-quality playing cards. The new paper they were being printed on was firm and glossy, producing cards entirely unlike those made of wood, while the various colors of ink meant that each suit could now be easily differentiated and decorated with beautiful visuals.

One autumn day close to the Harvest Festival, Brother Egmont suddenly visited the High Bishop's chambers with a single gray shrine maiden in tow. She looked sick with anxiety, and the sight caused me to defensively tense up a little.

"Brother Egmont, I do not recall you arranging a meeting..."

"Why would I need to when the High Bishop's gone and there are only gray priests here?" he retorted.

I glanced at Zahm, who smoothly disappeared into the kitchen. He was likely leaving through a back door to inform the High Priest of this sudden arrival, so I needed to buy time until they returned.

"My sincerest apologies. We have not welcomed a blue priest without an appointment before, and so we are somewhat unprepared. I can imagine some urgent business has inspired your arrival. May I ask what it is?"

"Take Lily back to the orphanage and get me a new attendant. Bring me gray shrine maidens."

I swiftly looked over at Monika, who spun around and exited the room at once to inform Wilma, before turning back to Brother Egmont. "My sincerest apologies once again, but we cannot accommodate such a request without advance warning."

"Why not?"

"The gray shrine maidens all have duties given to them by Lady Rozemyne. It will take time to gather them together, and given the manual labor they have been engaged in, they will not be clean enough to be presented so suddenly to a blue priest."

Brother Egmont crossed his arms, not really seeming to understand. He evidently wasn't familiar with the concept of a gray shrine maiden not being immediately presentable.

"If you are to be taking a new attendant, it is necessary that they look as beautiful as possible, rather than being brought in the midst of their work," I continued. "I believe it is in your best interests to return to your chambers for today and wait for the candidates to be prepared."

Despite his frustration, Brother Egmont ultimately agreed; he was a blue priest repulsed by even the thought of something unsightly.

"With that settled, might I ask why you are returning Lily to the orphanage?" I asked. "It is important for us to know how she has displeased you." My question was purely for appearance's sake, though. There was only one reason gray shrine maidens were ever returned to the orphanage, and so I simply kept my eyes down and pretended to write things on a form.

"She got pregnant," Brother Egmont said tersely, looking down at Lily with a disgusted grimace. "She's been whining about feeling sick for days, and now she's throwing up everywhere. I've never seen an attendant this useless in my life."

"I see. It certainly is unacceptable for an attendant to be unable to do their duties."

Seeing that we were in agreement, Brother Egmont lightened up a little, his tone now slightly less harsh. "Exactly. I need a replacement immediately."

"...That said, it is the High Priest who handles the ownership of attendants, not the High Bishop. I must ask that you schedule a meeting with him."

"Excuse me?! You're the High Bishop's attendant. Handle it yourself!"

Brother Egmont had been favored by the previous High Bishop, and so he was used to speaking solely to him whenever he wanted something done. Things were different now, though—the High Priest was working hard to return the temple to how it had been before the previous High Bishop's reign.

"The transfer of priests and shrine maidens comes under the High Priest's jurisdiction," I explained. "I am aware that such distinctions were at times ignored in the past, but that is no longer the case."

"You're pretty cocky for a gray priest!"

Brother Egmont raised a hand to strike me, but before he could, there came a small chime. I internally sighed with relief; that was the High Priest's bell, meaning Zahm must have returned with him.

"My apologies, Brother Egmont, but I have already arranged a meeting with the High Priest here. However, I will yield my meeting time so that you may settle this matter with him first."

"Ngh..."

He had no problem arriving unannounced when only gray priests were present, but he wouldn't be so rude to the High Priest himself. Members of the former High Bishop's faction remained uncooperative with the High Priest, and for that reason, their income was slowly being slashed, forcing them into more uncomfortable lifestyles.

"Fran, why is Egmont here?" the High Priest asked upon entering the room, meeting him with a displeased stare. "I believe I am already scheduled for a meeting at this time."

"Brother Egmont arrived without warning. It seems he wishes to replace one of his gray shrine maidens posthaste," I responded promptly.

"I see. The transfer of priests and shrine maidens comes under my jurisdiction, Egmont, so you are to arrange a meeting with me, not the High Bishop's attendants. Return to your chambers for today; my time is already occupied."

Brother Egmont dragged Lily out of the room, ultimately having no choice but to arrange a meeting at a later date. Zahm shut the door firmly behind him, at which point I knelt before the High Priest.

"I truly apologize for the disturbance."

"There is no need. I predicted that incidents of this manner would occur with Rozemyne gone, but replacing a gray shrine maiden, hm? I imagine she will be quite upset if she discovers I did not handle this as she would. What a pain."

Meanwhile at the Temple

The High Priest went on to explain Lady Rozemyne's will. She had been quite firm that while she did not mind gray shrine maidens who *wanted* to be attendants being given to blue priests, she would under no circumstances accept someone being forced into it, even if that necessitated her taking them on as her own attendants.

Lady Rozemyne truly is soft when it comes to the orphanage...

It was of course heartwarming, since it was so much like her, but it also made me worry for the future when Lady Rozemyne was no longer the High Bishop.

"Fran, I imagine that Egmont will send his request for the meeting without hesitation. I intend to meet with him at fifth bell three days from now. Be prepared to bring shrine maidens from the orphanage, with Rozemyne's will in mind."

"As you wish."

After seeing the High Priest off, I left the chambers to Zahm and went directly to the orphanage. There was no escaping that someone would be chosen to become Brother Egmont's new attendant, so preparations would need to be made before it was time for the meeting.

When I arrived, I was welcomed by a trembling Wilma, her hands clasped tightly in front of her chest. "Fran, what happened?" she asked me. Monika was at her side, looking worried for her.

"Lily has become pregnant. A new attendant is going to be selected for Brother Egmont three days from now."

"Three days from now...?"

"The High Priest has said we are going to respect Lady Rozemyne's will, so it should not be as tragic as you may think."

Wilma's fear of men meant she did not want to leave the orphanage, so her position as one of Lady Rozemyne's attendants was more than she could have ever hoped for. The other gray priests and shrine maidens stuck in the orphanage, however, saw leaving to serve a blue priest as moving up in the world. To many, even becoming an attendant for Brother Egmont was considered worthwhile.

There were more adult gray shrine maidens in the orphanage than before, with many having come of age just like Rosina and Nicola had, but there were still only twenty or so in total. They were all lined up, some tightly clasping their hands as they hoped to stay at the orphanage, others debating with themselves whether or not this was something they wanted, and still others looking ahead with sparkling eyes, eagerly looking forward to being chosen just as Delia had in the past.

"Do any of you wish to become Brother Egmont's attendant?" I asked. Four women shot their hands up in an instant. I gazed across them, completely ignoring those who still seemed to be unsure about the decision, then nodded. "Very well. You four shall accompany me to the meeting three days from now."

"Fran, won't you be bringing them all...?" Wilma asked, blinking several times in surprise. She was used to all shrine maidens of adult age being taken out of the orphanage, with the blue priests then choosing whoever they liked most.

"It is Lady Rozemyne's will that each orphan have the power to choose their future. Those who wish to become attendants will therefore be prioritized."

Three days later at fifth bell, I brought the four shrine maidens who had volunteered to the High Priest's chambers. Brother Egmont looked at them and frowned.

"Just four?"

"Many shrine maidens were executed by the former High Bishop. Were you not aware, Brother Egmont?"

"No, I was. Anyway... these girls aren't bad."

Meanwhile at the Temple

The former High Bishop had prioritized appearance above all else when choosing which shrine maidens to keep alive, so it was only natural that those who remained had praiseworthy beauty. Brother Egmont compared them with a vulgar look in his eyes, then pointed at one.

"Alright. You."

The selected shrine maiden was left behind as I returned to the orphanage with Lily and the other three. The High Priest would handle the contract himself.

I didn't know the specifics, but I was aware that those being assigned to serve blue priests were made to sign a magic contract preventing them from leaking details of Lady Rozemyne's recipes, workshop, or personal life.

Wilma was already waiting for us when we returned to the orphanage. "Welcome back, Lily. It must have been quite the struggle to work while so unwell. Here you may rest as much as you need to."

Lily suddenly burst into tears. Wilma stroked her back, listening compassionately as the girl sobbed about being deathly afraid of her body changing in ways she did not understand, and the blue priest she had served calling her useless and in the way. It had hurt her heart beyond words.

Deciding to leave Lily to Wilma, I exited the orphanage. This was surely the best possible result—just as Lady Rozemyne wished, a shrine maiden who desired to become an attendant had done so, while one who did not was allowed to quit.

In any case, there was now a pregnant woman in the orphanage, and that introduced its own problems. Lily had said that she did not understand the changes her body was going through, but neither did we. I asked the High Priest what he knew, but he merely said to ignore her, explaining that the baby would simply be born on its own after enough time. We all trusted his judgments, and as the whole orphanage seemed particularly relaxed about it all, Tuuli and Lutz visited to learn etiquette as planned.

"Ignore her?! Born on its own?! That's ridiculous!" Tuuli exclaimed. "Childbirth is a crazy big deal! Do noble babies just pop out of thin air or something?!"

"It's not somethin' you can do without preparing! You've gotta deliver the baby with a ton of people helping!" Lutz added.

The blood drained from my face. Tuuli had assisted when her mother gave birth, and as a boy, Lutz always raced to help when a neighbor was in such a situation, so their words held considerable weight. It was only then that I remembered commoners and nobles had distinct cultures and understood things differently. It was likely that they had their own understandings of childbirth as well, and given that the orphanage didn't have mana or magic tools, the commoner perspective was a lot more relevant to us.

With the High Priest's advice on the matter now no longer of use to us, we had no choice but to rely on outside help. But there was nobody in the orphanage with childbirth experience, and nobody in the lower city was eccentric enough to come somewhere so widely scorned to help.

If only Lady Rozemyne were here...

Her absence was painful. She had likewise seen her little brother's birth up close, and it would have been simple enough for her to gather commoners in the lower city to assist.

"My mom would come for sure, but I don't think she can do it all on her own," Tuuli said.

"I'll see what Master Benno can do," Lutz continued. "Corinna's given birth before, so I'm sure he knows what we'll need."

And so Lutz went to consult Master Benno, who had apparently responded with: *"Babies don't just come out on their own! It's too dangerous to have people that ignorant handle this! That woman's gonna die there!"* Everyone went pale upon hearing that, never having considered that this would be so difficult.

When Lutz and Tuuli asked Master Benno to think of a solution, his conclusion was to bring Lily to Hasse during the Harvest Festival. The monastery there had a better relationship with commoners than the temple, and if Achim and Egon asked for help after having spent the winter there on the High Bishop's orders, it was likely that at least a few women would volunteer. Furthermore, Master Benno had said that even the orphans from Hasse would know more about childbirth than the shrine maidens in the temple.

As expected of Master Benno... Thank you for providing advice even during these busy times.

Following Master Benno's recommendations, we made the necessary preparations to move Lily to Hasse. We also asked the Plantin Company what tools we would need for the childbirth itself and made sure they were at hand.

It wasn't long before I was boarding one of the carriages heading to Hasse for the Harvest Festival with Lily, Achim, and Egon. I had written a letter addressed to Richt in advance, requesting his assistance with the childbirth.

Lady Charlotte delivered the letter for me, then confirmed that he had agreed to help. As expected, Nora had previous experience assisting with such matters, so she played an important role inspecting everything we had brought, checking on Lily's health, and figuring out when she was likely to give birth.

"I'd estimate somewhere around the end of spring," she said. "When it's time for Spring Prayer, please bring a few extra shrine maidens. We don't need many men, since they can't come into the room while she's giving birth."

I see. Men not being allowed in explains why Tuuli and Lutz know different things...

Lily remained in Hasse as we departed for our next stop during the Harvest Festival. We were receiving Lord Wilfried and Lady Charlotte's assistance here as well, as planned, so we easily gathered what we needed for winter preparations.

We cooperated with the Gilberta Company to butcher the pigs, just as we had the year before, and everything was progressing smoothly—that is, until the end of autumn approached. Master Benno from the Plantin Company was summoned by the High Priest and told that he was to expand the printing industry. It seemed that Lady Rozemyne's mother, Lady Elvira, wished to establish a printing workshop in her family's home province.

"It will simply be impossible to begin right away. Even if we do leave immediately, not a single piece of paper can be made in a province with frozen rivers. Plus, how will you support us with food and materials when Haldenzel freezes over, trapping us there?" Benno asked, protesting the immediacy of the demand.

"I imagine Giebe Haldenzel would provide you with food, but it certainly would be pointless to send you there before any work can be done," the High Priest replied, falling into thought. I could tell from the troubled look on Master Benno's face that he was wishing Lady Rozemyne was present to support him.

"Every workshop will require its own preparations, and I will not be able to establish them all myself without first securing the assistance of the Merchant's Guild," Master Benno explained.

Meanwhile at the Temple

"Using noble authority to force matters will only breed discontent and cause problems in the future. Nobles, merchants, and craftspeople each have their own distinct customs. You and Lady Elvira surely both understand how necessary it is to lay the proper groundwork, correct?"

"In that case, prepare a list of everything you will require and have it delivered to me by the winter baptism ceremony. It is necessary to provide concrete evidence of what needs to be arranged before work can begin."

Master Benno left the High Priest's room, cradling his head as he trudged to the front gate.

He later returned for a business negotiation with Lady Elvira, with the High Priest present as the one responsible for the printing industry in Lady Rozemyne's absence. Lady Elvira had something that she wanted printed for winter socializing no matter the cost, and it was to that end that she required her own workshop, which she wanted to be constructed immediately.

"In that case, we will print what you need ourselves at the Rozemyne Workshop," Master Benno suggested. It would mean them abandoning winter preparations to desperately run the workshop at full capacity for a while, but his proposal was accepted, buying him some time before they needed to build a printing workshop in Haldenzel.

Master Benno went straight to the workshop to directly ask the gray priests for their help. Not a single person refused; they owed much to the Plantin Company, and so they wanted to do whatever they could to repay them. He promptly took out the manuscript that Lady Elvira had given him, with both Gil and Lutz frowning upon seeing how thick it was.

"It'll take too long to set the letters with this many pages. We don't even know how many characters this is," Lutz said.

"Yeah. We should go with mimeograph printing for this one," Gil agreed.

They both nodded, then headed to the orphanage with wax paper and their tools in hand. Everyone else had already started making the necessary preparations, having sprung into action the moment they heard the words "mimeograph printing."

Master Benno blinked, impressed at how well-organized their workflow was, at which point Fritz walked over to him.

"Master Benno, we intend to do everything in our power to help, but what about winter preparations? There is much we are going to lack if we miss the opportunity to gather in the forest."

"I went ahead and charged them a huge express fee. If we're going to make this happen, we'll need to buy most of our winter prep."

"In that case, I have a list of things we will need. Can I ask you to take care of them?"

"Yep. I'm the one forcing all this work on you, after all. That's the least I can do."

With Master Benno handling winter preparations for us, we would be able to keep working until right before winter socializing began.

"Thank you. In which case, you may return to your store now, Master Benno. I imagine we are not the only ones you need to discuss this with."

"Nope. Thanks, Fritz. See you later."

With that, Benno spun around and exited the workshop.

"Fran, it is as you heard. I will entrust the orphanage's winter preparations to you," Fritz said, pushing the workshop's list of necessary goods into my hands.

Meanwhile at the Temple

I went ahead to the orphanage, since I needed to collect a list from them as well. When I arrived, Lutz and Gil were already lining up tools on the dining hall tables.

"Rosina, can I ask you to make stencils for the letters, then have Wilma make stencils for the art?" Lutz asked.

"If there's anyone else who can write nicely, please have them make stencils as well," Gil added. "It shouldn't be too much of a problem for the pages to have kinda different handwriting..."

"I came here to teach music, but I suppose I can help," Rosina said with a single sigh as she accepted the manuscript. "Oh...? This handwriting is already quite elegant. We can make stencils directly out of these sheets."

"Perfect. Let's get more people making stencils, then. We'll just trace the handwritten pages we've already got."

As Lutz and Gil rushed around explaining the circumstances to everyone, I went over to Wilma and acquired the orphanage's winter preparation list. It was similar to the one Lady Rozemyne had prepared during her first year here, with everything organized so that one could tell at a glance what was and wasn't yet done.

"At Fritz's request, I shall be handling the orphanage's winter preparations," I explained. "Please do your best to help the workshop, Wilma."

"I thank you ever so much, Fran."

With Zahm and Monika's help, I organized what we needed the Plantin Company to acquire for us. The list was fairly sizable, since our preparations involved the High Bishop's chambers, the orphanage, and the workshop.

As for the food we had received during the Harvest Festival, I was trusting Hugo, Ella, and Nicola to prepare it all. We were all busily running around with far too much work for us to reasonably complete.

We all threw ourselves into our duties, leaving no time to even assist the High Priest with his work, and as a result we were just barely able to finish Lady Elvira's order before winter socializing began. The workshop was filled with glee, and as the workers burst into cheers, I started flipping through one of the books.

"Erm... Excuse me, Master Benno. It seems to me that the illustrations in this book strongly resemble the High Priest. Has he given his permission for this to be printed...?" I asked, recalling Lady Rozemyne complaining about him getting mad and forbidding her from printing any such pictures in his likeness.

Master Benno, looking slightly sicker and more exhausted than usual, shot me a glare. "He ordered us to print this himself, and we got the manuscript from Lady Elvira. Who are we to ask questions? Who's gonna pay for all our losses if *someone* doesn't keep their mouth shut and sticks their nose where it doesn't belong? Huh?"

The gleam in his dark-red eyes silenced me at once. I hadn't the will to argue with Master Benno when he was irritated and sleep-deprived, and it was indeed true that the High Priest had asked us to satisfy Lady Elvira's request by printing whatever it was she desired.

What in the world is going to happen at this year's winter socializing...?

It would soon be a year since the incident with Lady Rozemyne, but the High Priest had said she was still far from waking up. I did not understand the details, but it seemed her mana was so extremely compressed that it was taking an excessively long time to dissolve.

The High Priest instructed me to replace the feystones in the jureve while he examined Lady Rozemyne, grumbling complaints all the while. "How did you ever survive with this much mana inside of you, Rozemyne? How?" he muttered.

Meanwhile at the Temple

As I stacked a new book atop the growing pile beside Lady Rozemyne, I thought to myself that she had most likely lived due to the will of the gods.

Winter socializing began, and with the High Priest absent, we once again had to prepare for the Dedication Ritual without him. We were all used to this by now, and so things progressed smoothly even without an authority present to direct us.

Unlike last year, the High Priest did return once during our preparations, but he went back to the castle soon after checking on Lady Rozemyne. It seemed that feystones filled with her mana would once again be used for the Dedication Ritual.

At Tuuli's recommendation, we elected to compile a book explaining noble etiquette and euphemisms during the winter. Master Benno had concluded that while it would not sell to nobles, it would be popular among rich merchants and the authorities of towns and cities.

Spring arrived without any significant change in Lady Rozemyne's condition. The Plantin Company was busy hurrying about, not knowing when Lady Elvira's next request would come, and in the midst of all this, Master Benno graciously attended a meeting about Spring Prayer at our behest.

The meeting was held within the orphanage director's chambers, with Wilma and three gray shrine maidens who would be joining Lily in Hasse in attendance. As the Plantin Company primarily employed men, Tuuli was there as well, due in part to Master Benno having determined that her experience with the orphanage would make discussing matters with the shrine maidens easier.

"I expect that by Spring Prayer, Lutz and I will be in Haldenzel," he began. "I'll leave Mark behind this time to make communication easier, so just send word to him once it's time. The Gilberta Company would be fine as well with Tuuli there."

Tuuli nodded in agreement with a smile. Her etiquette studies had truly paid off, such that she looked naturally graceful even while seated.

"Is it safe to assume these four shrine maidens will be leaving to help with the birth?" Master Benno asked.

"Um, not quite... I am going to be staying behind," Wilma said quickly, shaking her head with an openly nervous expression.

Master Benno raised an eyebrow. "Aren't you the attendant Lady Rozemyne left in charge of the orphanage? That's how you were introduced to me. I'm pretty sure you should leave the orphanage to someone else and go help with the birth. There's a lot of stuff you'll need to learn to do."

"That is... That is certainly true, but..." Wilma trailed off, shaking her head over and over again as if fanning the air with her face. She then looked to me for help. I could imagine she was deathly afraid of even speaking to Master Benno, so I swiftly explained her circumstances to him.

"A blue priest tried to force himself on her, and she's been too afraid of men to leave the orphanage ever since, huh...?" Master Benno repeated. His previously calm face suddenly flashed with anger, and his voice dropped into a growl. "Don't make me laugh."

"Um..."

"You're in charge of the orphanage, right? Cut the crap! Who knows how many births you're gonna have to deal with from now on? How's this place gonna survive when the person in charge doesn't know jack about childbirth? Don't think Hasse is gonna help out every time. They're doing it this once as an act of kindness so you can handle it yourselves from here on out, and don't you friggin' forget it."

Master Benno fixed Wilma with such a wrathful, frightening stare that tears began to stream down her face. She desperately shook her head, not knowing what else to do.

"But I... I..."

"You came to me 'cause you had no one to rely on without Lady Rozemyne, and despite how friggin' busy I am, I agreed to help get you out of this mess. And what do I get in return? The very person who asked for my assistance saying she doesn't wanna do anything but stay locked up in the orphanage!"

"Th-That was not my..."

Wilma looked completely taken aback, likely having never expected to be chastised so harshly, but Master Benno faced her head-on and continued, not once breaking eye contact.

"Then what *was* your intention, huh? Stay locked up inside and pray that everything magically solves itself? This is your job! I don't have time to help someone who's not even willing to go out and learn for themselves. If you don't go to Hasse, I'm not lending you any carriages! It's just half a day away, right? You can walk!"

"Master Benno?!"

Lady Rozemyne had paid for carriages and guards such that the sheltered gray priests and shrine maidens weren't exposed to danger, but here Master Benno was suggesting that they walk a road that would take an average commoner half a day to travel.

"I don't have time for cowards with no motivation," Master Benno said bluntly, standing up from his seat. "I've got work to do. The Plantin Company has to prepare to depart for Haldenzel, so I'm leaving."

"Please, wait! I'll... I'll go! S-So please... grant us your help!" Wilma pleaded between sobs.

Master Benno sat down again, his brow knitted in a deep frown. We discussed what needed to be prepared for Spring Prayer, then concluded the meeting.

The very moment Master Benno left the room, Wilma collapsed onto the table, continuing to cry. I looked down at her with sympathetic yet distant eyes.

"...I understand the fear of being forced to do something that you do not wish to do, but you were rescued before ever being thrust into such a situation yourself. There are some people who never get saved, and are forced to do things against their wishes repeatedly. It is necessary that you learn to live on even in those situations and gradually conquer your weaknesses."

"Fran?"

"Does Lily wish for the child she is about to give birth to? I imagine not. But even so, she is fighting against her fear and doing her best to see it through."

Wilma raised her head, a look of realization slowly dawning on her face. I continued, now speaking more quietly.

"For how many years has Lady Rozemyne protected you? It was because of your encouragement that Rosina worked so hard to overcome her inability to do paperwork. Lady Rozemyne likewise worked hard in learning to live as a noble. You advised them both, and now I believe it is time for you to conquer your own weaknesses as well."

The Gutenbergs waited for Giebe Haldenzel to return to his home province before beginning their move. They departed for Haldenzel along with Gil and several gray priests.

Not too long after, it came time to leave for Spring Prayer. Tuuli came to see us off, since she was so worried for Wilma, and started encouraging her as best she could.

"Wilma, I am certain there is nothing to fear," she said, sounding far more like a well-raised noble than she had prior to her etiquette training. "Our father is among the soldiers serving as your guards."

"Our father...? Ah!" Wilma suddenly recalled that Tuuli and Lady Rozemyne were sisters, then looked over at Gunther, who was watching his daughter with a worried expression.

"There are none there who would mock or assault one of Lady Rozemyne's precious attendants," Tuuli assured her. "You may rest easy. I promise."

"I thank you ever so much."

Driven by Tuuli's encouragement and Gunther's silent approval, Wilma stepped forward on trembling legs and climbed into a carriage.

Spring came to an end, and we received word from Wilma that Lily had safely given birth. On an early summer day with pleasant weather, I requested carriages from Master Mark and departed for the monastery in Hasse. I then returned with Wilma, the gray shrine maidens who had gone to help, and Lily with her newborn baby.

Wilma's expression was much brighter now that she had experienced life outside the orphanage, and there was a strength in her eyes that made her seem much stronger and more reliable than she was before.

Everyone in the orphanage began taking turns looking after the baby, just as they had done with Dirk. It wasn't long before Wilma and Lily were wearing exhausted expressions at almost all times.

Summer too ended before we knew it. Lady Rozemyne had not awoken even by the time Monika came of age, but on one autumn day near the Harvest Festival, the High Priest gave a small smile after checking up on her.

"She has begun to move her fingertips. Her recovery is around seventy, perhaps eighty percent complete. All we must do is wait for her to awaken."

"I am glad."

After spending such a long time asleep, it was a relief to hear that she was finally showing signs of awakening. We still could not expect anything in the immediate future, but after enduring so many seasons without even the slightest change, even the smallest good sign was enough to fill me with joy.

"Good grief... Just how much trouble do you have to give me before you're satisfied...?" he asked the still sleeping Lady Rozemyne. Despite his tone sounding as annoyed as usual, there was both immense relief and intense worry in his eyes.

During the Harvest Festival, the High Priest returned to the temple every two to three nights by highbeast to check on Lady Rozemyne. "She must be immensely important to the High Priest," Zahm noted with a somewhat bemused smile after seeing him off yet again.

"...She is. Out of everyone he has ever met, Lady Rozemyne is the only one who has actively tried to reduce his workload. She sincerely worried about his health, scolded him for relying on potions so much, and challenged the archduke himself on his behalf—there is surely no other High Bishop in the world who would show him that much consideration."

My words prompted Zahm to rub his forehead and sigh, no doubt recalling the High Priest's current workload and unhealthy lifestyle. "I pray for his sake that she awakens soon," he said, looking toward the hidden room where she was asleep.

"Though I imagine that even then, his days of constant headaches will only begin anew..."

It was a number of days after the Harvest Festival ended that the High Priest informed me Lady Rozemyne had awoken and would need to be given a bath.

The Laynoble Guard Knight

"You are my brother, and this incident involves our entire family. You understand this, yes? Then tell me, Damuel—why did you propose to Lady Brigitte, then shamelessly refuse her when she agreed to marry you?"

Soon after I had turned down Brigitte on the night of the Starbinding, my brother—the head of our house—dragged me back to our estate. I now sat facing him and his wife Juliane in his quiet office, with all the servants having been cleared out of the room. Juliane was staring daggers at me with her narrowed green eyes.

"You had an entire year to prepare," she said. "Should you not have made arrangements ahead of time for Lady Brigitte to refuse you instead? She was surely deeply wounded that you would turn her down in public when you yourself were the one to propose. Do you not even remember why you defended her against Lord Hassheit? Was it not to protect the very honor you have now worked to undermine?"

I gritted my teeth. My intention had never been to hurt Brigitte. I had thought she would accept my proposal, and that would be that. Never did I think she would suddenly impose such a bold prerequisite, especially with everyone watching us.

"I thought we had agreed that I only needed to increase my mana capacity. I never thought she would suddenly force a new condition on me then and there."

My eyes had widened in shock when Brigitte asked me to move to Illgner with her, and it was then that I saw Lady Elvira watching me with a slight smile. The moment I saw the look in her dark-brown eyes, I heard her voice in my head: *"You certainly know much about Rozemyne, don't you, Damuel?"* It was a question she had asked me prior to Lady Rozemyne's baptism, when she and the knight commander summoned me to ask whether I would continue serving as her guard knight.

Lord Ferdinand and the knight commander had then warned me to, in their words, *"Think carefully and understand the significance of someone who knows so much about Rozemyne resigning from serving as her guard."* I couldn't quit serving her when she had allowed me to be her guard knight out of the kindness of her heart, and it was precisely because I knew her secrets and remained loyal to her that a laynoble like me had been given such an important role in the first place. Tragically, this was the very same reason that her guardians would never let me leave.

"I was more surprised than anyone when she asked me to come to Illgner..."

"What...? Hold on, are you saying that you expected not to marry into Illgner, but for Lady Brigitte to marry into *our* family?" my brother asked incredulously. I nodded, a little confused.

"Brigitte and I are Lady Rozemyne's guard knights. Would it not be unthinkable for the both of us to leave the Noble's Quarter at the same time?"

It simply wasn't an option for me to quit being a guard knight, and Brigitte was staying in the knight dorms precisely because she couldn't remain in Illgner. To me, it made perfect sense that we would stay in the Noble's Quarter after getting married.

"No, what's unthinkable is that you ever thought such a thing. Lady Rozemyne certainly does favor you, but you are a laynoble who everyone thinks should quit his position as soon as possible, and Lady Brigitte is Giebe Illgner's little sister. In what world would you not be marrying into her family? Who would waste their one chance to rise in status from a laynoble to a mednoble?"

It was then that I realized I understood things differently from other laynobles. They shifted factions constantly based on trends and happenings, but I was the odd one out, locked into my position due to secrets that I couldn't tell anyone.

"So you mean to say that everyone thought my proposal was founded on the idea I would marry into Illgner...?"

"Of course. It would have been beyond us to take Lady Brigitte into our own estate," my brother said flatly, leaving no room for argument.

Juliane looked at me with an absolutely baffled expression. "Could it be that you intended to have a mednoble like Lady Brigitte lower her status to that of a laynoble to marry you? How in the world did you expect to live in the Noble's Quarter after that?"

I was stunned into silence for a moment. My previous engagement had ended up getting canceled, but I had at least gotten halfway through the preparation phase before then.

"She wouldn't have been able to stay in the knight dorms, so I planned to rent a home in the Noble's Quarter after our wedding," I explained. "It wouldn't get in the way of us going to the temple and castle for work, and we would each have one attendant, which wouldn't be too different from Brigitte's current situation."

Both my brother and Juliane brought their hands to their foreheads in disbelief.

"Your previous fiancée was a laynoble, remember? Would you really force the mednoble little sister of a giebe to live like that?" my brother asked.

Juliane nodded in agreement. "That would make it difficult for Lady Brigitte to ask her family for help with matters related to her marriage and eventual childbirth, would it not? And it would certainly not be similar to her life in the dorm."

I blinked in surprise. The two of them had helped me with my marriage before, so I hadn't at all expected them to react so negatively to this.

"Damuel, I think being so friendly with the mednobles and archnobles serving as Lady Rozemyne's guards has blinded you to how significant a mednoble marrying down into a laynoble family truly is," Juliane said with a sigh.

She went on to explain what life after marriage was like for a woman. Socializing remained their primary endeavor, just as it was before marriage, but they had to socialize based on the status of their house.

"One's status changes depending on their marriage, so Lady Brigitte would be forced to live as a laynoble," Juliane summarized. "She would no longer be able to remain friends with those she had been equal to before, and when visiting her home province, she would be expected to bow in subservience to her family and relatives."

"Damuel, a landowning mednoble marrying a laynoble who isn't even the head of his house is just as significant as you marrying into a rich commoner family," my brother added.

I tried putting myself into that position. As a commoner, I would no longer be able to freely meet with my family, having to instead send word ahead of time, and I wouldn't be allowed to act as their equals. Just how much a person was distanced from their friends and family of another status became even clearer when I remembered the way Lady Rozemyne was forced to interact with those from the lower city. But while she had gone up to a higher status, Brigitte would have gone down.

As I was just a bachelor and a second son, my brother had always dealt with our relatives, which meant I hadn't thought very hard about what Brigitte's life would be like after marriage.

"It's true that I didn't think things through enough, but Brigitte became a guard knight to support her family, since canceling her engagement with Lord Hassheit had made it difficult for her to stay in Illgner. She herself said that strengthening her bond with Lady Rozemyne in the Noble's Quarter was important for her home province, and so I never thought she would want to return there after getting married."

I had thought Brigitte would be happier living in the Noble's Quarter, continuing to get Lady Rozemyne's support through my serving as her guard knight. My hands, still clenched on my lap, started to tremble.

"Did she not already solve that problem by securing Illgner's involvement in the expanding printing industry? It is only natural that her thoughts would shift to getting a husband and growing the giebe's family as much as possible to help support Illgner's future."

According to my brother, Brigitte canceling her engagement to Lord Hassheit had led to all the laynobles supporting Giebe Illgner leaving the province, meaning there were almost no nobles in Illgner at the moment. The giebe's family and the few remaining nobles were banding together to survive, and since their highest priority was getting more noble support, they wanted Brigitte and her husband to grow their numbers.

"Your marriage was accepted by Giebe Illgner despite your laynoble status precisely because you are Lady Rozemyne's guard knight, are not of an opposing faction, and are not the head of your house. He had originally planned for Lord Hassheit to marry into the family, so we can guess they always intended for you to do the same."

"...You sure know a lot about Illgner, brother."

"Our house would be tied to them if you married into the family; it is only natural that I would learn what I could about them. The real question is why you evidently never thought of all this despite having been the one to propose. Surely you spent the past year learning *something* about Illgner, no?"

In reality, I hadn't learned a thing. I was completely unaware that Lord Hassheit had intended to marry into their family, that Illgner had fallen into disarray after Brigitte's marriage was canceled, and that they were suffering such a serious noble shortage.

"When I visited Illgner with Lady Rozemyne, I did notice that there were exceedingly few nobles... but I didn't realize why that was, nor did it occur to me that Brigitte wanted to return home," I said, and as the words left my mouth, I remembered something—the time Brigitte had asked me what I thought about Illgner.

Could she have asked that with me marrying into her family in mind...?

Upon hearing me respond positively, she had beamed with delight and sincerely accepted my proposal. We were both trembling with joy over our hearts having connected, but it seemed we had misunderstood each other even that early on. I didn't want to believe it. I shook my head, trying to drive away that spine-chilling thought.

"I am a laynoble risen to the position of a guard knight due to Lady Rozemyne's good graces. I cannot quit my post without her permission, nor can I leave the Noble's Quarter. Brigitte should have known that from working with me," I said, trying to convince myself at the same time.

My brother's eyes widened with surprise. "Ah, I see... You are in a position that most laynobles would never find themselves in. The very idea that someone *should have known* your feelings, however, is nothing short of arrogance. Even as your family and someone who knows the circumstances behind your employment, I did not consider this. Everyone judges things based on their own perspectives."

Brigitte had interpreted things based on her own thoughts, whereas I interpreted things based on mine. As a result, neither of us had ever truly understood each other.

My brother, who had been staring at me intently, broke into a bemused smile. "Damuel, you certainly have worked harder than anyone expected. You increased your mana capacity to the point that you could feasibly propose to a mednoble, and while you maintain that this was thanks to Lady Rozemyne having taught you her compression method, increasing one's capacity is no simple task. As your brother, I am proud of what you have accomplished... but that is not good enough. Getting married takes more."

My heart wrenched at his remark. I gritted my teeth and lowered my eyes. To think I had come so close... I didn't want to accept that this failure was my own fault—that I hadn't been good enough.

"An equivalent mana capacity is the bare minimum you need—not even fellow laynobles can get married on mana and feelings alone. You two spent an entire year with the proposal in mind, and yet neither of you managed to deduce there was a line between you that could never be crossed."

His words stabbed into my heart one after another. I had worked desperately over the past year to increase my capacity as much as possible, believing that was all I needed to do for Brigitte to accept my proposal. But this ignorance meant that I hadn't considered the marriage carefully enough.

The Laynoble Guard Knight

"Marriage and love are not the same. For a couple to succeed in marriage, what's important is not the love that blooms between them, but rather their ability to live together. Lady Brigitte's and your visions of the future were simply incompatible. It would have been hard enough for you to live together given your difference in status, but with you two not even having understood each other, marriage would have proven impossible."

A tense silence hung in the air. Where would we live after marriage? What circumstances were we both grappling with? Brigitte and I hadn't once discussed these basic matters.

What should I have done? Could we have worked things out if we had just spoken about them ahead of time? If so, what should I have said to her?

I racked my brain, trying to put the pieces together.

If only Lady Rozemyne were here...

Perhaps then things would have gone differently. She had aided me in more ways than I could count, so there was no doubt in my mind that she would have helped me think this through. Maybe she could have gotten Lord Ferdinand and the commander involved.

But would it have been right to ask for even more help, after she already taught me her compression method...?

Neither Brigitte nor my brother knew this, but Lady Rozemyne was a commoner who had allowed herself to be adopted by the archduke to protect her lower city family. She ultimately wasn't in a position where she could defy the wills of her guardians, and me giving her a request that she couldn't grant would only hurt her young heart.

What kind of guard knight would do that to the one they serve?

I questioned myself over and over, digging as deep as I could, until I finally reached the conclusion that it was impossible for Brigitte and I to be together. A heavy sigh escaped me as I looked back up, only to find that Juliane had since left. Just my brother remained, sipping from a glass of wine as he watched me.

"Did you find an answer you're satisfied with?" he asked, a warm look in his eyes as he poured a glass for me as well. I accepted it from him and took a sip. The wine tingled and burned my throat.

"It seems the Goddess of Binding did not bless me after all. No matter how hard I think about it, I can't ever see us getting together—not when I can't quit my post as guard knight and Brigitte is so dedicated to Illgner."

"I see... In that case, be sure to apologize deeply to Lady Brigitte. Regardless of your circumstances, you proposed to a mednoble in public and then refused her despite being a laynoble yourself. As your brother, I will apologize to Giebe Illgner as well," my brother explained, before sighing as though a weight had been lifted off his shoulders. "To be honest, I am just glad that Lady Brigitte questioned whether you would be willing to join her family before accepting your proposal. If she had accepted without either of you noticing your misunderstanding, the wounds would have been much deeper when reality came to light."

Had our engagement been confirmed, it would have ceased being a problem between the two of us and turned into one that involved our entire families. My brother was the head of our house, and he wanted to avoid conflict with Giebe Illgner more than anything else.

I just wasn't paying enough attention to other people...

Marriage wasn't something that affected only the two directly involved, and by letting my emotions run wild, I hadn't given those around me even the most basic considerations.

I met with Brigitte at the temple the next day. It was painfully embarrassing, but better than having to talk to her at the knight training grounds with a bunch of nobles watching.

"Forgive me, Brigitte. When you said you couldn't return to Illgner, I accepted it without question. I never even tried to find out Illgner's circumstances or whether you did one day hope to return after all."

"No, the fault is all mine for not realizing that your position prevents you from leaving the Noble's Quarter. It took my brother pointing it out directly for me to understand. If only I had noticed sooner..." she replied with a sad smile.

I couldn't help but laugh bitterly. Neither of us had understood the situation until those we knew spelled it out for us. My brother was right—thank goodness we had found this out before the marriage and not after.

"Damuel... can you truly not leave Lady Rozemyne's side?" Brigitte asked, her amethyst eyes gleaming with a familiar determination. She didn't want to give up yet, nor did she want me to. My heart begged me to move mountains for her, but my brain reminded me that no matter what happened, our love simply wouldn't be possible.

"Brigitte, is leaving Illgner truly not an option for you?" I asked. Perhaps it was cowardly of me to respond to her question with yet another question, but my heart was screaming for me to ask it. I couldn't give up yet. If only she could stay in the Noble's Quarter, then everything would work...

Our eyes met, and it was clear we both still had strong feelings for the other.

After a lengthy period of silence, Brigitte let out a slow sigh and lowered her gaze. When she looked up again, I could tell from the gleam in her eyes that a rejection was coming.

"I am family to Giebe Illgner. I became a guard knight solely to aid my home, and so I cannot live in the Noble's Quarter as a laynoble. I seek only a marriage that will benefit Illgner."

I could practically hear the Goddess of Binding forever severing the thread that joined us. The strength drained from my body, but I gave a weak smile nonetheless. "It's a bit rude for me to ask, but... do you have someone else?"

"Lady Elvira spoke to my brother and is due to introduce me to someone from her faction. We need to hurry if I am to marry before I'm twenty, so she told me to resign from my post as guard knight sooner rather than later. Hah... At the very least, you won't have to feel awkward seeing me in the temple or at the training grounds..." she said with another sad smile before turning her back to me. "May we both meet the one tied to us by Liebeskhilfe the Goddess of Binding's threads."

The day after I said my final goodbyes to Brigitte, it was a training day for the archducal family's guard knights. Just thinking about how all my colleagues would antagonize me for refusing to marry a mednoble despite my position as a laynoble made my stomach hurt.

I could feel the stress building up inside of me as I arrived at the training grounds, where I found the knight commander Lord Karstedt and Lord Bonifatius waiting for me. The former wore a sympathetic smile, while the latter was punching the air with enthusiasm.

The Laynoble Guard Knight

"You're a good man, Damuel!" Lord Bonifatius shouted. "Takes a strong heart to have that kind of loyalty!"

"I-I'm honored..."

I had been petrified with fear over how I would be treated, but it seemed that my bosses actually held a great deal of respect for my decision to prioritize loyalty over marriage. Lord Karstedt was nodding along with the exceptionally pleased Lord Bonifatius, seeming to understand my situation completely. It was a big relief to know that the training grounds weren't filled with scornful people.

"I'm moved. As a show of respect for your loyalty, I'll train you even harder!" Lord Bonifatius declared. "To me, Damuel!"

Please go easy on me...

But of course, Lord Bonifatius had never gone easy on anyone in his life. My days of suffering both a broken heart and a broken body continued until the day Lady Rozemyne woke up.

One Handful of a Chef

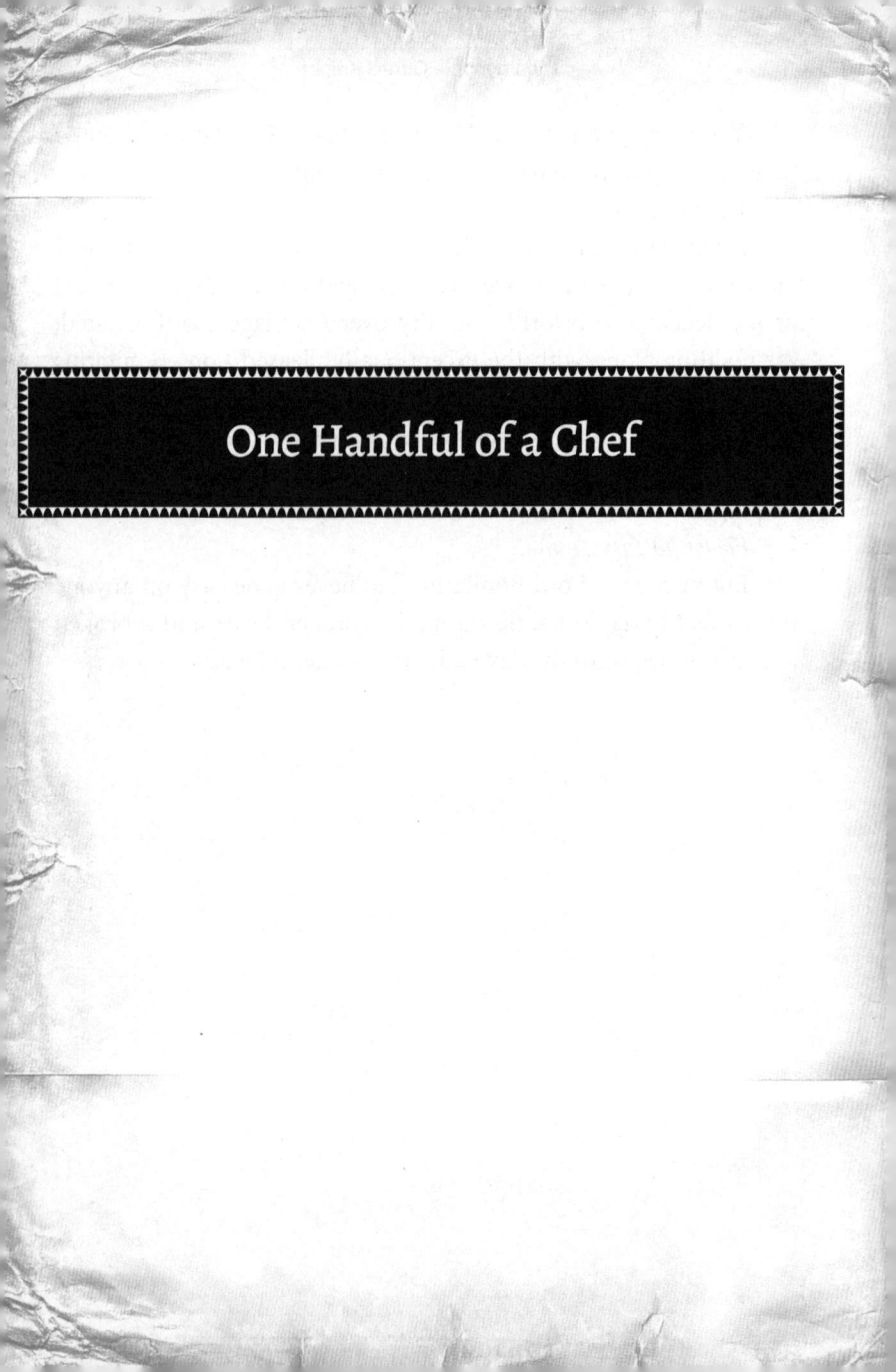

Yet another heavy sigh broke the silence.

Could you give it a rest already? Sheesh.

I furrowed my brow in annoyance, which earned me a worried glance from Nicola. "Um, Ella..." she began.

"I'm fine. Could you wash these fisha for me?"

For the past few days, a heavy atmosphere had hung over the kitchen that made it uncomfortable to say or do just about anything. I gave instructions to Nicola, then looked at the one responsible for the awkwardness. It was Hugo, hunched over with dead eyes as he stirred a pot.

I mean, I understand why he's depressed, but come on...

Our problems had started when the Othmar Company came asking for ways to expand the Italian restaurant's menu. They wanted at least one new recipe for the summer, when they received more customers from outside the city. We normally would've asked Benno to speak to Lady Rozemyne for us, but she was going to be asleep for a whole 'nother year.

Fran had shot them down fast and told them to think of something themselves, but Todd—the Italian restaurant's chef—hadn't managed to think of any good ideas. In fact, when Hugo had gone back to his home in the lower city, Todd had clung to him in tears asking whether he knew anything about Lady Rozemyne's recipes he could share.

Unable to refuse the request of an old work buddy, Hugo started to think up new recipes. But in the meantime, the Othmar Company determined that Todd couldn't handle this himself, and so they asked the guildmaster's personal chef Leise to think of some as well.

I didn't know what had gone down between Hugo and Leise when he went to the Italian restaurant to tell Todd his new recipes, but I did know that a competition had been organized by the time he came back. They were going to duke it out, and whoever made the better recipe would have theirs used in the restaurant.

Lady Rozemyne liked pretty weird foods, so even with a magic contract limiting what recipes we could share, Hugo and I had plenty of ideas from our time working as her personal chefs. So, he decided to challenge the competition with an original recipe of ours that she had loved.

However, he ended up losing to Leise anyway.

Hugo had been depressed ever since. He sadly hung his head even while in the middle of work, with his poor posture and distant gaze making him seem hardly alive. He usually looked so cool in the kitchen, but this was just pathetic.

He let out another heavy sigh. How many times was that now? I'd done what I could to cheer him up the day after he'd lost, but at this point, I was fed up with it.

So you lost once, what's the big deal?! All you have to do is win next time!

While I was angrily chopping up the fisha, Nicola finished washing the rest of them and sent a worried glance Hugo's way. He seemed to notice that, as he turned his gloomy face to her and gave a weak smile, no doubt hoping she'd console him.

One Handful of a Chef

The moment I saw that smile, something inside of me snapped. I dropped my knife, stomped over to Hugo, and punched him on the arm.

"I get that you're sad about losing to Leise, but how long are you gonna be a little baby about it? Just looking at you like this annoys me!"

"Wha?! Wh-Why so harsh?" Hugo stammered, widening his eyes in surprise then grimacing at my unexpected rant. But I was the one who should have been grimacing—not only was he damaging my opinion of him by being such a loser, now he was trying to be all cozy with Nicola right in front of me.

"If you want to try to beat Leise again, I'll do everything I can to help you, but being this much of a sad sack in the kitchen is just depressing. Your sour feelings are gonna make the food taste terrible. Just take some time off until you're back on your feet. Hate to say it, but you're just in our way right now, Hugo."

I glared at him, and Hugo glared right back, his lips bent into a frown. He then looked to Nicola in hopes of getting some support, but she was just watching us with eyes like saucers.

Sorry, but you're not gonna exploit Nicola's kindness here.

I grinned and went back to Nicola's side, where I picked the knife back up and chopped the rest of the fisha before adding them to a bowl filled with water. "Fran was saying we've still got a year until Lady Rozemyne wakes up, you know. Nicola and I can handle cooking for the orphanage just fine by ourselves, so there's nothing stopping you from taking some time off. Right, Nicola? Don't you think it'd be better for Hugo if he rested until he was feeling better? His depression's gonna seep into the food."

Nicola placed a finger on her chin, tightly knitting her brow in thought. "Mm, well, we can't really have the food start tasting bad... I'll ask Fran to let Hugo go back to the lower city."

"Er, no, Nicola! Wait a second!" Hugo exclaimed. "I'm fine. I'm all better now. You don't need to tell Fran anything, okay? Please?"

"Really...? You're better now?" Nicola asked, blinking with surprise.

Hugo nodded over and over again, now looking especially panicked. "Yup! Lemme get back to cooking!" he said, swinging his arm like an exaggerated windmill. I couldn't help but laugh as he tried to distract Nicola with the thought of delicious food.

Nicola was raised in the temple, so she didn't quite understand how some things worked. If she had told Fran that Hugo needed some time away because his food tasted bad, he would be considered a failure of a personal chef and fired—there was no point paying a chef who couldn't make good food, after all. But that wasn't something Nicola really considered, probably due to her upbringing. All she focused on was making and eating tasty food.

"Nicola, can you handle the pot?" Hugo asked. "Ella, once you're done with the fisha, come help over here."

I couldn't tell whether my yelling had actually whipped him into shape or he was just faking it well, but it looked like Hugo had kicked aside his depression. He picked up a knife to start peeling some potatoffels, apparently intending to make something fancy to both distract Nicola and show that he had fully recovered.

I drew some water from a jug and cleaned my knife, while Hugo plopped down into a chair next to me in the corner of the kitchen. He grabbed a potatoffel out of a bag fully packed with them and started to peel it.

"Curse you, Ella. I'll make you pay for this..." he grumpily muttered at me under his breath.

I waved a hand dismissively. "You can try, but I'm not scared of someone who lost to Leise and then tried to cozy up to Nicola for comfort."

"Wait! Never mind, I take it back. Forget this ever happened."

"Noooooope."

I don't want to forget a thing about the guy I like, so...

I chuckled at his expense and started peeling a potatoffel as well. Hugo sped through his one like he wasn't depressed at all anymore. Life had returned to his eyes and he was sitting up straight; in fact, he was looking kinda manly again.

There we go. This is *the Hugo I want to see at work.*

I hummed to myself as I continued to peel, earning me a raised eyebrow from Hugo. "You sure are in a good mood," he muttered out of annoyance—well, it was more awkwardness than annoyance. He was aware he had been killing the mood in the kitchen and was now trying to cover for it. The fact I thought that was cute probably showed just how bad my taste in men was.

I dropped my peeled potatoffel into a bowl and shot Hugo a smile as I picked up another. "Don't feel so down. There's gonna be another competition at the end of summer, right? All you have to do is beat Leise there. We should definitely use some mushrooms for the autumn menu. We could cook them through with butter, freshen them up with vinegar, or—"

"Ella, do you actually think I can beat Leise?" Hugo asked, sounding like he had suddenly lost all confidence in himself.

"Yep," I replied without missing a beat. Hugo's eyes widened in disbelief, but I really didn't understand why he was feeling so unsure. "I mean, you lost last time because you're just too good at making food Lady Rozemyne likes, not because you're a bad chef. You can win next time for sure."

"I'm surprised you can say that when Leise bashed the dish so hard…"

Hugo was starting to hunch over again, likely remembering all the things Leise had told him: that the recipes were innovative, but much too salty; that he should have added resha or pitses to draw out the flavor; and all sorts of other minor quibbles.

"Okay, quit it. That's enough."

I thrust a peeled potatoffel right in Hugo's face to stop him from hunching forward any further. He grimaced, and this time I returned a grimace myself. We'd finally gotten him to cheer up; I didn't want him getting himself all depressed again.

"You'd dominate any competition about making food Lady Rozemyne enjoys, but the one you lost was about a recipe for the Italian restaurant, right? Your problem was making a meal with Lady Rozemyne's tastes in mind. I mean, she likes her food salty, so…"

Hugo had lost the competition because he was too focused on Lady Rozemyne's own preferences. It was the job of a personal chef to learn what their boss liked, slowly change their seasoning to match their tastes, and not to use ingredients they weren't fond of. As such, the food they made was catered to the wants of a single person, not an entire restaurant.

"Todd asked for some new recipes from Lady Rozemyne, so that's what you brought him, right? That's why you lost."

"Yeaaah… I guess it's the rich merchants who decide on what tastes better. Only makes sense Leise would win when she just took normal noble food and added consommé to strengthen the flavor…"

The Italian restaurant's menu didn't need anything too unique; what mattered was having a traditional, slightly modified recipe that could be made with easily purchasable ingredients and seasonings.

"Guess I'd need to make something that appeals to more people than just Lady Rozemyne. The restaurant not having an ice room like we do didn't help either; I couldn't use most of the summer recipes I'm used to making."

"True. A bunch of Lady Rozemyne's summer recipes need things that can only be kept in an ice room."

Lady Rozemyne was weak to the heat, and her poor health meant she was often quick to lose her appetite. As a result, she mainly wanted light meals in the summer or slightly chilly things that could be eaten without much effort. But the ice rooms were made with magic tools, so it wasn't possible for the Italian restaurant to rely on them.

"So basically, I'm just thinking too much like a noble, huh? I need to think more about what commoners eat. Hm... Yeah. I'll have more options for autumn recipes."

Now that Hugo was facing the reasons he lost head-on, his mood was starting to brighten even without my efforts. I saw his lips rise up into a motivated grin, which made me grin myself.

There we go! That's the face I kinda like to see.

Satisfied that he was once again wearing the expression I most loved to see on him, I got back to peeling my next potatoffel.

"Um, Hugo?" I asked, noticing he was just sitting there in a daze with his knife. "You've stopped working. C'mon. Peel, peel, peel."

He quickly snapped back to reality and started peeling again, but it seemed like his heart wasn't properly in it. For once, he was actually peeling slower than I was, and the fact he kept glancing my way was really making me curious.

"Is there something else you're worried about, Hugo? You don't need to think up a new recipe for the competition right away, you know. There's still plenty of time."

"Y-Yeah... Right. I'll handle it later," he murmured. He was looking right at me, but it didn't sound like he was paying much attention at all. Whatever he was thinking about, it must have been important.

What is it this time? Gosh, he sure is a handful.

Was there anything else that Hugo had to worry about? Nothing came to mind. I pursed my lips in thought, trying to figure it out while I continued to peel.

"Hey, Ella..."

"Yeah?" I asked casually, leaning forward in anticipation of another discussion about a dinner menu or something.

"Want to get married?"

Did I... Did I mishear that?

It was so sudden that my mind went blank. There was such a slim connection between his question and what we had just been talking about that I couldn't believe my ears. I just stared at him, blinking in shock.

"Well, er, I mean... You always cheer me up, and, y'know... I was thinking it might be nice to spend my life with you," he mumbled awkwardly before slapping a hand against his forehead. His ears had gone red, along with the rest of his face. "Man, why'd I say that? If you don't want to, go ahead and tell me. I'm used to it."

Hugo grabbed the half-peeled potatoffel out of my hand, quickly finished it, then stood up with the bowl of potatoffels to flee to the other side of the kitchen. Without even thinking, I reached out and grabbed his arm to stop him.

"Actually, I'm... glad you asked. I, um... I like you too, so... I'm really glad. But could we at least talk about this when Nicola's not around...?"

One Handful of a Chef

Nicola didn't have enough common sense to read the mood and give us some space; instead, she was staring at us closely, like a kid interested in a conversation between adults. I naturally couldn't talk about romance with her watching like that.

"R-Right. Good point," Hugo stuttered. "I'll, uh, bring it up again after work. Right."

And so, he proposed to me again on our way home. My love for him had finally borne fruit, but that didn't make him any less of a handful.

"I can't believe this..." he complained. "Waiting for Lady Rozemyne means I don't get to be center stage for the next Star Festival either!"

We had gone to Fran for permission to get married, only to be told that no decision could be made until Lady Rozemyne woke up. Hugo was still agonizing over that, since he had been beyond excited to finally participate in the Star Festival as a groom.

I took his hand and consolingly patted him on the back as we walked away. He stopped grumbling once I intertwined my fingers with his, calloused as they were from holding knives all day.

"Anyway, Hugo—let's forget about the Star Festival and start thinking about that cooking competition that's coming up. You wanna beat Leise this time, right?"

"Yup, and I'm gonna. You think of a dessert for me, Ella. Something that uses rafels," he said, looking down at me happily. His brown eyes were filled with newfound motivation, and the moment I saw them, I knew he would win this time for sure.

Afterword

Hello again, it's Miya Kazuki. Thank you very much for reading *Ascendance of a Bookworm: Part 3 Volume 5*. This concludes Part 3.

This time, Rozemyne's ruelle gathering goes off without a hitch thanks to Ferdinand and Karstedt helping out. She obtains all the ingredients needed for her jureve, but as she's jumping for joy about finally getting to be healthy, everything falls apart.

Wilfried falls for a trap set by nobles during the hunting tournament while Rozemyne is traveling around for the Harvest Festival. She works her head at full capacity to think up a way to save him, ultimately managing to maintain the status quo as far as the public is concerned. But as for reality...

In the midst of all this, Charlotte appears for the first time. Rozemyne does her best to show off to her first little sister but ends up getting kidnapped, resulting in her needing to sleep for two whole years.

The short stories in this volume cover some of the things that happened while Rozemyne was unconscious; a lot changes in the castle, the temple, and the lower city. The two newly written ones are from the perspectives of Damuel and Ella, with both focusing on the conclusions to their respective romances.

A second popularity poll will be held to commemorate the end of Part 3. The biggest surprise to us on the publishing side was Damuel getting third place last time. I wonder if we'll see another surprisingly popular character this time around, too? I can't wait to find out.

Afterword

The cover art for this volume shows Rozemyne trying to stop Charlotte from being kidnapped, while her grandfather and Angelica rush to save them. Bonifatius appears in the color art, too. It's raining grandfathers! Charlotte's also so cute that my heart thumps just from seeing her. You Shiina-sama, thank you very much.

And finally, I offer up my highest thanks to everyone who read this book. May we meet again in Part 4 Volume 1.

July 2017, Miya Kazuki

THE NOW FAMILIAR...
END OF VOLUME BONUSES!

A COMFY LIFE WITH MY FAMILY
Art by You Shiina

HAAH! ROZEMYYYNE!

SHE'S DEAD!

CRACK

SQUEEEZE

WHAT IF BONIFATIUS FOLLOWED HIS HEART?

...

NOT SO SECRET ADMIRER

AWW, WHAT?

Don't "awww" me!

JUSTUS! STOP FOLLOWING ME! NOTHING'S GOING TO HAPPEN!

I WANT TO HUG YOU

Whoa. Squee! **LUTZ!**

MYNE! ♥ Oof. SQUEEZE SQUEEZE SQUEEZE

CHAAARGE

Acting on instinct
GYAAH CHAAARGE **ROZEMYNE!**

DEATH APPROACHING!

CONVERSATION

YES.

THE WEATHER IS EXCELLENT TODAY, DON'T YOU THINK?

SOME CASUAL SMALL TALK.

· · · · · · · · · · · · ·

IT'S ACTUALLY KIND OF SCARY, SINCE I HAVEN'T GOT A CLUE WHAT HE'S THINKING.

GRANDFATHER SAYS SO LITTLE, IT'S ALWAYS HARD TO KEEP A CONVERSATION GOING.

WHAT HE'S THINKING

What a fantastic day— I'm getting to s__k to my __ing grand___er, an_ __ looks jus_ __ __dorab__ __ always. N_ __hatte_ __ many tim__ __e her, her cuteness __ __ fade in the slight__ __ __ozemyne! Y__ __ __best gr__ __ __ould

JUREVE INGREDIENTS

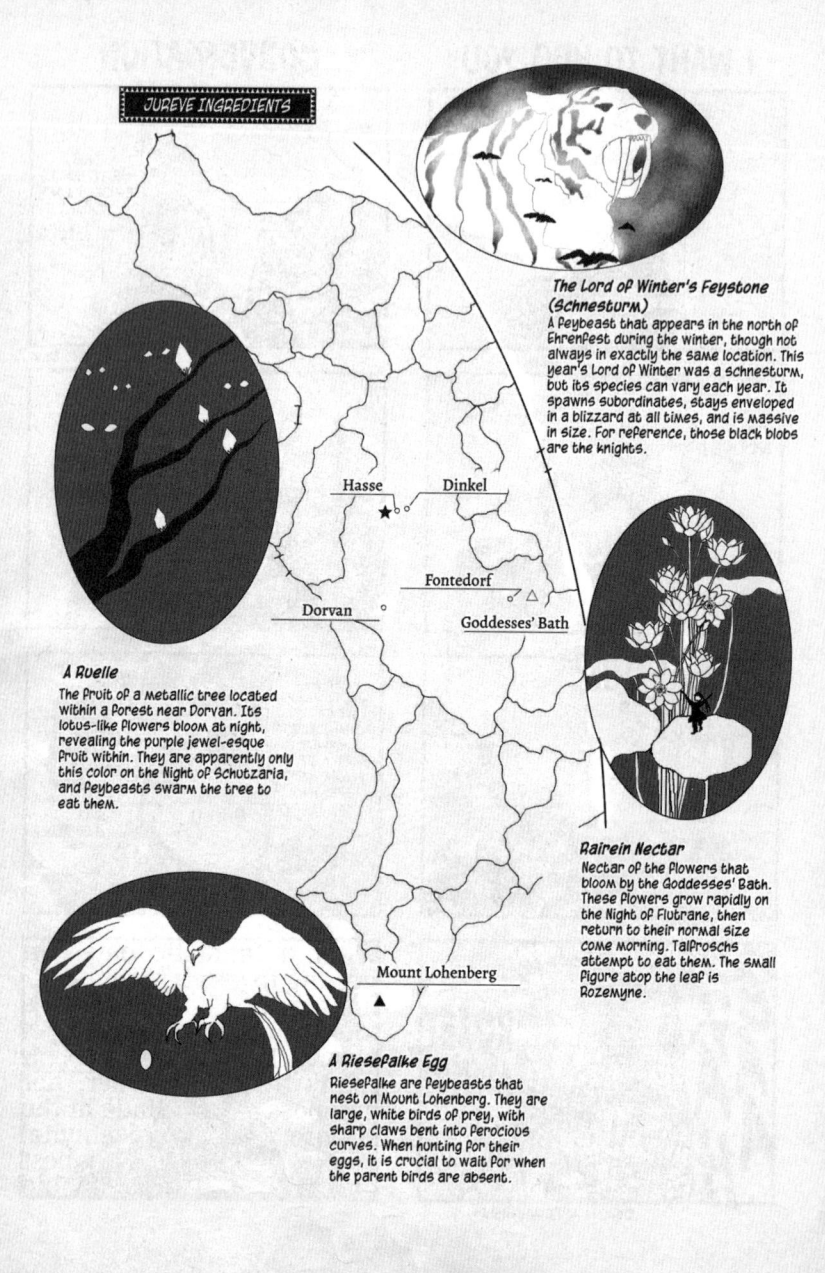

The Lord of Winter's Feystone (Schnesturm)
A feybeast that appears in the north of Ehrenfest during the winter, though not always in exactly the same location. This year's Lord of Winter was a schnesturm, but its species can vary each year. It spawns subordinates, stays enveloped in a blizzard at all times, and is massive in size. For reference, those black blobs are the knights.

Hasse — Dinkel

Fontedorf

Dorvan — Goddesses' Bath

A Ruelle
The fruit of a metallic tree located within a forest near Dorvan. Its lotus-like flowers bloom at night, revealing the purple jewel-esque fruit within. They are apparently only this color on the Night of Schutzaria, and feybeasts swarm the tree to eat them.

Rairein Nectar
Nectar of the flowers that bloom by the Goddesses' Bath. These flowers grow rapidly on the Night of Flutrane, then return to their normal size come morning. Talfroschs attempt to eat them. The small figure atop the leaf is Rozemyne.

Mount Lohenberg

A Riesefalke Egg
Riesefalke are feybeasts that nest on Mount Lohenberg. They are large, white birds of prey, with sharp claws bent into ferocious curves. When hunting for their eggs, it is crucial to wait for when the parent birds are absent.

ASCENDANCE OF A BOOKWORM

I'll do anything to become a librarian!

Part 4 Founder of the Royal Academy's So-Called Library Committee Vol. 1

Author: **Miya Kazuki**
Illustrator: **You Shiina**

NOVEL: PART 4 VOL. 1 ON SALE NOW!

MANGA: PART 2 VOL. 3 ON SALE NOW!

Author:
SATORU YAMAGUCHI
Illustrator: **NAMI HIDAKA**

VOLUME 11 ON SALE SEPTEMBER 2022!

11

My Next Life as a VILLAINESS: ALL ROUTES LEAD TO DOOM!

VI

VOL. 6
ON SALE NOW!

Tearmoon
Empire

Nozomu Mochitsuki
Illustrator: **Gilse**

THE FARAWAY PALADIN

The Lord of Rust Mountains: Primus

NOVEL HARDBACK 3 ON SALE NOW

MANGA OMNIBI 1-2 ON SALE NOW

Kanata Yanagino
Illustrations by: Kususaga Rin

Yuri Kitayama
Illustrator • Riv

OMNIBUS 6
ON SALE NOW!

Seirei Gensouki: Spirit Chronicles

Author: Kureha
Illustrator: Yamigo

VOLUME 4
ON SALE NOW!

The White Cat's Revenge
as Plotted from the Dragon King's Lap

4

HEY ////////
▶ **HAVE YOU HEARD OF**
J-Novel Club?

It's the digital publishing company that brings you the latest novels from Japan!

Subscribe today at

▶▶▶**j-novel.club**◀◀◀

and read the latest volumes as they're translated, or become a premium member to get a *FREE* ebook every month!

Check Out The Latest Volume Of
Ascendance of a Bookworm

Plus Our Other Hit Series Like:

- ▶ My Next Life as a Villainess: All Routes Lead to Doom!
- ▶ Tearmoon Empire
- ▶ Dahlia in Bloom: Crafting a Fresh Start with Magical Tools
- ▶ Dragon Daddy Diaries: A Girl Grows to Greatness
- ▶ Seirei Gensouki: Spirit Chronicles
- ▶ The White Cat's Revenge as Plotted from the Dragon King's Lap
- ▶ The Faraway Paladin
- ▶ The Tales of Marielle Clarac
- ▶ In Another World With My Smartphone
- ▶ How a Realist Hero Rebuilt the Kingdom
- ▶ My Daughter Left the Nest and Returned an S-Rank Adventurer
- ▶ My Quiet Blacksmith Life in Another World

...and many more!

In Another World With My Smartphone, Illustration © Eiji Usatsuka   *Arifureta: From Commonplace to World's Strongest*, Illustration © Takayaki

J-Novel Club Lineup

Latest Ebook Releases Series List

Altina the Sword Princess
Animeta!**
The Apothecary Diaries
An Archdemon's Dilemma: How to Love Your Elf Bride*
Arifureta: From Commonplace to World's Strongest
Ascendance of a Bookworm*
Bibliophile Princess*
Black Summoner*
By the Grace of the Gods
Campfire Cooking in Another World with My Absurd Skill*
Can Someone Please Explain What's Going On?!
Chillin' in Another World with Level 2 Super Cheat Powers
Cooking with Wild Game*
Culinary Chronicles of the Court Flower
D-Genesis: Three Years after the Dungeons Appeared
Dahlia in Bloom: Crafting a Fresh Start with Magical Tools
Demon Lord, Retry!*
Der Werwolf: The Annals of Veight*
Doll-Kara**
Dragon Daddy Diaries: A Girl Grows to Greatness
Dungeon Busters
The Emperor's Lady-in-Waiting Is Wanted as a Bride*
Endo and Kobayashi Live! The Latest on Tsundere Villainess Lieselotte
Fantasy Inbound
The Faraway Paladin*
Forget Being the Villainess, I Want to Be an Adventurer!
Full Metal Panic!
Full Clearing Another World under a Goddess with Zero Believers*
Fushi no Kami: Rebuilding Civilization Starts With a Village*
Goodbye Otherworld, See You Tomorrow
The Great Cleric
The Greatest Magicmaster's Retirement Plan
Girls Kingdom
Grimgar of Fantasy and Ash
Gushing over Magical Girls**

Hell Mode
Her Majesty's Swarm
Holmes of Kyoto
Housekeeping Mage from Another World: Making Your Adventures Feel Like Home!*
How a Realist Hero Rebuilt the Kingdom*
How NOT to Summon a Demon Lord
I Shall Survive Using Potions!*
I'll Never Set Foot in That House Again!
The Ideal Sponger Life
In Another World With My Smartphone
Infinite Dendrogram*
Invaders of the Rokujouma!?
Jessica Bannister
JK Haru is a Sex Worker in Another World
John Sinclair: Demon Hunter
A Late-Start Tamer's Laid-Back Life
Lazy Dungeon Master
A Lily Blooms in Another World
Maddrax
The Magic in this Other World is Too Far Behind!*
Magic Knight of the Old Ways
The Magician Who Rose From Failure
Marginal Operation**
The Master of Ragnarok & Blesser of Einherjar*
Min-Maxing My TRPG Build in Another World
The Misfit of Demon King Academy
Monster Tamer
My Daughter Left the Nest and Returned an S-Rank Adventurer
My Friend's Little Sister Has It In for Me!
My Quiet Blacksmith Life in Another World
My Stepmom's Daughter Is My Ex
My Instant Death Ability is So Overpowered, No One in This Other World Stands a Chance Against Me!*
My Next Life as a Villainess: All Routes Lead to Doom!
Otherside Picnic

Perry Rhodan NEO
Prison Life is Easy for a Villainess
Private Tutor to the Duke's Daughter
Reborn to Master the Blade: From Hero-King to Extraordinary Squire ♀*
Record of Wortenia War*
Reincarnated as the Piggy Duke: This Time I'm Gonna Tell Her How I Feel!
The Reincarnated Princess Spends Another Day Skipping Story Routes
The Saga of Lioncourt**
Seirei Gensouki: Spirit Chronicles*
She's the Cutest... But We're Just Friends!
The Sidekick Never Gets the Girl, Let Alone the Protag's Sister!
Slayers
Sometimes Even Reality is a Lie!**
The Sorcerer's Receptionist
Sorcerous Stabber Orphen*
Sweet Reincarnation**
The Tales of Marielle Clarac*
Tearmoon Empire
To Another World... with Land Mines!
The Unwanted Undead Adventurer*
Villainess: Reloaded! Blowing Away Bad Ends with Modern Weapons*
VTuber Legend: How I Went Viral After Forgetting to Turn Off My Stream
Welcome to Japan, Ms. Elf!*
When Supernatural Battles Became Commonplace
The White Cat's Revenge as Plotted from the Dragon King's Lap
The World's Least Interesting Master Swordsman

...and more!
* Novel and Manga Editions
** Manga Only
Keep an eye out at j-novel.club for further new title announcements!